I0561320

There are secret worlds that are known to
none … or is that so? Well no, actually.
If you listen with more than your ears, see with more than
your eyes, breathe and stretch your inner self out into
the universe, you will find you can touch, interact with,
see other places, other worlds … well, sometimes.
If fortune favours you, a door may open and your life may be lightly
touched by – who knows what – but before you know it, you have
glimpsed a world you never knew existed yet was there all along.
Therefore, the question is, 'Do you want to see one of these
worlds, to know more about it, to delve into it, to belong to it?'
Yes?
Then turn the page.

Hanging village of Pooreena
South East of
Tanglemire Forest
early morning

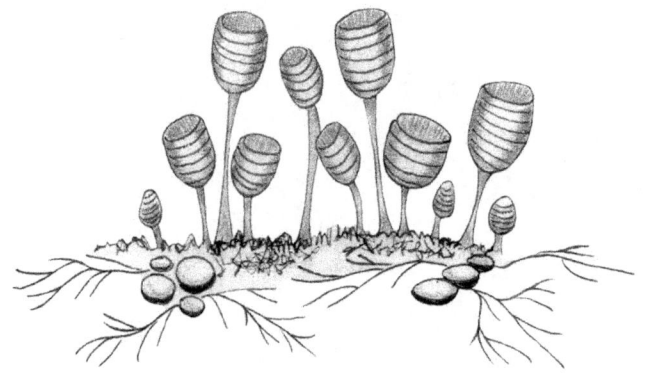

The Gribble's Gift

Tanglemire Forest
no ordinary world

Tanglemire Forest
no ordinary world

The Gribble's Gift

BY N.J. TIERNEY

The Gribbles Gift
First published in Australia by N. J. Tierney 2020

Copyright © N. J. Tierney 2020
All Rights Reserved

 A catalogue record for this
book is available from the
National Library of Australia

ISBN: 978-0-6488111-0-7 (pbk)
ISBN: 978-0-6488111-2-1 (hbk)
ISBN: 978-0-6488111-1-4 (ebk)

All illustrations by author N. J. Tierney © 2020
Cover design by Andrew McIntosh © 2020

Typesetting and design by Publicious Book Publishing
Published in collaboration with Publicious Book Publishing
www.publicious.com.au

Fourth print run

All characters and events in this publication are fictitious, any resemblance to real
persons, living or dead, or any events past or present are purely coincidental.

No part of this book may be reproduced in any form, by photocopying or by any electronic
or mechanical means, including information storage or retrieval systems, without
permission in writing from both the copyright owner and the publisher of this book.

Dedication

This book is dedicated to the three men who
came into my life and changed it forever.

To **Doug Reiser** (Gold Coast Show), who saw in me and my
miniature models something no one else did, and invited me to
display my models at the show. I have being doing that for the past
20 years. Because of him, I met -

Jeff Gilberthorpe (of the Icon Collection). If it wasn't for his
encouragement and belief in me, this story would never have been
told, and I may never have written again.

And to **Garry Luadaka** (my life partner) He has given me the time,
love, support and encouragement to pursue my dreams.

I lived in the shadow of my mind for over 20 years, then a book
appeared, written on the pages were the words;

> *"If you continue to do the things you have done in your past,*
> *You will continue to get in the future,*
> *The things you have always gotten."*
> By Anonymous

So I changed my life, one thing at a time, and look
I've written a book.

Prologue

The moon of Venra, draped in her cloak of starlight, danced across the velvet sky and took her position on the stage. For good or bad, none may say, for all fear what they do not understand. There are secret lives, in secret places, and none know what binds them together, or is that so?

In distant years past, when the earth was still young, Venra looked upon plants covering the ground, giving them the strength to grow tall and lean. Only the strong survived to stretch their limbs to the sky.

Then a day came when a single seed, red in colour, blew in on the wind to grow in the fertile soil. From where it came, none knew.

As the silver tree grew with a determination to stretch higher than all others, its magnificence became a remarkable sight. When Venra shone her light upon it, it proclaimed itself, the Founding Tree.

Many years passed before the tree perceived its time had finally come to send out sons and daughters, to share in its glory, its burden, its love. So now, bright red flowers, small in size, blossomed within its silver leaves in such numbers it was as if the tree itself had been set ablaze in a dazzling display, the sight of which shall never be seen again. Insects came from far and wide to feast on the sweet nectar and as they buzzed amongst the delicate petals, a spark of life was lit within one blossom, then another and another.

As the nights grew cold, a multitude of long, dark, red seed casings slowly twirled themselves down towards the ground. Within each one, a single seed grew. Then, as with all things, everything comes to an end, or a beginning, and the casings slowly drained of colour, grew brittle and cracked open. Each feathery bed of soft down tumbled free to allow the single red seed held within to be blown on the wind until, if fortune favoured it, it gently landed on soft soil where it could take root. If not, it withered and died.

These sons and daughters of the Founding Tree grew strong, becoming giants of the ancient strain of Silver Lunaria trees. A forest, older beyond the count of all days and seasons, now came to life. Many a creature, large and small, with their strange ways not understood by all, came to live within it.

The safety under its protection was never questioned.

But humans, who did not care for the life of trees, no matter how old and wise they might be, came into the middle of the forest with their axes and blades.

As each tree fell, the cries of pain filled the air and the Founding Tree looked upon their destruction with dismay. Its own fate was sealed, this it knew beyond all doubt. Therefore, with the love of a parent for its young, an urgent need grew to save them all. Deep within its core, a warm sensation started to swirl like a soft wind. The intensity grew, gathering sparks of red, blue and green as the essence, the spirit and the life force of the tree spread throughout every atom, cell and limb. Then it expelled its energy with such ferocity that a wall of protection ringed the entire forest, ensuring no human with defilement in their heart could ever penetrate it. Hidden away, forever safe, was now a secret world.

Then with sickening cuts the Founding Tree, too weak to resist, was felled, destroyed, laid waste, replaced by brick and steel. Bedlow Manor was built upon its roots, which to this very day still lie deep beneath it.

The wild trees, with long memories and even longer lives, now stand as sentinels surrounding the desecration. All have been branded with the name Tanglemire Forest.

1

Ebony was lost and she knew it.
She was too young to be walking in this forest
alone, and she knew that too.
If only she'd kept her promise.
But how could she?
So here she was standing, staring into the
darkness ... listening.

Thunder was grumbling its way across the roof of the world as if it was trying to grind the ancient forest into dust. Lightning was spitting shards of anger out across the heavens. Its radiated light danced in the canopy, plummeting past the towering trees, full of youth and vigour, penetrating deep into the forest, highlighting stunted oak and beech. The ancient trees, weighed down by the ravages of time, brooded in their own decay as their twisted roots anchored deep in the soil. The wind, high above, could only just be heard down amongst the rotting leaves, where it was cold and damp, and a stillness filled the air as if the forest had taken a breath and held it.

Ebony looked to her left. "Um." She was sure there was something out there ... hiding behind a tree ... watching.

You can cope with this, Ebony, she told herself. *You're twelve years old for goodness sake. You can do this!* But as she looked into the forest, doubt crept into her mind. Maybe she'd made a mistake.

A mistake! she grumbled to herself. *You have got to be kidding. Stupidity, more like. How the heck did you ever get into this mess?*

Ebony pondered on that. How long had it been since she'd set off walking to the orchard? It had been late, quite late in the afternoon actually. The sun had been trudging towards its inevitable end, and would soon disappear behind the canopy of the forest surrounding her home Bedlow Manor. She had already entered the wheat field to the south of the lake, before a rumble, slow and deep, vibrated through the air. She looked back towards her home. Its array of roofs and turrets were now crowned with dark clouds pregnant with rain. Sunlight was glinting off the many windows running along the face of the large three-storey Gothic building sitting upon the hill. A full moon, faint against a late afternoon sky, disappeared from view as the clouds grew in intensity.

Is there still time? Ebony wondered, even though a niggling feeling crept into the back of her mind that maybe she was wrong. Ignoring it, she smiled and spun around so fast her green skirt flared around her knees, allowing a breath of cooling air to brush against her bare skin.

She looked to the apple orchard in the distance and headed towards it. Just ahead of her, a long fluffy brown tail belonging to Scruffy, her pet dog, an Australian terrier, disappeared amongst the golden wheat stalks. Suddenly, she stood frozen to the spot. A feeling of immense loss overwhelmed her. A shiver cascaded through her body. A whimpering sound made her look at her feet.

Scruffy looked up with his brown sparkling eyes, worry written within them. She dropped to her knees and ruffled his left ear. "I've missed you so much, Scruffy. A year is such a long time. I hope I never have to go back to that boarding school ever again." Standing up, Ebony wiped a tear away and looked again towards the apple orchard where the trees were as old as Bedlow Manor, growing close, too close, to Tanglemire Forest.

Why are you doing this? she asked herself as a door in her mind slowly creaked open. Warm smiling eyes in a face old and thin, framed by fine silver hair, flickered across her mind's eye. Ebony's throat tightened and her eyes stung with tears as thoughts of her beloved grandmother threatened to overwhelm her. She looked down at the ground and watched a beetle scurry away, a cold hard hand squeezing her heart. Memories – sad, agonising, devastating ones – swarmed up from the depths of her mind. She thought she had been able to lock them away so long ago, but now here they were, threatening to escape. She slammed the door shut on them, not wanting to remember.

Instead, she looked at the fairy garden she was carrying with great care. She straightened the little twig sitting amongst the moss and flowers placed on bark that she had gathered from a tree near her home. She smiled at happier memories of her grandmother helping her to lay these tiny gardens at the base of the old apple trees, hoping fairies would find them one day. But those days were now gone, because she was gone.

Then the door to her memories flung open and a great sadness descended upon her. She sank to her knees. Tears flowed freely, and sad, desperate thoughts of the day her beloved grandmother had died crashed upon her like waves. Days, hours, minutes had ticked by on that dreadful, hateful day and the next, and the next and the next, until she thought they would never end. She felt lost, unable to grab hold of anything solid anymore.

Distraught at her loss, a day came, many months later, when Ebony found herself standing under the shade of the old apple trees, not knowing how she had got there. However, it was there she had found a small measure of comfort and a silence amongst the trees which had not been there before. It felt as if she was now standing in a church with its musty sunshine, and damp, safe, comforting warmth. Like a hug from her grandmother. She had then stepped forward and stopped. It had dawned on her that she'd interrupted a conversation. It was as if the very trees themselves had been talking, but had now stopped the moment she'd entered their presence. A feeling as if many eyes were watching her had made her fidget. Should she go on, or turn and run? Then, frowning with determination, she'd tiptoed through the grass and tentatively laid a fairy garden at the base of an old tree, just as she and her grandmother had done so many times before.

She'd frowned at the little garden with its twigs, moss and mushrooms. She did not even remember making it.

As she had stood looking around, wondering, waiting for what she knew not, a weight had slowly descended upon her shoulders like a cloak. Then a sudden urge had filled her up and she'd wrapped her arms around the nearest tree. With her lips close to its bark she had whispered, "I love you, Nan. I miss you *soo* much."

A tear trickled down Ebony's freckled cheek as the memory faded; over a year had passed since that day. So much had happened since then. She now looked upon Scruffy's worried face as he sat amongst the stalks of wheat, looking up at her. Ebony bent down and tickled him under his chin with its coarse hair and gave him a wry smile. He pushed his moist black nose against her cheek, then stood back as she lifted herself up and looked again at the fairy garden she was holding. How she had missed making them, missed getting lost in a miniature world, where the troubles of her life seemed to disappear.

Disappear. Now there is a thought, Ebony pondered. "Um."

The air shuddered and Ebony looked up. The afternoon light had gone dark. Her home now sat in shadow. Thick dark clouds, tinged with the green of impending hail, were tumbling over one another, rushing to fill every inch of the sky. Lightning flicked a long tongue of light across the dark clouds. Thunder roared like a wild animal demanding to be let loose. Birds screeched, taking to the air.

A shiver ran up Ebony's spine. An unknown fear instantly consumed her. All her senses demanded she run back home, but her legs refused to move. She just stood, waited and watched as the majesty of the heavens heaved and groaned above her.

Then, like an orchestra tuning up for the main performance, the wind roared across the countryside as if in pain, and before Ebony knew what had happened, it was upon her, grabbing at her clothing, whipping her long strawberry-blonde hair into a nest of tangles. Lightning flickered across the horizon, making her jerk. Heavy raindrops were now falling like stones out of the sky, pummelling her body. Scruffy yelped and, with ears flat upon his head, ran. Ebony spun on her heels to follow, but her windswept hair made it difficult to see. She tripped, landing on the muddy ground, staining her clothing. Stalks of wheat, whipped into a frenzy by the wind, lashed her face. Large hailstones now battered her young body. She cried out in pain and quickly scrambled to her feet, her fairy garden left forgotten in the mud. With her arms covering her head, she ran on, struggling to stay upright, looking upon a world like no other, as if all sense of it was lost.

Wind, rain, lightning, thunder and hail, all seemed to be battling one another for supremacy. Leaves from the nearby forest were flung high into the air to join the turmoil. A white mist had grown in density and was now rolling across the countryside like a wave. Then, it was upon her. It was as if she'd been swallowed by a cold, wet cloud, and she could only just see a few feet in front of her. A dark shadow, small in size, dashed past.

"SCRUFFY!" screamed Ebony, but her voice was lost on the wind. Her vision blurred, sounds were muffled and she wondered, was that him? "Scruffy!" she cried out in desperation, but saw nothing. "Where are you?"

Lightning zipped out of the clouds exploding into the earth nearby. Ebony screamed as the air sizzled with energy. She ran into the unknown as lightning split the sky to her left. She dashed to her right, slipped, picked herself up and rushed forward. Then, as if a switch had been flicked, it was over. She had plunged headlong into the dark, ancient, forbidden trees of Tanglemire Forest.

Trying to catch her breath, Ebony bent over and with one hand gripped the stitch in her side. She then turned and looked back through a frame of gnarled branches to where the elements of the air continued to battle on. The sight of a thinning mist sent a tingle through her nerves. It was as if a strange, magical, mysterious world lay beyond, and somehow she no longer belonged to it. She took a deep breath.

Ebony!

Ebony spun around with a thrill in her heart. She knew that voice. It was her mother's – but that was impossible! Still, she eagerly looked around, but only dark trees could be seen.

You promised. Her mother's voice resonated in her head, as her parents' scowling faces loomed in front of her mind's eye.

"But ..." protested Ebony, then huffed.

Her parents had made her promise repeatedly never to go into Tanglemire Forest, no matter the reason. Ebony sighed with resignation. She was going to be in so much trouble.

She absentmindedly rubbed her arms, which were sore from where the hail had battered them, and then noticed that the stitch in her side had subsided. She wondered what to do. Stay put! Any good book on camping worth its salt would tell her to do just that when a person was lost.

But I'm not lost, she pointed out to herself. *No,* but somehow the word did not ring true.

Ebony peered past the trees again out into the world beyond and wondered if she should try going into the storm again. Thunder groaned as if daring her to come and face the onslaught once more. Lightning flashed as if to press the point home. She bit her lip. *No. Not a good idea,* she decided. Then thoughts of Scruffy flashed into her mind. *I hope he's all right. I hope he made it home safely.*

She turned and looked back into the forest. It seemed to go on forever. The further back it went, the darker it became until all sight of the trees disappeared. Instead, a wall of shadowless night threatened to swallow up anything and everything that stumbled into it. A shiver ran up her spine. Scatterings of light now flickered through the boughs of the trees above as the storm raged on. A silence hung so thick amongst the tree trunks that Ebony felt she could have cut it with a knife. It was as if the dark sentinels were standing straight and tall ... waiting.

However, looking at the small trees nearby, and the damp ferns and dead branches surrounding her, she was unsure.

"Um." She sniffed the air and listened. It felt wrong. It held a shiver as if something was near. Something she was sure she didn't want to meet. A scuttling in the leaf litter nearby made her hold her breath and she stared hard into the gloom at her feet; nothing appeared, well, nothing she could see. *Nope. I'm not staying here.*

Well then, she told herself, *there is only one thing for it.*

Yes, I know, she answered. *And a grand plan it is, even if I do say so myself.*

Ebony knew if she kept walking under the safety of the trees near the edge of the forest, she would eventually reach the back of the mansion. The trees grew closer to the building there. From there she could make a dash for home. Her parents could not possibly accuse her of breaking her promise of never going into the forest, because, well, she hadn't *actually* done it, had she? *Surely they will understand ...*

Well, no ... not really. Ebony cringed at the white lie she was telling herself. *Technically this is still part of the forest. So I don't really think they will understand at all ...*

Oh, do shut up! she told herself as she took another deep breath, creased her brow, steeled herself and with her Mother's voice fading into the distant caverns of her mind, walked purposefully into the forbidden forest.

The edge of the forest seemed to have disappeared. *How did that happen?* Ebony asked herself. *I only walked around a fallen tree stump and sidestepped a clump of brambleberries,* she complained to herself.

Well yes, there was that ... and then skirted around the small shrub ...

"But ..." cried Ebony, throwing her hands in the air in frustration. Then she sighed. "I thought I was better than this," she said aloud. "All those camping trips I went on with Nanny Jones when I was much younger should have taught me something."

You were only camping on the lawn at the back of the mansion. It doesn't really count ...

"Ugh! ... Still!" protested Ebony.

Nanny Jones had gone to such an effort to teach me the names of the stars, how to extract water from the leaves of the trees, how to light a fire ... and ... and ...

"Stop! Stop! Stop!" she cried, grabbing hold of her head and squeezing her eyes shut. "I'm lost!"

Ebony squirmed because her voice sounded louder in the silence. Sighing, she let her hands drop to her sides and gazed upon a world of shadows filled with dark trees, and breathed air filled with the musty smell of damp leaves. She listened to water dripping from on high and could still hear the storm venting its anger out across the canopy of the ancient forest. Scatterings of light flickered amongst the leaves above.

She quickly looked to her left. Somewhere in the distance, bells tinkled.

What was that? she asked herself.

I don't know, she answered.

She listened, but the sound did not come again. Shivering, she took a step forward, then a tingling sensation vibrated through her body. She rushed on, stopped, spun around and looked back, but all that was there was the same dark forest she had been seeing for what seemed like hours. However, something had changed; she could sense it. She looked around but only trees blending into the shadows surrounded her. The only light, if she could call it that, came from green glowing fungi scattered throughout the forest. She pondered on that; she did not remember seeing them before, she was sure of it, but now they seemed to be everywhere, as if eyes, which blinked from time to time, were now watching her.

She froze. There was a sound in the distance, soft at first, as if a thousand drums were marching towards her, increasing in number, rushing forward, growing louder. Just as she realised it was rain, she quickly ducked beneath the protective branches of a nearby tree.

"Wow!" she cried as the dazzling display exploded all around her.

Each raindrop, landing on a leaf, turned silver with a sparkling inner light then split apart, rolled around like mercury and fell to the ground. Upon touching the other droplets, they grew into puddles of their own making. As the rain passed on, blue glowing threads, long and fine, now emerged from the leaf litter. Ebony watched with a fascinated horror as they grew in number, eventually covering the ground, the same way that fungus covers rotting fruit. Panic rose to her throat as she now found herself surrounded by a rippling, forever-growing blue carpet of threads weaving their way towards her. Grabbing hold of a nearby branch for support, she stood on her tiptoes, desperately wishing she could climb the tree to safety. The blue threads reached out. Ebony quickly lifted her left foot off the ground and teetering on the tips of the toes of her right, grasped the branch tighter. Then one single thread, slowly, as if it too was nervous, touched her mud-stained shoe and instantly shrank from it.

As quickly as the threads had appeared, they retreated amongst the leaf litter, leaving no trace of the silver puddles behind.

An uneasy relief surged through Ebony and she took a few steps forward. Thunder grumbled. The air vibrated as if giants were fighting in the mountains of the sky. Lightning flashed through the canopy with such ferocity that silhouetted trees, with craggy fingers clawing at the air, sprang out of the dark. Ebony screamed and ducked behind a tree, pressing her fingers against its rough bark, cowering within its wild roots. She brushed her long wet hair away from her face then listened.

A whimpering sound drifted through the air. She strained to hear where it had come from but no, it was gone.

"Could it be?" she whispered as hope sprang into her heart. "Could it actually be Scruffy?"

Ebony's pulse quickened and she stretched her hands before her, tentatively searching the shadows, grasping hold of trees as she moved forward, then stopped. There it was again. The sound was off to her left close to the ground. It was the sound of a creature whimpering. Frightened. Lost. And she knew it was Scruffy. It just had to be.

"Scruffy! Scruffy, is that you? Where are you? It's me. It's Ebony."

Radiated light broke through the canopy again, highlighting a hollow at the base of a large ancient tree. Poking out of it was a small hairy muzzle.

"Scruffy! cried Ebony, dashing forward. Sliding to her knees, she scooped him up and crushed him to her chest. "Oh, Scruffy! Scruffy! I've found you. I've found you. I've final-l-ly found you."

Tears streamed down Ebony's cheeks as she hugged his little wet body.

Scruffy whimpered and nuzzled against her.

"I know, darling," crooned Ebony. She loosened her hold on him, then settled herself amongst the damp leaf litter. "It's all right, I've got you now. It's all right."

She eased him onto her lap and Scruffy buried his face into the folds of her green skirt. She pulled her knees up close and patted him.

"You're safe now, Scruff," she lied.

Ebony looked deep into the forest. Light continued to dance in and out of the canopy above, allowing small sections of trees below to appear and then disappear. As the storm continued to rage overhead, the air tingled with energy and a shiver ran up Ebony's spine. She flinched. *Will this storm never end?* Cymbals crashed. Lightning flashed. Something exploded high above. A flash lit up hundreds of trees in an instant. Ebony screamed as Scruffy struggled against her grip. Then the light was gone, as if swallowed by some huge black maw. Sizzling stars cascaded into the depths, and Ebony bit her lip and held her breath as she watched them fizzle out before they reached the ground. Scruffy whimpered and she squeezed him tighter. Something of great weight was now falling, crashing through the trees somewhere off to her right.

Ebony, with Scruffy cradled in her arms, scrambled to her feet. Her heart, thumping in her chest, demanded to be let loose as she peered into the dark forest. She clenched her teeth and stood rigid as if turned to stone.

The thunderous crashing came to a sudden halt as something hit the immovable earth below. The ground shivered. The canopy swayed. A brisk wind blew through the branches, sending a torrent of leaves and twigs raining down upon her. A second later, the ground heaved and Ebony stumbled and fell, the force sending the air from her lungs. Scruffy flew from her arms and yelped as he too tumbled to the ground. Ebony moaned as she clambered onto her hands and knees, then Scruffy's claws raked the back of her legs, biting into the skin.

"Ow! Get off me!" she cried, rolling awkwardly onto the ground and pushing him away. Then gathering him to her chest, she burst into tears. Scruffy was shaking right down to his paws.

What are we going to do?

I don't know.

As the last of the smaller branches tumbled to the ground, a deathly silence fell all around. She strained to see what she could not, to hear sounds that were not there. As minutes ticked by, the silence grew thicker and her hands shook.

"Be brave, Ebony," she whispered to herself. "Be brave."

Shapes of tall dark trees were now peeling themselves away from the darkness. A pale yellow glow appeared close to the ground.

Ebony peered into the distance.

What's that?

I don't know.

Trees, silhouetted against the light that was growing brighter with every second, seemed to get darker, denser.

"We've got to get out of here, Scruff." But Ebony, filled with sudden fear, froze as the shadows now felt thick and heavy, as if a cloak were descending upon her shoulders, closing in all around her. She closed her eyes and wished she was anywhere but here. Suddenly, unable to stand it anymore, she said, "Come on, Scruff, off you get."

She pushed him onto the ground. He growled as if displeased but she took no notice. Then sudden pain stabbed through her left knee as she struggled to stand up, and she crumpled to the ground. Tears prickled in her eyes and a black mist of self-pity started filling her up again, making her feel like a broken doll unable to be mended.

NO! screamed Ebony back at herself. She would not give in to this feeling of hopelessness, not again. Not now. She had to be strong, if not … She closed her mind to the thoughts of what would happen if she failed this time.

Feeling as if her body was a great weight, she dragged herself up and leaned against a tree for support. She took a deep breath, and with determination to move forward, realised there was a taste of moss and damp wood making her tongue tingle. It was then she noticed a vibration was now tickling through her fingertips. She snatched her hand away, tentatively pushed her ear against the tree trunk and listened. A soft pulse vibrated from deep within the tree. She turned and listened to the forest.

"Can you hear that, Scruff? Someone or something is breathing … and it's not us … You know what? I think it's the trees." She looked around and shivered at the thought of being surrounded by a whole forest that was alive.

All forests are alive, you idiot, she scolded herself. *I know,* she bit back. *But not like this one.*

"Come on, Scruff, let's go. We'll head for the glowing light, it's better than staying in the dark."

Ebony drew closer as the light grew brighter and her pace slowed. She tiptoed her way forward with Scruffy staying close as if he, too, could sense something.

Should I go on?

Of course, you should, she argued with herself. *You can't back out now.*

But what if it's dangerous? ... Um. Good point.

Ebony quickly ducked behind a large tree, leaned back and took a deep breath. Then clenching her jaw, she gathered her resolve and slowly moved away from its safety. Twelve tentative steps she took, pushing her way through branches that seemed to have been broken, torn asunder, until the next tree barred her way. Looking out from behind it, she said, "Wow, Scruffy! Look at this."

Forests hold many secrets. Tanglemire Forest holds more than most. From deep in the soil, to high in the canopy, mysterious creatures survive, live and love. The forest beats with a heart that lies in every molecule, every atom, every breath. It grows unseen, yet never dies. From the moss on the ground to the giant Silver Lunaria trees scattered throughout the forest in their groups of seven, protection is assured for the villages that hang from their silver boughs.

That is until the moon of Venra appeared in the sky once more.

Scattered amongst the giant Silver Lunaria trees, the days in the lives of all the villages came and went as they had always done, but now rumours of Venra's return had been swirling around in the forest for days, weeks, months. Even the Gribbles grew nervous. Their long noses twitched with anticipation. Their round tummies complained from the stress of the unknown. Groups of Gribbles could be found huddled on suspension bridges high in the canopy, scratching their flat heads, complaining, questioning. Didn't the Elder know what was to befall them? Did he not know everything? See everything? Even the Scribes, whose task it was to keep the records, could give no answer. Much knowledge had been lost over many seasons.

The hanging village of Pooreena had been built within three of the seven giant Silver Lunaria trees located in the south. From high in the sunlit lands of silver leaves, to the dark shadows of thick branches where the canopy of the younger trees met, from one tree to the next, seventy-three cone-shaped homes were scattered. Each home was festooned with a wide variety of plants and fungi, some luminous, others not. A labyrinth of suspension bridges connected all the buildings to one another, but only the most knowledgeable could make any sense of the maze.

A dozen or more houses, located in the deep south closest to the forest, were bathed in filtered light. One house was festooned with large, ruffled, cerise-coloured blossoms.

Inside was a small kitchen where a large wooden table stood. Bowls of plump purple berries, nuts, seeds and aphids' cheese wrapped in soft leaves could be seen upon its surface. A small patchwork bag was being packed by a large plump female Gribble with red hair.

"Mama, you're going to fill up my bag with food!" a young female Gribble complained as she tucked her white shirt, covered in purple spots, into the top of her green trousers. She then ensured that her short fluffy tail was brushed and continued, "How am I ever going to be able to fit any treasure in it now?"

"No doubt, young Gribble," Mama's long nose moved about as if she was sniffing out smells, "you would have eaten it all up by the time you find any treasure, so *no* nonsense from *you*, thank you very much. That reminds me, Veeleeta. Have you finished your morning meal? I don't want you going out into the forest on an empty stomach."

Veeleeta's long nose twitched while she finished plaiting her long black hair.

"Of course. Do you really think I would take one step out of this house without some food in my belly?" Veeleeta rubbed her round tummy and smiled. She then moved to a small shelf next to a round stained-glass window and climbed onto a nearby chair. Stretching out her four stubby fingers, which twitched with anticipation, she picked up the Ocarina, the musical instrument her papa had recently made out of a large round seed pod, and smiled at the memory of when her papa had given it to her. Now, looking forward to her day of adventure, she slid it into the patchwork bag.

"Well, be off with you now," Mama said, pulling the two drawstrings of the bag together. "And make sure you come back home before dark. Rain is coming," she added, handing Veeleeta the bag then patting her on her flat head. "The air is full of its scent."

Frowning, Veeleeta hitched the long strap over her shoulder then pushed her mama's hand away. Seeing a flicker of sadness in her mama's eyes, Veeleeta quickly, standing on tiptoes to reach her, pushed the flat end of her long nose against her mama's cheek and gave her a kiss.

She then turned towards the front door and spied her baby sister crawling across the rug.

"Arleenar. Come here." Veeleeta picked her up. "Give me a hug. "Will … you … stop … *wriggling*?" she complained. "I only want to give you a kiss goodbye." But Arleenar squirmed her way out of Veeleeta's clutches, bounced onto the rug below and crawled off towards some nearby toys. Veeleeta shook her head and smiled, then moved towards the front door.

"Congar, will you get your head out of that bowl?" Veeleeta looked down at the little chestnut-coloured ball of fluff munching on some small purple Dodder berries. "Do you want to come with me or not?"

Congar, her pet Poogle, looked up with his beady black eyes, blinked and stuck his pointy snout, stained blue from juice, back into the bowl. His long fur slowly turning orange was his only reply.

"Fine, have it your own way. You're going to miss out on an exciting day." Veeleeta opened the door to the early morning light and walked onto the veranda surrounding her home. She then leaned against the woven railings, stood on her tiptoes to see over the top, and yelled, "It is a beau-ti-ful morning."

She looked in wonder upon a misted world where hazy lights shone through and took in a deep breath. Her head felt light as the delicate perfumes from the surrounding flowers wafted through the air and the taste of many pollens settled on her tongue. She smiled and looked down as Congar brushed his face up against her round tummy. His snout showed no sign of his juicy meal.

"Oh Congar, can you tell? Finga flowers and Ruby Sargess, and Giffers are in flower as well. Oh, you know what that means?

17

Honey, jellies and pies and cakes, yum." Veeleeta laughed and smiled at the thought of all that food.

The growl of the resident Kooreen bird, settling down for the day after a night of foraging for Fly Snails, resounded through the village. Birds twittered and cawed as they woke for a new day. The mist slowly retreated into the forest, exposing hanging houses, one after another, covered in a vast array of plant life, moss, fungi, some illuminated, others not, lying cloistered within the silver leaves of the giant Silver Lunaria trees. A multitude of glowing plants and fungi in a wide range of colours spread out into the distance. Fan-shaped Peeloo fungi, glowing pale yellow, covered branches by the hundreds. A soft breeze brushed past and Veeleeta smiled. "I love this time of the morning, Congar."

"I too," said Congar, as he glided on small unseen feet up the side of the fencing, then balancing on the railing he lifted his head and howled. The long deep howl travelled out into the village. It was answered by many others from somewhere within its depths.

Veeleeta smiled and with a twinkle in her eye, lifted her head and howled, copying Congar, who joined her.

"You two! Stop it!"

Veeleeta and Congar spun around. Mama stood in the open doorway scowling back at them, hands on hips. Then as if satisfied with the result, she turned and closed the front door. Veeleeta and Congar looked at each other and burst out laughing, causing Veeleeta to cough. Recovered, she smiled and looked out over the balcony again.

"Oh look, Congar, the village is waking up."

Puffs of smoke swirled from many chimneys. The illumination from plants and fungi was now fading as the daylight grew brighter. Rays of soft sunlight exploded from on high, stabbing down through the silver leaves deep into the forest below. Then almost as soon as they had appeared, they vanished. Voices drifted on the breeze. Gribbles were laughing and chattering as they walked over the many suspension bridges, heading back from their nightly trek of the forest. What they had been doing or where they had gone Veeleeta knew not, but desperately wished she could have gone with them.

A herd of nine multi-coloured Cloud Dancers flew out from the canopy of silver leaves and silently wove through the village towards the Supply Station. Each Cloud Dancer used its four small wings to guide it down to trot onto the wide veranda surrounding the building. Gribbles greeted them warmly and quickly tied boxes and bundles to their backs. No sooner had they arrived than they were lifting off into the air again.

"I wonder where they've all been to," sighed Veeleeta. "Or where they are going." Her long nose twitched at the thought. "I wish I could have gone with Papa when he went to the hanging village of MoreReeCar."

"Too young," said Congar.

"I'm not! I'm twelve seasons old."

Veeleeta looked upon the twenty or so hanging houses that formed her view of the much larger village, but knew it would not be long before the vast area of the village she could not see would be a hive of activity as well.

It then occurred to her: why had she never travelled to the other Silver Lunaria trees to investigate the rest of the village? She did not know. She supposed it had never interested her until now. Her interest had always lain behind her, in the wilds of the ancient forest. That was where she longed to be.

Daylight was now growing all around her. Gribbles were appearing on balconies, starting their day doing whatever it was they were going to do. Fan-shaped Peeloo fungi, growing in huge swathes on the nearby branches, were now losing their nightly fluorescence. Blossoms on nearby vines were unfurling their petals as the air warmed. Butterflies flitted on the soft breeze as insects buzzed close by, and the anticipation grew until Veeleeta could stand it no more. "Come on, Congar. It's going to be a great day. A day of adventure."

Walking on the veranda around to the back of her home, Veeleeta took a few steps towards the suspension bridge that led out into the forest. She could almost feel it calling to her, to tread its paths, to go out into the magical, mystifying world she loved so much. But then a familiar whistle pierced the air. She turned towards the sound and scanned the nearby branches covered with a vast array of blossoms in all manner of shapes, sizes and colours.

"Congar. Can you see Trillium? He must be there somewhere."

"Look to the Wandoo Kerloo," answered Congar. "They are the small orange blossoms growing—"

"Yes! Yes! Show-off. I do know."

Veeleeta's eldest brother, Trillium, waved at her from the fourth branch to her right as he flicked his long black fringe out of his eyes. She smiled and waved back. He pointed to a large bunch of Giant Blue Trumpet Wandoo lying to his left. Some were twice the height of Trillium, and Veeleeta knew that if she'd been standing next to them, amongst the tiny leaves at the base of each tubular vase-shaped flower, they would have towered over the very top of her. As it was, they were still curled up waiting for the sun's rays to strike the heavily ribbed, dusty-blue giant flowers with their indigo spots. Trillium walked over to one of them and gave it a gentle pat.

She smiled again and waved enthusiastically at him. He returned the greeting.

"I hope Trillium is taking good care of those plants, Congar," said Veeleeta. "Papa will be terribly upset if they are not ready by the time he gets back. It will not be long now until the other Gribbles start arriving for the festival. I cannot wait for it. The Festival of the Gathering." Her long nose twitched with excitement. "Papa will be so pleased. You know how proud he is to be the Guardian of the Wandoo. I also know," she said, turning to him, her nose twitching again, "that he can't wait for the other Guardians to arrive from the other villages. He desperately wants to know what they think of his crop."

"It's more important than that!" Congar stated, looking up at her with his beady black eyes. "The Gribbles must not miss collecting the pollen this season. All the other crops have failed."

"Yes. Yes, I know," said Veeleeta, in a bored tone. "They have to watch and wait. They only have one chance to collect it for a *whole* season. So you keep on telling me. I don't care. All I care about are

the stories and the parties. It's always such fun when all the other Gribbles turn up. I can't wait for the parties. Oh, the dancing and the music. I love the music, Congar." She picked him up around his plump tummy and twirled him around, then replaced him gently onto the wooden veranda. She smiled as she dreamily remembered past festivals, where Gribbles danced and played music long into the night.

Congar's voice broke into her musings.

"Little Gribble," he grumbled. "Without the pollen, a lot of creatures would be … dead."

Veeleeta wrinkled her long nose and flicked a condescending look at Congar. She then turned her attention back to her eldest brother. He was holding out both his arms indicating the Giant Blue Trumpet Wandoo, which were slowly unfurling fine large petals, each tipped with delicate scrolls, dark blue in colour. The sun's rays had finally pricked through the silver leaves and the flowers were now slowly turning to face its warmth.

"Bye, Trillium," yelled Veeleeta, standing on her tiptoes and waving enthusiastically one last time.

Heading over the suspended walkway, she stopped.

Whimbrel, her other older brother, stood in the middle of the

suspension bridge with his hands on his hips. "And where are you off to, young Gribble?"

Veeleeta blinked and looked at him, then smiled, raising her eyebrows in a condescending way. "Who do you think you are? Papa? Trillium? It's none of your business."

Veeleeta brushed past him, and even though she only came up to his chest in height, she stuck her long nose up in the air and confidently walked on by as he yelled out, "I'll come with you."

Veeleeta spun around and glared at him, hands on hips. "No, you will not! It is bad enough that my two older brothers fuss over me all the time when I'm at home. I will *not* have one of you coming with me *now*."

"You're too little," protested Whimbrel, crossing his arms over his chest, planting his oblong feet defiantly on the wooden boards. "You need someone to look after you."

"Honestly! I don't need *anyone* looking after *me*!" Veeleeta turned away and, with Congar by her side, stalked off into the wilds of the ancient forest.

4

Veeleeta hummed a tune as she, with Congar just ahead of her, travelled over well-worn tracks weaving across the surface of the tree limbs. Occasionally, they traversed the gaps from one branch to another via the many suspension bridges zigzagging throughout the canopy like cobwebs. The two of them wound their way over moss and lichen, around fungi and plants, and occasionally stood back to let an insect pass by.

A fluttering up amongst the silver leaves ahead made them stop. Veeleeta crouched and placed a firm hand on Congar's back.

"Look!" she whispered.

A vast colony of large black-winged moth-like creatures flew into view.

"Tooreens," answered Congar, in a hushed tone.

"Wow! It's not often you get to see them."

"Fifty all told," stated Congar.

A few pale lean solemn faces, with their large dull eyes, turned to look at them, only to turn away and continue their journey.

Their long black hair, cut into ridges tinged with dark brown, silently rippled along their long, thin bodies. A pair of equally long, thin, pale arms and legs trailed out behind them. Four large black velvet wings, stippled with silver, shimmered as they silently flew in and out of sunlit patches. In a matter of moments, the entire colony was swallowed up by the shadows of surrounding trees.

"*Well*," said Veeleeta as she stood up. "How can the day get any better after *that!*"

"Why does the colony leave?" mused Congar.

"Does it matter?"

"It might."

Veeleeta smiled as she sat leaning against the purple stem of a Dodder plant with its large curving blue leaves towering above her. "I'm starving. I'm glad Mama packed so much food," she said, sharing it with Congar.

She munched on some nuts, listening to the familiar sounds of the forest surrounding her, the twittering, cawing, squawking and screeching of birds. The chirping and chattering of insects by the hundreds fused with the humming of thousands of wings darting in and out of fragrant flowers. She leaned forward and smiled as she gazed upon the forest of old she called home and stared at it in wonder.

She sighed with contentment then picked out of her bag a biscuit made of powdered seeds and broke it in half, laying one half on some moss in front of Congar for him to eat. A small golden ball of fluff, with a green throat and a long tail covered in white wispy threads, flew down and landed next to Veeleeta, who eyed the bird with suspicion. She looked around her, but could see no more of its flock. *Well, maybe just this once,* she thought. She smiled and, breaking off a crumb from her biscuit, offered it to the bird. Within the blink of an eye, the air was alive with a multitude of tiny golden birds flying down to land on every plant nearby. Veeleeta gasped. "No you don't," she said, laughing. She should have known there wouldn't be just one of them; there never was. She quickly stuffed her biscuit back in her bag. "No way are you lot getting hold of that! You had better eat up quickly, Congar."

Congar looked up from munching on his biscuit. Shocked, he jerked back as he saw all the birds looking at him, eyeing off his piece of the biscuit. He quickly gobbled it up while crumbs that fell deep within the moss were quickly carried away by an army of tiny pink ants. Still, the birds did not leave even though there was now no trace of the meal left behind. They seemed to be waiting for something.

Veeleeta smiled. She knew what they were waiting for. She retrieved the Ocarina from the bottom of her bag, placed it to her lips and blew. The trilling of the music floated through the forest, winding its way around the head of an insect, which looked up as if it was trying to understand what was happening. The music caressed the giant trees of old, only to slowly drift apart until every single piece of music was eventually absorbed into the very fibre of the forest itself, just as all things do that die. Then the birds, as one, lifted into the air and Veeleeta laughed as they flew away and she watched them go.

"Congar," said Veeleeta, with happiness in her voice.

"Yes, little Gribble?"

"I was wondering. This forest is *so* big, huge in fact. How did it get here? I mean, surely it has not been here forever. Everything has a beginning and an end, I suppose. And, how did Poogles end up living with Gribbles anyway? Come to think about it, how did Cloud Dancers do the same? All of you must have come from somewhere. *Why is it* I do not know the answers to these questions?" Veeleeta turned an accusing eye upon Congar. "I thought you were supposed to teach me."

"You have never been interested in the history of Pooreena, or any of the other hanging villages scattered throughout the forest, thank you very much. You have shown *no* interest at *all* in its inhabitants even though I have tried *many* times to instruct you. I cannot teach you everything. There are so many things for a little Gribble to know to survive in a forest so ancient and *you* don't always want to listen."

"Well, I'm listening now," said Veeleeta, as she repacked her patchwork bag. Then she stopped what she was doing. "Oh look, Congar."

"Fly Snails," stated Congar.

Veeleeta watched in wide-eyed astonishment as each large, soft, single yellow foot, striped with purple and topped with a pale white shell, undulated across the top of the branch, leaving a fine trail of silver slime to mark their passing.

"Wow! I wonder if I could collect some of this."

Veeleeta pushed a stubby finger into the wet silver mucus. It instantly turned into dust and blew away on a faint breeze. "What? Umph." Veeleeta frowned and watched the silver particles scatter throughout the surrounding vegetation. "Drat! Why are they called Fly Snails, Congar? It seems such a strange name to give to a creature that moves so slowly. Maybe they've got—" Veeleeta stopped talking.

Each pale shell was now hinging open, revealing four small delicate translucent white wings unfolding from within. Each snail, with a flap of those wings, lifted its large glossy foot from the branch and flew down out of sight.

Veeleeta dashed to the edge of the branch. Hanging onto a nearby vine, she watched the Fly Snails disappear into the leaves of the plants below.

"Congar, can you imagine ... falling a-l-l that way? Wouldn't it be dreadful?" She shivered.

"Dangerous! Dangerous! Away! Away!" squeaked Congar.

"I wonder what lives down there." Veeleeta attempted to see past the greenery. "On the forest floor, I mean."

"Nartells and Carbuns," called out Congar.

Veeleeta looked back at him; he had turned yellow. "Oh don't be so silly," she said. "There is no such thing; they are only in tales told around Fire Stones. Still, it would be terrible to end up down there."

Gazing into the depths of the forest, she soon became dizzy. Her stomach started to churn.

"Veeleeta!" pleaded Congar. "Move away! Move to me!"

"Yes, I think you're right," her parched throat croaked. Veeleeta scrambled, with her feet feeling like huge weights on the end of her thin shaky legs, back towards Congar, who had now turned back to his normal colour. "Thank you, Congar," said Veeleeta, as she gingerly patted him on the head. "You're always here to save me. What would I do without you?"

Congar turned pink as if embarrassed by such praise.

As the day passed, they travelled higher into the silver-limbed tree than Veeleeta had ever gone before. They now trod where no paths lay.

The hours passed and the light started to fade.

"We need to return," stated Congar. "The night will be closing in soon and rain isn't far off."

Veeleeta sniffed the air. "Rain's a long way off. Just a little longer? ... What's that? ... Oh, look!" Veeleeta dashed ahead. She pulled the strap of her bag off her shoulder and dropped to her knees. She gazed with rapture at a long row of nine small, round, white balls, each stuck to the bark of the branch by a tiny shiny black stem. "What do you think these are, Congar?"

Congar sniffed them and stood back. "Eggs."

"Eggs? Of what?"

"The Crested Stickleback."

"Oh." Veeleeta looked at the delicate paper-thin casings before her. She was sure there was something moving about inside. "But ... what is that?" she asked.

"A creature that crawls with—" Congar stopped talking. Veeleeta turned to look at him when he didn't continue. "Leave!" said Congar, turning bright yellow. "We must leave."

"But why? I haven't found anything yet. I'd really like to continue looking." She stood up again, replacing the strap of her bag upon her shoulder.

"The air grows heavy," warned Congar. "Can you not feel it? There is a coldness in the air. It's time to leave ... Listen."

"I can't hear anything."

"Yes. That's the problem," answered Congar.

Veeleeta looked around. The constant noise, made up of the living breathing forest humming in the background of Veeleeta's life, which she was so used to she didn't even notice anymore, had ceased. The songs of birds, insects and even the trees were all silent and it was a silence that was deafening, unnerving, overwhelming. The colours had changed too. Gone were the bright silvery leaves splashed with colourful insects darting from one flower to the next. Now they were dull. A shadow descended upon everything and grew darker by the second. "What does it mean?"

"It means we must leave," urged Congar, as his fur changed to orange.

The leaves above Veeleeta's head began to sway in a stiff breeze and the two of them immediately turned for home. In the distance, a dull roaring sound grew and the sweet scent of summer rain filled the air.

"Leave! We must leave!" yelled Congar, as he rushed ahead, turning a brighter shade of orange.

"But it's only rain."

"Leave! We MUST leave!"

A shiver crawled up from beneath Veeleeta's feet to her head, as if the very branch she stood upon was telling her that something was wrong, terribly wrong. "I'm coming as fast as I can," she said.

Veeleeta staggered forward, her oblong feet pounding on the branch beneath as she rushed past a vast array of fungi, plants and vines growing on the huge branch. The wind grew in strength.

Thin branches above swayed with more vigour and the air grew thick. Alarmed, she quickly fumbled for the pouch attached to her belt, untied it, opened it and grabbed the little purple Messenger Bug from its protective luminous bed of fungus. She lifted it to her mouth.

"Get help," she yelled, panic rising in her throat. "Tell them where we are. We need help."

The tiny Messenger Bug took to the air as the wind whipped Veeleeta's long black plait across her face. She tripped on a row of Yellow Singa Cups, and as she fell, landing hard, they whistled twing-g-g … twing-g-g, twing-g-g … twing-g-g, twing-g-g … twing-g-g as they sprang back into position. Veeleeta, attempting to get her breath back, lay where she had landed. Then she spotted a couple of small blue feathers caught within some pink fungus next to her. "Wow!" Instantly forgetting her danger, she grasped at them just as the wind blew them out of reach. "Aagh! Drat!"

Reality came crashing back upon her as rain fell hard, stinging her body. What was she thinking? She had to get out of there. She quickly scrambled to her knees, hitching her bag upon her shoulder again. She staggered forward, fighting against the wind. The air was thudding in her ears as if it was breathing hard. The leaves all around her were lashing the air, snapping free, being flung around with fierce abandon. Rain splashed all around her. Insects darted for cover amongst mounds of moss, under roots of vines, burying themselves deep inside plants with such urgency Veeleeta could sense their desperation.

A suspension bridge came into view and she could see Congar heading towards it.

The rain fell even harder. The wind grew stronger, tugging at her clothes, lashing at her long hair.

"Congar! Wait!"

She ran on. Reaching the bridge, made from planks of wood wound together by rough vines, she stepped onto it, but stopped two boards in: the bridge had started to sway.

Congar, standing on the bridge itself, turned bright red in colour and yelled, "Too late! Too late!"

Veeleeta's mind spun. *What does he mean?* The bridge now swayed so much she froze, not daring to move. Terrified she yelled, "CONGAR! Please. Come back!"

Leaves flung against her face. A squall of rain dashed against her body. She sank to her knees and gripped a plank of wood so tightly her knuckles were white. The wind whistled past her ears with such intensity that one of the rope railings snapped free of its anchor, a nearby branch.

Veeleeta screamed as the bridge tilted to one side and she slid along with it. A squeal pierced the air and Veeleeta, shocked into silence, watched as Congar plummeted down, down, down into the depths, lost from sight as the wooden planks he had been standing on broke apart and descended into the shadows below. She was now teetering on the edge of oblivion; empty space lay before her. Instinctively, she quickly twisted herself around and scrambled back onto the silver branch, snatching at anything that would give her traction. She flattened herself onto its surface, gasping for air, as her mind could not, would not, grasp what was happening. Shuffling slowly away from the edge, she grabbed hold of a vine with both hands, squeezed her eyes shut and wished she was anywhere but here.

A deafening rumble high above her head rolled itself around. The air vibrated through the very fibre of the tree. Torrential rain was falling all around her, pummelling her tiny body. Lightning struck and a huge explosion cracked the branch above her head. Thousands of burning stars shot across the rooftop of Veeleeta's world. She screamed and hung on tighter. The sound of branches creaking, crunching and tearing asunder grew louder and louder, and a second later the branch she was clinging to shook so violently that she and it plummeted to the floor of the forest.

Ebony could see a bright yellow haze covering a vast clearing as if the stars had fallen from the sky, and plummeting to the ground, like a curtain of diamonds, was rain. Her gaze travelled to the outer edge of the clearing where trees, torn and disfigured, could be seen. A falling leaf fluttered into view. It hung as if suspended, twinkling with silvery light; a split second later, it was caught by the rain and dashed to the ground, disappearing into the haze below. The remains of branches with their silver leaves and broken limbs, snapped, torn and crushed beyond all hope, poked through the haze, and lying amongst them were two huge silver trees that had obviously crashed to the ground.

The rain stopped as if a tap had been turned off.

Ebony hesitated.

She pondered whether she should stay where she was or step into the clearing. Then before she knew what she was doing, she'd done just that. She gasped and wondered, *Why? How come?* Because she didn't think she had even made up her mind to do anything, and yet here she was now, standing out from under the protection of the trees where the air was colder. Goosebumps prickled over her bare skin. Even her feet felt cold. She looked down. Her white shoes were sinking into the mud and dirty water was seeping into her white socks.

I'm going to be in so much trouble, she thought.

Looking ahead, she saw a sea of luminescent yellow fungi on the ground like confetti scattered at a wedding. Ebony picked up a piece of fungus the size of her palm; it felt spongy, and she brought it up to her eyes to get a better look at its glowing flesh. It was shaped like a fan, its fluted edges with rings of growth showing up as deep yellow scalloped lines emanating from its base, which had a small piece of silver bark attached to it, just like a shelf sticks to a wall. *For fairies to use.* Ebony smiled at the thought.

She caressed its surface then placed it into one of the two side pockets of her green skirt.

She looked up at the canopy. There was a huge gap in it. The storm, exhausted from the exertion of war, had finally given in as all things must when their time is up. Now she could see the black velvet sky above with its twinkling stars, and the moon, full, bright and in all its glory, with a single cloud passing across its face. Ebony smiled at the beauty, but inside she felt a deep sense of foreboding. It was late. Very late. And she would have been missed a long time ago. Dread filled her with what was to come when she was found. *If you're found, you mean,* her inner voice said in a cool, unfeeling tone. *You could die out here, you know … Oh, do shut up!* Ebony growled at her inner self. Would it never be quiet!

Scruffy whimpered from his spot at the edge of the clearing. Ebony looked at him, put her hands on her hips and shook her head in disbelief. Drops of water were falling from the leaves above onto his back.

"You're such a duffer, Scruff. Why don't you just give up and come and help me find something? There must be *some* other interesting things in all of this stuff."

Scruffy lowered his head and, with drooping ears, glared back at her.

"Fine, have it your own way. I don't know where you get all this stubbornness from."

She shrugged her shoulders, picked up a small spiky plant and studied the swirling patterns on the fleshy grey leaves. The bruised and battered petals were various shades of pink with a spattering of fine purple dots around each edge. How she would love to be able to draw them, to paint a picture. *Yes.* Making up her mind to do just that when she got home – *If you get home you mean* – she stuffed it into the pocket of her skirt, ignoring her inner qualms. She then started searching for more plants. The floor of the forest was littered with a wide variety of flowers and plants, more than she had ever seen in her whole life, and none of them she knew.

As Ebony picked up another flower, the sound of bells drifted through the forest again. She quickly looked at Scruffy, unsure if he was safe. His head was to one side, his ears were up; he could hear them too, she was sure of it. Then he yelped and shot forward. A large leaf, unable to carry its load of water anymore, had caved in under the weight and drenched him.

"Oh, I'm so sorry, Scruffy," laughed Ebony. "Are you all right?" Scruffy abruptly stopped in front of her. His head was low, his ears sagged and he was dripping wet. He stared at her as if accusing her of something.

"It's not my fault," said Ebony, shocked that he would blame her. "Come here." She gave him a rub under the chin then turned and as she stood looking at the wonder in front of her, blue dots appeared in the undergrowth beyond the clearing off to her left. Ebony took in a sharp breath as she watched them blink on and off, becoming fewer and fewer, getting smaller and smaller as if they were moving away until finally they disappeared.

Scruffy whimpered and rubbed himself against her leg. Ebony bent down and gave him a reassuring pat.

"Um. We will be all right, Scruff," she said, hoping this was true. "Come on. I want to have a look at these silver trees. They are huge. They must have been hit by lightning. It's the only reason I can think of that they would come crashing down like that, causing all of this." Ebony spread her arms out to indicate the devastation surrounding her. She then walked up to the larger of the two trees, as Scruffy started sniffing his way through the nearby debris.

The tree trunk came up to her knees. Its silver surface was covered in patches of lichen, moss and the remains of vines and plants, but something seemed wrong. She'd never seen a tree with such an explosion of plants growing up its trunk before, but as it lay there on its side, she could almost believe that it was a branch, not a tree at all. As soon as she had thought it, the truth was there. This was a branch of immense size.

The tree must be huge!

She tentatively reached towards it. Her fingers easily slid across its smooth warm silver surface until they abruptly stopped. Red sticky sap oozed out of a large gash, one of many in its side. Frowning, Ebony looked into the wound. Layer upon layer of different shades of pink splintered wood could be seen as she peered into its depths. Blood-red sap was oozing out of its dark red heart. Sadness hung in the air. Ebony had not noticed it before, but now she felt as if the area was thick with loss and despair. Tears prickled in her eyes. Why? She did not know why. It was as if the sadness was seeping into her senses, awakening her own devastating memories, threatening to overwhelm her. She grew frightened as the feeling grew in intensity. Her heart started pounding and she felt it getting louder in her ears.

Scruffy barked.

Ebony flinched and the sadness within her instantly faded away.

Glad of the distraction, she looked to the far side of the clearing and could only just make him out. His head was down and his tail was up, waving frantically.

"What have you found, Scruff?"

S cruffy had found a small dark hollow created by three silver branches lying higgledy-piggledy over the top of each other.

"What is it?" said Ebony, quite excited at the prospect that he might have found something special, interesting, or maybe just downright boring or dangerous.

Ebony, putting her doubts to one side, sank to her knees wincing and shivering as the cold muddy water splashed against her legs, soaking the edges of her clothing. On all fours, with her long hair dragging in the mud, she hunched over, stuck her bottom in the air, and peered inside the hollow.

"Um … I don't know about this, Scruff." She sat back upon her heels and looked at him.

Scruffy looked back at her with expectant eyes. Ebony frowned. "Oh all right, but it'd better be worth it."

She picked up a thin branch with a small piece of glowing fungus attached, making an excellent torch, and poked it inside the hollow.

"Well … you're right, Scruff. … There is something in there." Taking a deep breath, she plunged her left hand into its depths, closed her fingers around something small and soft, and without another thought, pulled it out.

Ebony sat on a branch and carefully opened her hand. A rush of excitement threatened to overwhelm her as she looked down at the muddy object no larger than her thumb lying in the middle of her palm. She gently poked it. It did not move but felt soft in the middle. She then picked up the hem of her green skirt and attempting to be as delicate as she could be, rubbed some of the mud off it.

"Wow! Look at this, Scruff." Ebony pushed her open palm towards him. "It looks like a little person. A fairy. Finally!" *Oh, no wings.* "Um. Well. Let's have a look at you," she mumbled to herself.

She gently turned the object over one way and then another by twisting and cupping her hands. She stared at it in wonder. She was sure that even though it, whatever *it* was, was small, it had a long nose – or was that short? "Um!" If she was to describe it, she would say it was a very short, stumpy elephant trunk, with a pig's snout on the end of it. It was about the length of her little fingernail. She then looked at its face: the tiny eyes were shut. Ebony delicately touched the top of its head.

"It's flat." In raptures of disbelief, she exclaimed, "This is *amazing.* Scruff! Look! It's wearing clothes. See? There are little purple dots showing through the mud, there on the top half." Ebony pointed to them, and when she gently touched the area, it felt like fabric. "And it has a round tummy and these look like trousers. I think they are green, and look, the *tiniest* legs I've ever seen … and yet it has two large oblong feet. And *shoes!* Amazing!" Turning it over, she said, "Look, there is a long dark plait down its back." She gently picked up the end of it between her fingertips before releasing it. "And a tail! Fancy that. It's almost like a tiny rabbit tail but not so pointy. Wow! What an amazing creature."

Creature? Ebony questioned herself.

Of course, it's a creature. What else could it be? Look at it …

Is it alive?

Good question.

Ebony held it up to one of her ears. Sticking a muddy finger in the other, she closed her eyes, opened her mouth a little and concentrated. Allowing her mind to settle, she smiled. She could just hear breathing, very shallow, but it was definitely alive.

"Amazing," she said again, shaking her head as she looked at it, smiling.

Then turning to Scruffy she said, "Well, Scruff? What do you think?" He sniffed the creature and tilted his head to one side, cocking his left ear in the air.

"Tut! Honestly!" Ebony looked back at the creature again. "I wonder where it came from and what it is." She looked up to the gap in the canopy. "It could not have come from up there, could it? No, it must have been on the ground when the branches fell." Looking down at it she said, "You poor thing. I'm amazed you survived at all. Well …" Ebony paused as she thought of what to do. "I know. We will take it home, Scruff. Yes. That's a grand plan."

She carefully stood up, placed the creature in the pocket of her skirt, which held the collection of strange plants she'd collected earlier, and turned towards the dark forbidding forest. "Right, let's get out of here."

6

Ebony moved to the edge of the clearing, holding a small branch of glowing fungus, the illumination of which gave off a small circle of light. Scruffy leaned against Ebony's left leg. She was glad of the warmth and the feeling of having something solid up against her. It made her feel safe, although there was a niggling feeling inside her mind, suggesting that perhaps she wasn't as safe as she thought she was.

Even though the bright glow from the vast amount of luminescent fungi lying in the clearing behind her spread out into the surrounding forest, it didn't spread very far. Silhouetted trees could be seen close by, but as she looked into the distance, which was as black as a starless night, all sight of the trees was lost. Ebony shifted her leg and Scruffy took a step forward.

"Well, Scruff, I know we're both in this mess, but I can tell you now, I'm expecting *you* to get us out of it."

Ebony glared down at him. Scruffy cowered under her gaze but did not move.

"Well?" She placed her hand on her hip and frowned. "Which way do we go?"

Scruffy growled in reply.

"Don't give me that. Dogs are supposed to be good at this sort of thing, so get on with it. You don't expect *me* to try and figure it out, do you?"

Scruffy huffed and headed off, Ebony following.

As the two of them walked into the dark, dense forest, Ebony held the fungus torch in her left hand. It emitted a small ring of comforting light, but she flinched every time she heard the chirp of an unknown creature or insect. The sounds of things scuttling in the leaf litter made her nervous. She kept looking back but there was only the black of night to see. The light from the clearing had faded from view a long time ago.

The two of them trudged on for what seemed like hours and Ebony grew tired. Her shoulders stiffened, her left knee ached and she started to hobble, then she stumbled on a tree root.

"I've got to stop, Scruff," she said, rubbing her sore knee. "I've just got to sit down."

Ebony gingerly positioned herself at the base of a large tree, and sighed as she leaned back against the smooth bark. Scruffy clambered onto her lap and lay down.

"Hi there, Scruff," she said, gently laying her hand on his body. She then closed her eyes and fell into a dreamless sleep.

E bony awoke with a start. "What is it, Scruff?"

Scruffy's body had stiffened. A deep growl resonated through his chest. She pulled him closer. The occasional plop of water, dripping from one leaf to another, could be heard. Something moved within the leaves nearby. Bells tinkled in the distance. A streak of white light appeared then disappeared so quickly Ebony was unsure if she had actually seen it.

"What was that, Scruff?" she whispered. She peered into the depths and listened but the noise did not come again. "Come on."

Ebony gently pushed him off her lap then moaned as she stiffly clambered to her feet. Every part of her seemed to ache. She quickly hugged the nearest tree for support and realised how thirsty and hungry she was. Then she sighed, knowing there wasn't a thing she could do about it. Then again … She picked up a damp leaf, looked at it and wondered what it would be like to suck the dampness from it. "Um." She poked her tongue out and touched it. It tasted of damp earth and she spat out a glob of saliva. "Ukk!"

Nope! She dropped it. She remembered how Nanny Jones had once tied a plastic bag over fresh leaves to extract water from them. It had tasted just as terrible.

"I should never have stopped," moaned Ebony. "I hurt even more now, Scruff." She took a deep breath, steeled herself and said, "Right, let's go."

She looked at Scruffy who was lifting his leg against a tree, relieving himself. Ebony moaned, "If only it was that easy for me." She then screwed up her lip. *Should she dare?* Her insides had started to squirm and she could now feel the discomfort of not being able to relieve herself for hours. She'd been all right until she'd thought about it, but now the more she tried to ignore it, the worse she felt. In the end, there was nothing else she could do, she could not hold on any longer, and so reluctantly, she went and squatted behind a tree, feeling most awkward. Green glowing fungi pulsated amongst the nearby trees looking like eyes watching her. Once she was finished, she adjusted her skirt, admitting to herself that she did actually feel much better, except for the dampness in her knickers. It was decidedly uncomfortable and the faint smell of urine was unexpected. "Why does no one tell you these things?" she grumbled to herself. "Nanny Jones never said a word," Ebony huffed as she contemplated removing her underwear. *What? And walk around with nothing on? No way!* The thought sent shivers through her. Nope! She wasn't going to be doing anything like that! There wasn't a thing she could do about it now anyway, the damage was done. She could not have held on for much longer and she knew that.

She stood looking at the world around her. It never seemed to change. It was full of trees that looked dark and foreboding, silhouetted against the pitch black of nothingness. A soft pulsating sound always seemed to hum in the background. From where it came she could not tell, until she suddenly remembered, kicking herself for being so stupid, that it was the trees breathing. *Of course.* Drops of rain occasionally plopped onto the ground. Things moved in the leaf litter and a shiver ran up Ebony's back. They had to keep going, what else could they do?

"Come on, Scruff."

As they slowly walked into the unknown, the fungus torch dimmed and Ebony frowned, wondering how much longer it would last. She was growing tired again when something sharp tore at her legs. Frightened, she jumped backwards and stumbled and fell. Sharp thorns caught at her long hair, tore at her arms and legs, grabbed at her skirt and tore a hole in it. A long bramble cane slashed across her cheek, setting it on fire as it sliced open her skin. She dropped to her knees, letting go of the torch and grabbing at her face. Salty tears trickled into the open wound making it sting. Then, as the fire in the wound slowly died, she sat breathing hard trying to calm herself, trying to think of what to do. She gritted her teeth and pushed herself off the ground, then cried out in pain as strands of her long hair, entangled amongst the canes, were pulled from her scalp. She struggled against their grip. She instinctively grabbed hold of the bramble cane and pulled it away, then yelled as sharp thorns broke free, embedding themselves in her left palm.

"You idiot!" she yelled at herself as Scruffy barked in distress. "It's all right, Scruff," Ebony sobbed. She then pushed her back against the plant and as she freed herself from it, her skirt tore even further.

With tears in her eyes, she retrieved a hanky from one of the side pockets of her skirt and wrapped it around her hand, which had started to throb. *How stupid can you be?* Ebony scolded herself. *To walk straight into brambles. I can't believe you did that. Don't you know any better? ...* "Shut up! Shut up! Shut up!" Ebony yelled out loud as she slumped to the ground and cried. Injustice, hurt, sadness and grief consumed her, and her tears now had nothing to do with being lost in Tanglemire Forest.

Scruffy whimpered and brushed up against her. Ebony gulped, and through blurred vision patted him and tried to smile, but found she could not. Instead, she bent down and picked up her torch. She looked at it and bit her lip. Its light was only just glowing, giving off nothing of worth, except the knowledge that there was at least one speck of light in the immense darkness surrounding her. Even though it gave her a small measure of comfort, her heart felt heavy and she screwed up her eyes, desperate not to start crying again. She felt if she did, she'd never stop, not this time. *You have to be strong, Ebony,* she told herself. *Yes,* she answered. She knew that. She had to get them all home. But how? She didn't have a clue.

Ebony looked upon the forest, which still breathed in and still breathed out as it continued to grow all around her. She looked at the glowing green eyes of fungi blinking in the darkness, and then in a voice that sounded as if she was drowning, said, "Come on, Scruff. Let's go."

Scruffy trotted ahead and disappeared into the dark shadows surrounding her, then yelped.

"Scruffy! Are you all right?" Ebony hurried on, then she too cried out.

A crackling, tingling feeling flooded through her body. She spun around, thrusting the torch forward as if somehow it could protect her. Its light blinked out.

7

Ebony leaned forward. "Scruffy, are you there?" Her eyes strained to see something, anything, in the darkness that was as black as a raven's wing. All her senses tingled as she listened, watched and waited. It was as if she had stepped over an invisible line, or gone through one. No green luminescent fungi could she now see. Not even the sound of the trees breathing could she hear.

Something tickled the back of her leg and it made her jump. She felt a cold wet nose touch her skin. With realisation, she bent down and said, "Oh, thank goodness it's only you." She then patted Scruffy's head. He was shivering. "It's all right, Scruff." It dawned on Ebony that she could clearly see him. *Why?* She stood up and spun around, looking back to where she had come from.

In the distance, up in the canopy, a beam of white light was spreading through the branches, illuminating the forest as if bright moonlight shone upon it. It then turned direction and sped straight towards her. Ebony took a step back as a lump grew in her chest. A demand to flee filled her up, but fascination held her riveted to the spot and her inner self demanded to know what she was doing.

As the light drew closer, Ebony could see three glowing white balls lying within it, and the air was filled with the trilling of crystal bells. It was the same sound she had been hearing ever since she had entered Tanglemire Forest. A part of Ebony was pleased that she finally had an answer to what was causing it; another part of her didn't want to know and cringed in a deep dark corner of her mind, hiding away from the truth.

Scruffy barked.

The spheres suddenly stopped and hovered just above the forest floor a few feet away from them.

In an instant, the spheres exploded into thousands of bubbles. Ebony threw up her hands to protect herself and could feel Scruffy, who had yelped, cowering behind her legs. She watched through a web of fingers as the bubbles swirled around, gathering into three large long columns of light. They shimmered as if they were behind a windowpane made wet from rain.

Within the centre of each one was a bright light. Scruffy whimpered. Ebony blinked, desperately trying to get her eyes accustomed to the brilliance radiating all around her. She then dropped her hands to her side, stunned at what she saw.

Floating in front of her, the light formed into three immensely tall slim figures. Each had a long tail filled with sparkling incandescence. Each tail, tipped with voluptuous silken tail fins, was undulating in a non-existent breeze just above the ground.

Looking up, up, up, so high up, three blank featureless faces stared down at her. Long thin arms, each dangling with transparent strips of cobweb, stretched out towards her. Thin web-like hands beckoned her to come to them.

Ebony's heart skipped a beat.

"Hey, you!"

Ebony flinched and spun around to see who had yelled at her. Her eyes, filled with the white dots of dancing light, made it difficult to see anything. All she could hear were heavy boots resonating close by as they crashed through the undergrowth, coming closer and closer. Then crystal bells tinkled and Ebony turned just in time to see the three white balls of light disappear back into the dark forest.

Deep booming voices yelled, "Don't move!"

"We've found 'er!"

"She's 'ere!"

Ebony turned in the direction of the voices again, only to find a kaleidoscope of white dots of light flickering amongst colours of yellow, black and brown, making it impossible to see who was there.

Strong hands grabbed at her arms. She screamed, "LET ME GO! Let … me … go!"

Distorted faces appeared in the gloom. Lights bobbed amongst the shadows. Scruffy barked, snapping at unguarded legs, as heavy boots stomped all around him.

Ebony was picked up and thrown over a broad shoulder. She winced as her nose bounced into the rough cloth of a waistcoat smelling of sheep, and she found herself being carried through the forest. She lifted her head, heard a yelp, and watched horrified as Scruffy's body flew through the air.

"SCRUFFY!" she screamed, kicking and pounding her clenched fists against the back of the man carrying her. But strong arms clamped her legs tight, and Scruffy's mournful whimpering grew fainter and fainter, until the sound of his cries stopped. Ebony instantly screwed up her eyes, and whispered, "Scruffy!"

Time passed, how much, fast or slow, Ebony did not know. She was too tired, too worn out to even think about it. All she knew was that she'd been slowly rocked up and down, lying straddled across the shoulder of the huge man carrying her, for enough time to hurt. Her ribcage ached from being crushed against the man's back, making it difficult to breathe. Her back throbbed from being bent over his shoulder for so long. Her head ached with the blood rushing to her head, and even though she'd tried to hold her head up to elevate the pressure, eventually she'd had to give up and let it flop back down again. The only thing that helped ease the ache behind her eyes was closing them.

Now the taste of summer was drifting up from the ground. She opened her eyes and absentmindedly watched as ears of wheat swayed beneath her and she breathed in the night air cleansed by rain. It was then she remembered she was hanging upside down.

Panic gripped her as she watched the man's legs crash through the vegetation as if he was walking through the salty water of the sea.

What can I do?

I don't know.

Then the mountain of a man stopped. He dragged her from her lofty position and she slumped to the ground, her legs giving way. Firm rough hands grabbed her shoulders, settling her back upon her shaky feet. A lump stuck in her throat making it difficult to breathe, and she cringed. People surrounded her, their many faces distorted by the flickering yellow light of lanterns being held high, and the full moon, casting its eerie glow over the crowd, made the figures look dark and foreboding. Then everything started to swim in front of Ebony's eyes. The blood rushed from her head and she took a shakey step back.

"Miss Ebony!"

Ebony looked ahead of her. She knew that voice. She'd heard it before and a shiver filled her to her core. The voice sounded cold. Upset. Unforgiving. Ebony looked about and stammered, "Nanny? Nanny Windabothem. Is that you?"

The sea of people stopped rolling and crashing around, and all became calm. The shadow of a tall thin figure peeled itself away from the crowd and Ebony felt herself shrink away from it. A desire to flee flooded her whole body. She took another step back but found her way blocked by the same mountain that had delivered her here. She looked from side to side for a way out but saw none. Her thoughts were a jumbled mess, and yet relief filled her because there was actually someone here who would save her from all these strange people, take her back home, although that hope was tinged with fear. Did she really want to go home where people did not know what happened behind closed doors, to go home with *her?*

"Miss Ebony! Come here!" The voice filled with menace demanded her utter obedience, but Ebony did not move. "Come here!"

A strong hand at Ebony's back pushed her with such force she stumbled forward. Her arms flailed in the air and she felt herself falling. Faces seemed to sneer at her as she finally tripped over her own feet and slumped against Nanny's thin body. Bony hands landed heavily on Ebony's shoulders. Ebony struggled to stand up, but when she did, she found herself looking at a face distorted by the lack of light. Two large black empty sockets, sitting in a pale face, shocked Ebony so much she attempted to run, but Nanny Windabothem's fingers, tightening their grip, held her fast.

"What have you been doing?" snapped Nanny Windabothem. "Do you know how worried we have all been?"

Ebony felt herself being shaken. A chorus of whispering built up around her. The air grew thick as Nanny looked over at the crowd, quickly releasing Ebony from her grasp.

"But—" protested Ebony.

"Don't but me, young lady."

Nanny Windabothem's face, illuminated by nearby lanterns, showed sharp dark eyes glaring at Ebony as if they would bore deep into her, and see all her secrets. "I've had half the village out looking for you, for hours. Your parents are worried sick and they're on their way home. I have even called the police. How thoughtless can you be?"

Ebony opened her mouth to say something, to protest, but nothing came out. She winced as Nanny grabbed her forearm, digging her fingernails into the soft muscle. Silent tears trickled over Ebony's cheeks as she was dragged back home to Bedlow Manor.

8

High in the canopy, four long silver threads dropped out of the silver leaves. Like snakes glowing in the night, they slithered over unseen branches, descending into the black void below. Upon touching the muddy ground, each snapped straight and taut, from floor to treetop. Silence filled the clearing as they stood waiting … waiting … waiting …

Leaves rustled. Branches swayed. A cool breeze slowly swirled within the clearing, caressing each thread, causing each of them to split right down the middle. With delicate unseen fingers, the breeze slowly prised each thread apart, revealing a glowing ladder. Then lovingly, the breeze floated its way between the rungs of each one of them, playfully flicking at the sides of each thread causing them to vibrate.

Slowly, slowly, ever so slowly, a soft melodious tune grew in richness and shattered the stillness of the forest. It wound its way around where once young green saplings had stood straight and strong but now lay crushed, deformed and dying, leaning up against their older cousins for support. The music gently, lovingly, swirled itself within the very being of every branch, leaf and twig, which gave one last tremor, one last sigh, before the music reluctantly left them to their inevitable fate. Then as the ancient forest shuddered and looked on in dismay, the music continued to swirl itself out into the darkness only to be consumed, as all things are within the living fibre of the very forest itself.

Each ladder now shone upon discarded silver branches, whose leaves had turned black. They shone upon plants whose flowers lay crushed beyond all hope, and swathes of blackened fungi. All the debris lay higgledy-piggledy in the mud, the result of two huge branches, which had descended from the great heights of the towering trees above, crashing into the immovable earth below.

A party of four small Gribbles descended into the deep dark void, now stinking of decay. Their long noses twitched. Their bright eyes stared out into the gloom. Their large oblong feet, shod with well strapped shoes, made their way down the glowing ladders, one rung at a time. Then a Gribble asked, "Trillium. Will you slow down and answer some questions? Like, who are we rescuing?"

"Oh, for goodness sakes, Grigwell," said Trillium, not slackening his pace, his long nose scrunching up and making it look like a short snout. "I thought you knew. It's Veeleeta!" he called out, as he hitched his trousers up a little to ease his climb down the ladder. "It wasn't until Congar returned that we even knew Veeleeta was missing. He told us where to start looking."

"Veeleeta! How? When? ... Will you just stop! How can I know anything when you will not stand still long enough for me to be told? All I knew was that I was to meet you here and to bring Fluellen and Quintell. I had no why, how or what. I only had time to grab my waistcoat holding my Fire Stones. No one seemed to know anything really. I have managed to send some Messenger Bugs to the Master's Station to arrange for some supplies to be delivered to us, just in case we need them, but it's very difficult to put a rescue mission together when I *don't* even know who or what we are rescuing." Grigwell scowled at Trillium, scratched his scanty beard then continued to descend.

Trillium ignored him as he flicked his black fringe out of his eyes.

"Trillium," a soft voice said from Trillium's right. "When was Veeleeta last seen? Why did Congar not come with us? It would have been much better if he had."

"Fluellen," said Trillium, finally stopping, turning to look at her so fast his long black plait fell across his shoulder. "Congar managed to glide home and tell us what happened and where to look for Veeleeta. He will be alright, he only needs to rest. Poogle's are extremely resilient as you know. Honestly, I've told you all I know."

"Why were they so far away from the village?" asked another Gribble with silver hair.

"Oh, I don't know, Quintell! You know what Veeleeta is like," Trillium said. "She goes off collecting things all the time, stubborn as anything, will not be told. Honestly, I don't know where she gets it from."

The other Gribbles lifted their eyebrows. Fluellen giggled as she scratched at her round belly. "That reminds me," she said. "Why has Snailum not come with us? Does he not know what has happened?"

Trillium looked into Fluellen's sparkling eyes, her face framed by her two white plaits that were so long they came down to her waist.

"Papa's been away for many days," he answered. "He's travelling to MoreReeCar. Mama has sent a Messenger Bug to tell him what has happened, but it will take him an age to return to the hanging village. We could not wait."

"Look up!" shouted Grigwell.

The clouds had cleared and the moonlight was now pouring through the gap in the canopy. The search party, hanging in mid-air, watched as it plummeted past them, highlighting crushed and mutilated remains of trees. At the bottom of the gaping void, it ignited a minuscule spark of light in one and then another and another of the blackened fungi scattered across the clearing. As the light grew, it spread like a wave of water swirling in a pool at the base of a waterfall, until every single piece of the thousands of fungi now glowed with a pale yellow light. Revealed were two huge silver limbs, and thousands of smaller branches shattered to pieces.

As Trillium alighted onto the muddy ground, he and the other Gribbles released their grip on the ladder, which then slithered its way back up into the treetop and disappeared.

"Look at this place," Trillium whispered as he stood wide-eyed looking upon the devastation. "How could Veeleeta possibly have survived the fall?"

Scattered in all directions were branches whose bark seemed tarnished as if it had not been polished by the moon's radiance on many a night. A vast array of plants, desperately clinging onto where they had grown since seedlings, along with swathes of glowing fungi, hung limp.

"Look at all this *mud*," said Fluellen, as she turned to look behind her. "My tail's going to get covered in it. Trillium, could you just check?"

Trillium frowned as he looked down at Fluellen's stubby tail with its long blonde hairs sitting in the mud. "Fluellen! If you are going to start worrying about such things, you might as well go back to the hanging village right now, and go and *do* whatever it is that females *do!*"

Fluellen turned and narrowed her eyes. "I will remind you, Trillium, that I'm a Master Auror, and if you think my skills are any less worthy than Master Healer Quintell, or Master Tracker Grigwell, then you are sorely mistaken. And, if I want to worry about the state of my tail, that's *my* business!" Fluellen moved to stand next to Grigwell, then glared back at Trillium who frowned and looked down at his shoes.

Quintell shook his head, allowing his long plait of silver hair to slide off his shoulder and hang down his back. He sighed and walked over to one of the two huge silver limbs. He pressed his hands against its cold bark now stained dark with sticky red sap. He tapped it with four short stubby fingers. "I can feel its pain." He pressed his small ear against it. "It weeps. It knows it is dying … Fluellen, can I ask for your assistance."

Fluellen frowned then moved next to Quintell, who was now singing, very softly, a song of sorrow. She took a deep breath and closed her eyes as she placed both her hands on the branch. A bright green light slowly spread out from her hands, like water, until it covered the entire branch. The light then changed to blue and was slowly lost from sight as it was absorbed into the very fibre of the wood. Fluellen pulled away, breathing hard. She then slowly moved over to the second branch.

"What is she doing?" whispered Trillium.

Grigwell looked at him as if he was unsure he should say anything. "She is putting the branches to sleep so they don't suffer anymore."

"What! She is killing them?"

"They are dying already. She is making that as peaceful and painless as possible. Look!" Grigwell pointed as he lifted his head, allowing his long black plait to fall off his shoulder and down his back. Thousands of insects were lifting from the forest floor, heading for the canopy above.

"Where did they all come from?" asked Trillium, as his long nose followed their ascent.

"The moon of Venra has sent her rays to save them," said Fluellen, as she now watched the mass exodus. "It's guiding them back to the safety of the canopy, just as its rays have ignited the spark of life in the Peeloo fungi surrounding us. Although …" Fluellen's voice trailed off, and she turned to look around her. "It will not keep the fungi alive for long."

Quintell picked a small spiky plant out of the mud and touched the battered petals of the tiny white flowers protruding from its top. Six round orange bugs were crawling out from amongst the petals. He then picked out a fine blue strand from within its leaves, raised his eyebrows and placed the strand in the top pocket of his waistcoat.

"What is that?" asked Trillium.

Quintell looked at him. "It's a white Seafurl. It only grows on the branches of Silver Lunaria trees. In fact, it only grows—"

"Not … the … plant. That! The blue stringy thing."

"Oh, I'm not completely sure. It reminds me of something from long ago. It's just on the tip of my tongue. Oh well, I'm sure it will come to me … Look!"

The six orange bugs had now joined the rest of the flight to safety. All the Gribbles watched them lift themselves high into the air on their delicate wings. When they were lost from sight,

Quintell tucked the plant amongst moss on a nearby branch and gently patted it, then wished it well.

"Look at the Peeloo, they are dying." Quintell picked up a piece of the glowing fungus from the mud and caressed it with a stubby finger. A black line had appeared around its outer edge and was steadily growing thicker, swallowing up the light within. Moonbeams had started fading as the moon continued its cosmic dance across the night sky. The speck of light lying deep in the heart of every piece of fungus was growing fainter.

"Grigwell," said Fluellen, "Venra is moving on. The moonbeams will soon pass. Nothing down here will survive without her light. It will soon be pitch black."

"What a waste," said Quintell, letting the fungus fall to the floor to join its thousands of companions as dark shadows, which had been clawing at the edges of the clearing, now seeped under shattered logs and floated down from above.

"Fluellen, send for lamps," ordered Grigwell. "The other Gribbles should be near with the supplies I've ordered."

Trillium's eyes darted around. He planted his shod feet firmly in the mud, removed his cap, dusted it off against his large round belly, replaced it over his long black hair and found he could not drop his hands. They had started to tremble. He grabbed his cap, pressing his fingers against his flat head, attempting to steady them.

How were they ever going to find Veeleeta in all of this debris?

He closed his eyes and took a deep breath. When he opened them, he saw Fluellen reaching for a pouch attached to her belt that all Gribbles carried. She untied the thongs holding it in place and, as Trillium released his hold on his cap, she put the pouch onto a large clean leaf, tossing her long white plaits behind her. She knelt on a completely different leaf, ensuring it also was clean, and opened the pouch. Inside were two spongy pads, glowing pale yellow. They sat on either side of a thick piece of twine. Twelve Messenger Bugs were held within, six on each side. Each small winged bug, in two rows of three, was identical in shape and form but not in colour. Some were as bright and shiny as sunlight on dewdrops, and others as dull as dried leaves.

Fluellen picked out a fluffy brown bug with five metallic blue bands around its lower body. She placed it on the palm of her right hand and it started to glow purple. "Tell the Gribbles we need the supplies and torches now. We will call for help if needed."

She softly blew on its fine golden wings. The Messenger Bug took off into the air and headed straight for the canopy.

"I hope the other Gribbles aren't too far away," she said.

Within moments, there was a soft rustle in the leaves above. Three thin ropes began lowering themselves towards them. Each had a small brown sack attached.

"They are here already," said Grigwell. "Good."

The blue-banded Messenger Bug returned to the pouch Fluellen held open and snuggled into its respective space, its glow dimming as it settled.

The sacks reached the ground just as Fluellen closed the pouch and refastened it to her belt.

Two of the sacks contained backpacks, one for each Gribble. Each was full of supplies and had a bedroll attached to the top. The third sack contained four sticks with protective hoods covering something at one end. As soon as the sacks were empty, just like the ladders, they sprang up into the canopy and disappeared.

Each Gribble, after hitching on a backpack, picked up a stick and upon removing the protective hood, revealed a piece of fresh Peeloo fungus shining with a cheery bright yellow glow. It made an excellent torch. An instant later, the moonbeams disappeared. A split second later, the very faint spark of life that fleetingly rekindled itself deep within the heart of thousands of blackened Peeloo ... died.

9

Ebony was now standing in the foyer of the Victorian Gothic mansion she called home. She ached from head to toe and felt as dirty as her clothes looked. Her shoes were soggy and her feet were itchy from being wet for so long. She looked at them and wiggled her toes in an attempt to make them feel better. It didn't work. Her long dishevelled hair fell across her face. She plucked a dead leaf from the strands of her long strawberry-blonde hair and dropped it onto the black and white tiles, which normally would have been spotlessly clean, but were now covered in muddy wet footprints. All she wanted to do was go to bed and hide away from the sadness that was eating away at her. Scruffy was gone.

She hardly noticed the noise of shuffling feet and murmuring voices until a hush descended upon the crowd of people from the nearby village. They had been out all night searching for her. Some were now pointing to the huge chandelier in the centre of the foyer. Its sparkling light had attracted hundreds of flying insects, which danced in and out of the intricate maze of crystal drops as if mesmerised by the light. Some people were marvelling at the many artifacts resting on antique tables nestled against pale-papered walls. Some could not resist touching the marble statues and crystal vases, leaving dirty fingerprints spattered over them. The staff employed to care for the hundred-room mansion looked on in dismay. Two pot-bellied policemen stood silently to one side as their eyes took in every detail.

Ebony faced the sweeping staircase dominating the room. Nanny Windabothem was standing on the fifth step from the base of the stairs. She stood straight as a pole, running her trembling fingers across her dull black hair, drawn into a small tight bun sitting at the back of her head. She straightened the jacket of her brown uniform, which was covered in a spattering of mud. Her cold dark eyes scanned the crowd. She dropped her arms to her side and gave a small cough.

Silence filled the room as everyone turned to look at her. A tiny smile crept across her thin lips as if she was pleased to have such a large audience, but a split second later it was gone.

"Welcome everyone. I would like to thank all the people who have helped to find Miss Ebony and bring her home safely. I'm sure that Mr and Mrs Wood are most grateful. You have all very kindly left your warm and cosy homes to search for Miss Ebony in one of the worst storms this country has seen in many a year. You have searched for many hours in the cold dark night and have suffered much anguish and discomfort. It has been a long and arduous evening and there are refreshments for any who wish to partake in the ballroom. The servants will show you the way, but, before you go, I'm sure that Miss Ebony would like to thank you herself."

Nanny looked down at Ebony with piercing eyes, as if she enjoyed laying the blame at Ebony's feet for the distress she had caused everyone. Ebony looked at her with horror, then gulped and turned to face the crowd. Grim faces of hard-hewn men, who looked as if they had sprouted from the ground with their thick and wiry beards, stared at her. The women, who were obviously waiting to hear what she had to say, had a soft motherly look about them. Their eyes were filled with warmth and a tinge of sadness. Most looked as wet and bedraggled as Ebony did.

"I'm sorry," said Ebony, with tears prickling her eyes, "for putting you to so much trouble."

"And?" said Nanny.

"For coming and finding me." Ebony's heart sank to the floor with humiliation.

"And?" said Nanny.

Ebony pondered on that. What else was there to say? "Thank you ... I didn't mean to get lost."

Nanny straightened herself as if satisfied, then said, in a voice that cut the air like steel, "Isobel, take Miss Ebony to her room."

The young maid straightened and brushed down her white apron and took a step out of the crowd.

"And give her a bath. She is *so* dirty and she smells." Nanny Windabothem's nose wrinkled in disgust and she glared at Ebony as if she were something that had been stuck under her shoe.

Ebony blushed and looked at the floor. She then felt Isobel take hold of her hand and squeeze it gently. She looked into Isobel's warm, smiling, emerald-green eyes, and because she'd always trusted her, when she felt Isobel give her hand a slight tug, she allowed herself to be led up the sweeping staircase.

They were walking past Nanny's stiff body when Nanny called out, "Kate!"

Ebony turned to watch a young dark-haired maid sheepishly extract herself from the crowd.

"Make sure— What — is — that!"

Ebony stopped, forcing Isobel to do the same. Nanny's thin neck stretched in the direction of the large double doors still open to the night. Everyone turned to see a small muddy animal, its head held low, heave itself over the threshold and limp across the tiles, leaving muddy footprints in its wake.

"Scruffy!" Ebony cried out. Instantly, she wrenched her hand free of Isobel's and rushed down the stairs, skirting around Nanny Windabothem, who didn't seem to understand what was going on. Ebony pushed her way through the crowd and reaching Scruffy, scooped him up off the floor. "Scruffy! Scruffy!" she cried. He whimpered, snuggling his wet and muddy head against her neck. "Oh, Scruffy. I thought I had lost you. I thought you were dead."

A gasp came from behind Ebony, and the hair on the back of her neck stood on end. She slowly turned, to find the crowd were now looking at her. From the back, murmurings, whisperings came as if a wind was moving the people apart, allowing Nanny Windabothem to step forward.

Ebony hugged Scruffy tighter, and he whimpered. Nanny's face turned bright red as one eyebrow shot up and a purple vein in her forehead pulsed. A single hair dared to twang out of place. Nanny's dark eyes flashed from the reflected light of a nearby lamp as if a storm was brewing inside them. Silence and suspense hung in the air. Everyone waited as Nanny towered over Ebony.

Breathe! yelled a tiny voice in Ebony's head and she sucked in the cool night air.

Out of the corner of her eye, Ebony noticed the two policemen exchanging nervous glances.

"I apologise for being late," said a man in a croaky old voice. The air crackled, and Ebony flinched, as did everyone else in the room. An old man, bent with age, was standing in the entrance of one of the halls leading away from the foyer. His pale blue eyes were scanning the crowd.

Nanny turned towards him. Everyone relaxed. She stabbed her finger in Ebony's direction and said to the old butler, "George, get that ... *thing* ... out of here and clean it up."

"Righty-oh."

George shuffled over to Ebony. He took the whimpering Scruffy from her arms, giving her a small smile and a secret wink, and shuffled off in the direction of the laundry.

Nanny gasped. Ebony looked back at her.

"Look ... at ... the ... state ... of ... *you!*" Nanny's eyes narrowed and she looked down at Ebony as if she were a bug to be devoured.

No! Not again! Ebony yelled to herself, stepping back. She flicked her eyes from side to side, indecision screaming, *Run!* then yelling, *No! Don't!*

Murmurs came from the crowd. Nanny's eyes flicked in their direction, she then frowned, straightened her shoulders, tugged at the bottom edge of her brown jacket and brushed her sleeves. It was then she spied the mud smeared over the fabric when Ebony had tripped in the wheat field and fallen against her. Nanny slowly turned and glared at Ebony, then without another word spun around and quickly ascended the steps, disappearing into the depths of the building.

The Gribbles were plunged into darkness as the faint glowing haze hovering over the forest floor disappeared. They instinctively huddled together as their eyes grew accustomed to the lack of light. Only the area lit by their lamps and starlight now gave them a reprieve from the inky blackness surrounding the void. The echoes of unknown animals screeching and fighting in the undergrowth echoed out. A creature hooted; another answered. A suffocating shroud of shadows rushed towards them, stopped by the light radiating from their lamps, and yet underneath it all, there was a feeling of density, as if they were standing in a thick fog.

Everyone jumped when Grigwell said, "Fluellen, can you find any trace of Veeleeta?"

Fluellen picked up a nearby blackened leaf, ensured it was clean of any mud and knelt down upon it. She then took a deep breath, wiggled her fingers over the soil, and as her hand moved to the left she stopped and stabbed a finger in the damp ground to mark the spot. She then hit the ground with her fist. A white light leaped forward and disappeared into the earth. She stood up and stared into the dark. The other Gribbles did the same.

Thin trails of white light, a dozen or more, so soft and delicate they were barely there, appeared from the soil and whipped through the dark vegetation. They dived back into the ground only to appear further along, further apart from each other. They trickled off branches as if they were thinking, taking their time, then hurried on as if the light, growing brighter, had found something. Trillium, watching in awe, had the feeling that these tiny streaks of light were hunting, hunting for any signs of his sister, Veeleeta.

As time passed, the Gribbles continued to stand and wait. Quintell fidgeted. Trillium turned and looked at Fluellen, whose face was concentrated on the lights whipping their way through the debris. Then a smile came across her face. Trillium turned and looked into the distance: a faint white glow had appeared. All the trails of light were now speeding towards the same spot.

"There," said Fluellen, pointing to her right. "Her energy is very faint, and yet, there is something … missing."

All the Gribbles headed in the direction of the faint white haze, but as they traversed the broken and dead debris that loomed out of the dark into the light of their lamps, by necessity they were forced to spread out.

Trillium tripped. When he stood up to see what had caused him to fall, he realised it was a deep impression in the mud. He looked at it. There was something strange about it, something he could not put his finger on. Excitedly, he opened his pouch and blew on all twelve Messenger Bugs. They flew into the air to circle the Peeloo lamp he held high, twinkling like many-coloured stars, singing a curious tune, signalling the others to come to him.

Minutes ticked by. Trillium huffed and tapped his foot on the ground. "Why is it taking them so long to arrive?" he moaned.

A moment later, Grigwell appeared and Trillium pointed to the large imprint he had discovered. His long nose twitched with anticipation. "What do you think of this?"

Grigwell gazed at the ground while Trillium let the Messenger Bugs return and snuggle back into their respective positions in the pouch.

"I don't know," Grigwell said as he fingered his scanty beard. "I've never seen anything like it. But if there is one, there will be others."

Before long, a signal went up to the left, and both Grigwell and Trillium rushed towards it.

"Look." Fluellen stood to one side, pointing to a large mysterious print embedded in the wet ground, but there was no joy in her voice. "Grigwell," Fluellen said, turning to face him. "Everyone and everything in this forest is connected within a wide band of energy. The skill is to know where, within that band, one single particle of energy lies. The energy from this print does not lie anywhere within that band."

"What does *that* mean?" asked Trillium, with obvious frustration in his voice. He didn't like it when he didn't understand what was going on. It always made him feel foolish.

"It means," said Fluellen, turning to face him, "that whatever made this print has no connection to this forest. It means it has come from outside it."

Both Gribbles gasped.

"Grigwell," said Fluellen, facing him, ignoring their reactions. "We need to head to where the energy lights have indicated. They have found something, but what I do not know. We must hurry before it fades."

Grigwell nodded his head. "We shall, and I understand, but I must examine this print. Knowledge is power. The more we know, the more it will help us in our search."

"Then I will go ahead," said Fluellen. "I cannot wait."

Grigwell, after acknowledging Fluellen's decision, knelt down and quickly examined the size and shape of the print. He smelled the ground with his long nose and prodded the soil with his four stubby fingers. "Interesting," said Grigwell to himself in a worried tone.

"What is interesting?" asked Trillium, but Grigwell did not answer.

Another signal went up, off to their right. The two of them rushed towards Quintell. He had found another print. After Grigwell had examined it, he announced, "This has been created by a large creature. See!" He spread his hands out in front of the four deep impressions making up one print. "It has four feet, and its tracks are heading in the same direction as the energy lights."

"Can you tell us anything else about them?" Trillium asked Grigwell.

"Not at the moment, but give me time."

"Time! We don't have time," grumbled Trillium. "We have wasted so much of it already."

Grigwell glared at him and walked off. Trillium huffed then

followed the group of rescuers heading towards the energy glow, which never seemed to get any closer. Trillium had the unnerving feeling that it was fading.

They crawled under huge branches many times larger than themselves, clambered over others small enough to do so. They tramped in and out of depressions for what seemed like hours.

"Stop! Everyone, come here!" yelled Grigwell.

"What's up?" the others asked as they looked around, their long noses twitching.

"Can't you see?" said Grigwell, indicating the ground. "We're all standing in a large depression. We've now been through three. This print is the same as the one Trillium found earlier. It belongs to something big, *very* big. We're dealing with two creatures here, not just one."

"Two!" said Trillium, shocked. He looked around as if the creatures would suddenly appear out of the darkness, but he could see nothing, he did not have the skill.

The group found Fluellen sitting on a log with her head in her hands. She looked as if her world had fallen away from her.

"Fluellen? Can you see anything?" asked Grigwell.

Fluellen just shook her head. "No. I'm sorry." She then looked up. "Not ... really," she added.

"What do you mean, not really," snapped Trillium.

"I mean," said Fluellen, with agitation in her voice, "that there is something on the edge of my sight, something here." She shook her hands on either side of her head. "Something on the very edge, but every time I turn to look at it, it's gone. I ... I ... I just feel it's on a different energy wavelength. A wavelength I cannot connect to. I can't see it. Also, too much time has now passed. The fleeting ghost energy of where Veeleeta once was in is no longer here. It has dissipated."

"What are you talking about?" grumbled Trillium. "Can't you ever say anything straight out?"

"It means," said Fluellen, standing up and facing Trillium with anger in her voice, "that the energy we saw when we first arrived has gone, *disappeared*, if that makes it easier for *you* to understand. It was only phantom energy anyway. I feared as much. As I said, this is where she's been, but is no longer."

"What do you mean, no longer?" asked Grigwell in a gentle understanding tone.

Fluellen just shook her head. "She isn't here."

"Well, can you find where she was last?" asked Grigwell.

Fluellen shook her head and looked very sad. "No. I'm sorry. Once it has gone it cannot be found again. All energies linger for a little while, some more than most, but once it has lost its strength it can't be found again."

"I see. So, it's up to me. Everyone, stay here while I search the area," commanded Grigwell.

"What do you mean?" called out Trillium, but Grigwell was gone. "What do you mean? What does Fluellen mean? I don't understand," yelled Trillium as he rushed after him.

"What? What! Oh, go and wait with the others, will you?" grumbled Grigwell as he studied the ground. "I need to think. I need to be quiet. You want me to find Veeleeta, don't you? Go and sit with the others."

The night dragged on. Trillium, who refused to be left behind, occasionally looked up to see two specks of light indicating his two companions sitting patiently, watching and waiting, on what he assumed must have been the top of a large branch.

Grigwell, in the meantime, had been crawling into deep hollows, sniffing the ground, pointing out tracks leading them into yet another hollow, and then another, and another. Trillium helped by looking inside nooks and crannies.

Suddenly, Grigwell sat down on a branch and sighed.

"What's wrong?" asked Trillium. "Why have you stopped?"

"I'm tired."

"Oh."

Trillium pulled up a large black leaf and sat down opposite him.

Grigwell stared at the ground.

"You're going to be able to find her, aren't you?" asked Trillium, with a sadness in his voice that threatened to overwhelm him.

Grigwell did not reply.

Trillium looked at the patterns in the mud and wondered how Grigwell ever made any sense of them at all. They made no sense to him. *Why was that?* he wondered. He knew the answer before he had even asked the question. It was because he had never bothered to learn the skill. Well, he was going to change *that*. He was going to learn about the mysteries of tracking, then next time a tracker was needed, it would be him. Then he would understand.

He looked back at Grigwell, who had suddenly stood up. Without a word, he moved towards a small hollow created by three silver branches and poked his fungus torch inside. Trillium watched as Grigwell crawled inside. Silence seemed to fill the air. A few moments later, Grigwell had backed out and collapsed in the mud.

"What's wrong?" said Trillium, rushing to Grigwell's side.

Grigwell held up a small shoe and a little patchwork bag.

Trillium snatched the items out of his hands. "Is she ... dead?"

"She is not here. I think the two creatures have taken her. Look at the signs in the mud."

"What!" Trillium hugged the items closer. He could see no signs of strange creatures, no signs of anything other than their own oblong footprints. "What can we do?" he asked, telling himself, *I have to learn this.*

"Don't worry. We will bring her back," Grigwell assured him, releasing all of his twelve Messenger Bugs, summoning the other Gribbles to come to them.

The Messenger Bugs were still twinkling overhead, singing their curious song, when the other two members of the group finally arrived. Upon being shown Veeleeta's belongings, the other Gribbles were overjoyed.

Fluellen held out her hands. "Do you mind if I hold Veeleeta's items, just for a moment?"

Trillium reluctantly gave both of them to her and watched with concern. As soon as Fluellen took them, she closed her eyes and immediately scrunched up her face as if in pain. Her fingers started twitching, then she gasped and froze. She opened her eyes; tears welled in them as she returned the bag and shoe to Trillium.

The other Gribbles stood looking at her, waiting for her to say something.

Silence lingered.

"Well?" asked Grigwell, as the Messenger Bugs all returned to his little pouch.

"It's as we knew," answered Fluellen, with sadness in her voice. "Veeleeta fell because of the storm. Lightning hit the branch above, and when it came down it took the branch she stood upon with it. There are blurred energies of something grabbing at her, guiding her, but what it was I cannot tell. There isn't anything more. Blackness is all I see."

Trillium looked at Veeleeta's patchwork bag with sadness in his eyes. He then opened it and placed the shoe inside for safekeeping. Inside, he found Veeleeta's Ocarina, and slowly, hesitantly placed it to his lips. As he blew, a sweet tune drifted into the darkness, and as everyone listened, it was slowly absorbed, as all things are, into the very fibre of the ancient forest itself. When it had completely disappeared, Trillium, with his hands shaking and tears flowing over his cheeks, replaced the musical instrument in the bag and secured it onto his backpack. He then frowned and stared at Grigwell. He found he could not, dared not, speak.

Grigwell nodded as if he understood, and then retying his pouch to his belt announced, "We need to find the rest of the tracks leading out of this place. The quickest way to do that is to move ourselves to the outer edge of the clearing, and walk the perimeter until we find them."

Time passed slowly as the group traversed the edge of the clearing. Trillium's head ached, swimming with questions that had no answers. Finally, Grigwell stopped and held up his hand. "I've found them. The tracks are here."

"Oh thank goodness," said Fluellen.

"Come on," said Grigwell, leading the little group of rescuers out of the clearing and into the trees.

But they had taken not more than a dozen steps when he stopped. A soft tinkling sound, like thousands of tiny crystal bells, drifted in the darkness.

"Selenites!"

11

Ebony lay in the bath, with bubbles up to her ears. She'd managed to ignore the initial sting of her wounds upon stepping into the water. She was now just happy allowing its warmth to seep into every pore. She ached from her head to her toes and was tired beyond belief.

She rubbed her right shoulder. It felt cold. *Why?* She looked up at the sash window located a small distance above the bath. She could now feel the cool night air seeping its way through the gaps in the window frame. The fine netted curtain, only covering the bottom half of the window, did very little to halt its progress into the room. She frowned and looked around her. The room was cold enough with all the black and white tiles on the floor and the white tiles halfway up the white walls, let alone having a window that did not keep out the cold.

Why would anyone in their right mind put a window in such a spot in the first place? she complained to herself. *It is right next to you when you're having a bath. Who designs these rooms?* she moaned. *Oh, do stop complaining,* she said to herself. She was too tired to care. *Does it really matter? Nothing matters.*

There was a soft knock on the door.

"Come in, Isobel." Ebony always knew it was her by the way she knocked. It was almost as if she was apologising for having to disturb the occupant of the room.

Isobel popped her head around the door and smiled. "Ah, good, good. Good to see," she said, hurrying over to the bath. "Now, the water is not too hot, is it?"

"No, it's just right. Thank you."

Isobel shuffled a small stool over to the side of the bath and sat upon it. She then proceeded to adjust her apron with a bit more fuss and vigour than was really necessary. Ebony tried to ignore it. Isobel started bouncing the hairbrush she held in one hand, up and down in a rhythmic manner on the top of her knee.

Ebony shut her eyes and sighed. Isobel always did this, fidgeting when she had something on her mind. "Yes, Isobel?"

"Miss Ebony," Isobel finally said with a sigh in her voice, "why'd you run away like that? You have only been home from boarding school for such a short time. Four weeks. Not long, not really. Are you really so unhappy?"

"I didn't run away," replied Ebony, slipping under the water, wishing the question had not been asked. When she re-emerged, unable to hold her breath any longer, Isobel was still there waiting for an answer. "I didn't. The storm was so ferocious. I just sort of … ended up in the forest."

"Well, at least you're home now safe, and that's all that really matters. Come on, we'd better remove all this shrubbery." Isobel pulled at a small twig entwined in Ebony's long wet hair.

"You're hurting me," yelled Ebony, as Isobel continued to tug.

"I'm sorry but this will never do. Here, you'd better do it. Your hair looks like a bird nest gone wrong." Isobel stood up and handed Ebony the hairbrush. "I'll go and get your night things but you make sure you remove all that mud. I'll be back soon."

Ebony grabbed a hank of hair and gritted her teeth as she dragged the brush through the tangled mess. Bits of leaves and twigs came away, as did long strands of her strawberry-blonde hair. She dropped the remains onto the tiles below. She frowned as she looked at the pile and once finished brushing, she rubbed her fingers through her sore head. She then leaned back and shut her eyes. Memories of Scruffy's little body flying through the air and disappearing into the shadows of the forbidden forest came crashing into her mind. She shook. The sight of glowing fungi flashed into her mind's eye and she bolted upright.

"My skirt!"

She looked over to the wicker chair in the corner where her wet and muddy clothes lay. She saw the bathroom door was still shut and, with her heart pounding in her chest, scrambled out of the bath. Ignoring the pain in her knee, and every other part of her body that now complained, she dashed over to it. *Hurry! Hurry!* her inner voice yelled. *She'll be back at any minute.*

Ebony pulled out the plants she'd gathered and the little creature from the side pocket of her skirt. She quickly looked at it, but it was still unconscious, unmoving, and covered in mud. She glanced around the room.

Where to hide you? Where to hide you? she thought. *Hurry! Hurry! Will you just be quiet? I can't think,* she snapped at herself. *There!* She opened the door of a long thin linen cupboard. Stacked inside were bundles of neatly folded white towels and face flannels. She grabbed a flannel, placed the creature and the strange plants in the middle of it, carefully folded the fabric and then stuffed it at the back of the second shelf. She dashed back to the bath and lowered herself into the water. The door creaked open.

"What do you think you are doing?" Isobel was standing in the doorway, glaring at her. She was holding a tea tray and had Ebony's nightwear draped over one arm.

"What? Oh, err, nothing," said Ebony, as she slipped further into the frothy water up to her chin.

"Why do I not believe you?" answered Isobel, looking at the wet footprints on the tiles.

Once Ebony was dressed in her nightie, dressing-gown and slippers, she entered her large bedroom. She found Isobel had lit the fire and the room felt toasty warm. Scruffy was lying on the hearthrug asleep and Ebony sighed. She was finally home, safe.

Isobel flipped the light switch, but the lights did not turn on.

"Drat! The light globes must have blown. How did that happen? They were fine an hour ago."

She placed the tea tray down on the bedside table and switched on one of the two bedside lamps. A small portion of Ebony's four-poster bed, with its carved wooden bedposts and dark-green brocade curtains tied back against them, was revealed. The rest of the room lay in shadow.

Ebony moaned as she removed her dressing-gown, her shoulders aching. Pain stabbed her body as she slowly crawled between clean sheets smelling of lavender and lay back against the mountain of lace-edged pillows, sighing. There had been times during her ordeal when she had wondered if she would ever see her home again. Now she slid her feet down beneath the covers to where she knew a hot water bottle would be. She smiled as a foot touched its knitted cover. Isobel never failed to put one in the bed when there was a chill in the air.

Ebony lay back, listening to the soft crackling of the fire and the never-ending ticking of the clock on the mantlepiece, and Isobel tucked her into bed.

"Thank you, Isobel. It's *so* good to be home."

"That's all right," Isobel answered, straightening herself. "Here." She handed Ebony a cup of hot chocolate and placed on the bedsheets a little plate with a plain biscuit on it. "Drink up, and don't get crumbs in your bed."

"Oh, thank you," said Ebony. "I'm starving."

"Ah, well, I'm sorry it can't be anything more substantial, but it really is too late for you to have anything more. Honestly, if I had known what was going to happen, I would never have let you go for a walk. I'm just so glad you're home safe. We were all so worried about you. Have a good night's sleep, Miss Ebony." Isobel turned for the door.

"Isobel."

Isobel stopped and turned to look at Ebony.

"I'm sorry if I got you into trouble with … Nanny. I didn't mean it."

"I know. Don't worry. Your father has …" Isobel stopped talking and lowered her gaze. When she looked up. She smiled. "Everything is all right."

"My father?"

"Goodnight, Miss Ebony."

"Goodnight, Isobel."

Ebony lay in bed and nibbled at her biscuit, watching the firelight flicker on the two high-backed armchairs either side of the fireplace. She watched the glow of the fire stretch golden fingers across the polished floorboards and drank her hot chocolate, loving every mouthful, but silently she was counting, "One ... two ... three ... four ... five."

Crawling out of her comfy bed, gritting her teeth against the pain, she put on her slippers and dressing-gown, tiptoed over to the bedroom door and slowly opened it. She tentatively stuck her head out, looked up and down the hallway. No one was around. Only the chime of the grandfather clock deep in the depths of the mansion could be heard. She tiptoed across to the thick carpet and made her way to the bathroom. Reaching it, she dashed into the room, quietly closed the door and leaned up against it.

She took a deep breath, the cold air caught in her throat and she coughed. She threw a hand across her mouth and frowned at her lack of self-control. Switching on the light, she grabbed a towel and kicked it into place at the base of the door, hoping the light would not be seen from the hallway. Moving to the linen cupboard, she fished out the small bundle and, with her heart pounding in her chest for fear of being caught, popped it into the pocket of her dressing-gown.

Back in her room, Ebony looked around.

Where can I hide it? Where can I ... Ah, ha. There. She rushed to the wooden chest of drawers and pulled open the top drawer. The contents were in deep shadow but Ebony knew where her white cotton vests lay. As she placed the package on top of the vests, she felt movement within the bundle. Ebony froze. She lifted the package back up to her face, picked up an edge of the fabric and started to peel it back.

"Click!"

She spun around.

The bedroom door had opened just a crack, and a sliver of light now shone through.

Don't open. Don't open, Ebony whispered to herself, her eyes staring at the door.

"Isobel. There you are."

It was Nanny.

Ebony quickly turned back to the drawer, placed the package inside and whispered to the creature, "Sorry." She carefully pushed the drawer shut, desperately trying to be quiet. A muffled voice answered.

"Is Miss Ebony in bed?" asked Nanny.

Ebony turned, holding her breath, watching the door again. It didn't move.

"Yes, Nanny," answered Isobel, as if she was now standing close to the bedroom door.

"Good."

Ebony sighed with relief. The door had still not opened further.

She ran to her bed, gritting her teeth as pain shot through her aching body. She scrambled to remove her dressing-gown.

"Have you taken her dirty clothes down to Kate?" asked Nanny.

Ebony finally extracted herself from the sleeves of her dressing-gown. She dumped the fabric onto the camphorwood chest at the base of her bed, just as Isobel answered, "No."

"Then go and do it!" growled Nanny.

Ebony jumped into bed, winced as the pain in her body complained, then yanked the covers up under her chin. *Breathe calmly. Breathe calmly.*

A split second later, the bedroom door flew open, and in walked Nanny Windabothem.

12

"What are Selenites?" asked Trillium, straining to see anything, but only darkness looked back. He shivered and clung more tightly to his torch as it gave off its small ring of comforting light.

Images of Pooreena, the village he called home, popped into his mind. He smiled at the memory of his friends trekking through the vast forest, always getting themselves lost, and yet always, somehow, managing to find their way back home. Of Moon Flowers ablaze with a glittery light in the brightest part of the village where sunlight streamed down through the silver leaves; of the wonder, and yet dread, of the Gribble houses located in the deepest, darkest shadows, and wondering why any Gribble would want to live in such a dark place; of his mama's hugs and berry pies. How he wished, at this precise moment, he was back there.

Now, here he was, standing alongside his companions looking into the dark forest. Not a speck of light could be seen other than their torches. There were no familiar sounds of creatures scuttling in the night, no howls from Poogles echoing through the village. Now only darkness and the smell of rotting vegetation seeped into his nose and clung to him, like pollen covers the backs of bees. He rubbed his eyes and peered into the forest. Green glowing eyes blinked into existence. He tensed, unsure what to do. He looked towards his companions for confirmation that all was well, but he didn't get it. He flinched as a bunch of fungi on the trees nearby started glowing green in colour. Then the light blinked out, only to reappear as if the fungi had been watching him. "Oh thank goodness," he said, almost wilting on the spot as he realised what they were. Trillium could feel the tension in the air as the Gribbles waited for something else to happen.

A tinkling sound resonated through the silence.

"What are Selenites?" asked Trillium, again. Grigwell and Fluellen had exchanged knowing nods. The sound grew louder, echoing, bouncing off tree trunks, making it impossible to tell its direction.

"What are …?" Trillium's words died in his throat.

A tunnel of white light was speeding towards them, highlighting hundreds of trees, as if moonlight had suddenly illuminated the forest. Three balls of light seemed to be in the middle of it.

The tinkling music grew louder as the light wove between the tree trunks, heading closer. Trillium stood mesmerised. It stopped a few feet from him, hovering just above the ground. His nose twitched, anticipation growing.

The spheres suddenly exploded into thousands of coloured bubbles. The Gribbles threw up their hands to protect their eyes. Grigwell and Fluellen yelled, "Don't listen to them."

Trillium's heart beat faster. *RUN!* his mind screamed, but his little legs did not move. His head spun. He slowly opened one eye, then the other, and blinked.

Thousands of bubbles were swirling and whirling, rushing towards three central points. They gathered into three long columns, shimmering like dewdrops, twinkling with morning sunlight.

Finally, the lights became three immense, finely sculpted figures, shining like starlight, each with a plump tail ending in a large elegant voluptuous white fin which gently swayed as the creatures hovered above the floor of the ancient forest.

"Aren't they beautiful?" whispered Trillium, his mouth falling open in awe.

The Selenites' bodies filled with swirling smoke then changed to a multitude of colours, as if thousands of tiny stars were flashing within them. The creatures swayed in a mesmerising, fluid motion and Trillium's eyelids grew heavy while a musical voice echoed inside his mind.

Trillium, come to us-s-s-s … Sleep forever-r-r-r in the caverns of the

West. Come and rest from the trials of your world-d-d-d. We will care for you forever-r-r-r._

"Don't listen to them!" someone yelled from close by.

Trillium scrunched his eyebrows and blinked several times. Fluellen's frowning face slowly came into view.

Trillium looked around. Quintell looked as if he was going to be sick. Grigwell didn't look much better.

"Are you all right?" asked Fluellen. Trillium nodded, and relief was written across her face.

"What happened?" asked Trillium. "I thought I was floating ... in light. There were voices."

"It's all right, I understand, but you must not listen when they start calling to you. They'll take you with them if they can."

Trillium stared at the three Selenites. They did not look as if they would harm him.

Their bodies transformed, looking as if hundreds of white butterflies were fluttering inside them, desperately wanting to be free. Then the bodies turned frosty white as three high-pitched voices chimed in unison, _"The forest wails at the loss of one of its own-n-n-n."_

Long strands of hair, resembling strings of seed pods, cascaded over the creatures' shoulders.

"Woe to you-u-u-u," the Selenites chimed, the sound seeming to be everywhere. _"Your quest has failed before it even begins-s-s-s. You search in vain-n-n-n. ... Your kinsman is lost."_

Trillium mouthed the word. Lost. _What did they mean, lost?_

"Explain what you have seen, Selenites of the West," demanded Grigwell.

"Your kinsman has been attacked-d-d-d by creatures from the outer world-d-d-d," the Selenites answered in their sad and melodious tone, which vibrated through the very being of every Gribble, through the forest itself, into the very ground they stood upon. _"Woe to you for she has been dragged away-y-y-y to where none may go-o-o-o. Your kinsman is lost forever-r-r-r."_

The Selenites spread their fragile arms towards the Gribbles, and the attached strips of transparent cobwebs gently swayed with the movement. They beckoned with their long webbed fingers. *"Come to us-s-s-s,"* they chimed. *"We will care for you forever-r-r-r."*

"Concentrate, everyone!" yelled Grigwell.

"Don't listen to them!" shouted Fluellen.

"Do they mean," Trillium looked at Fluellen then to Grigwell for an answer, "what I think they mean?"

Grigwell nodded yes. Trillium's eyes widened and his legs felt weak and finally giving way, he collapsed to the ground. He put his head in his hands and started rocking. "How could this have happened? How am I ever going to be able to find my sister now?"

A soft comforting hand rested on his shoulder. He looked into Fluellen's face. There was concern written there. Trillium stood up and, addressing no one in particular, said with defiance in his voice, "Where have these creatures come from anyway? How can we believe them?"

Images sprang into his mind of dark dense caves filled with sharp white crystals, so immense in shape and size it was impossible to see where they began or where they ended. The feeling of something living, breathing, brooding somewhere deep within those caves seeped into his brain and he shivered with revulsion. There was something ancient, rare and frightening hiding within those caverns, something that imprisoned … what? Trillium's mind filled with a red glow and within it he could hear crying.

Trillium grabbed Fluellen's sleeve. Tears tumbled down his cheeks. "Fluellen, I have to find her. I can't give up. We … we can't give up. Not just like that. How could this have happened? What am I going to do? What will Mama and Papa say?"

"It's all right," said Fluellen. "It's all right. No one is giving up. Don't worry, we will find Veeleeta."

Trillium nodded, and as he stood up the Selenites disintegrated back into three balls of light and melted back into the depths of the forest, lamenting, *"Woe to you, Gribbles of Pooreena. Your kinsman is lost forever, forever-r-r, forever-r-r-r."*

Nanny Windabothem entered Ebony's bedroom and crossed the floor to stand at the edge of the shadows. Ebony watched with distrust as she waited for her to say something, *do* something, but Nanny just stood very still, with her hands by her sides, as if she too was waiting. She was watching the door.

Rushing footsteps could be heard thundering up the stairs, a commotion came from the hallway. Ebony's parents burst through the door still dressed in their evening wear, having just come from the theatre, although they didn't look as neat and prim as she would have expected. Their faces were flushed, distress was written in their expressions. "Ebony!" they both cried out as they rushed to her bedside.

"Are you all right?" her mother asked, stroking Ebony's face with a white-gloved hand.

"Ebony, what happened?" her father said, sitting on the bed with sweat beading across his brow, his black shoulder-length hair hanging limply. He was looking deep into her eyes as if somehow that would tell him the truth. "Nanny Windabothem has told us what she knew but I wanted to hear it from you. Are you all right?"

"Yes, I'm fine," answered Ebony, with glee that her father was actually here, talking to her and yet trepidation mixed in her heart, how long for? Her parents were finally home. She herself had been home from boarding school for a month now, and at no time had they come to see her. Phone calls had been her only means of communication with them, until now. *It only took me being lost in a forest to do it.* The sullen thought popped into Ebony's mind. Then guilt sank into her heart; were her parents really so thoughtless? She hated it when she felt like this. "I'm fine," she answered again.

"Miss Windabothem," Ebony's father said as he rose to look at Nanny. "How can I thank you for everything you have done? Our little girl is home safe."

Nanny Windabothem's cheeks flushed and she nodded her head in acknowledgement but said nothing.

Ebony was horrified. *Did these people know nothing about this woman?*

"Hello, Mr Wood." An old man with a deep timbre to his voice walked into the room. He was carrying a large black bag. "Mrs Wood," he said, nodding his head in greeting as he saw Ebony's mother who was now moving to stand at the end of the bed.

"Dr Waters. Thank you for coming so late at night," Ebony's father said as the doctor walked up to his patient.

"Err." Dr Waters stopped and looked at Mr Wood. "You have to speak up. I'm not as young as I used to be."

"Thank you for coming so late at night," Ebony's father repeated more loudly this time.

"Huh! You mean morning, don't you, Mr Wood?" Dr Waters answered with agitation in his voice, louder than would have been normal in a younger man.

"Yes, yes. You're quite right," answered Mr Wood.

"Speak up!"

"Yes. You're quite right!" bellowed Mr Wood.

"Not so loud, young man. I'm not deaf, you know."

Ebony's father's forehead furrowed and his cheeks flushed.

"Why is this room so dark?" Dr Waters stood and looked at the condition of the darkened room as if seeing it for the first time. "How do you expect me to see my patient using only bedside lamps and the light from the fireplace?"

"I do apologise," said Ebony's father, as he loosened his bow tie and undid the buttons of his white brocade waistcoat. He turned to Nanny. "Miss Windabothem, surely there must be some light bulbs somewhere?"

Nanny Windabothem turned her head in her employer's direction and said, "My apologies, sir. I've sent for young Harold to bring some up from the cellar. I did mention it before."

"I see. Then he is taking a heck of a long time about it. I suppose we will just have to wait." There was a soft knock at the door. "Yes. Come in. Ah, Isobel. Yes, come in."

"Excuse me, sir," said Isobel, as she entered the room. "I've brought the bowl of warm water and the towel the doctor requested."

"Thank you, Isobel."

"Mr Wood, more light if you don't mind?" the doctor asked again as Isobel placed the bowl on the bedside table.

"Miss Windabothem," said Mr Wood, turning to look at her again. "Will you please open the curtains? It is a full moon tonight. That should help the good doctor see what he is doing, considering we still have no light bulbs."

Nanny looked in Isobel's direction. "Isobel."

Isobel nodded and scurried to one of the four banks of dark blue floor-to-ceiling velvet curtains. She drew them back, revealing two sets of windows with a striped orange padded window seat beneath. Bright moonlight flooded the room. Isobel then drew back the three other sets of curtains running the length of the room. The moonlight made everything instantly take on a razor-sharp appearance, and all the shadows became much darker.

Ebony's father raised his eyebrows as if he could not believe that Nanny Windabothem would order Isobel to do what he had asked her to do, as if the task was below her. He frowned and then moved over to the mantelpiece and leaned against it as Dr Waters said, "I suppose that will have to do."

The doctor then turned his attention to Ebony. "Now, young lady, what have you been doing to cause all this fuss and bother and get me out of my warm comfy bed at this hour of the night or should I say … morning?"

"She has been lost in Tanglemire Forest … for hours." A soft, silky voice came out of the shadows on the far side of the room.

Ebony's mother, still dressed in a long emerald-green satin evening gown, appeared in the light to stand near the bedside lamp.

The doctor lifted his bushy eyebrows, stuck a finger in his ear, twisted it, then said, "What did you say? Speak up, girl. Don't twitter like that."

Mrs Wood looked perplexed but repeated what she'd said a bit louder. Her husband smiled.

"Has she now?" the doctor said, turning to look at Ebony.

"Well, we—" Ebony started to say.

"Don't mumble, girl. Speak up." Dr Waters leaned in closer towards Ebony.

"I said we, Scruffy and I—" Ebony started to explain in a loud voice which she was unsure if she could keep up.

"Oh, yes of course, silly of me, I forgot about the dog," interrupted the doctor. "It's been a while since I've seen you. I remember now, you two never go anywhere without each other, do you?"

Dr Waters then picked his stethoscope out of his bag and stuck the silver disc under his armpit.

Ebony raised her eyebrows.

He removed it, felt it, breathed on it, felt it again, nodded as if satisfied and said, "Now sit up, young lady, and lean forward and—" The doctor started waving his arms up and down as if deciding how best to get the stethoscope under Ebony's nightie. Eventually, he put it down from the top, moving her long hair out of the way to do so.

Pressing the disc up against Ebony's rib cage on her left side, he held her shoulder with one hand and said, "Cough!"

Ebony did the best she could. The doctor then moved the stethoscope to her right side and said, "Cough!"

"Well, that's fine," he said, removing the instrument and putting it back in his bag.

He then picked up her right arm and pressed against some dark bruises on the inside of her forearm. "Ummm." He leaned in even closer and looked at them. Ebony squirmed and removed her arm from his grasp. *The less he knows about them the better,* she decided.

He stood up and put his hands behind his back, looked over the top of his round glasses and stared straight into Ebony's eyes.

Ebony looked away, ashamed that he might have guessed where the bruises had come from. "Ummm ... Go on," said Dr Waters.

"Well, um ... we, err ... we went outside." Ebony darted a look at Isobel who flicked a nervous look at Nanny. Ebony followed Isobel's gaze to find Nanny's cold dark eyes glaring straight into hers. Ebony quickly looked down at her green woollen blanket. "Go on," the doctor, prompted, examining her other arm which was covered in scratches and welts from hail.

"Oh ... well ... um ... we ... we were heading towards the apple orchard, but I got distracted by the butterflies."

The doctor now examined her legs, which were in the same condition as her arms, except for the added scratches from Scruffy's claws and the brambleberries. "I chased them," Ebony continued, "and they flitted onto the Scotch thistle flowers. We then went and-"

"Pardon?" her father asked as he moved towards her. "What? What thistles?"

"There is a large plant next to the lake. They have such beautiful flowers, don't you think? Such a lovely colour."

"Colour. Beautiful flowers! Huh! I can't believe it, after all these years. I thought we were rid of them all. Evelyn," he said, turning to his wife. "Remind me to talk to the head gardener. What's his name? Flag. Yes, that's it, Flag. I will not have those plants on this property. You let one live, you might as well have a thousand, then there will be no grass. Sheep are not goats, they do not eat thistles."

"Err!" said Dr Waters, scowling at Mr Wood as if he didn't understand what was going on. Then turning back to Ebony he said, "Anyway, my dear, please do go on with your story."

"Yes ... um ... well, we went and sat down next to the lake. I caught some tadpoles in my hands."

"Ah, haha. I remember doing that when I was a wee tyke. Did they suck on your fingers?" asked the doctor, as he retrieved a pair of large silver tweezers from the black bag sitting on top of Ebony's bedcovers.

"Yes, they did," said Ebony, giggling.

"They tickle, don't they? Well, only the big tadpoles, the little ones don't seem much interested." Dr Waters then took hold of her left hand.

"Yes, they do … Hey. Hey. Ouch. Hey. Hey. What are you doing? That hurts."

"I'm sorry, my dear, but that thorn had to come out. So do the rest of them, I'm afraid. If I leave them in they would become septic and that would never do."

Ebony looked at the tweezers which now securely held a large sharp bramble thorn. The doctor held it up and examined it through his round spectacles then peered over the top of them. "What *have* you been doing to yourself?"

Ebony pushed herself back into her pillows. She didn't like the way he was looking at her. "Well, we, err …" she continued, "we then walked down to the apple … Ow … Hey … Ow-w-w … Ah … Tut … orchard." The doctor retrieved another thorn.

"Which one?" her father asked.

"The one next to … Ah … the forest," she moaned as another thorn was removed.

"I see, and what did you do down there?" Her father's tone warned her to tell the truth.

"I … I built a fairy garden."

Fairy Garden

Ebony's cheeks flushed red. *Was she too old for fairy gardens now?* She pondered on that thought. She had not thought so before the storm, so why did it make a difference now? "I wanted to place it at the base of one of the ... Ow ... apple trees." Another thorn came loose.

A cough from her father cut her off. Ebony looked down at the stitching holding the satin edging to her green woollen blanket.

"Well, it looks like that's the last of them. One, two, three," Dr Waters mumbled as he counted the thorns, "four, five. You did get yourself into a pickle, didn't you?"

The doctor put the thorns into a small glass bottle. "Do you want to keep them?" he asked Ebony. "As a memory?"

Shocked at such a thought, Ebony shook her head. "No! Thank you."

"Are you sure? I still have my first lock of hair from my first haircut you know, from when I was three, and that was a long time ago. And my first tooth!"

Ebony blinked and shook her head, not knowing what to say to that. She doubted if her parents had kept her hair from any haircut, let alone her very first one, or her teeth for that matter. Ebony shivered at the thought. It was not something she actually found appealing in the slightest.

"Are you sure? Oh well, I will keep them, just in case you change your mind." The doctor shrugged his shoulders as if perplexed as to why she wouldn't want to keep them. He kept lots of specimens in his office, he loved the stories that went with them. They were a memory key to him, especially as his memory was not the best these days. He returned the bottle and tweezers to his bag. He then took out a small white china bottle and undid the cork stopper. He poured some yellow liquid into the bowl of water sitting on the bedside table. With a damp wad of fabric, he started dabbing the wound on her face. It stung and she flinched.

"What did you do after that?" he asked as he moved to the wounds on her hand.

"I ... err ... we never made it to the apple orchard. It started to rain. It grew dark, and the clouds rumbled and tumbled over the tops of one another. The wind blew so hard that I was tossed around like a rag doll. A rag doll, mind you." Ebony waved her arms around. Her mother smiled. The doctor mumbled something, grabbed hold of one of her arms to steady it and continued his work.

"Thunder and lightning were everywhere," continued Ebony. "It was all around us. It wouldn't stop. The hail ..." Tears trickled down her cheeks. "The rain poured down in torrents. Torrents!" Ebony threw her hands out in front of her again, causing the doctor to miss dabbing her wounds.

"Will you stop doing that," he grumbled.

Ebony frowned. She was rather enjoying telling her parents about her story. It wasn't often she got to tell then anything that happened in her life, they never stayed home long enough for that, and since she'd been at the boarding school she'd hardly seen them at all this last year. Now they were home, she was desperate to talk to them, to tell them anything, as long as they would listen to her, and now the doctor wanted her to stop! Never!

"The rain stung my face," she continued, "and the wind was churning the wheat around like I was in a washing machine. I don't know what happened. I just found myself in the forest."

Ebony blinked and looked around at the occupants of her bedroom as memories rushed upon her.

"I finally found Scruffy," she whispered. "He was very frightened, and then we ... um..."

Don't tell them.

Everyone was looking at her, waiting. Every bone in her body said not to tell them what she had found deep in the forest.

"Well, we ... um."

Don't tell them.

"We ... um."

Don't tell them.

"We got lost." Ebony dropped her eyes, thankful she'd kept her secret.

"Well, luckily, you are home safe and sound, sort of," said Dr Waters, as he retrieved a large black jar and unscrewed the lid.

The room filled with the scent of summer flowers. "My own blend," he said with pride in his voice and a smile of satisfaction. He then lifted Ebony's right arm and smeared some orange cream onto her wounds. "I think it was lucky your Nanny was able to find you."

Ebony looked towards Nanny Windabothem to find she was still staring at her in that cold disinterested way that always made Ebony think she was up to something. A shiver ran down Ebony's spine and she flinched. The doctor stopped what he was doing and stared at her, puzzled.

"Now," he said slowly. "Keep your arms out straight so I can wrap them in this special cloth. It's my own invention, you know, it's made out of potato skins impregnated with five herbs, a secret blend. It will help bring out the bruising and heal them much faster than more conventional ways."

When the doctor had finished bandaging Ebony's arms and legs, he removed from his bag a small purple glass bottle and a glass tumbler.

"Drink this." He filled the tumbler with thick blue liquid. "It will help you sleep. I'll just finish up."

Ebony took it, eyed the contents with suspicion, glanced at him, sniffed it, screwed up her nose and drank it down, spluttering when she'd finished. "Why is medicine always so disgusting?" she moaned.

"You're going to be very sore for the next couple of days, and other than a leg falling off, you will be fine." The doctor smiled, taking the tumbler back and wrapping it in paper before returning it to his bag, as Ebony opened her mouth in horror.

"It was a joke," said Dr Waters, smiling.

Ebony lifted her eyebrows, glared at him then huffed. She didn't think much of his joke. He should stick to being a doctor.

"Dr Waters," asked Ebony. "Um. Could you please check Scruffy? I'm sure he has been hurt."

"I'm not a vet!"

"Don't worry about Scruffy," her father said. "The kennel master has already checked him over. He just has a sore hip. He will be all right when he has rested … Dr Waters. Thank you for coming."

"That's perfectly all right. I will send you the bill. It'll pay for my next holiday."

Ebony's father seemed lost for words.

"I'm joking," the doctor said with a wry smile.

"Yes, yes of course," answered Ebony's father, as if he didn't know what to think.

"Before I go, a word with you if I may, Mr Wood." The doctor gently took Mr Wood's arm and guided him away to stand next to the bedroom door. He then looked around him as if he didn't want anyone else to hear what he was saying. Then leaning towards Mr Wood, he said, "I'm glad to see you took my advice about sending Ebony to boarding school."

Ebony's ears pricked up at the mention of her name. Dr Waters, obviously thinking he was whispering, was actually talking so loudly she could hear every word he said; so could everyone else in the room.

"I know you and your wife had great reservations about this course of action, but once Nanny Windabothem had explained to me how distressed Ebony was about the loss of her grandmother, well, I started to make inquiries. When the *incident* happened two months after the funeral ... well, I do think that sending Ebony to the Black Hawk Boarding School for Girls was the only option. They are excellent at helping young girls who have, shall we say, a delicate disposition of the mind. Anyway, even though there has been this, err, shall we say, *mishap* tonight, there is a definite improvement in her wellbeing. This is only high spirits, high spirits."

Ebony froze at the words she was hearing. She was stunned. She'd never known the real reason her parents had sent her away just over a year ago, when she had needed them the most, and now she did. Bitterness swelled within her so much she could taste it. An old man, with old ideas, had destroyed her life. *How dare he do that to me! How could her parents possibly have listened to him? But it really wasn't him at all,* Ebony realised. *It was her.* Ebony slowly slid her eyes towards Nanny Windabothem. She was looking back at Ebony with eyes which were so dark they gave *no* indication of the depths she would not go to, to get what she wanted. There was no remorse there.

"Thank you, Dr Waters. I quite agree," said Mr Wood as he turned to face Ebony.

A secret door opened in Ebony's mind and memories flickered across her minds eye. Her grandmother was dead. She had died two months earlier. Then a day came when Ebony had found herself lying upon the green grass, looking up through the dappled leaves of the ancient apple trees, not even caring how long she'd been there, nor how she came to be doing it. As she had lain there on the soft soil, which felt like a comfy mattress, a warmth had surrounded her like a blanket and slowly seeped into her body. A soft wind had rustled amongst the branches. A single pale yellow leaf had drifted towards her. She had watched it slowly drift down on the gentle currents of air. It alighted onto her chest, and she breathed in the scent of autumn and sighed. Then another dying leaf drifted down, then another, and another as the wind rustled the leaves above. A drop of rain had landed on Ebony's cheek as if it was a tear, but still, she did not move. The strength of the wind increased. Leaves tumbled to the ground, carpeting it in yellow, green and fawn, and still she had lain there, as still as a stone. Rain pattered across Ebony's face. The warmth grew within her as a cloak of damp leaves covered her from head to toe, and she had wondered, *Is this what it feels like to be buried?*

Time passed, how much she did not know, nor did she care, as a swirling sensation began to flow through her mind. She felt she was being carried away down a gentle stream that was quickly picking up strength. The water lapped around her body as she lay with her long hair trailing in the current. Ebony's brow had furrowed, she was feeling cold. She was heading for a waterfall. Panic rose in her throat. She tried to cry out, but no sound could she make. Closer and closer the edge came; colder and colder she felt. Mist rose high into the air. Thunder resounded in her ears. Terror rose within her, she was going to be dashed against the stones at the base of the waterfall. Then, time slowed down; her grandmother, full of youth and vigour, was there, smiling, waving from the foreshore.

"Not yet, dear heart," she called out as Ebony lifted away from the water. "The time is not right. One day we will meet again, but not yet. Not yet. Not yet. Not yet."

Then Ebony felt herself being carried away by strong hands that had picked her up as if she were as limp as a rag doll.

Voices spun around her on the edge of her senses. Worried, upset they were. Then warmth, love and gentleness filled her up and drove away the cold that had bitten deep into her core. Suddenly a light appeared in Ebony's consciousness and rushed through the corridors of her mind. Her eyes opened, but it was as if she was looking through a long tunnel of rainbow light upon the worried faces of her parents looking small, off in the distance, but Ebony pondered, why were they so worried? She felt herself gently drift on soft clouds further and further away from them, feeling warm and safe.

Then a wrinkly hand came into view and placed itself across her brow. Instantly Ebony was back in her room, back in her bed, back in her body, and back in her mind.

"The fever has broken," the old voice croaked. Relief now showed on her parents' faces.

A day came when whispers could be heard in the corridor beyond her bedroom door. Bags were packed and Ebony went to live at the Black Hawk Boarding School for Girls.

Ebony looked around her bedroom and a tear trickled down her cheek as the memory faded.

"Isobel," said Mr Wood, turning to face her. "Could you see the doctor out when he has finished, and don't forget to close the curtains before you leave."

"Yes, sir," answered Isobel.

"Excuse me, Miss Windabothem," Ebony's father said, now turning to Nanny. "We would like to have a talk to Ebony." Nanny

Windabothem looked as if she didn't understand what he was saying. "*Alone,* if you don't mind." He indicated the door.

Nanny Windabothem raised her thin eyebrows slightly, nodded and moved towards the exit. Her sensible black shoes echoed on the polished floorboards and her crisp brown uniform crunched in the silence as everyone watched her leave. As she opened the door, she turned and said, "Excuse me, sir. Have you given some more thought to our discussion earlier on the phone, about the dog being placed in the kennels with the working dogs?"

"Yes, actually I have, and as I said before, Scruffy is to stay by Ebony's side. I think it is for the best … In my opinion."

Nanny stared at Ebony's father as if weighing up if she should say anything more. Obviously deciding against it, she left the room, closing the door behind her.

Isobel quickly drew the curtains shut then rushed to open the bedroom door again. As the door clicked shut behind Dr Waters, a soft voice crooned, "Ebony dear."

14

Ebony slid her eyes towards her mother, crossed her arms, hunched her shoulders, pushed herself further back into the pillows and waited. She figured she knew what was coming.

"We have both been very worried about you," her mother said, sitting on the side of the bed. "When Nanny contacted us, saying you were missing, well, I was beside myself. I mean, we … we were beside ourselves."

Ebony bit her lip, drew in a deep breath and watched her father as he leaned against her chest of drawers. He was glaring at her. He started to fiddle with the handle of the top drawer.

Don't open it. Don't open it, she whispered to herself, and inwardly sighed with relief as he moved away to lean on the mantelpiece instead.

Her father's shoulder-length black hair was dishevelled and he had creases across his brow. His white brocade waistcoat was unbuttoned, as was his shirt collar. His black bow tie lay limp around his neck, and he had pushed his shirt sleeves up above his elbows.

He looks so tired … and it's all your fault, Ebony snapped at herself.

Ebony's mother turned to look at her husband. Quickly turning back to look at Ebony, she pursed her lips together and frowned. She then straightened her evening gown and ran a hand across her hair; the same colour as Ebony's. She paused to finger a delicate headband covered in tiny white pearls. She fiddled with her pearl earrings and matching necklace, and clutched the pair of long white gloves now lying in her lap before saying, "How many times have we told you not to go into Tanglemire Forest, young lady?"

A blank look was Ebony's only reply as she remembered the instant she'd stepped into the forbidden forest, with her mother's voice resonating in her head. She had broken her promise. *But what else could I do?* Ebony answered herself.

"Oh honestly, Ebony, how can you have forgotten. We've been telling you for years not to go into that forest. Under *any* circumstances."

"Yeah, yeah, all right," grumbled Ebony, under her breath. "I forgot … sort of."

"The villagers have warned us, time and time again, about people going in and never coming out," her mother said, "and *you* promised."

"But!" Ebony protested. "I didn't mean it."

"Don't but us, young lady," her father snarled as he moved towards her. "You lied to us."

"But!" Ebony pleaded again, backing further against her pillows.

"Agh!" Her father groaned and stomped off.

He never listens, Ebony grumbled to herself, yawning.

"Ebony … dear," her mother said.

"Do you have any idea what you have put us through tonight, young lady?" her father said as he returned. "Have you got the slightest idea how hard it was to get permission to fly our jet out of Paris at this time of the morning?"

"Now, dear," Ebony's mother said turning to her husband, "there is no need to go into—"

"No need! No *need!*" he said, interrupting her again. Then glaring at Ebony he continued to say, "I can't believe that you're turning thirteen tomorrow—"

"Today," stated Ebony's mother.

Ebony's father looked down at her. "Is it?" She nodded to indicate yes. "Well, today then. But that does not excuse you, young lady! Why don't you just *grow up?* You can't go gallivanting around in a forest – that we have forbidden you to go into, mind you – and for us *not* to have something to say about it."

"Why can't Nanny Jones come back?" Ebony said, knowing the answer before she'd even asked the question. "And why do I have to go back to boarding school?" *Why did you listen to that old man?* Ebony thought with resentment. "Why can't I just stay home? Why can't *you* two stay home?"

Something flickered across her father's face, but then it was gone. He stood up straighter. "You know very well why Nanny Jones can't be here. And *you,* young lady, have just destroyed all our plans. When your holidays are over, you will be going back to boarding school where they will keep an eye on you. I now have to pick up *all* the pieces and try again."

Ebony glared at her father, not understanding everything he had just said.

"And while you're *here,*" he continued. "Nanny Windabothem will put an end to all this childish behaviour. We were supposed to be entertaining buyers tonight. Not dashing back here having to deal with a disobedient child."

"Now, John!"

"No, Evelyn," he said, "we were in the middle of some very important negotiations." He leaned in closer and shook a finger at Ebony. "Negotiations that were going to change *all* our lives. We had to leave those people standing in the foyer of our hotel instead of taking them to the theatre, for crying out loud. Do you know how hard it was for me to get those theatre tickets? You know I hate getting dressed up like this. I feel like a damn penguin."

Her father paced up and down on the Persian rug, then sat down on the edge of the bed next to his wife, putting his head in his hands. "You do realise we've lost them, Evelyn, don't you? Our plans are all gone."

"John. … dear," her mother said, putting a comforting arm around his shoulders. Ebony's father ran his hands through his long hair, making it look even untidier than before. A twinge twisted in Ebony's stomach. "John, you know perfectly well there will be other buyers out there," Ebony's mother continued.

He suddenly stood up, stuffed his hands deep into his trouser pockets, glared at both of them and started stomping up and down in the shadows again.

Ebony's mother sighed, shook her head and turned to face Ebony. "Ebony. Dear. How many times have we told you about the little girl who went missing in the forest? She's never been seen since, and there are all those—"

"That was twenty years ago!" interrupted Ebony.

Her mother's bright blue eyes narrowed as she continued to say, "As … I … was … saying, she went in and never came out. And there are all those weird noises we've been told about. Well, granted we have not heard anything, but that is not the point. Half the village was out looking for you tonight, as well as the police." She shook her head and scrunched up her gloves, her hands trembling. "I'm sorry, dear, but there are no excuses."

"But Scruffy?" Ebony darted a look in the direction of the fireplace. Scruffy's silhouetted form lay asleep on the hearthrug, oblivious to what was going on.

"We understand all about Scruffy, but look at you, covered in scratches, clothes torn to shreds. Crumbs, Ebony, anything could have happened to you. What were you thinking? And you promised."

"Yes, but when I made that promise," yelled Ebony, as she leaned forward, "I didn't think a storm would chase me in there, did I! And lucky I did go into the forest or I would never have found Scruffy if I hadn't!"

Her mother scowled and slowly stood up. Ebony shrank deep into her lace-edged pillows, as a little voice from somewhere deep inside her, squeaked, *You shouldn't have done that.*

"For crying out loud, Ebony." Ebony's father rushed to her bedside and stood over her. "You should know better. You are not a little girl anymore. I can't believe that you have behaved like this."

Standing up straighter, he announced, "Right, young lady. That's it. Until you can prove to us that you can be more responsible, you're banned from going anywhere – without supervision anyway – and that's that!"

"What!" Ebony sat bolt upright. "You can't do that!"

Her father glared at her, and she slowly sank back into her pillows. *You've done it now,* she said to herself, feeling her body grow warm and heavy. Her mother and father exchanged a knowing glance, and then looked at Ebony.

It's typical they'd agree with each other. Ebony sank further into her pillows and yawned as her eyelids fought to stay open. *I could have died out there,* she grumbled to herself. *Don't be so stupid,* she answered. *You didn't, did you? ... I could have.*

"John, I think we should leave this to another day. I do believe we have made our point."

"Yes. Yes. You're quite right, as always. Goodnight, Ebony."

The bedroom door finally clicked shut. Ebony stared out through a gap in the curtains. The morning sun was just starting to break through the night sky; the clouds streaked in shades of white and grey were kissed with pink. In the distance, the ancient forbidden forest was silhouetted against it. Snuggled in her warm bed, her eyes finally unable to stay open, Ebony gave up the fight and shutting them, mumbled, "Scruffy, how the heck did we ever get into this mess?"

15

Trillium watched his feet drag in the dust, his mind filled with questions that had no answers. It was only then that he registered Fluellen walking next to him, and wondered how long she'd been there.

"Grigwell will never let you down," she said. "Nor will Quintell, nor will I."

Trillium stopped. "Leave … me … alone! Do you have any idea how I feel?"

Fluellen shook her head and whispered, "No, not really. I can—"

"My sister is missing," Trillium interrupted, not caring what she had to say. "The Selenites have just told us that I … that my whole family will never see Veeleeta again. I don't want, or need your sympathy. Go … away."

Fluellen's bottom lip quivered, her long nose scrunched up and her eyes went glassy with tears that she blinked away without success. She walked off, shoulders bent, to join her companions. They had stopped further ahead and had turned to watch. Trillium stared at them. Guilt sprang into his heart. He looked at the ground, kicked at the soil, then noticed that the large crusty face of an insect had peeked out from over the edge of a nearby leaf. It was waggling its long purple fluorescent antennae in his direction. He turned away from it.

The temperature had now dropped and dew was settling on the forest making everything damp.

"Thank goodness, morning is finally here," said Quintell, as sunlight filtered through the canopy.

As they continued, the light brightened so they stopped and replaced the hoods on the fungi torches to preserve their luminous ability. They then hitched them to their backpacks and walked on, but not more than a few steps later Trillium asked, "Did you feel that?"

"Was it a tingling sensation?" inquired Quintell.

"Yes, but it's gone now," answered Trillium.

"Fluellen, can you see anything?" asked Grigwell, turning to see that she was further behind. "Can you feel anything?"

"Feel what?" shouted Fluellen. She stopped moving, and looked around. "Now you mention it," she said as if to herself. "It's a … strange … um … I can feel Selenites. They have been here … but … there is some … thing … else." Fluellen slowly moved forward then stopped again. Her eyes opened in surprise, then closed as she spread her arms out wide.

The others gasped. Fluellen had started to glow, and seeping out on either side of her body, or at least that was what it looked like, was a wall of light filled with a multitude of tiny white stars. Its fingers wove along the forest floor like a snake slithering its way through the trees, eventually disappearing far into the distance. The Gribbles looked up to see that the wall had now speared straight up into the air, to be lost high in the canopy above. Fluellen opened her eyes and turned around on the same spot; it was as if the wall of light was made of liquid. It instantly filled in any gaps she might have created. Then bringing one arm to her side, she continued to hold the other out in front of her. She slowly stepped back towards her companions, and the wall enclosed all around her arm, until only her fingertip was left pointing at its surface, as if there was a connection between her and it. Then Fluellen pulled her finger away, and the wall of light was gone. She collapsed to the ground.

"FLUELLEN!" All three Gribbles rushed forward. Quintell reached her first. "Are you all right?"

Fluellen moaned as he helped her sit up.

Grigwell handed her a flask of water he had retrieved from his backpack. Trillium looked on, unsure of what to do.

Silence filled the air as Fluellen took a long drink. When she'd finished, she handed the flask back. Grigwell, with concern in his voice, asked, "Fluellen, are you sure you're al—"

"What was that!" Trillium interrupted.

Fluellen turned to him and frowned. "I'm fine, Trillium. Thank you very much for your concern."

"Oh." Trillium looked to the ground then whispered, "Sorry."

"But ..." Fluellen suddenly looked shocked, and slowly looked around her. She blinked several times, rubbed her eyes and looked at Quintell. "No!" She shut her eyes again and held her head in her hands.

"Fluellen!" Quintell patted her shoulder, and looked on with deep concern, as did the other Gribbles. "What is wrong?"

Fluellen was crying. Then slowly she stopped and lifted her head. She looked as if she'd aged ten seasons with worry. "I'm ... I'm sorry," she said. "It's just such a shock."

"What is such a shock?" Grigwell asked.

"It's my own fault, Grigwell," Fluellen said as she gingerly stood up with Quintell's aid. "That was ... is an energy field." She shook her head. "I should never have tried. I've paid the price all Aurors dread. I've never felt anything like it. When I entered the energy field, I used all my skills to feel deep within it. What I found there was old. Older than I've ever known anything to be, and it has many energies flowing through it. I had been taught that energies disperse over time, but this has not. If anything, it felt as if it is growing stronger, even now. Where it has come from, where it is going, I cannot say. I cannot even say why it is here. All I can say is that I have an inkling, with no facts to back it up, but I think this energy field spreads further into the forest than I can see. There is a feeling within it that makes me think it links up as if it surrounds the entire forest. That it is somehow protecting it."

"But how? Why?" Grigwell asked, looking towards the wall of

light that was now invisible. "The forest continues on from here," said Grigwell, confused, and he turned and pointed behind him as if somehow questioning what Fluellen was saying.

"Yes," answered Fluellen, slowly looking out into the trees beyond. "But the energy of these trees is low, very low. It's so low it's almost as if the trees are asleep. I can't see them. It's like the footprints we found in the clearing. The energies are here on the very outskirts of my sight." Fluellen raised her hands and shook them on either side of her head. "But I can't grasp them. All is dark to me now."

"What! You're not blind, are you?" Quintell asked with obvious concern in his voice, waving a hand in front of her face.

"No. Not blind to this world, just blind to its energy. I normally see everything bathed in its own colour of energy. Here it is dark, as if a shadow has descended upon my sight. There are no colours here unless you want to call black and grey colour."

"But that's what we see," Trillium pointed out, looking around.

"Interesting," said Fluellen, turning to look at him. "But that's not what I would normally see. Well, used to see," she added, as if a great sadness now lived inside her. "That's all gone. Now I feel like … like … I don't know what I feel like … Empty, I suppose." Fluellen heaved a sigh and looked at the ground.

"Listen," said Quintell. "The trees. I can't hear them breathing. And the green fungi have all disappeared."

Everyone looked around.

"Why would that be?" asked Grigwell.

"I wouldn't have the slightest idea," answered Quintell. "But if I ever get the chance to find out, I will."

"Come on," said Grigwell. "We will find no answers here, not today. We had better be getting on. Fluellen, are you well enough to do so?"

Time moved slowly as sadness lay deep in Trillium's heart. The words the Selenites and Fluellen had said went around and around in his mind. He walked on as if he didn't really know where he was going, which was good because he didn't. Then something inside him told him that the other Gribbles had stopped walking. He looked up. They had indeed stopped ahead of him. He walked up to join them to see what they were looking at.

Destruction lay all around. Plants lay flattened. Branches were broken. It was as if a herd of adult Babacoots had been bouncing around in the area, destroying everything, but that was unheard of, and it would take a thousand to cause this much damage. *It could not possibly be,* Trillium concluded. *They live in the Glade of Sharoon, which is many days' flying from here. No, there must be another reason,* he decided.

Grigwell silently and deftly moved out into the desolation. He signalled with his hand for the others to follow. "Look!"

Huge imprints lay everywhere like craters. The ground was churned up as if animals of immense size had been rutting amongst it.

"But …" Trillium started to say but found no words would follow.

"No!" Fluellen suddenly cried out. Everyone spun around to find she had not moved into the desolation before her. She just stood rigid with her hands over her eyes, wailing, "No! No! No! No! No!"

"Fluellen!" Quintell rushed to her side.

She eased one hand away and squinted at Quintell, and instantly crumpled to the ground, crying, "No! Please! No!"

"Fluellen!" Quintell bent down and grabbed her by her shoulders in an attempt to raise her. Tears were tumbling down her cheeks. Her eyes were shut tight.

"My head! My head!" mumbled Fluellen.

"What is wrong?" asked Quintell.

"My head! It hurts! I feel it is trying to split apart."

"Get her away from here," commanded Grigwell, as he and Trillium rushed to her side. "Take her away, quickly. I will follow later."

Quintell and Trillium each grabbed an arm of Fluellen's, and half-dragged, half-carried her to stand upon her shaky legs, stumbling back the way they had come. Trillium flicked a look behind him and called out, "How will you find us?"

"I'm a tracker," answered Grigwell, "Of course I will find you."

Fluellen, now sitting under the shade of a large fern holding her head in both hands, cried, "It hurts! Please make it stop! It hurts."

Quintell quickly rummaged around in a little pouch, one of many attached to his belt. He retrieved a small container made from a seed pod and undoing it, said, "Trillium, grab Fluellen's hands away from her head."

Quintell quickly spread some red cream across Fluellen's forehead and instantly she relaxed and stopped crying.

Kneeling down next to her, Quintell took her wrist and felt her pulse. "Are you feeling better?" he asked.

"Yes! Yes. Much better. Thank you."

"What happened?"

"I could see the light. So much energy. It—"

"Is Fluellen all right?" asked Grigwell, as he emerged from the surrounding vegetation.

"Yes," answered Quintell. "She was just about to tell us what happened."

"There was so much energy," she repeated, squinting at Grigwell. "I saw lights, on the very edge of my sight. As tall as trees it was. Terror. I felt a great terror. In the air. Everywhere."

"Hatred?" asked Trillium.

"No, not that. Relief! Anger! Indecision! Sorrow. Great sorrow. I don't know. I can't make it out. It hurt my head. I've never felt anything like it. I can't understand all this. I've never had to deal with this sort of thing before. I ... I ... just ..." Fluellen held her head in her hands again and started sobbing.

Quintell put a comforting arm around her shoulder.

"I've investigated the prints we found," said Grigwell. "The only conclusion I can come to is, giants have entered the forest."

"What!" exclaimed Quintell.

"No!" Fluellen whispered, dropping her hands away. Looking up, she said, "Oh!" as if she suddenly understood something.

Trillium frowned. "But what has that to do with Veeleeta?"

"I'm pretty sure the giants have attacked the creatures we have been following," explained Grigwell. It seems that one of those creatures was a giant as well, smaller, a child for any better explanation than that. It has been attacked." He shook his head in disbelief. "In the vast clearing, where we started our search, I was confused with the tracks," continued Grigwell. "They were small for one so big and were mixed with tracks I had never seen before. But there," he said, pointing back to where he had just come from, "there is no mistaking it. A giant has taken Veeleeta, and it has now been attacked by its own kind. The giants have taken them out of the forest. We need to hurry. Fluellen, are you able to carry on?"

There was silence. Trillium looked up, confused, as if he could not comprehend what he had just heard. "But—"

"We need to get going," Grigwell urged, helping Fluellen to her feet.

As the group continued to move through the trees, they and the surrounding shrubs became sparser, and daylight grew brighter. Eventually, the Gribbles pulled a large leaf to one side, and morning sunlight burst upon them. They blinked as they emerged from the forest. In front of them stood a wall of thin stalks, golden in colour, twenty times the height of a normal Gribble, and it was barring their way.

16

Trillium now began to comprehend the sheer size of the creatures they had been following. He and the other Gribbles had walked up and down the wall of long golden stalks to find large areas had been damaged, some even squashed flat. It was clear that the giants had caused it all.

"What are we going to do now?" Trillium moaned. He turned to find the other two Gribbles looking expectantly at Grigwell, who had now raised his eyebrows in reply.

"Well, all right," answered Grigwell, as if he understood that they were expecting him to solve the problem. "Let's climb a tree."

Finding a suitable one, they climbed it until they found a branch they deemed high enough, and as they turned to look out beyond the confines of the forest, they were shocked by what lay before them.

All Gribbles spend their entire lives within the forest surrounded by an uncountable number of trees and plants, as well as noise created, season upon season, night upon night, day upon day, by a vast number of animals, birds and insects, not to mention the very trees themselves.

Even though Trillium had travelled with his papa to a number of the other hanging villages scattered throughout the ancient forest, he had never been able to see further into it by more than a few trees. He had never ventured to the very edge of it. He had never looked at what lay beyond it. Now he was doing just that, dread filled him at what he saw.

A huge emptiness, with the dim light of daybreak shrouded in a cold grey mist, stretched before him. An overpowering silence hung in the air with no hint of life beyond. A hazy golden ball of light rose above the veiled horizon, and as its long fingers of sunlight inched across the countryside, the mist fled before it, revealing a huge expanse of golden vegetation. Bright red flowers, dotted amongst it all, unfurled their large silken petals and swayed as a breeze caressed the sea of gold. Dewdrops sparkled like diamonds across its surface before the sunlight kissed them goodbye.

Trillium looked to his left and saw a long curve of dark trees disappearing behind a large dark shape. To his right, he saw another line of dark vegetation disappearing into the distant hazy horizon.

"There isn't anything there," said Fluellen, with tears in her eyes. The others looked at her in confusion.

"Nothing?" questioned Trillium, unable to understand. *What is she talking about? It looks beautiful, and yet ... it's full of terror.*

She turned to face them. "As I've said before. We Auras see the energy within all things, even the colours they produce. But here, there is nothing. No light, no colour, no energy. I can see none of it, and yet here it is, a world existing without it. I ... I had heard of such tales, whispers of worlds with no light, no energy, but I never believed it until now." Fluellen turned to look back at the expanse before her.

"Then what do you think this world is?" asked Quintell.

"Tales tell of worlds living on the edge of our existence," answered Fluellen, as if she was in a dream.

Trillium screwed up his eyebrows. This was more than he could understand.

"There are worlds that live at a different frequency from ours," continued Fluellen. "There is no connection between the two. It would answer why I can't see it, and yet, I don't know how to solve that." Fluellen turned to look at Trillium. "I ... I can't help find Veeleeta anymore, Trillium. I can't see her, or any of your light for that matter. You are all dark to me. Ever since passing through the barrier of energy, I can see none of it."

"What!" cried Trillium, frustrated that he did not understand. "But you said you were not blind."

Fluellen laughed, but it was a laugh full of loss and heartache.

"No. I'm not blind," she said, as if her heart was breaking. "Only blind to the energy, to the light of all living things." She looked past the branch down to the ground, then slowly lifted her head and said, "I ... I will return to the village. I'm of no use to you now."

"But you can't do that," said Trillium, rushing up to her and grabbing her arms. "There ... there might be something, anything you can do. You can still see energy even if it's only here," he said, moving his hands to the edge of his eyes. He had at least managed to understand that much! "You can't go." Trillium stood up tall and frowned at her. "I will not let you."

Quintell patted Fluellen on her shoulder and smiled at her. She returned his smile with one of her own and nodded her head. "All right, I will stay. Although what use I will be to you, I do not know."

"Now," said Quintell, turning to look out before him. "How do we cross this?"

Trillium looked out over the wide expanse and felt as if the air around him had suddenly become solid. His eyes stung from tears and for a moment his mind went blank with indecision. How could he ask the others to go on in all good conscience? They had done so much, come so far, and now, Fluellen had lost everything because of it. But to do so on his own? He shivered. How would he survive? But Veeleeta? He had to try.

Then breathing deeply, and with resolution in his heavy heart, he turned to his companions and slowly and deliberately said, "Thank you, everyone, for coming this far with me, but I ... I'm going to go and find Veeleeta by myself." The others looked upon him with surprise. "Fluellen," said Trillium. "I know what I've just said, but ... but you have already paid such a heavy price for coming on this expedition. I ... I can't ask you all to do more." Turning to Grigwell he said, "I don't care what the Selenites have said, Grigwell. I thank you for everything you have done, but I can't ask you all to come. I know that without you all I would not have even been able to get this far ..." Trillium's voice cracked and he lowered his gaze. He didn't think he could go on.

"And without me, you will get no further," said Grigwell.

"And without us, you will not come back," said Fluellen, in her soft soothing voice. Trillium turned and looked into her bright smiling eyes knowing that they looked upon a dark world. "We started this and we will finish it, just as you said before." Her voice, filled with determination, continued to say, "What would Snailum say if we didn't care for his son?"

The other Gribbles nodded in agreement. Trillium stood silent in front of his papa's friends. He then heaved a large sigh, and his long nose twitched. Relief surged through him. He knew he would have tried to carry on, but he also knew that he feared that they were right, he would have failed.

"Grigwell," asked Trillium, unable to hide the tremor in his voice as he pointed out to the horizon. "Are you sure Veeleeta has been taken out there?"

"The tracks we have been following lead straight out into it," said Grigwell. "See how the many trails weave through the vegetation from the edge of the forest? They head towards that large circular area of flattened stalks way out in the distance. I'm sorry, Trillium. I had hoped I was wrong, but this proves the Selenites have told us the truth for once." He pointed to the black structure in the distance. "I'm not sure, but I think we might find Veeleeta there. It might be where the giants live." Shrugging his shoulders, he said, "It's as good a place to start our search as any."

Back on the ground, Trillium pointed at the golden edge of the field. "It will be impossible for us to walk through all of that."
"Yes, you're quite right," said Grigwell. "That's why we're not going to. We will just go over the top of it."

"Cloud Dancers, you mean?" said Quintell, surprised.

"Yes, we will need five," answered Grigwell. "That is if the mistress of the herd will let them come."

"Five, but there are only four of us," said Fluellen.

"We need one to carry the supplies and Veeleeta if we, eh I mean, when we rescue her," answered Grigwell in a gentle tone as he saw Trillium flick a look in his direction.

"Oh yes, yes of course. I knew that," said Fluellen, nodding her head and looking away.

Each Gribble retrieved a Messenger Bug from their pouch.

Trillium whispered to his favourite bug, the one he had had since he was young, "Tell Mama we have found signs of Veeleeta, we're heading out of the forest. We are requesting Cloud Dancers. I'll keep in touch."

Trillium watched as his and the other Messenger Bugs released by the other Gribbles glowed a variety of colours, flying out into the forest, back towards the hanging village of Pooreena.

"I've requested five Dancers," Grigwell said. "I've also sent a Messenger Bug to the Gribble Elder telling him what has happened, and what we're planning to do. I've asked him to arrange the delivery of our supplies to the Supplies Station. The Cloud Dancers will pick them up from there. Now, it's going to take some time for them to reach us, so I suggest we have something to eat, then rest."

"What do you think has happened to Veeleeta's Messenger Bug?" asked Fluellen.

Everyone turned to look at her. Quintell shrugged.

"You don't think it's ... dead, do you?" she asked.

No one said anything. Trillium's mind went blank again.

"It's just ... well, it's been with her ever since she was born. It would never leave her unless ... it had no choice."

"Fluellen! Stop it!" Trillium glared. "I'm sorry, but don't! Please!"

"We don't know the answer, Fluellen," said Grigwell. "Her Messenger Bug is only young, as you know. It can't fly very far. Come. Sit. We have things to do."

"I'm sorry, Trillium. I didn't mean anything by it," said Fluellen.

Trillium nodded. "I know." He went and sat down next to Grigwell who had retrieved a bunch of little round white rocks, Fire Stones, from the pocket of his waistcoat. Trillium watched as he rubbed them together causing them to glow. He then piled them into a hollow in the ground. Trillium stretched his hands out to embrace their warmth as a slight chill in the air made his skin tingle.

Quintell and Fluellen then cooked up some much-needed food, and once everyone's bellies were full, they all settled under a thorny shrub and lay back on the warm soil.

Trillium placed his hands behind his head and watched as insects darted amongst bunches of delicate white flowers scattered along the thick thorny canes, listening to their buzzing. A soft breeze kissed him on his cheek and he closed his eyes and fell into a dreamless sleep.

Ebony awoke to find a pair of warm green eyes staring at her. She instantly threw her bandaged hands over her face and groaned. A split second later she dropped them. "Don't do that!" she said, scowling at Isobel. "You scared me to death."

"Oh, I do think that's a bit of an exaggeration, don't you?" said Isobel, standing up, folding her arms and smiling. "You're still clearly alive."

Ebony frowned. "What do you want?"

"Nanny. She wants you to get up."

"I can't. I'm too sore. My knee hurts. My shoulders ache. My whole body is just too sore. I don't want to."

Isobel glared at Ebony until finally, she huffed, "Oh, all right." Ebony gingerly clambered out of bed and flicked a look at her top drawer where the creature still lay secretly wrapped in cloth. She sighed, knowing she would not be able to check on it until Isobel left the room.

Resigned to her fate, she allowed Isobel to help her out of bed.

Ebony, to show her protest, complained more than was really necessary as she struggled to slide her bandaged arms through the sleeves of her dressing-gown. Isobel then helped her shuffle over to one of the two high-backed armchairs next to the cold fireplace and eased her into its comforting arms.

"I'm just too sore for all of this," complained Ebony again, as she rested her head back and closed her eyes. She breathed in the spicy scent of the small white bunches of roses that were just starting to poke their heads through her open window three storeys up. A calmness settled within her.

"I'll go and get—" Isobel started to say. "Oh. Look who's finally woken up." She smiled.

"Hello, Scruff," said Ebony, leaning forward and looking down at him sitting on the hearthrug. "How are you? Are you feeling as bad as I am?"

Two dark brown eyes looked back at her, reproachfully. Ebony frowned.

"What has happened to *you?*" Scruffy's bushy eyebrows waggled in reply. "You've got no hair on your head and why are you wearing a jacket? It's summer."

Scruffy, dressed in a dog jacket spattered with a pattern of small white bones on a black background, slowly and very stiffly sat up.

Ebony glared at Isobel. "What's happened to him?"

"Yes. Well." Isobel rubbed her hands together. "As you know, George took him to be washed and cleaned. He was very dirty."

A rumble emanated from deep within Scruffy's chest.

"Isobel! What … has … happened … to … him?" Ebony demanded, staring at Scruffy.

"Um … Yes, yes, of course. Sorry. The only thing George could do with him was to give him a bit of a trim. He was in such a mess, you see. George said … well, he said, it was all he could do. You're lucky you have not suffered the very same fate, young lady."

Ebony went and kneeled next to Scruffy and tickled him under his chin.

"Don't worry, Miss Ebony," Isobel said as she removed the dog jacket. "It's only a hair … cut!"

"He's been shorn like a sheep! Not even his tail has been spared! Why did George do that?" Ebony looked at Isobel with accusations on her lips and tears prickling her eyes. "What's poor Scruff going to do now?"

Scruffy lifted a paw, looked at it, turned, looked at his tail, then raised his head and howled.

"Oh, Scruffy," said Ebony, her bandaged hand patting his bald head. "It will be all right."

Suddenly the bedroom door flew open and Nanny Windabothem walked in, carrying a large rectangular box, white, thin and shiny.

"Good morning, Miss Ebony," she said in an unusually buoyant voice. "It's about time you were awake."

Scruffy growled. Surprise flitted across Nanny's face for a split second as she looked down at him before her eyes narrowed. A cold steely glint flashed inside them. Scruffy whimpered and moved closer to Ebony, who moaned as she struggled to pick him up and put him on her lap, putting a protective bandaged arm around his chest.

"Are you feeling well this morning?" asked Nanny, slowly dragging her eyes away from Scruffy to settle her gaze on Ebony.

"I'm feeling very sore actu—"

"Isobel," interrupted Nanny as if she really was not interested in anything Ebony had to say. "Get Miss Ebony ready and bring her downstairs, and don't take too long about it."

Nanny placed the white box on the bed, patted it as if she was very pleased with it, glared at Scruffy and then left the room.

"What's that? As if I really need to ask." Ebony knew a delivery carton when she saw one. It had obviously not been sent by her mother. Not one of the hundreds of cartons Ebony had received over the years from the exotic countries her mother had travelled to had ever been just a plain white shiny box. She could never see her mother lowering her standards to that level. No. Handmade, out of silk, with ornate patterns over each one, was her mother's custom, not this. This was different, she could feel it. Something wasn't right about *this*.

"It's a gift from Nanny."

Ebony eyed the box with suspicion. "I knew it!"

"She bought it for you while she was in town yesterday," Isobel informed her.

"What! Why?" Nanny had never given her anything ever before. In fact, it had been the total opposite. So why now?

"You need to get yourself ready, Miss Ebony I think under the circumstances a birdbath is called for."

"A what?" Ebony looked at Isobel. "I'm not a bird."

"Very funny. Let's get on with it. We have to get you dressed."

"Dressed for what?"

"No time for questions."

18

Veeleeta's older brother, Whimbrel, was sitting at the base of a large mushroom wondering what had happened to his sister. He was also wondering why he had not been allowed to go and help find her. The last time he had seen her was on the suspension bridge. She had walked out into the forest, something she always did, and simply vanished. He should have gone with her on that day, no matter what she had said. He was her older brother, for goodness sake. Was it not up to him to take care of her? He huffed, picked himself up and headed home.

"Oh, there you are," said Mama, as Whimbrel walked through the door. "Quick, the Cloud Dancers are leaving."

"What?"

"Trillium has sent a Messenger Bug. They have found signs of Veeleeta. They are leaving the confines of the forest and the Cloud Dancers are going to go with them. Quick! You must hurry."

Whimbrel dashed out of the house. He rushed over many suspension bridges, climbed down a ladder and, breathing hard, ran across the decking surrounding a small abode hanging from the tip of a thin silver branch. Grabbing hold of the doorframe, he called out, "Freeschum, Freeschum."

The Cloud Dancer, jet black in colour, lying on the floor amongst aromatic herbs, heaved himself up to stand on his four, long, flat, padded feet. He flicked his fluffy tail, flapped his set of four black silken wings and stretched his long neck, making the black fluff that lay between two large horizontal ears sway. He then looked at Whimbrel with his large round bright eyes and said, "Yes?"

"Veeleeta is missing and I'm allowed to go and look for her. You must take … Oh, err … Sorry," Whimbrel apologised, as Freeschum frowned. He was a creature of free will, and one didn't just demand that he, or any Cloud Dancer for that matter, do anything. You asked, then you might get it if they felt like it. "Will you take me?" Whimbrel pleaded, "Please-e-e?"

"Yes," came the answer.

Whimbrel, beaming a wide smile, dashed to the back of the abode where a saddle chair and blanket lay. Struggling under their weight, he finally got them onto Freeschum's back, ensuring the belly strap was secure around his round tummy.

"Have you not forgotten something?"

Whimbrel looked up. His mama stood in the doorway, a backpack in one hand, a wriggling chestnut-coloured Poogle in the other.

"Thanks," Whimbrel said, grabbing the backpack. "What's he doing here?"

"I've had a vision, a dream. Don't ask questions. You have to take him."

"Why? I don't want to. You know what he's like."

"I ... I don't know why. I can't make any sense of it. I just keep seeing a field of white, and somehow Congar's involved. All I know is that it's important he goes with the rescue group. Also, I want you to give this to Trillium."

Whimbrel took the little cloth bundle tied up with string she handed him.

"What is it?"

"Never you mind. Just make sure you give it to him."

Whimbrel shrugged his shoulders and placed the bundle inside his vest pocket. He then returned to Freeschum. He attached his backpack to the rear of the saddle chair.

"Now, you need to go to the Supplies Station," said Mama. "The other Cloud Dancers are waiting, they'll be leaving soon."

"Don't worry," said Whimbrel. "We will get there in time, won't we, Freeschum?"

Freeschum didn't reply as Whimbrel pulled on the small step attached to the saddle chair, allowing it to cascade down. He climbed up and settled himself in the seat. He then pulled on the string attached to the base of the steps; they immediately folded up and Whimbrel tied them in place. He leaned against the backrest, putting his feet in the stirrups straddled across Freeschum's shoulders. "Congar, come on then if you're coming," called Whimbrel.

The Poogle, turning purple, flung himself out of Mama's arms, and seeming to glide along the floorboards, sprang into Whimbrel's lap and settled down.

"Now, remember, Whimbrel. Once you have given Trillium the package and delivered Congar to him, you are then to return immediately to the village."

"What? No!" Whimbrel cried out.

"Yes!" said Mama, with a stern look as if to push the point home. "You are too young to go on the expedition. It will be too dangerous. I will hear no more about it. You are to come straight home."

19

The Gribbles were awakened from their slumber by a familiar hum and they scrambled to their feet. Four Cloud Dancers were flying into the campsite. Each was a different colour. Each had a saddle chair securely strapped around its large round belly, and each, using its four small wings, hovered for a moment, before lightly touching down.

The Gribbles crowded around them as the Cloud Dancers pawed the ground with their large, round, flat feet. They tossed their long necks in excitement and their large round eyes seemed to smile as if they were pleased to see them.

Grigwell approached the stately pale-blue Cloud Dancer with a white chest. "Stellman. Thank you for coming."

The Cloud Dancer nodded his head but said nothing in reply.

"It's good to see you again, my old friend," Grigwell continued. "We have a long and, I fear, dangerous journey ahead of us, and I thank you for offering to help. I'm in your debt, yet again."

"Where are the supplies?" asked Quintell.

In answer, all four animals turned their heads towards the way they had come.

Three more Cloud Dancers, again different colours from one another, flew through the trees. Two carried supplies and the other, a jet-black one, had a young Gribble riding it.

"Whimbrel! What are you doing here?" Trillium placed his hands on his hips, planted his oblong feet on the ground and glared.

"Hello, brother," said Whimbrel, pushing his brown fringe out of his eyes. "It is nice to see you too."

A high-pitched squeal rent the air and Congar, now a blue ball of fluff, leapt from Whimbrel's lap and streaked across to Trillium, throwing itself at his chest. Trillium instinctively grabbed hold of him.

"What did you bring *him* for?" A long pink tongue darted in and out of a pointy snout, attempting to lick Trillium's face.

"I didn't have a choice!" Whimbrel yelled above the din. "Mama insisted on it. She said I had to bring him."

Trillium looked down at the blue ball of fur wriggling in his arms. Congar was trying to bury his pointy snout into his armpit. "Congar! Stop it! Behave yourself." Trillium pushed him onto the ground then turned to Whimbrel. "The last thing we need on a trip like this is a Poogle, especially this one."

Congar cowered and his fur turned yellow. He slunk back to Whimbrel who, having dismounted Freeschum, picked him up and stroked his head. Congar's fur turned back to its normal chestnut colour.

"Ever since Veeleeta went missing, he's been moping about changing to the same colour as the floor," Whimbrel said. "Mama kept stepping on him all the time. Even when she placed him outside, he squealed so much all the neighbours complained. You know what he's like when he doesn't get his own way. When he saw your Messenger Bug turn up, well, there wasn't anything else for it. I had to bring him. See, he's looking much happier already."

Trillium screwed up his face, crossed his arms and glared back at his younger brother, as five glowing Messenger Bugs flew past him returning from their trip to the hanging village of Pooreena.

Whimbrel shrugged, turned to look at the others and cheerfully announced, "We've come to help with the search for Veeleeta."

"I told you to stay home and look after Mama," grumbled Trillium, as his Messenger Bug bumped against the pouch hanging off Trillium's belt. It seemed to be demanding to be let back in. Grumbling, Trillium unhooked the pouch, opened it and, as the bug repositioned itself within the pad, continued to say, "You're too young to come on an expedition like this." Retying the pouch to his belt he added, "Why is Congar *really* here?"

"Mama had a vision," said Whimbrel. "That's why we're both

here. Oh, that reminds me. She sent you this." Whimbrel handed the cloth bundle to Trillium. "She could not make any sense of the vision except there was an expanse of white, and that somehow Congar is involved. She just knows we have to be here."

Whimbrel watched Trillium looking at the cloth bundle and with determination, said nothing about the instructions his mama had given him. He had spent the time travelling to the campsite, arguing with himself about whether he should do as he was told and go straight back to the village after delivering Congar and the package to Trillium, or take the risk and disobey his mama and go on this journey instead. He had to admit the argument had not lasted long. There was no way he was going to miss out on this adventure, no matter what his mama said, and he was prepared to pay the price for his disobedience.

Trillium took the package and cradled it in his hands.

"Fortunately," continued Whimbrel, "Freeschum let me ride him, so here we are."

Trillium tutted, and went and sat under the large leaf of a nearby plant. He watched Grigwell, who was ensuring each Cloud Dancer who was to carry a Gribble was correctly saddled, and that a bedroll and two flasks of water were attached to the back of each saddle chair. Trillium then turned his attention to the cloth package.

Inside was a small drawstring pouch made of cobwebs and coloured silk. Attached to it was a length of plaited twine, enabling him to tie it around his neck.

He pondered. Should he look inside? He had never been allowed to before. The one and only time he had seen this package, many years ago, his papa hadn't let him even touch it, or answer any of his questions about it. He had just taken it away and Trillium had never seen it again until now.

Peering closely, Trillium noticed a note lying within the folds of the wrapping. He picked it up and read:

Trillium, what is held within this pouch is to be kept secret. It's only to be used if a dire need presents itself. All my blessings go with you in bringing our little girl home.

Trillium put down the note and opened the pouch. He stared at it. Should he look? Curiosity finally got the better of him and he tipped it upside down onto his palm. Nothing came out. He turned it up the right way and peered inside, but only darkness peered back. He stuck a stubby finger inside and wiggled it about, but he could feel nothing. He turned it upside down again and shook it. Still, nothing dropped out. Frustrated, and not knowing what else to do, he drew the pouch shut, tied it around his neck and shoved it under his shirt, then rejoined his companions.

Grigwell was now standing in the middle of a huddle of Gribbles and Cloud Dancers. He was saying, "Just to make sure everyone understands what we're doing, I will give you a brief rundown of our problem. Veeleeta, you know, is missing. It's been established without a doubt that a giant has taken Veeleeta out of the forest."

"No!" yelled Whimbrel. The Cloud Dancers stomped their feet and shuffled about, causing some Gribbles to move out of their way rather quickly.

"Trillium," continued Grigwell, "will you explain everything to Whimbrel later, not now? I suggest we all head towards, what I assume, is the home of the giants. It will be as good a place to start our search as any."

The Cloud Dancers, agitated again, shuffled about.

"Stellman, please introduce us to the Cloud Dancers who have bravely volunteered to help us with our quest."

Stellman, his head held high, announced in a deep voice, "Leedrum."

A purple female Cloud Dancer, with a hint of white around the base of each foot revealing the five toenails on each foot, stepped forward and walked up to Fluellen. The two of them bowed their heads.

"Thank you for coming, Leedrum," said Fluellen, as she climbed into the saddle chair.

"Torix," Stellman called out.

120

A strong grey male, with darker spots spattered on his hindquarters, walked up to Quintell and they both bowed. "It's a pleasure to see you again, my friend," said Quintell as he too climbed into the saddle chair.

"Teasel."

A very elegant-looking white male, with powder-blue spots splashed on his hindquarters, moved forward. Trillium, who had never met Teasel before, nodded a greeting to him and seated himself without saying a word.

"Tortula and Tillia."

A green male and a pink female Cloud Dancer stepped forward with bundles of supplies on their backs. They both bowed their heads.

"I thank you all," said Grigwell, spreading his arms wide to indicate all the Cloud Dancers. "I thank you too, Freeschum, for offering to help us."

Trillium looked over to the jet-black Cloud Dancer who nodded his head. Whimbrel was already sitting in the saddle chair, leaning against its high back. He had quickly pushed his feet into the stirrups attached to the rod located across Freeschum's shoulders and Congar was now sitting on his lap.

The other Gribbles, when ready, took off into the air on their mounts as the sun, not more than three hours old, was emitting a warm glow. The real search for Veeleeta had now begun.

Ebony washed her face, a feeling of dread filling her as she did so. Her mind squirmed but no matter how she twisted her thoughts, she could not work out why Nanny Windabothem would buy her anything at all. She was up to something, she was sure of it, but what?

Now, with the tips of her hair damp, and her cheeks rosy from a good scrubbing, Ebony returned to her bedroom in her dressing-gown and looked at the box on the bed with suspicion.

"Right, Miss Ebony," said Isobel excitedly, "let's open your gift." A moment later, with white tissue paper scattered over the floor, Isobel lifted out the dress from within and held it up. Scruffy growled. Ebony just stared, shocked. She could not *believe* what she was looking at. It was pink! And, as if *that* wasn't bad enough, it had a pink satin bodice covered in tiny black spots, and a skirt with three ruffled layers, each a different shade of fuchsia pink shimmering in the morning light. "It's horrible. I knew it would be," she said. "I just *knew* it."

"Oh, no it's not. It's just … pink." Isobel put on an apologetic smile as she spread out one of the short puffy sleeves edged with lace. Ebony folded her bandaged arms tight against her chest, planted her feet on the Persian rug and scowled at Isobel. "I'm not wearing it! Nanny Jones would never have made me wear this, even when I was young. I hate pink, it's worse than brown. Which … I … hate!"

Isobel sighed, placed the dress on the bed and picked out another item from the box. It was a puff of white tulle. She shook it. It became a pile of many pleated petticoats which would allow the dress to sit out like a fluffy feather duster.

Ebony's mouth dropped open, horrified. Isobel then picked out a wide sash, a pair of ankle socks with lace edging and a pair of sandals, all in white. She held them out to Ebony, who did not take them. Instead, she glared at Isobel with cheeks that felt on fire with frustration.

Isobel shook her head and placed the items on the bed, then dug back into the box to find a white vest and underpants all trimmed with lace and a long, thin, pink ribbon for her hair.

"I'm not wearing it! None of it! I refuse! I'm not three years old!"

"You are an extremely trying child at times, Miss Ebony. You will need to learn when to fight your battles, and I can tell you now this is *not* one of them."

"And I'm telling you," yelled Ebony, "I'm not wearing it! None of it! You can't make me. No one can!"

Ebony placed her hands on her hips and, feeling herself getting very hot all over, frowned at Isobel.

"What is all this noise?"

Ebony spun around at the same time as Isobel did. Nanny Windabothem stood in the doorway. Her gaze scanned the two of them then locked onto the empty box.

"Isobel? I thought I asked you to get Miss Ebony dressed."

"Yes, Miss Windabothem. Sorry, Miss Windabothem. We were just doing that, weren't we, Miss Ebony?"

Ebony slowly turned to face Isobel and looked upon her with utter loathing.

"Then get on with it," said Nanny Windabothem. "Enough time has been wasted. I shall now have to wait for her."

Ebony sighed and as her shoulders slumped, her hands fell to her side.

Isobel handed her the new underwear. Ebony took it.

Ebony stood in front of the full-length mirror looking like a kewpie doll from a fairground, or a mummy dressed in a pink frock, she could not quite decide which. Scruffy rubbed his skinny shorn body up against her bandaged leg and whimpered. Tears welled in Ebony's eyes, then splattered onto the polished floorboards. It dawned on her what this was all about; how could she possibly have forgotten? *My birthday. Do these people know nothing?* she said to herself. *How can they do this to me?*

Slowly, Ebony turned towards Isobel with eyes that pleaded to make it all go away. Isobel looked to the floor, blushing.

"You look … acceptable." An awkward smile crept across Nanny Windabothem's thin lips as she moved towards Ebony. Nanny flicked a scrawny hand in Scruffy's direction. "Get away!"

Scruffy slunk back to the cold fireplace and returned to sit on the hearthrug.

Nanny, obviously pleased with how the pink dress looked, patted the layers on the skirt and pulled at the short puffy sleeves. When satisfied, she straightened the flaps of her own brown jacket, placed a bony arm around Ebony's shoulder and guided her to the door. Ebony's heart filled with sadness.

"Come on, Scruff," Ebony said as she looked behind her to find Isobel putting Scruffy's jacket back on him. She glared at Isobel and then turned away, disgusted. She had trusted her.

Ebony walked ahead of Nanny Windabothem, and every time she slowed, desperate to delay the inevitable, she was pushed in the back and told to keep moving. Isobel and Scruffy brought up the rear. Ebony felt herself grow hot with anger, desperation growing within. A whirlwind of questions and accusations swirled in her mind. She grew so hot inside she felt she could tear the whole world apart if only to stop this, but in the end, she knew she would be the coward she always was and do as she was told.

The procession continued to walk down the three flights of stairs and across the checkerboard tiles of the foyer to stand in front of the dining-room door. Miss Windabothem turned and fussed over Ebony's dress and straightened her socks again. She then stood up and straightened her own jacket. She ran a hand over her dull black hair drawn tightly into a bun, took a deep breath and grabbed the door handle. Ebony edged back. It was now or never. She needed to make a run for it but as she dithered, indecision scurrying around in her brain, like a mouse who could not find the way out of a trap, the door instantly flung open and Ebony was pushed through it.

21

Whimbrel flew through the air, a vast golden expanse of vegetation spreading before him, and as he looked into the distance, it and the sky had become one.

A breeze rushed upon him and tousled his fringe. It seemed to laugh as it raked its fingers through the vegetation below, leaving dark honey-coloured trails in its wake.

Whimbrel looked back at the forest. It spread like a green smudge for as far as he could see. It was so big. *Why did no one tell me?*

He turned back around and leaned into his saddle chair. Congar squirmed on his lap. Whimbrel breathed in deeply, then frowned. Strange pollens coated his tongue. He mused on their taste and texture as a small voice inside his mind called out, *Listen!*

Whimbrel tilted his head and concentrated. He strained to hear across the enormous space before him but could hear ... nothing. There wasn't the breath of a beetle, not a single butterfly singing its song of change, not even a bird greeting the morning sun. The only sound he heard was Freeschum's wings beating the air.

Whimbrel sneezed.

Shimmering up from the depths of the never-ending sea of gold was heat mixed with a sweet musty smell. It filled all his senses and made them feel dull, then he yawned and looked across to the other Gribbles flying alongside him to see that they too were yawning.

He looked upon this strange world surrounding him, breathed in deeply and sneezed again. As the group flew on, his eyelids slowly grew heavy and his long nose drooped.

He smiled as hazy images of his village, with sunlight filtering through the leaves, drifted in front of his mind's eye.

Then the images faded like smoke on the evening breeze as Fluellen, who had flown up beside him, yelled, "We're stopping for a rest!"

He was now wide-awake. The Cloud Dancers were wheeling in a tight circle, heading for a bare patch of ground deep amongst the golden stalks.

Once dismounted, Whimbrel stood up and rubbed his bottom, looking at the forest of vegetation surrounding them.

"Whimbrel!" snapped Trillium. "Don't just stand there. Go and see if the Cloud Dancers want a drink."

Whimbrel scowled and watched Trillium walk away. Then, slouching, he went and did as he was told.

When everyone was fed, the Gribbles leaned back against the stalks of vegetation to rest.

"Is there no end to this stuff?" Fluellen moaned.

"How much further do we have to go, Grigwell?" asked Trillium.

"I don't know," Grigwell answered. "I'm going to have to risk flying higher so I can get my bearings. We need to find a suitable place to camp for the night."

"Camp for the night!" said Trillium. "Are you telling me we're going to have to stop out here, for the whole night? In this stuff? How much further do we have to go?" he repeated, folding his arms across his chest, huffing and pointing his long nose in Grigwell's direction.

Whimbrel shook his head and looked down at his shoes. Was his brother ever going to change?

Grigwell, without responding, got up and walked over to his backpack, retrieved something from it and returned to sit down again. He unfolded a sheet of paper and looked at it.

"Grigwell! Do you know where we're heading, or not?" said Trillium. "How long is it going to take us to get there, wherever *there* is?"

"Yes and no," answered Grigwell, taking a drawing stick out of the top pocket of his waistcoat.

Trillium glared at him.

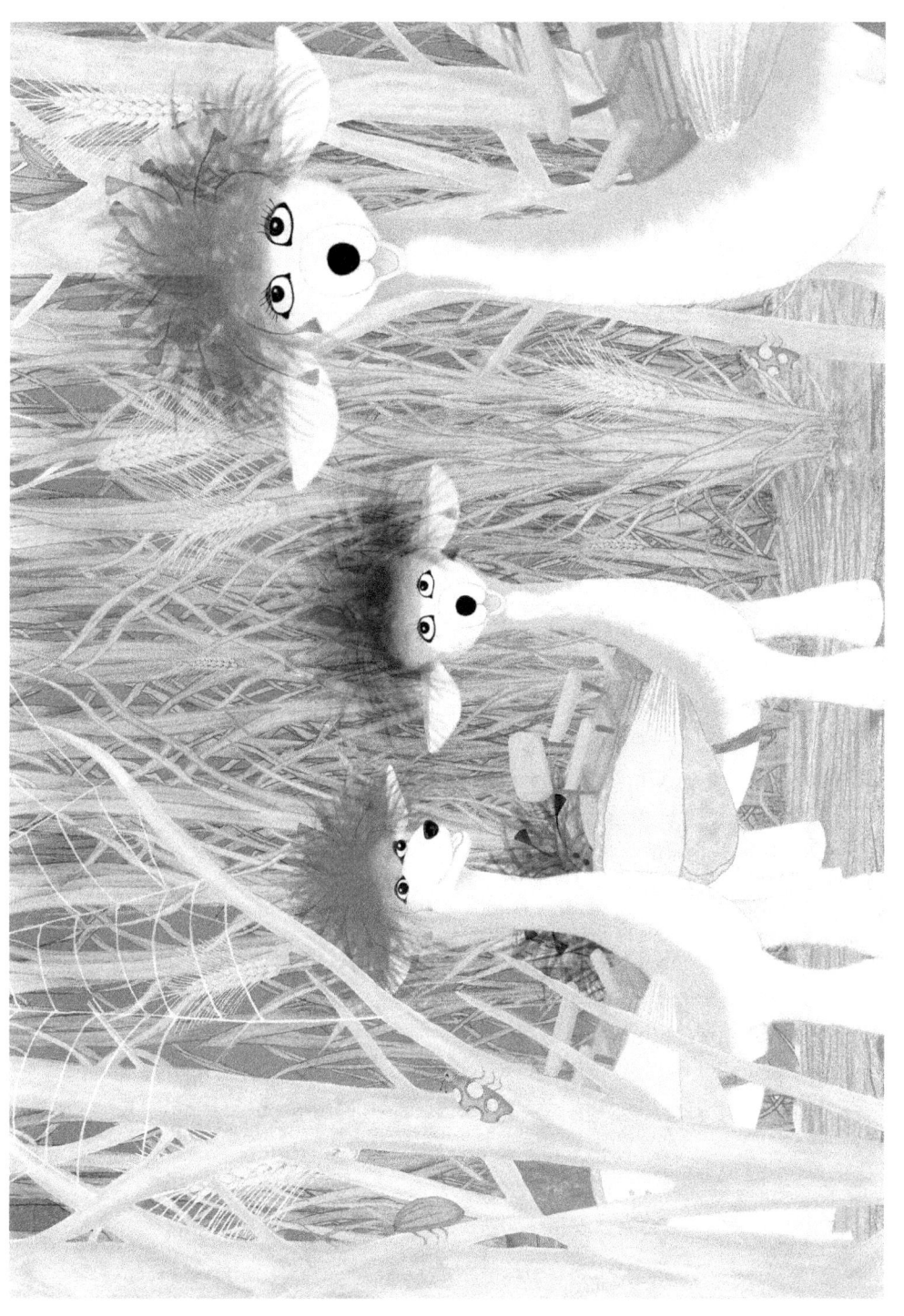

"Oh, all right. I'll explain things as best I can. Gather around."

Everyone huddled together. Congar wriggled his way forward and sat down. The Cloud Dancers poked their heads up over the top of the group, then silence fell upon them.

"Now this map is very rough … Congar! Will you get off?" Grigwell flicked his hand. Congar's fur turned orange as he moved off the map, then he went and sulked next to Whimbrel. Within moments, his colour changed back to its normal chestnut when Whimbrel placed a comforting hand on his head.

"I'm making this map up as we go along," said Grigwell. "We started approximately here." He pointed to the bottom right-hand side of the map. There was a circle with the word 'Home' written in the middle of it. "This is where I think Veeleeta has been taken." His finger pointed to the top left of the map where he had drawn the shape of a square, with the word 'Giants' written in it. "The tracks were heading in that direction." He tapped the paper several times and his nose bounced up and down in time with it. "Now, of course, the idea is to get to—"

"Where are we now?" interrupted Trillium.

"I think we're about here." Grigwell pointed to the lower section of the map, waving his hand in a small circle.

"Where are we going to camp for the night?"

"I don't know."

"What about tomorrow?" asked Trillium. "When do you think we will get to the giants' house?"

"I don't know," repeated Grigwell. "As I've said before, I need to fly higher to get my bearings."

Trillium's shoulders slumped.

Grigwell picked up the map. "Trillium! We don't have a clue what is out here, or what we're facing, so please … be patient."

Upon returning to the skies, the group hovered just above the tips of the vegetation. The sun was higher, hotter and brighter, hanging in a cloudless, cornflower-blue sky. Whimbrel placed a hand above his brow and watched as Stellman, with Grigwell aboard, flew above the rest of the group. They flew high into the sky, so high they looked like a dark dot. Then a screech rent the air and the dot plummeted out of the sky.

E bony entered the dining room with a bit of a stumble. A crowd of people turned to look at her and their murmurings ceased. The only sound drifting in the air was soft classical music. Ebony bit her lip and took a step back. She bumped into Nanny Windabothem, who pushed Ebony forward with fingertips that felt like steel rods boring into her back.

"Ebony."

Ebony's mother wore a bright floral summer dress. "You look so … lovely?" her mother said, shooting a nervous look at someone Ebony could not see. She then took Ebony's bandaged right hand in hers and dragged her into the centre of the room.

"What a lovely dress," someone said.

"You do look so grown up," another person said as Ebony's cheeks flushed with embarrassment.

Are these people crazy? Ebony thought. *Look at me! I'll be scarred for life because of this! … Oh don't talk rubbish,* Ebony scolded herself.

"Happy birthday, Ebony. You *do* look lovely."

Ebony spun around to find her father smiling at her. He too was dressed in summer colours. Pastel pink trousers, lavender shirt and a dark, highly embroidered waistcoat with gold threads entwined within the design. His long dark hair was neat, tidy and tied back in a ponytail.

"Would you like a drink?" her mother asked. Ebony nodded yes, and her mother guided her towards the dining room table covered with a delicate handmade white lace cloth. Spread before her were crystal bowls filled to the brim with sandwiches, salads, nuts, cakes and sweets, all twinkling in the light of two tall lamps, aglow with stained-glass lampshades. Large vases filled with summer flowers sat at the back, and in the middle of it all was a round birthday cake, decorated with red, yellow, pink and white roses, with thirteen candles dotted amongst the green leaves. Written in purple icing were the words *Happy 13th Birthday Ebony.*

"Thank you," said Ebony, as her mother handed her a crystal cup full of punch. Ebony looked at the chunks of strawberry and pineapple bobbing about in the pink fizzy drink. She took a sip and using a silk napkin as a plate, picked up a curried egg sandwich and started nibbling at it.

She scanned the gathering in front of her. People, who she recognised as the staff, were chatting and laughing amongst themselves. Ebony eagerly looked around to see if Nanny Jones was amongst them.

She's not here, she thought with a sinking feeling settling in her heart. *Why would she be? After what you did … what you said.* Ebony felt herself getting hot, her eyes stinging with tears. *Don't do this to yourself, Ebony. Everyone's looking at you. Look at something. Look at something.*

She looked down to find Scruffy faithfully sitting at her feet. She blinked away the tears threatening to overwhelm her, pinched off the corner of her sandwich and gave it to him. "At least I've got one friend," she said, as a pang of loneliness closed its fist around her heart.

Scruffy spat the food out onto the floor.

"Tut! Honestly. You're such an impossible dog sometimes."

Using her napkin, Ebony picked up the soggy lump. Scruffy placed his cold wet nose up against her cheek, leaned back and looked at her with his bright eyes. She smiled an awkward smile at him, tickled him under the chin, then stood up.

Ebony's father cleared his throat and everyone became silent. He walked over to Ebony, took her by the hand and led her to stand near a small round wooden table where her gifts sat. He then turned to the crowd.

"Today we are here to celebrate Ebony's thirteenth birthday." Turning to Ebony, he said, "You're growing up so fast. We will put aside the dramas of last night and just enjoy the fact that you are here with us today. Now some of the staff—" here he indicated the crowd with a wide sweep of his hand "—have given you some gifts. Also, I must thank Miss Windabothem for giving Ebony her beautiful party dress. That was very thoughtful of you."

Nanny straightened her shoulders, raised her sharp nose in the air, cast a look around the room, then nodded in Mr Wood's direction. Ebony blinked, desperately attempting not to scowl. She could not *believe* what she was hearing.

"Now, Ebony," her father said. "Would you like to say something before opening your gifts?"

Ebony flicked a nervous look at her father, then blushed and smiled shyly. Placing the napkin on the table, she turned to face her guests.

"Um ... Thank you, everyone, for coming to celebrate my birthday. I ... I will never forget it."

Embarrassed, Ebony quickly turned and picked up the gift closest to her. It was about the size of a shoebox wrapped in bright orange floral paper and tied with a bright pink ribbon.

"What is the name on the gift, dear?" her mother asked. Lifting up the nametag, Ebony blinked. *Crumbs!*

"It's from Nanny." Ebony, who was slightly shocked and even more embarrassed, turned and looked at Nanny Windabothem.

"Err. Th ... thank you very much." Everyone was watching her. She gulped.

"Open it, dear," her mother said with an excited edge to her voice. She always did love the opening of gifts, even if they were for other people.

Ebony hesitantly and very carefully undid the wrapping, lifted the lid from the box within and removed a small white leather handbag. She lifted it up to see it better.

"Oh, how nice" and "Isn't that lovely" could be heard from the guests.

"Thank you, Nanny ... It's lovely." And it was. Ebony was amazed by how Nanny could possibly have chosen something like this, so elegant, and yet choose a dress that was just so ... wrong.

Ebony placed the empty box and the handbag down on the table. She then picked up a small parcel about the size of her hand, wrapped in old brown paper. It was from George the butler, who never was one for formalities. She thanked him. His prune-like face broke into a smile. Ebony ripped at the covering, letting it fall to the floor. Her parents giggled. Nanny frowned. Ebony then held up a new blue dog collar embedded with small round silver-coloured studs.

"Oh look, Scruff, isn't it lovely?" She showed it to him, but he scowled back at her and hid behind her bandaged legs. "Honestly, Scruff, that's not very nice."

Scruffy slowly poked his bald head out from behind her legs.

"What's George ever done to—? Oh, yes, of course. The haircut. Um." Ebony looked at George. "He loves it really, George. Thank you."

George chuckled.

Ebony placed the collar on the table next to her new handbag and picked up another gift. It was a soft package neatly wrapped, from Isobel. Within was a set of six white lace hankies. In the corner of each one was a large embroidered letter E with tiny wildflowers entwined throughout.

"I embroidered them myself," Isobel told Ebony, her voice full of pride and a sparkle in her emerald-green eyes.

"Thank you," said Ebony. "They are lovely. I shall treasure them always."

The next gift was squat, round and heavy. She knew what this was. She'd had them before, and without having to read the tag, she went and hugged Agnes, the old head cook. "Thank you. You know how much I love your shortbread biscuits."

Everyone *oohed* and *ahhed*. Ebony knew they all secretly wished they too had been given some of Agnes's award- winning biscuits.

Ebony returned to the table to open her last gift. It was tall, wide and heavy. Ebony carefully undid the wrapping to find a beautiful white vase with strange-looking blue birds painted over it, as if they were long in body and wide in wingspan.

"It's a gift from Mrs Salix, the head cleaner," her mother said. "She is sorry she can't be here today, but she's had to rush home. It's her little boy's birthday today as well. She hopes you like it."

"It's lovely," Ebony replied, admiring the delicate designs and hoping that one day she could paint as well as Mrs Salix.

There was a rough cough from the back of the room.

"Excuse me, sir," said Mr Flag the head gardener, still dressed in his overalls with only socks on his feet. "But I've just gathered these for Miss Ebony from the rose garden. I know they are her favourite flower."

"Oh, thank you *ever so much*," Ebony crooned as she rushed up to him and took them into her arms. She stuck her nose amongst the soft petals, breathed in the heady perfume from the many varieties, then placed them in the vase.

"Now, Ebony," her father said. "Before you get your present from your mother and me, Nanny Jones has sent you this." He produced from his waistcoat pocket a little red box tied with a fine golden ribbon.

Ebony stared at it then gently took it and held it for a few minutes within her bandaged hands before placing it inside her new handbag.

"Aren't you going to open it?" her father asked.

"I'll … I'll open it later," Ebony answered in a whisper that could barely be heard. She then turned back to look at her father. He smiled as if he understood.

"Now, we have a gift for you." He pointed to the other end of the dining room. As the guests parted, they revealed something tall covered in a white sheet. It was taller than Ebony, in fact, it was almost as tall as her father and she was amazed she'd not noticed it before.

"Go and see what's under it then," he said when she did not move.

Ebony, knowing every eye was upon her, walked up to it as if her legs were made of lead. She grabbed the sheet and, cringing as pain shot through her left palm, pulled as hard as she could. The sheet slid off, falling into a heap on the floor. Her mouth dropped open.

"Wow!" said many guests.

"Look at that!" said someone else.

"Isn't that amazing?" said another.

It was a model of a castle made out of light-coloured stone. It had five long thin towers, their roofs capped with light grey tiles.

There were balconies and stained-glass windows, and surrounding the base were models of mossy rocks, shrubs, flowers and delicate vines climbing up the castle's façade.

Her father pulled on two gargoyles situated on a tower on the right-hand side of the castle. A wall sprang open, revealing rooms both large and tiny, sweeping staircases, little alcoves, wooden cupboards and ornate fireplaces, with many, many doors leading off to other unseen rooms.

Oohs and *ahhs* exploded from the guests again as they all pressed forward, craning their necks to get a better look.

"You can open up other sections of the castle by pressing down on other gargoyles," her father said with pride in his voice. "We thought all those crazy little soft toys you and Nanny Jones had made together could come and live in it. I can just see the pink octopus hanging out a window, the purple-haired fairy standing on a balcony, the blue donkey somewhere. Well, he would be a bit of squeeze, but I'm sure you can fit him in somewhere. They would look really good, don't you think?"

Ebony, dazed, looked up at her father, then looked back at her gift. Her throat tightened and she feared she might not be able to keep breathing. Tears prickled her eyes. *How can I tell him?*

Her mother's arm was now on her shoulder. Tears finally tumbled over Ebony's cheeks and she buried her face in her mother's dress.

"I'm sorry," said Ebony, once she'd recovered. "I didn't mean to upset you yesterday."

Her mother got down on one knee, smiled back at her and gently held Ebony's bandaged hands in hers.

"We know you didn't mean it, dear. You know we still love you, no matter what you do." She stroked Ebony's long ponytail. "All that matters is that you're home safe and sound." She gave Ebony a hug, and her delicate floral perfume enveloped both of them. Ebony drank it in, allowing it to flow through her senses. Her mother slowly pulled away. "You cannot expect to go running off like that and not get into a little bit of trouble now, can you?" She hugged

Ebony again. Ebony smiled, nodded and went over to her father, who swept her up in his big strong arms and gave her a bear hug.

"All of us," he said, placing her back on the floor a bit faster than he used to when she was younger, "we're just so worried about you last night. We thought we had lost you forever, and then what would we do?" He looked at the castle. "You do like it, don't you? You're not too old for it now, are you? It's just that it took a bit longer than I thought to have it built. The man started building it nearly two years ago. I was beginning to wonder if he would ever finish it but I must admit I am really impressed with it."

Ebony looked up at her father, stunned that he had thought of having this built so long ago, before so many things had happened to change their lives forever.

"No. No, I'm not," Ebony answered. "And yes, I love it."

"Here." Her father pulled a nearby wooden chair towards her. "Stand on this." He handed her a cloth package, long and thin. "Put these in the tops of the turrets of the towers."

Ebony gingerly took the wrapping and using two fingertips, pulled back the top layer. Beneath sat five long metal spires all in different lengths, each coloured metallic blue, each with a golden tip. One had, atop it, a banner, long and fine, that looked as if a gentle breeze had blown undulating curves through the yellow fabric, but now it was frozen, permanently stuck in position. It was emblazoned with the family crest of a white swan with a crown on its head, on a shield of blue with a variety of symbols in red and green.

Ebony, standing on tiptoes, reached up and gently but firmly stuck a spire into the top of each of the five shingled roofs on the towers, making sure the flag emblazoned with the family crest was placed on top of the roof on the highest turret. She then leaned back to admire the result. It definitely finished the castle off. It had looked a bit odd without them, but she'd not realised that until they had been added. She then turned, smiling, wanting to say thank you, when a slight movement at the other end of the room caught her eye. Nanny Windabothem was sneaking out through the dining-room door.

23

The party was over. The guests had dispersed, where, Ebony did not know nor did she really care. There was only one thought in Ebony's head, well, several actually, but the most important one was that if she was quick enough, she could just check on the creature in the drawer. She had to know, was it still alive?

Taking the stairs two at a time until she ran out of breath, she stumbled because her knee gave way. "Idiot!" she grumbled. Her excitement had, momentarily, made her forget about her sore knee.

Scruffy, who had followed her, rushed to her side. She ruffled his head and smiled. "I'm all right, Scruff."

Hobbling to her room, she placed her new handbag on the bed, then hurried over to the chest of drawers and stopped. She took a deep breath to calm herself down. Her heart was fluttering as she slowly opened the top drawer and looked down.

Sitting in the middle of the cotton vest was a muddy creature, no bigger than her thumb … trembling. Its tiny long nose was moving about as if sniffing out smells.

"You're alive. Oh, thank goodness," whispered Ebony, bringing her face closer.

The creature snatched at a corner of the fabric and held it up in front of its face. Its tiny terrified eyes looked into Ebony's then flicked them from side to side, as if looking for a way out. Nervously it looked back at Ebony again.

"Are you all right?" Ebony lowered her face to the top of the drawer. "We will not hurt you," she said in a soft soothing voice, hoping it would help the creature understand. "We found you in the forest. We brought you back here to keep you safe." Indecision squirmed inside Ebony. *Was that really true?*

The creature lowered the fabric a little. Its nose had stopped moving about.

"Scruffy found you stuck under some branches in the mud. It's a wonder you were not squished flat."

The creature said nothing, and Ebony looked down at Scruffy who now sat at her feet.

"What do we do now?"

Scruffy looked up at her and blinked as if he didn't know what she was talking about.

"You're no help," she said. Then it dawned on Ebony that she had a real problem on her hands. What *was* she going to do with this creature? What if it ran away? It would be like trying to find a mouse in a hundred rooms. Impossible. It could hide anywhere. She needed a cage.

A cage!

The thought was abhorrent to her, but what else could she do? She needed to keep it safe until she worked out what to do with it.

You should have left it where it was, Ebony's inner self snarled at her. *Well, I didn't,* she snapped back at herself. Yes, she should have left the creature behind, she knew that, but if the truth be told, admitted to … she had not wanted to.

Muffled voices could be heard coming up the stairs. Ebony turned to listen. It sounded like male voices, one was her father's. She frowned, bent down low towards the creature and held a finger to her mouth. The creature leaned back, lifting the fabric to its face again. Ebony whispered, "People are coming. Please, be quiet. I will be back soon."

When she shut the drawer, two tiny, bright, terrified, white eyes looked back at her from the darkness.

Ebony turned and rushed into the hallway as guilt about the creature continued to flicker across her conscience.

She looked over the top of the stairs and smiled. The roof of the turrets belonging to her castle, with their five metallic blue spires aloft, bobbed into view. An unknown man appeared above the landing walking backwards, bent in an awkward manner. He was thin and wore grey well-worn overalls, a baggy cap sitting crookedly on his head. As he took a step, and then another, more of the castle appeared, as did another stranger off to his right. He too was dressed in grey overalls, bent with the effort of carrying the castle up the three flights of stairs. His thin face was kind, but flushed, and his large brown moustache moved like bellows above his lip as he puffed with the effort of carrying such a weight.

The whole structure now seemed to float in mid-air. Then her father's face suddenly poked out from behind the castle walls. His face was bright red, and he was huffing and puffing as if he was really struggling to stay upright.

He's going to drop it, a little voice inside her mind squeaked. *No, he won't,* she assured herself.

"Now keep 'er steady, lads. I've reached the top step," said the first man. "Now's takes the weight."

"I's got it, Fred," said the second.

"No! Wait! Wait!" Ebony's father called out. "I'm losing my grip." He was still standing on the stairs, and the whole structure teetered at an awkward angle. The castle wobbled. Ebony frowned and bit her lip. Her father's head disappeared behind the castle walls, followed by muffled sounds as if he was struggling to stand up.

"Hold it, Harold!" Fred cried out.

"I's got it."

"Is everything all right?" Ebony called out as she dashed forward. "You didn't damage it, did you?"

"Don't you worry, missy. 'tis fine, just fine," answered Fred.

"Father, are you all right?" Ebony called out.

Her father's face appeared again and he nodded yes, but his eyes told a different story, one of struggle, one of not wanting to let his daughter down.

Ebony bit her lip, unsure if he was going to make it to the landing.

With a bit of a struggle, sideways, then lengthways, the castle only just fitted through the doorway. Then the delivery men finally lowered it onto the rug in the middle of Ebony's large room. Her father grabbed at his back. Ebony, unable to keep her excitement contained, clapped her hands and bounced up and down, smiling.

"I'm glad you like it."

Ebony turned to see her mother smiling.

"It's just *soo* lovely. Thank you ever-r *soo* much," Ebony cooed. "Thank you." She gave her mother a big kiss on the cheek, who then smiled and looked to her left. Ebony turned to see her father now sitting on one of the striped orange padded window seats. His shoulders were bent and his arms hung between his knees.

Ebony rushed up to him, grabbed him around his neck and cried, "It's just *soo* lovely. Thank you ever-r-r-r *soo* much."

He patted her tenderly on the back several times. "Oh … Well … Yes … Yes, I'm glad you like it, but I'm sorry, my dear, I really must go and lie down." Ebony stood back from him as he heaved himself off the seat then headed for the door.

"Well, we will be off. Sir. Ma'am," said Fred.

"Ebony. What do you say?" asked Ebony's mother.

"What? I mean pardon?" Ebony turned to look at her mother, who used her eyes and a slight nod to indicate the delivery men, and so much more, like *Where are your manners?*

"Oh, yes of course," said Ebony, realising that in all the

excitement she'd totally forgotten about them. So she turned to look at the men, put her hands behind her back, straightened her shoulders and with a slight nod said, "Thank you very much, gentlemen."

"Yes. Thank you for your help, gentlemen," said Ebony's father, as he now stood next to the doorway with a bit of a bent, damaged look about him.

"Tha's not a problem, sir. Tha's what we're 'ere for," Harold said, removing his cap from his head and dusting it against his overalls.

"Don't forget to go back to the kitchen, gentlemen," called out Ebony's mother. "Agnes the cook has made you another cup of tea, and I understand that there is some more apple pie, the one with the marzipan in the base. Always my favourite." Mrs Wood flashed a smile, then continued, "We do appreciate you waiting so long for us to finish Ebony's party."

"T'ank you, ma'am," they both replied as they nodded their heads and smiled to each other, then quickly turned and left the room. The sound of their feet could be heard rushing down the steps. Mrs Wood smiled again.

"Excuse me, sir," said Isobel, as she brushed past Ebony's father to place the new vase full of roses next to Ebony's bed.

"Ebony dear." Ebony turned to look at her mother. "We will see you at tea time. Um, may I ask, what did Nanny Jones send you?"

"Oh." Ebony looked down at the carpet, then looking back to her bed, she whispered, "I have not opened it yet."

Her parents looked at her with puzzled expressions, and then as if they finally understood both gave her a slight smile.

"I see," her mother replied, as she slipped a comforting arm around her husband's waist.

Ebony watched them go. She turned and watched as Isobel moved towards her chest of drawers. Ebony held her breath. Her smile was gone. Her brow furrowed as she watched Isobel's hand slide past the top drawer. She breathed with relief when Isobel opened the small hankie box sitting on top of the dresser and placed the set of embroidered hankies she'd given her within it.

Scruffy's new collar and the box of shortbread biscuits were then placed next to it. Isobel turned to face Ebony.

"Well, I think everything went very well today, don't you? How about we get you out of your party dress?"

E bony, now dressed in a green dress, with a zip that went from hem to neck in the same style as her other dresses, stood next to her castle and flicked a look behind her. Isobel was finally leaving the room. Inspiration hit her. She now had the perfect place to put the creature in, to keep it safe. Her castle. But how to get it to understand this? "Um."

"Ebony-y-y."

Ebony stopped moving towards the chest of drawers and spun around to look at her bedroom door. It was still shut. She looked around her room. Only Scruffy was in it. He was sitting on the hearthrug in front of the cold fireplace with his ears pricked as if he too had heard the voice.

"Ebony-y-y." The voice, soft, almost in a whisper, like a dandelion seed floating through the air, seemed to be everywhere and yet nowhere.

"We are here-e-e."

"Who, who is … here?" Ebony asked, moving closer to Scruffy as if, somehow, he could protect her.

"Come."

Ebony continued to look around, trying to find where the voice was coming from. She stretched out her hand to touch Scruffy, only to find he was no longer there. He was walking towards her bed. Ebony found herself doing the same thing as if she was being pulled forward by some unseen force. It dawned on her that she should feel frightened, but she just didn't.

Scruffy had jumped onto her four-poster bed and picked up

her new handbag. He was shaking it. The gift from Nanny Jones dropped out of it and lay on the bedding. Ebony, now standing beside the bed, stared at it.

"Come," the voice said again.

Ebony's eyes opened wide. She looked at Scruffy who was now nudging the small red box with his nose. The voice had come from *it*. She was sure of it.

Taking a deep breath, and with some hesitation, Ebony climbed onto the bed and sat cross-legged looking down at the red box.

With trembling fingers, she picked up the little gift Nanny Jones had sent her. She held the box in her bandaged right hand and ran a finger across the surface, leaving a white trail as she did so.

Maybe it's special cardboard, she told herself, and maybe she might have believed it, if it had not been for the tingling feeling that went along with it.

Tentatively, she undid the gold ribbon. With her heart beating as if it was in her throat, she lifted the lid. Her heart sank. Revealed within was a smaller blue box, tied with a white ribbon. She tipped it out and her purple fingerprints were left on its surface. Undoing the ribbon, she lifted the lid to reveal another, even smaller box inside. It was black, with a silver ribbon this time.

Ebony scowled. "Scruffy? Why would Nanny Jones send me a box full of boxes?"

Upon removing the black box from the blue one, Ebony touched it with the tip of her finger, which tingled with such a vibration that it bounced across the surface, leaving red smudges behind. Ebony snatched her hand away. Then with curiosity getting the better of her, she quickly undid the silver ribbon, removed the lid and looked inside. "Oh!"

24

Shouts went up, and Whimbrel looked to the sky. Grigwell and Stellman were no longer there. A screech, so much closer this time, froze him to his seat. Congar squealed and turned bright red. In a blur, a curved beak and a keen piercing golden eye flashed past. Razor-like lethal talons glistened in the sun, outstretched, ready to grab their prey. Whimbrel watched, horrified, as Stellman sped down, down, down towards the safety of the vegetation, being chased by a huge bronze-coloured bird, like none he had ever seen before.

All the other Cloud Dancers flew at the bird, attacking it. Freeschum grabbed a bird's tail feather in his mouth and flew sideways. Whimbrel, panic-stricken, hung on to the arm of the saddle chair with one hand, while the other held Congar. The bird's flight faltered and Freeschum released his grip.

Whimbrel looked back to see two Cloud Dancers pulling feathers on the bird's neck. A third pulled at the dark feathers on its back while others circled near its head. The bird was snapping at any who came too close. Then the bird veered away to one side, and sped higher and higher into the sky. The Cloud Dancers, as one, turned and flew down to join their companions.

Freeschum pushed the stalks apart with his body at great speed, causing them to flip back along his sides, smash against his wings and whip against Whimbrel's body and face. Congar screeched when Freeschum landed with a stumble on dry ground. Whimbrel and Congar tumbled out of the saddle chair and landed with a thud and a squeal. Whimbrel lay on his back, looking up at the patch of blue sky far above, watching the silhouette of the bird as it wheeled its way up, up, up into the heavens until finally it disappeared.

If there were other sounds, he could not hear them. He just lay quiet and still, then Freeschum's dark face appeared looking down at him. Whimbrel slowly held up a hand and stroked Freeschum's velvety nose.

"Up!" demanded Freeschum.

"Yes. Yes. I'm coming," answered Whimbrel, without moving.

Freeschum's large round foot pushed against Whimbrel's body as he repeated the word. "Up!"

"I'm up! I'm up!" Whimbrel moaned, and gingerly heaved himself into a sitting position. "It wouldn't hurt if you asked if I was all right."

He glared at Freeschum who was glaring back at him. Then Whimbrel noticed Congar was curled into a little ball of red fur lying in the dust. "Are you hurt?" he asked. Congar's little nose poked out and sniffed the air. His eyes blinked. "Are you all right?" Whimbrel asked again.

"All right? All right!" yelled Congar as he uncurled himself. "No, I'm not all right. I've just been tossed about like a Tufa bird."

He then lifted his head and howled.

"Up!" repeated Freeschum.

"I'm up, I'm up. All right," groaned Whimbrel, and finally stood up, grabbing at his back, and after checking that Congar was really all right, he followed Freeschum through the forest of stalks.

Freeschum led him and Congar to a small clearing, where the other Cloud Dancers and Gribbles were huddled around Grigwell. "I'm sure the area I've seen will be suitable," Grigwell was saying.

Whimbrel's back hurt, his head ached and all he wanted to do was curl up and go to sleep. The other Gribbles were rushing from one Cloud Dancer to the other ensuring they were well. Quintell had opened a little pouch attached to his belt and was proceeding to administer creams and lotions to any member of the party requiring it, including Freeschum. Guilt consumed Whimbrel as he now noticed the cuts on Freeschum's and Stellman's wings and the bump on Grigwell's head. It had not occurred to him that anyone else would have been harmed, he had only considered himself when they had landed. Whimbrel now looked down at the ground and wondered what he could do to make up for his selfishness, to make himself feel better. He quickly went and got the water bottles and made sure everyone had a drink, but he found his shame didn't diminish as he had hoped, it only grew and sat, brooding, in the depths of his mind.

Sometime later the rescue party lifted off the ground. As time passed by, without any hint of the bird's return, Whimbrel started to feel hot again.

My eyes hurt, he said to himself, shutting them away from the glare of the sun. *And my head hurts.* He wriggled his bottom, trying in vain to find a better place to position it. He watched as the fingers of the breeze raked over the sea of gold, tickling, tantalising it, continually making it sway. The only thing breaking up the mesmerising haze was the occasional bright red flower with its large silken petals. All the colours now started to merge in front of him so he closed his eyes. His headache eased just a little as the caress of the warm lazy breeze brushed against his cheek.

"Oh, this feels *soo* much better," he said to himself as he drifted off into a fog, partway between waking and sleeping.

A horrendous scream split into his brain and he awoke with a thud.

"What ... what happened?" Whimbrel looked around at misty images hovering in front of his eyes. His body hurt even more than before. Somewhere at the back of his foggy brain he heard Congar crying.

"Don't do that again," a voice grumbled.

"What again?" Whimbrel tried hard to work out who was speaking.

"Are you all right?" another voice asked. Whimbrel blinked and rubbed his eyes. Congar had stopped crying, but who was that? *Yes, Fluellen, of course.* The fog had started to clear.

"You must be more careful," stated a voice Whimbrel now recognised as Quintell's.

"Careful!" Congar's high-pitched voice squeaked. "Of course he should be more careful. A Fly Snail could take better care of me than this … this … this little Gribble could ever do."

"Congar, please," pleaded Grigwell.

"Twice I've been thrown to the ground. Twice!"

"Are you all right, Congar?" asked Fluellen.

"All right! All right! Of course, I'm *not* all right. Why does everyone keep asking me if I'm all right, when it's plain to any creature with eyes in its head that I'm *not*! I will not tolerate this again. Beware the wrath of a Poogle, it's a sight to behold. You have *all* been warned." Congar lifted his head and howled.

"Congar!" said Grigwell. "Enough! Please!"

Finally, Congar fell silent and sat brooding.

"You're lucky Freeschum tried to break your fall," said Grigwell to Whimbrel.

Whimbrel looked up. Two Cloud Dancers hovered above him.

"What happened?" asked Whimbrel.

"You fell asleep and fell out of your saddle chair," growled Trillium. "That's what happened."

Whimbrel's cheeks flushed as he dug his fingers into the cool dark earth beneath him. He turned his face away from his brother, frowned and grumbled to himself, *Why can't they just leave me alone? It's not my fault.* Slowly, he pushed himself off the ground and walked over to Freeschum.

"Thank you," he said, but Freeschum looked away. Gingerly, Whimbrel clambered back into the saddle chair. Fluellen handed Congar back to him.

"Thank you," he whispered to her, then looking down at the chestnut coloured ball of fluff, said, "I'm sorry."

Congar remained silent as Freeschum took to the skies once more.

25

Ebony looked upon the silver heart-shaped pendant sitting upon a small black velvet cushion. She very carefully, with the tips of her fingers, retrieved it from the box and hung it from its fine silver chain, bringing the pendant up to her eyes. Ebony could now see it wasn't a heart at all. It was actually two wings of a swan making them look like a heart, and cupped between them was a ruby. Ebony had seen rubies before. Her mother owned a beautiful ruby necklace with earrings to match, but they looked like dull stones compared with this beauty. It was the reddest ruby Ebony had ever seen. An inner light seemed to smoulder in the ruby's very depths. The longer she looked, the more her eyes were drawn through a tunnel to the depths where a distorted face looked back.

Startled, Ebony quickly moved away from it. *Don't be so stupid,* she said to herself. *There can't be anything living inside a ruby.*

"Um, I don't know about this, Scruff. It's just so beautiful, but then again …"

Scruffy drew closer, sniffed the pendant and sneezed.

"Bless you. Do you think it's all right to wear? There can't really be anything living inside it, could there? I mean, that's impossible."

Ebony looked at him for confirmation that she was correct, but he went and lay down at the end of the bed, put his head on his paws and stared at her.

"Umph! I don't know why I bother asking you anything," Ebony said, frustrated that he could not do more than be silent!

Ebony, unsure of what to do, peered inside the black box. A tiny piece of paper could just be seen poking out from under the cushion. Carefully laying the necklace on the bedding, she again used the tips of two fingers to pick out the little cushion and retrieve the paper beneath. She read aloud:

Once what was mine is now given to you. Close your eyes and hold on tight. Heart's desires unleashed. Courage bursts forth. Worlds within worlds are revealed and the delight of my eyes will be set free.

"What do you think *that* means?" said Ebony, looking into Scruffy's deep brown eyes. He lifted his head, blinked, tilted his head as if to say he didn't know, then came and sat on her lap. "Yes, I don't know either," Ebony answered.

Tentatively, she secured the necklace around her neck. Why? Because it felt like the right thing to do. She then clutched the pendant. Why? She did not know why. It had felt warm against her skin, and now a tingling sensation pulsed through her hand and worked its way up her arm. Ebony looked at the pendant and tried to release her hold, but found she could not. Panic rose within her and she grabbed hold of Scruffy with her other arm as if somehow he could protect her.

The sensation now rushed to her chest, where she felt it split apart, speeding into her other arm around Scruffy, who fidgeted as if he too could feel the sensation. The feeling also travelled right up to the very top of her head and out through every strand of her long hair, while speeding down each leg and disappearing out of the end of each toe. Ebony took in a deep breath and the pendant slipped from her grasp.

"What was that?"

It dawned on her that her hand had stopped hurting. She quickly let go of Scruffy and removed the bandage from her left hand. All her injuries were gone. She pushed herself off her bed and rushed up to the full-length mirror. The large scratch across her cheek had disappeared. There wasn't even a scar. Ebony then removed the rest of the bandages from her arms and legs and revealed that all the scratches had disappeared. Even her chest and back had stopped hurting. In fact, as she thought about it, all her aches and pains had vanished.

Scruffy rubbed up against her legs. Ebony looked down at him then dropped to her knees.

"What has happened to you?" She quickly took his jacket off. "Huh … How? … All your hair has grown back!"

Ebony looked at her palm and then looked back at Scruffy. A tiny thought bubbled up from the depths of her mind, but before she could discern what it was, it disappeared.

She sighed and stood back up, looking at her reflection.

What just happened? she asked it.

I don't know, she answered.

Her brow furrowed as her eyes slowly drifted to the reflection behind her and she gasped, spun on her heels and stared wide-eyed at her room.

All Ebony's paintings were back, hanging up all over the walls as if they had never been removed so long ago. Her box of paints and all her craft materials now sat where they had always sat. All her toys, and even the models Nanny Jones had helped her build when she was much younger, were sprawled across the floor. They were even back on top of the wardrobe that had held them captive for well over a year and a half.

A shiver ran down Ebony's spine as images flashed through her mind of that fateful day, one of many. Nanny Windabothem had warned Ebony, "If you repeat those silly stories your last nanny filled your young head with, I will be most displeased, do you understand?" At the time, Ebony had thought, *No. I don't understand.* She was only eleven and a half after all.

A week later she'd been sitting on a window seat in a hallway talking to Scruffy.

"Scruffy, how do you resuscitate a rubber chicken?" Ebony looked into Scruffy's brown sparkling eyes and smiled. "Give up?"

Scruffy frowned.

"The same way you do a turtle, silly. Ver-r-y carefully." Ebony laughed, then looked at Scruffy who was still frowning. "You're no fun. All right, then, I'll tell you a story Nanny Jones told me. Once there was a Gribble known as Snailum, and he lived in a hanging village high up in the trees. One day—"

Nanny Windabothem appeared around the corner. Ebony stopped talking. A shiver ran down her spine as Nanny gave her a small tight smile and walked on by.

The next day Ebony and Scruffy had been made to stand next to her four-poster bed and watch as two male servants placed an enormous wooden cupboard at the end of her bedroom. When they left and the bedroom door was shut, Nanny, without saying a single word, packed all of Ebony's toys into boxes. All her paintings were taken off the walls. All the models and creatures she and Nanny Jones had made were gathered up. All her craft materials were packed away. All the beautiful clothes her mother had given her, from all the exotic places she'd travelled to, were packed away as well, and in their place she was given four simple uniforms to wear, blue, black, green and brown. And for best she had one green skirt, one blouse and one cardigan. She also had seven sets of white cotton underwear, including socks. Everything else that Ebony had ever held dear to her heart was locked away in that cupboard and Ebony was made to watch as Nanny turned the key.

That night, she'd cuddled Scruffy and cried herself to sleep.

She'd dreamed of an empty bedroom, except for a large wooden cupboard that was the only thing in it, and as she'd stood watching it, it had started shaking, moving towards her, or was she moving towards it? She could not tell. Noises came, rustling and murmuring from the walls, no, from the cupboard itself. She knew, though she did not know how, that her grandmother, her parents and Nanny Jones were inside.

The doors shuddered. It was as if someone or something was trying to escape. Two small pale hands grabbed at the brass handles, shaking the doors, but they had refused to give. The cupboard shuddered violently. The doors remained tightly shut. Crying? Sobbing? Echoes reverberated throughout the room. The sobbing grew louder and louder until the whole room shook with the vibrations.

Then, the cupboard had started falling, falling, falling on top of Ebony. The weight was immense, it was suffocating. She was going to be squashed out of existence. Screams echoed throughout the room, throughout the unseen house. The air vibrated with the very words, *"Help me! Help me! I can't do it! You've got to save me!"*

Tears flowed down Ebony's cheeks as the memory of the dream faded. Scruffy rubbed his face against her leg and whimpered as if he could sense her distress. She picked him up, buried her face in his neck and sobbed, "I can't do this, Scruffy."

Ebony sighed, and eventually putting Scruffy back on the floor went and picked up a small white plastic polar bear sitting amongst a pile of toys near the cupboard. Images of her mother's smiling face popped into her head.

"Oh look, I'll show you," her mother had said as Ebony and her father had watched her place the polar bear on top of the dining room table. She'd then pressed a long delicate fingertip on top of its head.

It made it bend down low, causing its little tail to lift up high and poop out an edible chocolate drop. Her mother had laughed and then repeated it over and over again, laughing even harder as more chocolate drops pooped out onto the top of the French polished table.

Ebony smiled as she remembered how her father, as usual, could not make up his mind whether he should laugh or frown, and had ended up having a coughing fit. This had sent her mother into another gale of laughter as she slapped him on the back several times. Finally, she'd collapsed into a dining room chair, saying, "Do you like your gift from Alaska?"

Ebony lovingly put the polar bear back amongst her other toys, lying in piles around the room. She then spied a toy Nanny Jones had made, one of many, and picked it up. It had a long white face with large pale eyes, and four large black velvet wings embroidered with silver scribbles. It reminded her of an oversized moth, except that it had two long white arms and legs dangling beneath it. Memories of the stories Nanny Jones used to tell her rushed upon her. The little houses hanging in the trees, the glowing fungi, the creatures that lived amongst it all. Gribbles, Cloud Dancers, so many things she could not remember them all. How she wished she could see them all for real.

She went and looked at each picture she'd painted so long ago, returned to the walls as if they were old friends who had been lost, but were now found. She stopped in front of one and scratched her skin where the pendant lay. It had grown warm.

The picture had two large houses, each in the shape of a triangle, each hanging amongst dark grey leaves, each with a wooden decking surrounding it. Ebony absentmindedly rubbed that area of her skin where the pendant lay against it. It had started to feel warm again. She frowned as she watched the leaves in the picture sway. One by one each leaf changed colour from dark grey to silver. Cautiously, she moved closer to the picture. She was sure her eyes were deceiving her. *How could this picture change colour like that? And yet ...* The painted moss and flowers covering the roof of each building were changing as well. She smiled as leaves sprouted along the vines, intermingling within the coloured fungi growing in small clumps. Beneath it all were lime-coloured shingles belonging to the roof of a house.

Smoke now drifted out of the many chimneys hidden within the leaves. She jerked when a little window flew open, and tiny curtains could be seen fluttering as if a breeze was passing by. She blinked and stepped back when a little front door opened, and then gasped as a Gribble stepped out onto the decking. It stretched its arms wide, its long nose twitched as it watched a flock of small yellow birds fly by. When it started to walk across the suspension bridge towards the other hanging house, Ebony finally reached out her hand. *It's not real. It can't possibly be,* she said to herself, *but it looks it … yes, I know … but it's not. It can't be.* The instant her fingertips touched the surface of the paper, the image returned to a static picture of two houses hanging amongst dark grey leaves. There was no smoke, no open window, and … no Gribble.

"Why can't you be real," Ebony sighed aloud, refusing to remove her hand from the image. "Nanny Jones talked about you as if you were."

Grow up, Ebony, a cold voice said that drifted up through the dark corridors of her mind. *You're too old to be daydreaming like this.* Ebony felt herself shrink away from the voice, then slowly she straightened her shoulders, stared back at it and defiantly said, *I don't care.*

She went and leaned out of her bedroom window and breathed in deeply, a cool afternoon breeze brushing her cheek, and she closed her eyes and sighed as she felt her body calm down. She looked towards the canopy of the forest and watched as the leaves rustled in the wind. She then froze. The lace curtains next to her were dancing in the breeze and she saw, out of the corner of her eye, someone watching her. She turned to see it was her own reflection in a windowpane. She absentmindedly rubbed the area where the pendant lay against her skin; it had started to feel warm again.

As she continued to look at the reflection, it started changing into a sad shadowy face with a tear slowly welling up in the soft blue eyes that looked back at her. The face grew younger and younger until her four-year-old self looked back at her.

"This can't be true," she whispered.

Sadness filled the eyes of her reflective self who reached out a shadowy hand towards her.

A feeling deep down in Ebony's stomach, warm and sickly, started to build. Her heart felt a sharp stabbing pain as tears bubbled up. Ebony watched the child mouth words she could not hear, but somehow she knew that it was frightened and lonely; a loneliness Ebony could feel. It was like a weight sitting in a deep, secret, lost part of her heart.

The windowpane grew dark. The girl now seemed older and was sitting amongst fine netting in shades of purple, blue and black. She was in a cold shadowy corner with her hands in her lap, as if resigned to her situation. She was looking up at Ebony with red-rimmed eyes that had been crying for a very long time.

Ebony looked down at a dead fly on the windowsill. She stared at it, and a tear dropped off the end of her nose and plopped into the dust. *I don't understand,* she said to herself. *That can't possibly be me. I'm not sad, not like that.*

But Mother and Father are never home, a child's voice stated from the corridors of her mind. *They started going away when you were young. When you were four, wasn't it?*

Yes, there is that, Ebony answered herself.

And Nanny Jones left to get married and have children of her own.

Yes, there is that.

And Grandma died when you were eleven and a half.

Yes ... There ... Is ... That!

And you were sent away to boarding school.

Yes, there is that.

And Nanny Windabothem is still here.

Yes ... there ... is ... that.

Ebony shuddered at the thought; she felt her body grow heavy. She looked back at her reflective self. The child was gone. Splinters of memories now dissolved into the recesses of her mind before she could even look at them. Then as if a roll of film had spluttered into life inside her head, Ebony could see her much younger self, and Scruffy, faithfully following Nanny Jones down to the apple orchard to make fairy gardens again. She saw all three of them watching clouds drift past, watching stars at night, sitting amongst little pink and white daisies, scattered in the grass by their thousands, making daisy chains for each other. Then, suddenly, Nanny Windabothem's face leered down at her.

No! Ebony pushed the memory of the first day she'd ever met her back into the deepest darkest corner of her mind. She didn't want to remember that!

Then memories of the day Nanny Jones left to get married, to have children of her own, flashed across her thoughts, and the film flickered to an end. Ebony screwed up her face and buried her head in her hands. "No ... I don't want to remember," she said, sobbing. "Please! No!"

Snap out of this, Ebony, she scolded herself. *This will never get you anywhere. Grow up! There isn't anything you can do about that. About what you said, what you did. You can't go back into the past and change it no matter how much you wish you could. Do not waste your time on something that is impossible to achieve.*

Ebony's sad eyes looked back at her thirteen-year-old reflection in the windowpane. *We will be all right, you know,* she said to herself. *Somehow we will be all right.*

Ebony dragged herself away from the window and went to her bed. Standing there she looked down at the empty boxes and the little note. She slowly replaced the note in the bottom of the black box, repacked all of the boxes with their respective ribbons and hid everything under the bed in a dark dusty corner, hoping no one would find them.

She then looked towards the top drawer of the wooden chest of drawers and remembered that she had to think of the creature held within, not herself. It would rely on her for everything from now on. Alarm flared within Ebony. Did she want to be so responsible for the life of another?

You should have left it in the forest!

Yes, but … I didn't want to.

Ebony shook herself. "Get it together, girl," she scolded herself. She now had a plan, well, the beginning of one at least, that was something. She moved towards the chest of drawers and tentatively pulled at the handles.

Someone knocked on the bedroom door. Isobel walked in. "It's time for tea, Miss Ebony." Then she stopped and looked at Ebony. "Your bandages? Where are they? What have you done?"

Ebony gave Isobel a blank look. She'd forgotten what would happen to her when she was found without the bandages on.

And Scruffy. Crumbs. How the heck was she going to explain that?

"Um," she answered.

"What have you done? That was very wrong of you to remove them," said Isobel, standing with her arms crossed and glaring at her.

"Yes, I know. I know," scowled Ebony.

"And what do you think Nanny is going to say when she sees this? She is a person who wants things done in a certain way. Let me look at you." Isobel took hold of Ebony's hands and looked at her palms. All the injuries were healed. She looked up, disbelief in her eyes, as she took Ebony's chin in her delicate fingers and looked at her face, twisting it from side to side, as if she really could not believe what she was seeing. "I don't understand what has happened," Isobel said as she peered even closer. "There isn't even a scar on your cheek. I just don't see how all your injuries could have healed so fast."

Ebony looked into Isobel's green eyes and shrugged her shoulders.

Isobel frowned, stood up and crossing her arms, continued to look down at Ebony for a long time. "Um. Well. It's all very strange, that's all I'm saying."

"All?"

"Well …" Then Isobel looked at Scruffy and her mouth opened in surprise. "How? What?" Isobel pointed to Scruffy, who was still lying on the bed looking at both of them. "How did all his hair grow back?"

Ebony shrugged her shoulders again. "Magic?"

"Nanny will never believe it. Whew." Isobel sighed. "Well, all right," she said, as if everything was far from being all right. "Let me think. Right! You need to put those bandages back on and … and … Scruffy will have to have his jacket put back on and stay in your room until … until … the doctor arrives tomorrow. Yes, that's a grand plan."

"But …" Ebony protested.

"No buts, young lady. Unless you want to face the wrath of Nanny, you will do as I say. She likes to have everything done the way she likes it done. Everything has a place and everything is in its place, as she keeps on saying. Come on, we need to get going."

With the bandages back in place and Scruffy wearing his jacket again, Ebony picked him up and placed him on her bed. "Now you have to stay here," she said, looking into his eyes. "We don't want Nanny to see you."

As Ebony went to shut the door, she turned and looked at him and said, "Sorry." Scruffy looked back at her as if he could not understand why she would do this to him, and a pang of guilt slashed across Ebony's heart.

"Anyway," said Isobel, as the two of them proceeded down the hallway. "I must say I'm glad to see you have put all your paintings back on the wall. The room did look decidedly unloved without them." Ebony stopped moving. Isobel continued to walk on then stopped when she realised Ebony was not walking with her. "Nanny told me how you had hidden everything away," said Isobel. "I could never understand it myself, but I suppose the doctor and Nanny Windabothem knew what they were talking about."

"Pardon?" Ebony said.

"Well, about the loss of your grandmother, and Nanny Jones leaving. Everybody grieves in different ways."

Ebony didn't answer.

"Anyway, I'm glad to see they're all back where they belong. You must be feeling much better. It's good to see."

26

The heat of the day was waning. Whimbrel scratched his left arm and huffed. As the group flew on, he grew hot and itchy again. "Will we never reach the end?" he moaned.

The gentle hum of the Cloud Dancers' wings drummed in his ears. His stomach groaned from lack of food. His eyes started to close and his mind filled with fog. *Keep your eyes open,* he said to himself. The fog in his brain grew thicker. *Concentrate,* his inner voice said, but it grew fainter and the sky grew darker. His eyes closed, and pictures of sunny days in the canopy flickered through his thoughts again.

CONCENTRATE! he screamed. His eyes snapped open and he blinked several times. The sun hung lower in the sky. Spread before him was a vast expanse of water. This was no mossy dewdrop or even a puddle of water held safely within a crook of branches; this was a jewel of the earth sitting within the setting of rippling gold.

His eyes opened wider as they desperately tried to absorb the beauty before them. He didn't want to miss a smidgen, not a single jot of what he was looking at. He might never see anything so beautiful again in all his life.

He watched, mesmerised, as the fluidly moving colours of black and blue, splattered with green and brown, swirled together. Whimbrel was sure that if he could only look at it a little bit longer, a little bit deeper, he would see something moving in its depths. He took in a deep breath and watched as the breeze whipped ripples across its surface, causing sunlit diamonds to twinkle like a cascade of stars, forever flickering light across its surface.

A flock of brown birds took off from the water's surface, creating long white trails beneath them as they left the water behind, and flew up into the sky. Other birds arrived and skated back across the lake, then bobbed about like autumn leaves.

The shadows grew long and the distant forest darkened as the sun sank behind it. The sunlight continued to dance off the water's surface, sending sparks of light into Whimbrel's tired eyes. The rescue group descended into ever-decreasing circles, towards the water's edge. Whimbrel reluctantly, and yet thankfully, shut his eyes as Freeschum finally landed on the foreshore. Tumbling out of the saddle chair, Whimbrel lay face down on the cool, damp earth, making no attempt to move as a drumbeat echoed in the corridors of his mind. All other sounds dulled and he desperately squeezed his eyes shut, attempting to ease the stabbing ache within them. As he lay there he didn't care if he never got up again.

A screech reverberated through the cool night air and the Gribbles staggered to their feet. Whimbrel stumbled about with sleep in his eyes. He breathed in the tang of the damp air and coughed as tall, dark, shadowy stems loomed all around him. His eyes slowly focused. He looked up. The tips of the stalks, silhouetted against the blue-black of the night sky, swayed high above him. Another screech rent the air, and Whimbrel scanned the sky. The moon was high, and the twinkling stars were suspended in the stillness. It was as if the world was holding its breath, waiting to do something amazing, something stupendous, something ... terrifying.

"There is no fear," a deep voice said, from somewhere behind Whimbrel's left shoulder. "It comes not for you."

Another screech drifted lazily, terrifyingly on the air. Some of the Gribbles looked up while others, including Whimbrel, turned to look behind him. Shards of moonlight highlighted the Cloud Dancers as they heaved themselves up from their slumber.

"Stellman, you speak," Grigwell called out.

"I speak," a voice answered from the back of the herd as seven pairs of white eyes blinked into existence. Whimbrel flinched.

Another screech echoed in the distance.

"You know what creature calls?" asked Grigwell.

"I know."

"What is it?"

"A creature that hunts, but it hunts not for you. Sleep," answered Stellman.

"A bit more information would have been helpful," mumbled Whimbrel, under his breath.

"Quiet!"

Whimbrel turned to see Trillium standing next to him, glaring down, and he quickly looked away, only to find Stellman had turned his head towards him as well. Whimbrel cowered under the pair of glowing eyes blazing in his direction. It was as if Stellman didn't like what he saw.

As everyone settled back down, Whimbrel found that sleep eluded him. He tossed and turned and grumbled with himself, *I can't sleep.* He rolled onto his side and huffed as he felt a lump under his blanket. *What is that?* He rolled over onto his other side. *Not another one,* he complained as another lump dug into his ribs. He stood up, grabbed the blanket and ripped it away but with the lack of light he could not see the offending object. With an unshod foot, he kicked at what he thought he was looking for and winced when he found it. He huffed, puffed and frowned as he laid his blanket back down and rearranged the backpack he was using as a pillow, then sighed, closed his eyes and whispered to himself, "Calm … down."

His eyes sprang open. Voices were whispering all around him. He stiffened and lay as still as he could. His ears strained to listen to the husky words drifting in the air.

"They sleep. They sleep. They sleep."

Who's that? Whimbrel asked himself, but before he could answer more words came.

"Move closer. Move closer. Move closer. The morning is near. The morning is near. They are coming. They are coming."

Who's coming?

Instantly, thousands of whispering voices exploded all around him and a stiff breeze blew through the stalks high above his head. He jumped up and hugged his blanket tightly to his chest.

"They are coming," the words continued. "The morning is near. We warn you. We warn you. They are coming. Coming. Coming. Coming. Coming. Coming."

As the voices slowly faded into silence, the breeze passed by and the multitude of stalks stilled. Whimbrel stared intently into them, but only shadows could be seen. A silence fell all around him, and it was a silence he didn't like.

A few minutes later he cautiously lay down. His head ached from lack of sleep. He still felt every lump and bump under him as he closed his eyes, then snapped them open again.

What's that? His sensitive hearing had picked out a snuffling noise. His eyes followed it as it moved in the undergrowth coming closer, closer, then as it passed on by it grew softer, and softer. All his muscles ached. He sighed as it, whatever *it* was, finally moved away.

I can't stand this, he complained to himself, dragging himself up. *How's a Gribble supposed to sleep with all this racket going on?* He frowned as he looked over at the dark lumps indicating his companions still cuddled up in their warm blankets, sleeping.

He shivered as the air grew colder. Everything including himself was now damp from dew. He clasped the end of his long nose and warmed it with his hands. He then wrapped the blanket around his shoulders, quietly moved to the outer edge of the campsite and started stamping his bare feet up and down, rubbing his arms to warm himself.

Whimbrel watched as pale morning sunlight slowly chased away the darkness, allowing its delicate fingers to stretch between every leaf and stalk. The forest of the night, with its dark and mysterious shadows, changed from black to grey to brown, then golden hues exploded high above his head. He stood in awe as the light licked the tips of the vegetation gently swaying above him.

He wrapped the blanket tightly around him as a single shaft of sunlight plummeted onto the dark soil off to his right. He rushed towards it and stood in its warmth. He held his arms out wide, and as his blanket fell from his shoulders he closed his eyes, lifted his face to the warmth and drank in the fresh morning air. Then a chill ran through him and upon opening his eyes he could see the sunlight had moved on, leaving him in shadow. He rushed towards the beam of light, stood in its warmth again, then as it moved, he was forced to move with it. He stood wiggling his toes. They felt cold and wet. He looked down and watched as the four toes on each foot squished in the mud. He looked up and found he was standing on the edge of the lake.

"Wow!"

27

Early morning light stabbed its way through a chink between the curtains in Ebony's bedroom. The soft light slowly glided over the polished floorboards, travelled up a wooden leg of the four-poster bed, slid over the bridge of Scruffy's nose as he lay sleeping at the end of it, journeyed over the covers, lingering just long enough to tickle Ebony's eyelashes, before continuing to glide up the wall and disappearing.

Slowly Ebony awoke and hitched herself into a sitting position, grabbed at a pillow, dragged it forward and hugged it. She lay back and watched the dust motes gently fall, like a silent snowstorm, through a single shaft of sunlight.

She looked over at the chest of drawers, then down at her toes wiggling under the bedcovers.

It can't be dead, she said to herself.

It didn't move last night ...

It was dark ... I could not see, she argued with herself.

I suppose. No, it has to be alive. It was breathing, wasn't it?

Yes. Yes, you're quite right. Of course, it was.

Ebony slowly clambered out of bed, retrieved her necklace from under the pillow and put it on. She walked over to a set of dark-blue velvet curtains that hung from ceiling to floor and dragged them apart. Bright summer sunlight flooded a part of her room and she looked over to her chest of drawers again. As she took a step towards it, one lonely little dot of a rainbow shimmered on the polished dark floorboards in front of her. She looked up at the stained-glass pattern winding across the top of the windowpane to her left.

Her eyes searched for the crystal dewdrops embedded within the petals of red and purple flowers poking their faces out from amongst a bed of green leaves. She held her breath, expectation growing, and watched the sunlight slowly create a checkerboard effect of dark and light glass as it travelled along with the pattern, and then, as it found a crystal, shot through it. In an instant, a bright star of light was born. She smiled as she watched as another, and another appeared. Then clapping her hands and laughing, hundreds of tiny dots of rainbows exploded all around her, dancing over everything. Scruffy awoke and looked about, bewildered at the sight.

Ebony held out her bandaged arms, smiled then twirled on the spot, stopped, turned her left palm up and caught one single dot of colour in the middle of it. The dot sat quivering. She blinked. A small fairy now stood there instead. Ebony blinked again. It was still there, smiling up at her, and as she smiled back she rubbed her skin where the pendant lay, finding the area had grown warm again. The fairy, with its thin green-stockinged legs, tiny green cap and lemon waistcoat, held up its arms above its head and, with wings shimmering in an array of transparent colour, danced a little jig.

"Where did you come from?" whispered Ebony, moving it closer to her face. It danced on in silence. "At least Nanny can't lock you in a cupboard."

The fairy stopped, tipped its cap, bowed and stood up straight. It smiled at Ebony who smiled back. "You're a boy."

Scruffy barked. Ebony looked over her shoulder. His front paws were up against the chest of drawers and he was looking towards the top drawer.

The rainbows instantly disappeared. She looked down at her palm. The fairy was gone and Ebony sighed. *What a shame.*

Scruffy barked again.

"What is it, Scruff?" Ebony asked, knowing the answer before she'd even finished asking the question. Excitement grew in the pit of her stomach as she walked towards him. With her heart thumping Ebony slowly pulled open the top drawer and looked inside.

"Why did you bring me here?" a little voice squeaked. The creature was balancing on the soft fabric with its feet apart, and hands on hips in an attitude of defiance.

"Wow!" was all Ebony could say as she absentmindedly rubbed the area of her chest where the pendant lay against her skin. It felt warm again. "Phew! You can talk. I mean, we will be able to understand each other."

"Why did you bring me here?" the creature said again, glaring at Ebony.

"Um, we found you unconscious in the forest," said Ebony, a bit taken aback by the attitude the creature seemed to be displaying. *Didn't it realise I saved its life?* "I … I didn't know what else to do. I could not just leave you there. You could have died."

The clock on the mantelpiece ticked away a minute as silence filled the room.

"How does a giant speak our language?" the creature eventually asked, relaxing its tone and removing its hands from its hips.

"Giant! I'm not a giant. Well … maybe … to you, I suppose I am. … What's your name?"

The creature looked at Ebony but said nothing. The silence grew as the clock on the mantelpiece continued to slowly tick away the seconds.

"Veeleeta," it finally answered. "I'm known as Veeleeta."

"That's a pretty name. Mine is Ebony. Ebony Wood. Um … err … I hope I'm not being rude, but are you a boy or a girl?"

Veeleeta frowned.

"I mean, are you a male or a female?"

"Your meaning?"

"Well, I've never seen anything like you before, and you're so muddy, and I'm … I'm sorry but I … I just can't tell, err … what are you? Although …" Ebony's heart had started beating fast, with a hot rushing feeling growing inside her as if she already knew the answer, but somehow it had slipped from her grasp.

"What are you?" asked Veeleeta.

"Oh, err. Um," said Ebony, distracted from her thoughts. "I'm a girl … err, a female."

"I'm a female too," answered Veeleeta. Then she smiled and Ebony smiled back.

"Where am I?" Veeleeta looked around as if she was taking everything in, although Ebony doubted very much if she could really see a whole lot from where she stood so low down in the drawer.

"You're here. In my bedroom," announced Ebony, as she looked into Veeleeta's round eyes.

"I see ... So now you will take me back home ... to the forest?"

Take you back! Ebony's mind yelled. *But you've only just got here.* But she answered, "Ah ... well ... actually, there is a bit of a problem with that. I'm not actually allowed to go near the forest anymore. In fact, I'm not allowed to go outside at all. Well, without being supervised that is, which means, of course, I'm not going anywhere, because Nanny Windabothem will never let me go. I am sure of it."

Veeleeta looked up with a frown on her little face and a touch of confusion as if she didn't understand everything Ebony had just said. "You will not let me go!" Her eyes darted around the room again.

"No, no, no, no. No, nothing like that." Ebony held up her hands and Veeleeta flinched so Ebony dropped them and went on to say, "No. It's just that I'm in a lot of trouble with my mother and father."

"Yes," said Veeleeta, in a sad tone. "My mama and papa, and the other Gribbles, come to think of it, will *all* be upset with *me* when they find I'm missing." Veeleeta looked down and shook her head.

"Oh," whispered Ebony as a twinge of guilt twisted in her stomach, and she fell silent for a few seconds. Then she looked up, and said, "What? Gribbles. Did you say Gribbles?"

"Yes," answered Veeleeta, looking confused.

"You ... are ... a ... Gribble?" asked Ebony, leaning in closer.

"Yes ... of course. I am but—" Veeleeta stepped back.

"Wow! This is great." Ebony looked down at Scruffy sitting at her feet and said, "Did you hear that, Scruff? This is a *Gribble*. A real live *Gribble*."

She leaned towards Veeleeta again and asked, "Do you live in houses high in the trees?"

Veeleeta leaned back and lifted the fabric to her chest as if she was frightened by Ebony's enthusiasm. "Yes. We live in the trees. Not the top of them of course, that's only for the— Why?"

"Wow! This is just amazing," Ebony laughed. "I *knew* it. Well almost knew it. Years ago, and I've never forgotten this, Nanny Jones told me all about you. Well, not about *you*, yourself, of course, but all about the Gribbles, I mean. Well, maybe not *everything* about Gribbles. I suppose she doesn't know ev-er-y-thing about Gribbles. How you all live high in the trees, and how there are lots of you. Not you, of course, I mean lots of Gribbles. I thought you were a lot bigger, but really, you are really quite tiny, aren't you? And you don't look like a Gribble. Nanny Jones drew pictures and you don't look like them. Maybe it's all the mud and ..." She took a deep breath and rushed on, saying, "Isn't ... this ... just ... great. It's amazing. I thought Nanny Jones just made you all up, but look, here you are. Real. Actual-l-y real." Ebony stopped babbling, stood up straight, took another deep breath and smiled the biggest smile.

Veeleeta stared up at Ebony with her little mouth open, as if shocked by what Ebony had just said.

Scruffy barked. Veeleeta suddenly dived down on to the soft fabric, threw some of it over her head and cringed.

"It's all right, Veeleeta, It's only Scruffy ... Scruffy, shh!" Ebony looked down and frowned. "You're frightening her."

Scruffy growled.

"None of that, thank you very much." Ebony picked him up and hitched him under her arm, then turned back to Veeleeta and asked, "Are you all right?"

Veeleeta pulled the fabric to just under her long nose. Her eyes opened wide and she shrank back. "What is that?"

"This is Scruffy, my pet dog. I think he wants to meet you. He was the one who found you."

Scruffy growled.

"Now you be nice," Ebony scolded Scruffy again, shaking a finger at him. "She's only tiny."

Scruffy frowned at Ebony and she tickled him under the chin.

He then looked down into the drawer and Veeleeta's hands dropped to her side, allowing the fabric to fall away. Her tiny mouth opened, her long nose drooped and she just stared at him in shock. Scruffy's black nose twitched and he leaned forward, placing one paw on the edge of the drawer. He lifted his ears, sniffed and then sneezed. Veeleeta instantly cried out, threw the fabric over her head and sat shivering.

"Veeleeta, it's all right," Ebony said with obvious concern in her voice. "I know he looks a bit ... err, big, but he won't hurt you. Will you, Scruff?" Ebony scratched him behind his ear and pulled him away.

"He ... he ... he's huge," Veeleeta exclaimed as she slowly pulled the fabric from her face. "Everything is just so big." Veeleeta's eyes scanned the room again.

"Well, yes, I suppose he is ... to you ... but to me, he's only small. And the room." Ebony looked around her. She'd never thought about it before. "I suppose it is all about perspective."

Ebony absentmindedly put Scruffy back on the floor and almost accidentally poked him in the eye as she patted him on the head. She stood back up and smiled.

"Are you going to keep me trapped?" asked Veeleeta.

"Trapped!" said Ebony, with shock in her voice. "But! Um ... " *I never thought of it like that. Well, I mean ... Um!*

Ebony looked with concern at Veeleeta, who was moving forward to lean on the rim of the drawer. Then Veeleeta yelled as she placed her tiny hands on the wooden edge. She instantly let go.

"What's wrong?" cried Ebony, moving forward to see what had happened.

"It's my arm. I can't put any weight on it." Veeleeta held her left hand near her right arm but didn't touch it.

"You must have hurt it when you fell out of the tree. Honestly, it's a wonder you didn't break your neck. Um ... don't worry. I'll do something, um ... I know, I'll get a hanky and bandage your arm. Yes, that's a grand plan. Just wait there a minute. Don't go anywhere."

Ebony opened the little handkerchief box sitting on top of the dresser and grabbed out a white hanky. *Are you mad?* she scolded herself. *Its arm is so tiny ... Scissors.* Ebony dashed off to get them. She lifted the edge of the white hanky, placed it between the blades of the scissors when Scruffy barked. Ebony stopped what she was doing, looked at him and flinched as he jumped up and pulled the hanky out of her hand.

"Hey, what's up with you?" Ebony snatched it back. Holding it between the blades of the scissors again, she noticed a large initial E embroidered with tiny wildflowers entwined throughout it. "Crumbs! I nearly … Ah! Isobel would never have forgiven me."

"Isobel would never have forgiven you for *what?*"

Ebony looked up with a start. Isobel was standing in the doorway. Ebony quickly snatched her hands behind her back, hiding the incriminating evidence. "Err … nothing. Don't you knock anymore?"

Isobel turned, knocked on the door and then turned back towards her and with a scowl, said, "What are you up to?"

"Err … nothing. Did you want something?" Ebony moved as casually as she could, in front of the drawer Veeleeta was sitting in, and gently leaned back, hoping Isobel wouldn't see she was shutting it.

"Yes, actually." Isobel took a step closer. "You're to come down for breakfast. Don't change the subject; what are you trying to hide?"

Ebony's heart started beating faster. Isobel's piercing green eyes stared straight at her. Ebony quickly glanced around the room, looked back at Isobel and said, "Nothing."

"I don't believe—"

"What is going on?" asked Nanny Windabothem, as she entered the room.

28

Whimbrel looked out upon a cloud of mist bleeding past the confines of the surrounding vegetation, spreading out across the water's surface. He looked to his left, then to his right. The mist hung so deep within the forest of stalks surrounding the water that he could not see into its depths. He smiled at the shadowy silhouettes of long, thin, strap-like vegetation; it was beautiful, and yet so silent and eerie that a shiver shuddered up his spine. He looked behind him. The mist had now surrounded him and he wondered how far he had travelled from the campsite. Whimbrel turned back to look at the lake as the early morning breeze rustled his long brown hair and caressed the end of his nose.

Suddenly, thousands of tiny round white fluffy creatures appeared as if out of thin air. Using their four delicate frosty wings, they darted in and out of the mist and hovered above the water, as two long fine tentacles, with a small hook on the end of each one, trailed behind them. Thousands more started landing on its fluid surface, using six delicate legs to balance on its rippling skin. Each then pushed down into the liquid beneath, and as they withdrew their tentacles, a minute green creature was caught on a hook. Each insect then flew back into the mist, lost from sight, while others came down to take their turn. Whimbrel smiled as he thought, *This is amazing ... I should tell the others.* But he did not move. He stood, mesmerised, watching clouds of the creatures sway to and fro, from one part of the lake to another, all the time landing on its surface, only to take off and be lost in the cloud once more.

I should tell the others, he absentmindedly told himself again, but still, he did not move. He just stood and watched.

Minutes later he gasped in awe as huge long black insects, each

with four iridescent black-veined wings, flew into view. They zipped through the air whirring at a frightening speed. Their jet-black beady eyes, perched on either side of their large round heads, constantly swivelled, and six long, sharp, thorny legs dangled beneath their long, thin, black, armoured bodies.

A twinge twisted in the pit of Whimbrel's stomach. He bit his lip and frowned. Something was wrong. As the seconds ticked by, more of the large insects emerged through the mist.

The smaller creatures moved out of their way in huge swathes, like clouds moving in a storm.

Whimbrel counted the larger insects as they flashed past. "One, two, five, twelve … er … sixteen … um, twenty … two."

He watched, fascinated, as they started swaying in unison as if they were dancing. One darted off to its left, and the others mirrored it. It was as if they were reflections of the one. It was mesmerising and yet …

Whimbrel's frown deepened. The feeling that something was definitely wrong was growing. He could sense it.

The insects broke up into groups of four or five and sped through the mass of creatures. As they did so, cries of pain filled the air and a shiver ran down Whimbrel's spine.

As each black insect emerged out of the cloud, speared on the cruel barbs running down the back of each of its six legs, bodies of the small white furry creatures were wailing and thrashing for a few seconds, only to go limp and lie silent with their long fine tentacles trailing behind them.

Whimbrel's eyes opened wide, his nose drooped and without thinking he screamed, "STOP IT! You can't do that!"

The instant the words left his mouth he regretted them.

The mist vanished. The white creatures were scattered to the winds and the huge black insects darted around as if they were looking for something they could not find. Then, as the sunlight glinted off their black armour, they slowly, en masse, gathered into a pack and turned in Whimbrel's direction.

29

Ebony and Isobel turned to see Nanny Windabothem glaring at both of them.

"Nothing," both of them answered at the same time.

Frozen silence filled the room as if Nanny Windabothem was considering her next move. She held her hand out. A letter was in it.

Ebony slowly moved towards her and reluctantly took the envelope. The air was thick with dread. She knew what it said before she'd even read it. She'd received enough in her short life.

"Your parents have gone away for a short trip. I'm to take care of your needs," said Nanny Windabothem, as if the idea repulsed her. "Seeing as you are up so early I require you downstairs in …" she looked at the watch on her wrist "… thirty minutes for your breakfast then your school lessons shall start on the dot of nine a.m."

"But I'm on holiday," Ebony dared to say with Isobel in the room.

Nanny glared at Ebony. "As you don't seem to be able to keep yourself out of trouble, young lady, I believe occupying your time constructively with learning is the best solution. It will also keep you out from under my feet. Isobel, please come with me. I've something I want you to do before you get Miss Ebony dressed for her school lessons. I want her looking her best for her tutor. I will not have him say that I've asked him to teach a ragamuffin, at such short notice."

Ebony watched them both leave, and cringed as Isobel turned and looked at her with an expression that seemed to say, *This conversation is not over.*

"Whew!" she said to herself as the door shut. *I'll have to come up with a really good excuse. Isobel's not going to let this go, and school lessons! I can't believe it.*

Ebony then looked at the envelope and threw it onto her bed unread.

Ebony washed her hands in the cold bathroom. *Doesn't this room ever warm up?* She'd just been to the toilet and she'd had a thought. It was an uncomfortable thought. *What do Gribbles do to relieve themselves? What is Veeleeta going to do?*

Even though the subject of a person's bodily functions was unpleasant to think about it was, she decided, a problem that needed a solution.

"Um …" Ebony bit her lip. How does one go about asking this type of delicate question? Maybe she didn't actually have to ask at all.

"Ah, yes. Right, flower pots." *That what I need. Gribbles live in the forest with plants and stuff. Flower pots have flowers … and stuff, soil. That's it. Now, where do I find one? … Yes, of course, the back step. There are heaps there.*

Ebony pondered whether she should risk dashing down to the back step now while still in her dressing-gown. What if she got caught by the wrong person? She shuddered at the thought of Nanny Windabothem catching her. No, she decided. The risk was too great.

She returned to her room, and not willing to just hang around in her damp dressing-gown, dressed herself in a blue dress with a zip from hem to neck. Goodness knew when Isobel was going to turn up. She was far too old to be dressed by someone else now. She looked at the brown dress hanging up in the wardrobe and vowed she would never wear it. She hated brown.

Ebony spied the letter from her parents still lying on the bed. She picked it up, and as sadness settled in her heart, she hooked some strands of her long damp hair behind her ears and said, "They're always going away, Scruffy."

Tears welled in her eyes as she sat on the edge of the bed, and Scruff came and lay next to her putting his muzzle on her lap.

"Why can't one of them stay home for once, Scruff?" Ebony stared at the envelope. "Surely it wouldn't be that hard. I'm only here for a few more weeks."

She reluctantly retrieved the letter and read:

Ebony dear,
An unexpected phone call later last night. There has been a landslide near one of the diamond mines in Australia. We will be home as soon as we can. Sorry, we've had to dash off.
Miss Winderbotherm will take care of you until we return, and Ebony, do as you're told this time.
Love always M+D

Ebony turned and looked at Scruffy. "Well, I suppose looking on the bright side of things, they might bring me home another one of you." Scruffy sat up and looked at her as if he wasn't impressed with that idea. "Well, you never know, Scruff. I mean to say, you were born in Australia and that's where they have gone to … *again*." There was resentment in that last word, and Scruffy growled. "Oh, don't worry, Scruff," Ebony said in a brighter tone. "I'll still love you, no matter what you do."

Ebony looked at the letter again. *Honestly, it wasn't my fault we got lost. It's not like—*

Scruffy barked. Ebony looked up to see he was now standing in front of the chest of drawers, looking up.

"Veeleeta! Crumbs, I forgot about her."

Dashing over to where Scruffy stood, she quickly opened the drawer. Veeleeta toppled onto the soft fabric below.

"Oops. Sorry, Veeleeta. Nanny and Isobel arrived, there wasn't anything else I could do but close the drawer. You don't realise how difficult it is to keep you a secret." Ebony smiled, but Veeleeta just remained silent and looked up at Ebony as if she was unimpressed.

"Um … Now …" *Use tact, Ebony,* she told herself. "I know you want to go home."

"I demand you release me!" yelled Veeleeta.

"Oh, err. Yes, yes, I do understand that," said Ebony with regret at Veeleeta's attitude. "But it needs thought. I can't just take you back to the forest, not yet. There are lots of other giants living and working in this house …"

Veeleeta's eyes darted around the room again, then settled on Ebony.

"… and I don't want any of them to find you," Ebony said, thinking about Nanny Windabothem and dreading what would happen if she ever found Veeleeta.

"If you will trust me, I will show you why it's not so easy to let you go." Ebony lay her bandaged hand down palm up in front of Veeleeta. "You will have to climb up onto my hand for me to show you."

Veeleeta looked at the open palm and hesitated. "You will not squash me!"

"Oh my goodness, no!" Ebony answered with total shock at such a thought. "I would never do such a thing."

"We Gribbles," Veeleeta said, looking at Ebony with a stern expression, "hold to our word, so I will hold you to yours." She then, with a deep breath, carefully walked up onto Ebony's palm and sat down in the middle of it. Ebony cupped both her hands, to ensure she didn't drop Veeleeta, then slowly and steadily walked over to the windows that were still closed. With a bit of a wobble, Ebony climbed onto a cushioned window seat, knelt down and raised her hands up to the glass. She looked upon the grounds of Bedlow Manor covered in a dull misty day that held no joy. Dark clouds trudged heavily across the sky. A wind was blowing through the tips of the trees, and drops of rain had started pattering against the glass. The mist was also seeping into the heart of Tanglemire Forest.

"If you look to your left you can see the long line of dark green trees over there at the back of the wheat field?"

"Yes," answered Veeleeta as she looked out through the windowpane.

"That's where we found you," continued Ebony. "Somewhere out there, amongst all those trees." Ebony looked at Veeleeta and noticed that Scruffy had stood up on his hind legs, put his front paws on the back of the window seat and was now looking out at the view as well.

"It's so far away," said Veeleeta, resting her little hands up against the glass, "and it's so big."

"Well, it's not really very far away, not for me anyway," explained Ebony. "The trouble is I'm not allowed to go anywhere near it anymore."

"Oh," sighed Veeleeta, as if she'd suddenly realised that she wouldn't be able to leave this place as easily as she'd first thought.

"I wonder ..." said Ebony, as if to herself. "I suppose there is the roof."

"The roof?" asked Veeleeta.

"Oh ... err ... um ..." stammered Ebony, surprised she'd been overheard. "Well ... I just thought that if we went up to the roof we would be able to get a better view of the forest from there."

"Can we do that?"

"Oh, err, not at the moment. We will have to wait until the mansion is much quieter, in the afternoon when people aren't moving around so much. There are far too many people at the moment."

Ebony lifted Veeleeta up so she could see her better. "I do understand you want to leave, I really do, but I need to think about it, and I need to keep you safe. You see that castle over there?"

Ebony swung around as slowly as she could, trying to make sure that Veeleeta didn't topple off her hand. "I can open it up and lock ... hide ... um ... put you in a safe place, if you like?"

Veeleeta looked alarmed.

"It's not for long, I promise, but I have to keep you safe. I'm sorry but I have to go. Nanny will come looking for me soon, and I assure you, you ... we ... don't want that to happen."

Veeleeta stared at Ebony as if she was weighing up her options. Then without much enthusiasm, she said, "Can I get out?"

"Sort of? I would have to let you out."

Silence came between them.

"And you would do that?" asked Veeleeta.

"Well, yes. Of course," answered Ebony, knowing she would.

Silence fell again.

Veeleeta looked out of the window again, then looked at the huge room, then hunching her shoulders as if resigned to her fate, nodded her head and whispered, "Yes."

Ebony carefully carried Veeleeta over to the castle, cradling her against her chest. She pulled down on one of the gargoyles her father had pulled the day before, revealing many rooms. She delicately set Veeleeta on the floor of the undecorated room.

"I've got to go to breakfast, but I will bring you back something to eat as soon as I can," Ebony said. "I'll just shut the wall up. But hang on a minute …"

Ebony dashed off to the chest of drawers, picked up the vest with the remains of the wild plants (which now looked shrivelled and dark) and placed it on to the floor next to Veeleeta.

"Here you are. Just so you have something to sit on until I can get you some furniture."

Veeleeta looked alarmed. "You're sure I will not be trapped in here?"

"Trapped!" Ebony said with shock in her voice. She didn't like this idea of locking Veeleeta up, but what else could she do? "But! Um … No!"

Ebony spun around, instinctively slamming the wall of the castle shut; the bedroom door had opened.

Isobel had returned early and quietly shutting the bedroom door behind her, slowly turned around to face Ebony.

"I thought you—" Ebony didn't finish what she was saying.

The air in the room suddenly felt thick with emotion. Isobel's green eyes bored into Ebony's.

"Right, little miss, what were you playing at?"

Ebony put on a look of total innocence.

"If I thought you were going to treat my gift with such little regard," said Isobel, obviously not falling for Ebony's acting, "I would never have spent weeks embroidering those hankies." She slowly walked towards her.

"Oh, no, no. No! No! It's nothing like that! I'm sor—"

"If you think," Isobel interrupted, "that I'm going to let you get away with whatever it is you were going to do to them, you have got another think coming, my girl." Isobel crossed her arms and glared at Ebony who suddenly had a spark of inspiration.

"I … I wanted to make a little dress … for one of my tiny dolls," said Ebony. "I just forgot. I was looking for fabric and I … I … well, I didn't mean to use your handkerchief. I didn't actually cut it up. Not once I realised," whispered Ebony, looking at the floor.

Isobel looked as if she wasn't sure she could believe the tale she was being told. "Um. Well," said Isobel, as if she was reluctant to give in. "I suppose having you back to your old self making things is good. All right, we will let bygones be bygones. Now, while I open up all these other curtains, can you please find yourself a cardigan? It's looking a bit gloomy out there," Isobel stated. Then as she looked out to the grounds below, she said, "Well, it's worse than I thought, a storm is building."

30

Whimbrel froze. The cluster of black insects, immense in size, hovered above the water, then using their whirring wings, slowly moved towards him. He started to carefully, deliberately, walk backward. He dared not turn his back on them. Then he stumbled over his own feet and fell into the mud. He scrambled to pick himself up, turned around and screamed at himself to *"RUN"*, no matter what, just RUN! He sprinted back the way he had come.

A sound, like seeds rattling in their dry casings, rose behind him. He rushed on, pushing through the forest of stalks. Everything looked the same. He dashed to his left. The sound grew louder. His heart pounded in his ears, sweat burst across his brow and his throat tightened as he took in deep raking breaths. Panic gripped him as the way before him blurred. He screamed at himself to calm down or all would be lost. Walls of stalks seemed to bar his way, then there to his left, a gap. He dashed on, zig-zagging his way through the vegetation, tripping over stones and debris as he screamed at himself to run, to just keep on running.

The sound behind him was getting closer and closer, growing louder and louder. *Don't look back,* he yelled at himself. *Don't look back!* He looked back. Bodies. Black with cruel barbed legs. A blur of iridescent wings was all he could see. He turned back and screamed, "TRILLIUM! HELP ME! I can't find you! Please! Help me!"

"Over here!" his brother's deep voice boomed. It came from amongst the stalks to Whimbrel's left. Whimbrel turned and ran on, faster and faster. A stitch gripped his side. He crumpled then stumbled and fell. "GET UP!" he screamed at himself as he forced himself to drag his body out of the dirt, forced himself to run on and on, stumbling as he went.

"Quickly!" his brother's voice came again. "We hear them coming." Whimbrel grabbed his side and squeezed it hard. He forced his lungs to breathe in more air. All the while the sound of his pursuers loomed closer and closer.

He turned a corner. The campsite came into view. Relief surged through his body at the sight of his brother, and then he stumbled and fell face first into the dirt.

"WHIMBREL!" Trillium's frightened voice screamed. "Run!"

"Come on!"

"You can make it!" the other Gribbles yelled.

Whimbrel looked up. His companions were running towards him. "I can't! I can't! I just can't," he sobbed.

"GET UP!" Trillium screamed again. "GET UP!"

Whimbrel dug his stubby fingers into the soil and dragged himself forward. His head hurt. His lungs ached. His side felt as if it wanted to break him in two and his legs trembled.

A hand came into view. He lunged for it and missed. He landed nose first into the ground again. Bleary-eyed, he looked up then realised the Gribbles had now encircled him. As he remained slumped on the ground, a squeal made him flinch. He looked down to find Congar looking back at him. He picked up the shivering ball of purple fluff and cradled him in his arms. "It's a … It's a … It's all right … Congar." Whimbrel willed himself to calm down, to breathe slowly. "It's … It's … It's all right. I've got you now."

The pain in his side slowly subsided, his legs stopped shaking, the ache in his head eased and he slowly stood up and pulled Congar to him. It was then he realised he was trapped within a protective circle of his companions. All he could see were the backs of the other Gribbles as they stood waiting.

"They'll try to drag us apart!" Grigwell yelled.

Whimbrel saw through a gap in the bodies before him Fluellen thrusting a Peeloo torch in front of herself. She was facing some of the huge black insects hovering above the ground. The force of their whirring wings against the earth billowed dust into the air. A rattling sound echoed all around and yet, the air seemed to be filled with a strange silence. It hung suspended in the air as if it was waiting for something to happen.

Then, as one, the insects rushed the group. A kaleidoscope of giant whirring wings, black shiny swivelling eyes, glinting nippers and thorny legs seemed to be everywhere. The Gribbles yelled as they lunged with Peeloo torches, desperate to defend themselves.

A terrifying screech of pain filled the air. A second later a sizzling sound could be heard. A sickening stench of burnt hair made Whimbrel slap a hand over his mouth. He groaned as an elbow knocked him in the face. The air filled with the sound of battle and he heard Grigwell screaming, "KEEP TO-GETH-ER!" The Gribbles pressed closer to one another. Whimbrel, who was bumped from side to side, ducked down and coughed as the stench of burnt hair filled his lungs, making him feel even sicker. Congar squealed and turned bright red. Whimbrel attempted to stand up but found himself being knocked down. He attempted to crawl between the bodies of his protectors to join in the fight but found his way blocked. He looked up through the tiny gap to the sky above. Tillia flew into view. She spat out a black veined wing before disappearing and Whimbrel moaned, "Even the Cloud Dancers are helping … but I can do nothing."

The horrendous sound of a dry death rattle resonated in the air then suddenly, there was silence. The noise of the battle ceased. The ring of Whimbrel's protectors broke apart and Whimbrel, holding Congar in his arms, looked out upon a land of desolation. Large black bodies were scattered about, some crumpled into unnatural shapes, either dead or dying. Huge black-veined wings detached from the insects' bodies were caught high in the stalks. The stench of burning flesh hung thickly in the air. Whimbrel instantly dropped Congar to the floor, who squeaked in agitation. Whimbrel pushed himself off the ground, rushed to his left and threw up.

Eventually, he staggered back towards the campsite. Trillium, holding out a cup, was walking towards him.

"Well done, Whimbrel," he said. "You did well."

"Did what? I did nothing."

Somewhere in the back of Whimbrel's mind, he registered the sound of strong wings thumping the air. He noticed out of the corner of his eye that some of the other Gribbles were running towards him, their hands held out wide. They seemed to be screaming at him but he could not tell what they were saying. He only half-registered that the cup his brother had held out to him a second ago had now fallen to the ground. Time seemed to slow down and he watched the water splash into the dusty soil. He looked up into his brother's wide eyes and wondered why they were full of terror.

Instantly, he was bumped forward and all the air was pushed out of his lungs. Then he screamed, and excruciating pain seared through his body as he was stabbed in the back. Large black-veined wings flapped in front of his questioning eyes and as darkness filled his mind, his body went limp and his feet lifted away from the safety of the ground.

Ebony hurried up the stairs carrying a small pot plant and a china cup which contained some fruit from her breakfast table cut up into tiny pieces. Reaching her bedroom she found the door shut so using her arm she pushed the long door handle down and ran to the castle. Scruffy rushed up to greet her but Ebony took no notice of him as she eagerly peered through a small section of clear glass within the stained-glass window. Veeleeta was standing in the middle of the same room she'd been left in. Ebony quickly placed everything on the floor, then dashed over to a little basket full to the brim with miniature bits and pieces belonging to doll houses she'd had in the past, but for some reason or other were no longer here in her room. She thought they had been relegated to the attic, a room where all the lost and unwanted things ended up.

Rummaging around for the little plastic plates she was looking for, and not finding them, she up-ended the entire basket in frustration. All the contents went sprawling across the floor. Spying two plates, she picked them up and hurried back to the castle. Opening the wall, she smiled. "Hello."

Veeleeta quickly put her hands over her ears.

Ebony pondered why. Small ears. Echo in a room. *Oh! I'm too loud.*

"Sorry," she whispered. "Hello."

Veeleeta lowered her hands but didn't say anything.

Scruffy growled.

"Oh hi, Scruff," Ebony said without looking at him. Instead, she said to Veeleeta, "I've brought you some food." Ebony showed her the cup, tipping it slightly so Veeleeta could see inside it. "They are grapes and a peach. I've cut them up for you."

Once she had placed the fruit on the plates, she gently pushed them inside the room. Veeleeta fled to another room and peeked out through the doorway as Ebony removed her hand.

"Um, I've also brought you this," whispered Ebony.

Ebony showed Veeleeta the small flower pot filled with purple and white violas growing within it. "Well, I know it's going to get a bit squished, but don't you worry about that I will get it in there somehow."

Veeleeta's eyes opened wide, not moving from the door frame.

Ebony jiggled the pot across the wooden floor, scraping gouges in the wooden flooring. Veeleeta instantly put her hands over her ears again as the sound vibrated through the air. Finally Ebony managed to get it in without squashing the plant too much. "I know it's a bit tall. Hang on a minute."

Ebony dashed to the back of her room and rummaged through her toys. She found a ladder, a table and a chair. She then leaned the ladder against the side of the pot. She quickly put the table and chair in the room.

"Er, I … er … thought you might need to go to the toilet, and … it's the only thing I can think of."

Veeleeta said nothing as she dropped her hands to her side and Ebony wondered if she actually understood what she meant. If not, how would she explain? "Is everything all right?"

"I … I … demand you let me go," Veeleeta said as she tentatively walked forward.

Ebony blinked, pulled away and sat on the floor. Her smile left her. "Oh."

"I can't stay here." Veeleeta rushed forward. "Please. You have to let me go. My mama, my papa. My brothers and sister …" Veeleeta burst into tears.

Ebony held her breath. *Oh, dear.* Sadness filled her heart. "But …" Ebony didn't know what to do. She'd been *soo* pleased, *soo* happy to have someone to talk to, a friend, but she should have known better. *Everyone leaves in the end,* she thought. Ebony's heart sank. *Now what?* She bit her lip as Veeleeta wiped her tears away.

"Veeleeta … Um … Please. I will think of something, I promise. In the meantime, would you like a bath? To wash all that mud off."

Veeleeta nodded her head. "Yes. Thank you." But there was no enthusiasm in her voice.

"Right, just wait there." Ebony rushed off and rummaged amongst her toys again, picked up a couple of likely objects and went back to the castle. "You're in the way, Scruff."

She placed a rug on the floor of the little room and set a small porcelain bath on top of it as Veeleeta stood to one side. Ebony picked up a miniature bed and another rug and placed them in a room connected to the room that held the bath. She hurried back to her pile of toys, tripping over Scruffy in the process.

"Will you get out of my way?"

Ebony picked up a small cupboard, a lamp, a vase, a tablecloth, a tiny towel and the smallest doll she possessed. She returned and knocked against Scruffy again. "Go and sit on the bed."

Scruffy dropped something out of his mouth.

You shouldn't treat him like that, Ebony scolded herself as she watched him slink away. *Oh, he'll be all right,* she told herself even though a tiny niggling feeling in her stomach squirmed within its depths. She picked up what he had dropped, glanced at it and threw it back amongst her toys. *What does Veeleeta need with a toy frog anyway?*

Ebony headed for the castle. Upon reaching it she dropped to her knees and hummed a tune as she placed the items in the rooms and fiddled with the furniture until she was happy with their placement.

"Right!" She stood up straight, put her hands on her hips and scanned each room. "That looks good. Yes, yes, happy with that. Good." She leaned forward and shifted the bed to the middle of the room. "Um, well, all we need now is some warm water and soap and we're done."

Taking a glass jar she used to wash her paintbrushes in, she slunk off to the bathroom, filled it up with warm water, grabbed a bar of soap and a clean flannel, dashed back to her room and filled up the little bath.

"Hang on a minute," Ebony said as she noticed that the bath came up to Veeleeta's shoulders. *How's she ever going to get into that?* She returned from rummaging around in the pile of toys with a plastic step ladder that folded in half so it could straddle both sides of the bath. It had belonged to a set of small plastic dolls who had sat around a swimming pool. "Now you can climb in and out. The bath's a bit big but it's the only one I have. I placed a bar of soap next to the bath." Ebony pointed at it. "You use it to wash with, and that flannel is to dry yourself with, also there is a bed in the next room," Ebony pointed to an open doorway to Veeleeta's right, "through there. I have put a little white vest on the table. You can wear that, as your clothes are so dirty. I took it off the smallest doll I own. I know it's a bit big but I can make you a new dress later. Right. Um, I'm sorry, but … I'm going to have to shut you up again."

"No! Please!"

"I have to. There are other people about, Nanny for instance. She can't find you. I've got to keep you safe. I'll figure out what to do, I promise, but it's not so easy."

She smiled to herself as she securely closed up the castle and turned to leave the room. *I actually have a Gribble in my bedroom.* She walked out of her room, shutting the door while deep in thought, not realising she had left Scruffy behind once more. *I need to keep it safe. No one must know. What am I going to do with it?* she questioned herself. *Do with it? It's not a pet.*

"Miss Ebony!"

Ebony looked up with a start. Nanny's face scowled back at her. "What have you been up to? You are late for your class. Your tutor has been waiting for you. Hurry up!"

"Yes, Nanny."

Trillium stood paralysed as time slowed. The cup of water slipped from his hand and slammed into the soil below, as he watched four large transparent wings flap with laborious movements towards his brother. Sunlight twinkled across the wings of shimmery membranes crisscrossed by thin black veins. Whimbrel's startled face reflected through every panel.

Trillium's brow creased as he watched, as if in slow motion, a sharp barb speed towards Whimbrel's back, then the air filled with an ear-splitting shriek from Whimbrel's mouth which shattered time, air and Trillium's heart as Whimbrel fell forward. Horrified, Trillium watched Whimbrel's limp body as it was lifted away from the ground.

"WHIMBREL!" Trillium screamed.

Dashing forward to where Whimbrel had stood but stood no longer, Trillium watched as the insect, carrying its burden, disappeared over the tips of the sun-kissed vegetation,

"Noo!" he cried, falling to his knees with tears blurring his vision.

"It's heading towards the lake," someone yelled as Trillium whispered, "Whimbrel."

Trillium had gone numb. Beads of sweat burst upon his brow. He grabbed his head, trying to keep the words that yelled inside it from escaping through his mouth. *I've lost them … I've lost them both.* Shadowy visions of his mama's sad face looked up at him. *My babies?* it said. *Find them … You MUST get them back!* Then his papa's frightened face reared up and yelled, *Get them back! What have you done?* Trillium's eyes filled with tears. Their shadowy faces slowly faded away and he collapsed to the ground.

Firm hands picked him up. Muffled voices murmured all around him. A vision of Whimbrel's face flickered on and off in front of Trillium's open eyes and he frowned.

"Trillium," a voice called.

As Trillium's eyelids rapidly blinked, Quintell's face replaced his younger brother's.

"I lost them, Quintell," Trillium's strained voice croaked. "I've lost them both." He grabbed Quintell's shoulders. "Whatever will I do?"

"We will find him," said Quintell, laying a comforting hand on his back. "We must go."

Grigwell yelled, "Everyone mount up!"

"What about Veeleeta?" Trillium's hands shook, refusing to let go of the only support they had, his nose drooping towards the ground.

"We need to find Whimbrel first," said Quintell, grabbing Trillium's wrists. "We can't let the trail go cold."

"But Veeleeta?"

"We will find her. Don't worry. We have to go." Quintell prised Trillium's hands free and Trillium stumbled forward. The ground beneath his feet seemed to have turned to liquid. Then a calm voice bubbled up from deep within his mind and said, *Get Teasel.*

Trillium stopped, took a deep breath, frowned and called out, "Teasel! Come to me."

All seven Cloud Dancers skimmed across the tops of the vegetation, heading towards the lake. Upon reaching the water's edge, Grigwell held up a hand and signalled them to come closer.

"Grigwell," called out Quintell, "it will be impossible for us to search all of this. Let the Bugs loose. Let them search it. They can look in places we never could."

"Good idea, but Quintell, you and I will keep a Messenger Bug each just in case we need to contact the other Gribbles. We will split up and search the foreshore. You, Torix, Fluellen, Leedrum and Tillia, search that half of the lake." Grigwell pointed to the area to his right. "We will do the other half, and if you find anything, send a bug to tell us."

Trillium, with Congar sitting on his lap, flew alongside Grigwell. Ahead, bugs, glowing in a variety of colours, darted in and out of the long strap-like green plants. Each one was lost from sight only to reappear further along within the thick vegetation.

Cloud Dancers darted around tall stems swaying on the edge of the lake. Some of the bugs flew high, while others flew low. A stiff breeze brushed the reeds. A loud chatter could be heard drifting upon the wind; it seemed to be saying, *Find Whimbrel. Find Whimbrel. Find Whimbrel.* Then Trillium looked to his left. Hundreds of green stalks swayed, their long, thick, velvety, brown seed heads nodded in the wind.

Is it possible? he asked himself. *Could they tell us where Whimbrel is? This isn't the forest,* his subconscious answered. *You can't feel them … You can't hear them … They are dead to us … No … It's just the wind, just the wind.*

Trillium sighed and looked to his right. He could just discern the other Cloud Dancers on the opposite side of the lake, mimicking his group of Cloud Dancers, which was flying high, flying low, darting in and darting out of vegetation.

"Congar will find Whimbrel," a tiny voice squeaked.

Trillium looked down at the pointy face looking back at him. He knew Poogles were amazing creatures, having so many skills, some of which he was sure he did not know, but even so, he wondered how Congar could help. All he said was, "Thank you, Congar." Trillium rubbed Congar's fur; it felt warm and a comforting, tingling sensation prickled the tips of his fingers. The warmth rushed up his arm and settled in his heart. For a split second, a slight smile crossed his face, and he silently thanked Congar as a spicy aroma surrounded him.

As the group flew on, large brown birds quacked, skidding into the middle of the lake, then sitting, bobbing like autumn leaves, turned to watch the rescue party pass by. Winged insects danced in their metallic armour of red and blue amongst strange plants. Huge olive-green striped webbed feet clung on tightly to thick stems of tall plants, as large bulbous golden speckled eyes, licked clean by a long pink tongue, watched them pass by.

The breeze buffeted Teasel. Congar whimpered. Instinctively, Trillium held him more tightly as they rocked in the saddle chair. He looked around. The other Cloud Dancers were being tossed about as well, fighting the wind to stay in a tight group. Several Messenger Bugs could be seen struggling to reach Grigwell.

Trillium leaned forward, urging Teasel to move closer to Stellman, as the Messenger Bugs landed safely on the arm of Grigwell's saddle chair.

"What is it?" yelled Trillium, as Teasel fought to stay close. Grigwell turned and putting his hands to his mouth, yelled back, "Found something. Not sure."

Grigwell removed his purple Messenger Bug from its pouch, whispered something to it and the instant he released it a gust of wind blew it out of sight.

"Come!" yelled Grigwell, waving his hand forward. Stellman turned to his right and Trillium and the others followed.

33

The wind grew stronger, the clouds grew darker, the air heavier, as the group flew closer to the vegetation in a vain attempt to find a reprieve. They dived over and under large leaves that paddled the air. The tips of long strappy vegetation whipped Freeschum and Tillia's hindquarters. They reared up with their front legs kicking at the wind only to veer away.

Trillium leaned forward and squinted against the unforgiving onslaught of the wind. With one hand he held on to Congar, with the other he held on tightly to the arm of the saddle chair. A long dark-brown object came into view. It was a log, half sitting in the water, while the other half leaned out across a bank of mud.

Grigwell held up a hand and pointed to it.

"I hope it's hollow," moaned Trillium, as the group flew towards it, and then before he knew what had happened, he found that it was. Its entrance appeared like a dark gaping mouth which disappeared as he flew inside the log. The clatter of the Cloud Dancer's feet echoed like a solemn drum on the dark, damp, rotting wood inside the ancient log, and Teasel came to a skidding halt. "Thank goodness," Trillium sighed. "This wind is getting worse."

"We're going to have to hole up here and wait for the others," said Grigwell, dismounting. He patted Stellman on the neck, who was panting hard, as were the other Cloud Dancers, recovering from fighting the wind.

Trillium dismounted as well and set Congar onto the dark uneven wood. He turned and looked out of the entrance. Stems of plants thrashed as large drops of rain sprinkled across his view.

"Cloud Dancers!" called out Grigwell. Trillium automatically turned in response as Grigwell continued to say, "Let the others know where we are."

All four Cloud Dancers closed their eyes then opened them again. "They come," said Freeschum.

"Are they all right?" asked Grigwell.

"They come," answered Torix.

Trillium spun around as the air filled with the sound of voices, wings and heavy breathing. Four Cloud Dancers suddenly flew into the sanctuary with their feet thundering across the wooden surface. Congar squealed and he and Grigwell jumped out of the way.

"Are you all right?" asked Grigwell.

"It's getting worse," answered Quintell, as he and Fluellen quickly dismounted.

"This place smells like home," pointed out Fluellen as she pushed her wet hair out of her face.

"What are we going to do?" asked Trillium.

"Settle down … settle down!" yelled Grigwell.

All became silent; everyone turned to look at him, and as the wind continued to blow past their sanctuary, he said, "I'm glad to see everyone's safe."

"What about the bugs?" asked Fluellen, as the rain fell harder, the sound drumming in their ears.

"They'll find places to hide until this settles down," answered Grigwell. "Then they will return. They will be able to find us."

"What!" Trillium looked straight into Grigwell's eyes. "But we can't wait!"

"Look at it out there." Grigwell pointed at the entrance. "It's getting worse." He glared at Trillium. "We would be mad to stay out there."

"I know but …" answered Trillium, defeated. "But we have to find them." He finally dropped his eyes, knowing there wasn't a thing any of them could do but wait.

"Let's settle down, have a bite to eat and warm ourselves," Grigwell suggested.

34

Veeleeta watched with concern as Ebony shut the castle wall with a bang. She thought she looked sad. Instantly, she threw her hands over her ears until the echoing sound caused by the action dissipated. Panic rose in her throat. She was trapped!

A need to flee suddenly filled her up and she rushed into the other rooms, one after another, trying to find a way out. No windows could she reach to see if they would open. Doors only led to stairs too steep to climb, or to other rooms, or down to black gaping tunnels, to where she did not know, nor would she risk finding out what was at the end of them. Dejected, she slowly made her way back to the room where the bath lay. Everything was so oversized. The room itself was huge, the chair, the table, the bath, even the pot with the plant reaching to the ceiling. Everything made her feel very small.

She sighed. Her panic had now left her, replaced by resignation to her situation. Then a twinge inside her made her bite her bottom lip. She needed to relieve herself. How long had it been since the last time? She looked up at the plant and the ladder leaning against the brown pot covered in moss. There wasn't anything else for it. What else could she do but climb it? Fortunately, she'd grown up in a forest, and if she was good at one thing, it was climbing. So with her hand on the first rung, which she only just managed to grab hold of, she pulled herself up and hooked a leg up onto it. Huffing from the effort, she sat and looked at the second rung. This was going to take a long time, only six more to go.

As Veeleeta finally squatted over a small hole she'd dug in the soil, the smell of the earth filled her senses. She looked upon the unusual flowers, with their smiling faces that were seemingly painted across the petals. They were poking out of the large dark-green crumpled leaves. The sight tugged at her heart.

Upon finishing, she covered the hole with soil. She then found a piece of dried plant stem. She twisted it into a twine between the palms of her hands, then coiled it into a round flat circle. With the ends anchored, so it would not unwind, she laid it over the spot of soil, as a marker, so she knew not to dig there again. She then walked around to the other side of the plant, sat down and leaned against it.

She closed her eyes, once more breathing in deeply the smell of the earth and the plant, and imagined she was home in the forest. But she wasn't a Gribble who lived in fantasy worlds. She never had been one to delude herself with untruths. How she wished, at this moment, she could be different, but it was no use. She was who she was and so she had to face the truth of the situation. She was trapped, and the only thing she could do was rely on a giant to feed her, protect her and set her free. Or was it?

Her thoughts drifted to Congar and tears trickled down her cheeks. Had he not told her a story once? Why did she never listen? Veeleeta calmed her mind and breathed deeply. He had taught her that if she wanted to remember something, she had to breathe, and calm the mind. She visualised a day when they had sat under a purple Dodder plant and could hear him telling her … what? She knew it was important. He had said … something … but what? Yes! That was it! Gribbles, in the past, could reach out with their mind and send their thoughts to another, no matter where they were. Yes, that was it! But it was a skill that had been lost, and most Gribbles didn't have the ability anymore. Veeleeta sighed and slumped, depressed, her hope of reaching out beyond these walls gone.

The memory of Congar falling into the depths of the forest flashed across her mind. It was as if she could actually see him, bright red in colour, screaming, as the suspension bridge fell away from him and he plummeted to the forest floor. She burst into tears.

"Congar," she whispered. "How I wish you were here. I miss you terribly."

Be brave, little Gribble. Be brave. I never left you.

Veeleeta instantly stood up and looked around. *Was that him? But … but … but he is dead.* Sadness lay heavy in her body. She knew she was deluding herself, but how? She never had before. Her mind started to spin. She felt she was going to break into tiny pieces. Then a longing to talk to Congar overwhelmed her. Rightly or wrongly, delusion seemed better than the truth.

"I'm in trouble, Congar, and I don't know what to do." Her voice cracked, tears sprang to her eyes again and her throat tightened, making it hard to breathe.

Solve one problem at a time, dear heart. One problem at a time.

Yes, that was it! How many times had he told her that before? So Veeleeta took to the task. She wished she had a writing stick, and paper, or at least a dried leaf, but she had none to write her list upon. She always liked making lists. She always found it easier to see what her problems were when she wrote them down. Sometimes she found if she solved one problem, other problems seemed to dissolve along with it.

So sitting up straight and taking a deep breath, she closed her eyes and mentally imagined herself writing her problems down on an imaginary sheet of paper, suspended in mid-air. Granted, she felt rather strange doing this, as she had always considered herself to be such a practical Gribble, like her papa. But she had no time to be worrying about such things. So with determination, she decided to write down a problem she had already solved. She was sure that by crossing it out, it would make her feel better because she had at least succeeded in solving one of her many problems.

My List
1 relieving myself – solution - me
2 food to keep up my strength – solution - Ebony
3 to clean myself – solution - me
4 to rest to keep up my strength – solution – me
5 to get out of this trap and get back to
the forest – solution me + Ebony?

200

Veeleeta examined her list in her mind's eye. "Um." She had to rely on Ebony to give her food, and she now remembered Ebony had given her some fruit to eat. She just hoped it was safe. That solved two problems.

To clean herself — well she could do that, there was the bath Ebony had supplied her with. There was another thing she could do — the bed in the other room, she could use it.

The next item on the list would have to wait. Feeling a lot better, she went to descend the ladder, stopped and said, "Thank you, Congar."

Veeleeta now stood on the ladder straddled across the bath, looking down at the water. It didn't look too deep. She was used to splashing around in rainwater which collected in the crook of tree limbs, but she'd always been able to touch the bottom with her feet. This might prove to be different. It did look inviting though. Returning to the floor, she undressed out of her mud-stained clothing which felt rather stiff now her clothes had dried out. She left them in a pile on the floor.

She then struggled to undo her plaited hair which had become entangled with mud. Slowly she climbed into the bath; it turned out to be not too deep. Her skin tingled, her nose twitched, and as she slipped under the water, allowing its warmth to seep into her tired and bruised body, all the strains and stresses she'd felt slowly drifted away. Fine trails of liquid mud seeped from her long black hair into the water. As she lay there, she thought of trying the thing Ebony had said would clean her. What did she call it? Soap. But it looked so big, huge actually, and she didn't know what it was made of. It might be dangerous. It might make her sick. No, she could not risk it, not if she was going to get herself out of this place. Plus she would have to get out of the warm water to go and get it.

She leaned against the wall of the bath. Above the waterline it felt cold, below it was warm, so she slipped down so she could lie with her chin just above its surface. She looked up at the two long stained-glass windows on the opposite wall. She stared at the hazy patchwork of warm colours reflecting onto the surrounding wall, and her thoughts drifted to lazy sunny days in the canopy high above the floor of the forest.

Her thoughts went to her personal Messenger Bug. *I hope she made it home,* Veeleeta thought. She had been with her for twelve seasons now; in fact Veeleeta had been there at its hatching, so her mama told her, but of course Veeleeta could not remember such a thing as she herself had only just been born. Veeleeta squirmed. She was unsure if it did actually know how to find its way home. She knew that if it didn't know, and therefore could not tell the Gribbles where she was, it was actually her fault. It was her responsibility, after all, to ensure her Messenger Bug was trained in many things, and one of those things was how to find its way home when lost. "Umm!" Veeleeta had to admit that she had not been very diligent when it came to its training.

She sighed as she now looked around the room and wondered how she'd ended up in it.

Visions of sizzling stars cascading all around her filled her mind's eye. She could almost hear the branch she had stood on creaking and groaning. Then Congar's ear-splitting squeal resounded in her mind.

She remembered how her head had grown light as the wind whipped around her body. She had looked on with horror as she could feel her four stubby fingers loosening their hold. Desperately she had tried to force them to grip the vine she was holding, hoping she could stop herself from falling. Eventually, though, no matter how much she willed her fingers to hang on tight, they didn't, and they were prised free. As her last finger had given way, she was flung away, tumbling through the air for what seemed like an eternity, never knowing which way was up or down, screaming until there was no more breath to use.

The colours around her had blurred. Her stomach had churned;

her mind lost all cohesion of its thoughts of the world around her. Knowing she would never see her family ever again, she finally gave herself up to her certain doom, when visions of a pale solemn face appeared. Long pale arms snatched at her, black velvet wings, stippled with silver, enveloped her like a blanket. Then they were gone, replaced by silver leaves. She felt a soft thud, then she registered that she was tumbling across something soft and squishy, then ... silence.

In the deepest, darkest corridor of Veeleeta's mind, there was a slight register of nothingness. How long this lasted Veeleeta did not know, then slowly, darkness surrounded her, and a feeling, ever so slight, of movement, occurred. It went on for how long? No time was kept. The mind did not know.

Then softness and darkness that somehow felt warm, then slowly, ever so slowly came a recognition that Veeleeta should wake up because someone kept calling her name.

"Vee-lee-ta. Vee-lee-ta. Dear heart. We are here. Come to us. We are here."

Bright red light flared in her mind, but it was a light she could only sense, she could not see it. Her eyes refused to open. There was movement, ever so soft and gentle. She awoke to darkness. She placed her hand in front of her face. She could not see it even though she knew her eyes were now open. Then the sound of grinding, groaning, wood on wood, and the roof of her world disappeared and bright light exploded all around her. Darkness was replaced by the huge face of a giant! It was as if the fables told around the Fire Stones had come true.

Veeleeta burst into tears as thoughts of her home danced through her mind, and she leaned forward in the water that now held no warmth. Tears streamed down her cheeks.

She slowly crawled out of the bath, and with a flannel, so large she could only wrap a small corner of it around her body, she struggled to drag the rest of it behind her as she made her way into the bedroom. She found the little white vest Ebony had left her and put it on. It came down to the floor. She then tumbled into bed, pulled the blanket up around her chin, hugged the pillow and burst into tears again.

Restless dreams filled every part of her mind. Congar screamed as he fell to his doom. Red glowing lights danced around her. Her body was falling, falling, never stopping. Veeleeta awoke with a start. Visions of her parents' smiling faces floated in front of her mind.

"Do they even know I'm missing?" she sobbed.

Ebony sat at her desk with her head in her hands, thinking. Her tutor's voice droned on like a fly buzzing against a window in summer. She watched the hands of the clock on the wall slowly, slowly, ever *so* slowly, tick away the minutes. She then turned and looked up at the long row of windows. The rain was dashing against the glass. The world beyond was now hidden. *I wonder what Gribbles do when it rains.*

"You can go now, Miss Ebony," her tutor called out. Ebony did not move. "Miss Ebony. You can go now."

"Oh, ah … ah, thank you."

"Where has your mind been this morning, Miss Ebony, because it certainly has not been here with me?"

"Um, sorry, sir … err … I'll … I'll do better this afternoon."

Ebony had only taken a step out of the library, which was being used as her classroom, when she bumped into Isobel.

"Ah, there you are. Your lunch is on the table. You're to be back here," Isobel looked at the little black-strapped watch on her writst, "in one hour. Do you think you can amuse yourself? I'm very busy at the moment."

Ebony wolfed down her food and dashed back to her room to quickly look through a window of the castle. Veeleeta was asleep. Deflated, Ebony slunk back to her own bed, sat on the edge of it and waited. Scruffy rubbed up against her arm, but she took no notice. She just kept looking at the castle. Time and time again she checked if Veeleeta was awake until finally she was summoned back to her lessons.

36

Trillium sat on the edge of the log, the top of which jutted out like a roof over a doorway. He dangled his legs over the ledge, looked out at the sheet of rain falling in front of it and subconsciously registered that Congar had just cuddled up next to him. He looked down at his shoes and watched the occasional drop of rain splatter onto their surface. He rubbed his sore eyes as the sounds resonating around him, thundering rain, wind, the speech of his companions, all faded and the internal voices rumbling deep in his mind grew louder.

Whimbrel? ... Veeleeta? ... I have to do something. There isn't anything that can be done. Why am I just sitting here? What can I do?

Trillium flinched as a hand fell onto his shoulder. The inner voices dropped to a whisper and went and hid in the shadows of his mind.

"Is everything ok?"

He looked at Quintell now sitting next to him.

"Why can't Fluellen find Whimbrel?" asked Trillium. "Surely she can feel his energy."

"No," answered Quintell, with sadness in his voice. "She can't. Ever since she went through that wall of light she can feel no energy at all, not even from us. She is finding it very distressing. She has never had to deal with a loss such as this. She thinks we have all entered into a world with a different frequency, and she can't work out how to break into it. She is so upset at being unable to help."

"I see," said Trillium, hanging his head low.

"Trillium, we will find Whimbrel," said Quintell, as he stroked Congar's head then returned to his companions sitting around the Fire Stones.

Trillium frowned and the inner voices became silent.

The sky grew dark. The air grew cold. The constant tapping of millions of raindrops resounded like distant drums around him, and still, Trillium did not move away from the entrance of their sanctuary.

A wooden bowl was placed in his hands but he remained staring out at the darkness, his mind only half-registering Fluellen's voice saying, "Trillium. Come and sit around the Fire Stones." A small thud sounded next to him as another bowl was set on the wooden floor. "Here you go, Congar, eat that."

The warmth of a blanket being draped around his shoulders comforted him, and the heat of the bowl warmed up his hands. As the smell of the hot fungi stew wafted into his nostrils, he looked down at it. He took a mouthful and sighed as the warmth flooded his empty stomach. He watched as shadows danced on the walls beside him and he turned to see the others gathered at the back of the log around the glow of the Fire Stones.

Trillium, with the blanket still wrapped around his shoulders, finally went and sat down amongst his companions. Quintell gave him a smile, took up a flute and played a tune that echoed its mournful notes out into the raging storm. Trillium stared down at the glowing Fire Stones and wondered if he would ever see his brother and sister again.

"Well, I know you will be sorry to hear about this," said Isobel, with a smile. "But today, Saturday, is my day off. There is no schooling today but the doctor will be here in one hour. Nanny Windabothem will see him in, then we can stop playing this charade with your bandages. Scruffy will also be allowed out of your room, instead of sneaking him out to go to the toilet. Now if you could just get yourself dressed and down to breakfast I would be most appreciative, as I will be able to get off a lot earlier. I'm off to the movies and then I'm going sailing with my beau."

"Bo?"

"Boyfriend."

"What! You have a boyfriend. So you will leave one day as well," said Ebony, sulkily.

"Someday, but not until you do not need me anymore."

"That will never happen."

Isobel smiled at her. "Thank you for the compliment but you will be surprised how quickly it will happen."

Ebony, holding some fruit from her breakfast table, peered through the windows of the castle again. Veeleeta was *still* asleep. "How long do Gribbles sleep, for goodness sakes!" Ebony complained. "She has been asleep since yesterday."

Ebony placed the fruit on top of the chest of drawers and as she turned away, with a dark sullen look upon her face, Nanny Windabothem entered her room followed by Dr Waters. Ebony stopped; she had forgotten he was coming.

"Good morning, Miss Ebony," said Dr Waters, laying his black bag on her bed.

Ebony stood looking at both of them but said nothing.

"Now, let me see how your wounds have healed." He turned towards Nanny Windabothem and said, "I'm expecting great results from these special bandages that I embedded with my secret formula."

As he slowly unwound each bandage from Ebony's limbs, he smiled and chuckled to himself. "I knew it," he mumbled. "Look, Miss Windabothem, success. I'm going to be *soo* rich."

Eventually, the examination by the doctor was over and so was the charade. Fortunately, no one took notice of Scruffy with his newly grown hair so they had got away with it.

Now free of bandages and dog jacket, the two of them walked the silent halls of the mansion. As Ebony listened to the echo of her heavy footsteps stomping down the stairs, she mused, *This place is always so quiet. I never see anyone. I wonder where everyone goes.*

The two of them walked into the large warm kitchen. The aroma of the midday meal bubbling on the stove drifted into Ebony's nostrils.

"Agnes, can I help you bake some biscuits?" asked Ebony.

"Oh … I'm sorry, my dear, but I've finished my baking for today. You could help by putting the washing up away and helping to clean the table so I can get everything ready for lunch."

Even though Agnes was one of Ebony's favourite people, and she did do as Agnes had asked, it was done with no enthusiasm. Eventually, the two of them wandered into the library and Ebony lazily thumbed through a few of the thousands of books on the shelves and moaned that nothing was worth reading. She then went back to her bedroom only to find Veeleeta still asleep, so she flopped onto her bed and stared up at the covering above the bed. She spied a cobweb in one corner and wondered if Kate knew it was there. Eventually, she nodded off.

"Miss Ebony!"

Ebony bolted upright and stared around her, wondering where she was. Nanny Windabothem had come into the room.

"It is time for lunch."

"This is ridiculous," grumbled Ebony, stomping out of her room again with Scruffy rushing ahead of her, heading down the hallway. "I never knew Gribbles slept for so long."

Ebony huffed as she moved along one of the many long hallways in the mansion. Then she stopped and stared at it.

She had always made a deliberate effort not to come here, and yet here she was. Why? She did not know why. She didn't like this hallway with its dark red walls covered in large paintings of people she knew not. She thought they might be her relatives from long ago who had lived in Bedlow Manor. But these people meant nothing to her. Some looked cruel, others sad, but she knew there were none she would ever want to meet in person. A shiver ran down her spine. The tiled hallway held a strange feeling as if people were listening, watching everything she did.

She stepped onto a thick rug, one of many, coloured purple and black, with strange designs woven within them running up the centre of the tiled floor. Small wooden tables nestled against the wall along the length of the hallway, some with strange statues on them, others vases of flowers. That was another thing that niggled at Ebony's mind. Why flowers? Who would ever see them? She'd always wondered why her parents insisted on keeping everything in this hall. If she had the choice, she would get rid of it all.

She stopped. Had the air just felt colder?

She was turning to leave when Scruffy scampered up to her, dropping a ball at her feet. She stopped and looked at it then looked into his smiling face, his tail whipping the air.

"Yes, you're quite right, Scruffy. I'm sorry. I'm being silly."

She picked up the ball and threw it up the hallway. Scruffy raced off, scuttled across the rugs and caught it in his mouth. He rushed back and dropped the ball at her feet again, then barked a happy, playful bark.

"There you go," said Ebony, throwing it a bit further this time. He took a flying leap and grabbed it in his mouth. Ebony laughed out loud and clapped her hands. He rushed back towards her. She took a step back, bumping into a small wooden table nestled against the wall. She spun around and her eyes opened wide, as a large crystal vase full of dark red roses started wobbling.

"No!" she yelled as she instinctively held out her hands a split second too late. The vase toppled off the table and smashed onto the tiled floor below. The hall filled with the tinkling sound of thousands of tiny shards of crystal bouncing across the hard surface. Water and red blossoms scattered in every direction. Nanny Windabothem walked around the corner.

T rillium's nose tickled as it grew warm. His sleepy eyes opened to the pale morning light inching its way into the hollow log. Throwing back his blanket, he dragged himself out of his bedding and grabbed at his back; a sharp pain twinged within it. As the pain subsided, he moved closer to the edge of the entrance and looked out.

A sunny day greeted him. On the other side of the lake was a stand of tall, thin, strappy, green vegetation swaying gently in the breeze. The mud had disappeared beneath the rising water level. A flock of small brown birds flew out from amongst the vegetation and a cloud of minuscule insects skimmed across the surface of the water below. As Trillium stood watching, he breathed in the warm air full of the scent of strange pollens and damp moss, and stretched his arms. He stiffened as the sound of large wings filled his ears. He dropped his arms to his sides and looked to his right. A swarm of large long-bodied black insects flew straight towards him. He took a step back and watched from the safety of the shadows.

I must warn the others, he told himself.

Something soft rubbed up next to him and he froze with fright. He looked down and whispered, "Congar. Don't do that!" He dropped to his knees and placed a firm hand on Congar's body. "Look!"

He pointed to the parade of large black insects that were now so close he could see the whir of their large iridescent wings. "Will you go and wake the others, and tell them to be quiet."

A short time later soft footfalls came from behind, and Trillium turned to see Grigwell coming up from the back of the log. Trillium put his finger to his lips and pointed towards the entrance. Grigwell nodded and silently moved up next to him. The insects were now flying so close to the log that the sound of their wings thumped the air inside, causing it to vibrate. Moving closer to Grigwell, Trillium whispered, "Where have they come from?"

Grigwell hunched his shoulders to indicate he did not know. He then whispered, "I'll go and tell the others."

Trillium returned his gaze and watched as the last of the insects flew out of sight.

"Look," Congar's soft voice said, "Whimbrel lies there."

Trillium looked down to see Congar pointing his nose to his right, indicating something that lay beyond the entrance. Trillium screwed up his eyes and peered in the direction, but all he could see was the bank of long, dark-green thin-leafed plants, pale-blue sky above, and wisps of white clouds drifting by. He frowned then said, "Come on."

The group was waiting for him at the back of the hollow log.

"What's happening?" whispered Fluellen as all the others leaned forward to listen.

"Congar says he's found Whimbrel," Trillium called out as he picked up a saddle chair and blanket and placed them onto Teasel's back. "We have to go." Everyone else then started to do the same.

"We don't have any time to waste." Trillium climbed into the saddle chair then yelled, "Teasel, quick! Go!"

"Wait!" growled Grigwell, as he waved his arms but Teasel tossed his head and trotted past him, taking to the air.

"Where we are to go?" asked Teasel as he hovered over the water.

"I don't know," answered Trillium, realising he didn't have a clue where Whimbrel was.

"You know not?"

"Well ... Um ..." stammered Trillium, just as Congar called out. "Quick! We must hurry." Trillium looked to his left. Leedrum was hovering next to him. Fluellen, with Congar sitting on her lap, was frowning.

"We must hurry," repeated Congar.

"I know, but where is he?" called out Trillium.

"If only you would wait," snarled Grigwell, as he and Stellman glided up next to Trillium.

"What? Wait? We don't have time to wait. We need to find Whimbrel."

"If you had just waited instead of dashing off like that, wasting time, we …"

"What?" yelled Trillium. "I'm not the one wasting time, you are!"

"Hurry," squealed Congar. "We must hurry."

Trillium glared at Grigwell, then turned and yelled out, "Congar, lead the way."

Thick-stemmed plants loomed in front of the group. Congar directed Leedrum to land at their base in the middle of a patch of moss on the muddy bank. As the Gribbles dismounted, Congar sprang from Fluellen's lap and glided off to Trillium's right.

Trillium, along with the other Gribbles, rushed after him. Upon reaching the edge of the small clearing, they stopped and Congar scurried around whispering, "Quiet! Everyone quiet. There is danger still. Come. Hurry." He then turned and headed out into the forest of stems.

Everyone followed only to find the Cloud Dancers could not pass. The stems were knitted together too closely. Being too wide to fit, the Cloud Dancers reluctantly agreed to await their return.

When the Gribbles emerged on the other side of the vegetation they stood in disbelief at what they saw. A huge tangled mass of thick silver-grey stems stood in front of them. Every leaf was large, every stem was strong and tall, and every section of the plant was covered in a mass of long, sharp, deadly, needle-like spines. At its base lay a skirt of dead brittle leaves, each still clinging to their protective covering like spears protecting the plant from attack. Trillium looked up into the dizzy heights. Above, dancing on a soft breeze, were puffs of purple flowers blending into the azure sky. He then peered into the interior of the plant, but all he could see were deep shadows. He shivered with the thought of what lay beyond.

"Congar," whispered Trillium, as he bent down close to him. "Whimbrel can't possibly be … He can't …"

Congar turned and looked up at him as if he understood what Trillium's mind would not, could not, did not want to accept, when all of a sudden Fluellen whispered, "Is he in there?"

They both looked at her. Trillium frowned and put his finger to his mouth. Grigwell knelt down next to Congar, and whispered, "Go and find Whimbrel. Return with the news."

Trillium watched as Congar moved in and out of the shadows, his fur constantly changing colour, allowing him to blend in with the background. In the end all Trillium could see was a shimmer, a slight shape until finally, Congar disappeared from sight.

Trillium and Grigwell fidgeted and sighed as they waited in the shadows of the tall plants. They flinched when Congar suddenly reappeared before them, his fur changing from grey to its normal colour of chestnut. "Whimbrel has been found. Come."

"Is he alive?" asked Trillium.

Congar looked up at him. "Unknown. One creature stands guard. Come."

Trillium's mind went blank. Whatever it was he was expecting to hear that wasn't it.

"Wait," cried Grigwell. "Fluellen and Quintell aren't back with the torches yet … Ah, here they are. Everyone take one and let's go."

Grigwell patted Trillium on the shoulder as he passed him by, then keeping low, everyone followed Congar and they skirted around the plant to the left. Eventually, they all stopped and huddled under some large green leaves and looked upon the tangled mass beyond. A dark opening lay only a few steps away. Congar looked up at Grigwell and said, "Come."

Silently, deftly, they edged past the sharp spines, always moving further into the shadows as they carefully manoeuvred around each stem, then they stopped. Everyone sniffed the air.

Trillium's long nose screwed up as the stench, which only comes from decaying flesh, made him want to cough. He slapped a hand over his mouth. Fluellen did the same. Holding his breath, he willed his stomach to settle as a sickening sensation swirled within it.

Congar quickly glided on, the Gribbles followed and then stopped again. Just above their heads, speared upon a sharp spine, was a single small, round, white, furry creature. Two long white tentacles hung from the base of its abdomen and trailed down the wall. Pale frosty wings hung limply by its side, and two pale green eyes, devoid of all life, stared out at them. The Gribbles stared back, then turned and reluctantly moved forward.

39

As the Gribbles moved further in, the sunlight dimmed. The number of bodies hanging on thorns grew in number. It was like some macabre display, or larder, and Trillium shivered at the thought of unseeing eyes watching them walk on by.

As the Gribbles turned a corner, they stopped and gasped at the sight that lay before them. They had entered a large, dimly lit circular cavern, made from the spiky stems of the huge plant with its woven walls of thorns surrounding them like a basket. White fluff covered every surface of the basket except the floor they stood upon.

The Gribbles huddled together; the air was thick with the stench of rotting flesh. Tears sprang into Trillium's eyes. Through the dim light, halfway up the far wall, he spied Whimbrel, hanging by a large sharp spine. His head lay limp against his chest. His eyes were shut. He was unmoving. He was amongst a wall of fluffy white bodies; every single creature surrounding him was … dead.

His mama's words popped into his mind. *All she can see is an expanse of white.*

A scuttling sound came from Trillium's right. Everyone spun around. They peered into the deepest darkest part of the clump of stems but could see nothing.

Grigwell indicated with a wave of a hand to follow him. Silently, everyone glided from one shadow to the next, eventually arriving at the base of a thick stem. They looked up. Whimbrel's limp body was just above them. Grigwell slowly touched everyone on the shoulder, Congar on his head. When everyone was looking at him, he put a finger to his lips. He pointed into the darkness where a scuttling sound could be heard, patted his chest, pointed to Fluellen and stabbed his finger to the ground. He then touched Congar, Trillium and Quintell and pointed to Whimbrel.

Trillium shivered as he watched Congar immediately glide over one white lifeless body to the next as he made his way towards his brother. Quintell then did the same. Trillium took a deep breath and instantly regretted it as the stench of death filled his lungs again; nonetheless he solemnly slung his blacked-out torch over his back and started climbing. His stomach churned but he told himself, *Keep going. Keep going.* His foot slipped. He fell forward and cringed as he felt the soft remains of the dead body beneath his fingers. His body shuddered, he felt sick to his stomach. Shutting his eyes, he yelled at himself, *Keep going ... I can't,* he moaned to himself. *Whimbrel cannot be left here. Keep going!* Trillium opened his eyes and stared straight into the lifeless green eyes staring back at him. He shivered with revulsion, then with a determination he did not know he had, he pulled himself up and clambered over the rest of the remains until he reached his brother's feet. They were bare, caked in dried mud. Hesitantly, Trillium moved his fingers out towards them. *What if he's dead?* He quickly withdrew his hand, pulled himself further up until eventually, he reached Whimbrel's left hand. He willed himself to touch it. It felt cold. He snatched his hand away. *No! Don't be dead. You can't be.* Tears sprang into his eyes.

A loud crunching sound reverberated throughout the shadows below. Trillium glanced into the gloom but only dark eerie shadows looked back. He returned his gaze to Quintell who had now positioned himself on his brother's right side, silently beckoning Trillium to move closer.

Trillium looked at the cruel sharp barb protruding through Whimbrel's shoulder, through his clothes. Blood was smeared on its surface, staining the fabric. He looked at his brother's face. His skin was a sickly yellow colour and his long nose lay limp. There was no sign of life. Trillium dragged his gaze away and watched Congar, who had climbed up next to Whimbrel's small ear. He was whispering, "We are here, dear heart. Don't despair. We are here." Congar pushed his cold wet nose up against Whimbrel's cheek. A tear tumbled over the rim of Whimbrel's eye and slowly slid down towards his chin. Trillium and Quintell sucked in their breath, then looked at each other and smiled. Relief swirled in Trillium's heart as he watched Congar continue to whisper, "Fear not, dear heart. All is not lost."

A rattle of clicking sounds resonated through the air. Trillium looked down. A single large black creature had now entered the area below and was staring straight at Fluellen and Grigwell. He felt it could not believe that they were even there. Its cruel black pincers clicked. Its large translucent wings flapped. Suddenly a yellow torchlight lit up the macabre chamber. Grigwell and Fluellen had obviously removed the hoods from their torches. The creature squealed and backed off, then advanced, and Grigwell yelled as he lunged at it with his torch. It squealed again, backing off, then charged. The air filled with a high-pitched screech and a new stench of burnt hair drifted up from below as Fluellen pulled back her torch from the shell of the creature.

"GET HIM DOWN!" screamed Grigwell.

"Trillium! Quickly! Help me!" cried Quintell.

"Right." Trillium scrambled to be above Whimbrel's head and moved to position himself above his right shoulder.

Grigwell's voice yelled, "Hurry up! Get him down!"

Quintell lifted Whimbrel's right arm and pulled as Trillium, leaning up against the dead bodies lying at his back, closing his mind to the thought of them, used one of his long oblong feet and pushed up against his brother's right shoulder. Quintell pulled again, Trillium pushed again, as Whimbrel moaned, his limp body slowly dragged free from the thorn. Quintell pulled again. Trillium pushed with all his might, then as Whimbrel's hand slipped out of Quintell's grasp they both screamed, "NOO!" Whimbrel's body tumbled to the earth below.

Congar rushed down towards him. Trillium and Quintell quickly followed. Reaching the floor, they picked up Whimbrel's arms and legs. Someone yelled, "Move!" The two of them staggered under the weight of their burden, back towards the other Gribbles.

The black insect advanced, clicking and thrashing its head around in agitation. Grigwell and Fluellen waved their torches in front of its head and drove it back. As the group retreated, the insect advanced, and then stopped, lifted its head and made a string of rapid clicking noises. A few seconds later the air filled with the sound of humming wings.

"HURRY!" screamed Fluellen. "They are here." She slung her torch behind her back and seized one of Whimbrel's legs. Grigwell did the same with his torch, grasped one of Whimbrel's arms, and the group ran.

The sound of many wings shifted, making it impossible to tell where the insects were coming from. Trillium looked ahead: stems were becoming sparser, the light was becoming brighter. The rescue group rushed around a corner. Bright sunshine flooded across their path. With relief, they dashed towards the exit, their only means of escape, when suddenly they all skidded to a halt. A wall of large black creatures had descended from the sky and was hovering in front of the entrance, barring their way.

40

Nanny Windabothem cast her cold eyes across the devastation of dark red blossoms and crystal shards scattered across the tiles; they then slowly settled upon Ebony. As quick as lightning, she stepped forward, grabbing Ebony's forearm, pinching the muscle hard.

"Ow! You're hurting me," cried Ebony, as Nanny pulled her up close.

"Be quiet if you know what's good for you." She turned and dragged Ebony along the hallway.

"Let go of me," whimpered Ebony, as Nanny squeezed tighter. Tears flowed down Ebony's cheeks while Scruffy barked and snapped at Nanny's heels.

"Scruffy! Please! Stop!" pleaded Ebony.

Scruffy yelped as Nanny kicked out at him, and he backed off and barked again. Nanny opened a large, solid oak door, pushed Ebony into the room beyond and slammed the door shut behind them. Instantly, Scruffy's barking was cut off like a switch.

Silence filled the room. Nanny spun Ebony around, pulling her forward, forcing her to stand on her tiptoes. Their faces were so close now that Ebony cringed.

"You stupid little girl," spat Nanny. "Your parents will blame me for that, not their precious daughter." And with those words she let her arm go.

Ebony shivered as if ants were crawling up and down her spine. She tried to glare into Nanny's eyes but found she just could not do it.

"Turn around. Face the desk," barked Nanny.

Ebony turned and did as she was told, feeling like a coward

for not standing up to Nanny Windabothem who was now slowly walking up and down behind her. Ebony's shoulder blades stiffened, as the sound of Nanny's sensible shoes hitting the wooden floorboards echoed through the room. Her heart beat faster, beads of sweat burst forth upon her brow, as she waited. *How the heck am I ever going to get out of this?* she said to herself as she waited. *You've never managed it before,* she replied as her shoulder blades now started to ache. Then the shoes stopped. Ebony cowered as Nanny leaned forward and hissed in her ear, "You have caused me nothing but trouble since you arrived home from boarding school. If it had been left up to me you would still *be* there."

Nanny came around to the wooden desk and sat down in her straight-backed wooden chair. "Fortunately, your father showed great foresight in engaging me to run this household and none too soon. It has taken me well over a year and a half to bring the running of this household back into shape, and just as I get it the way I want, *you* come home, and now I'm expected to be a nursemaid."

Nanny sighed. "Well, I suppose it's only for another few weeks then you'll be gone, back to boarding school, exactly where you belong. You have only been here for four weeks, refusing to eat perfectly good food, running up and down the hallways, making a terrible racket, speaking out of turn, telling childish stories, getting lost." Nanny glared at Ebony, and continued, "I understand that you have been complaining about the loss of those frivolous dresses of yours. It's the price you paid for your disobedience all those months ago. I will not tolerate it. Do … you … understand? It's a lesson you need to learn, young lady. It's one you *will* learn, because if you do not learn from your mistakes you are doomed to repeat them, and will be punished accordingly."

Ebony opened her mouth to say something but nothing would come out, and inwardly cringing at her lack of gumption, she shut it.

Nanny sighed again and lowered her head, then lifting her narrowing eyes up to Ebony, a slight twitch of a smile slid across her thin lips. "Every action has a reaction," she said. "Every decision has a consequence. *A price.* It's another lesson you need to learn early on in life, young lady. I did, and look where it has got me. Now ... how do you think *you* should *pay* the price for breaking such a valuable item, and more importantly, for disobeying me the other day?"

Ebony lowered her eyes to the floor. She'd been dreading this. "You had been told by your parents *never* to go into Tanglemire Forest."

Ebony said nothing.

"Were you not?"

Ebony was silent.

"Were you *not!*

"Yes, Nanny."

"But you did it anyway. How do you think that made me look in the eyes of your parents?" Nanny Windabothem leaned back against her chair. "I blame it on that last nanny you had. What was her name? Jones. Yes, that was it. Nanny Jones. Frivolous. No discipline. That's something else I will not tolerate. She filled your head with those airy-fairy ideas. Fairy gardens! Honestly! How pathetic! And all those paintings, and those ridiculous models.

"Well, I'm glad to see that since I've been here you have stopped wasting your time doing *them*. Excellent! Your father showed great foresight getting rid of her and sending you to boarding school."

Ebony looked up. Heat had suddenly risen in her belly and words rose in her throat. It was all wrong. That was not what had happened. It was because of Nanny Windabothem that she had ended up at the boarding school, not her father. It was because of *her* she had been ripped away from the only home she had ever known. Then a voice inside her head pleaded with her to say nothing, it was not worth the pain, and the words instantly died on her tongue.

Nanny picked up a wooden ruler from the desk and pointed one end of it towards the right-hand corner of the room. "Go and stand over there."

Ebony glared at her but did not move. *Don't do this, Ebony,* a frightened voice said from deep inside her, but still Ebony did not move.

223

Do as you are told! Ebony pleaded with herself, as she stood looking at Nanny.

No … I have to stand up to her …

Don't! Please! Ebony argued with herself. *You know what will happen … Please!*

The seconds ticked by. Nanny started tapping the ruler on the wooden desk.

Don't! Ebony pleaded with herself again. Tears were welling inside her as she could feel herself giving in again. She sighed, reluctantly turned and walked to the corner of the room. Sadness filled her heart. *Was this ever going to end?*

"Turn around and stare at the wall," growled Nanny, and Ebony did as she was told. "Straighten up. Don't slouch. Don't move a single muscle, or else I might have to find a better use for this ruler. How many times have we had to go through this since you have been back?" Nanny's voice droned on. "I will turn you into a young lady if it's the last thing I do. You will learn to obey, just as I learned it. You should count yourself lucky. I'm being very *lenient* with you. It's a failing of mine. My unc—" Nanny instantly stopped talking. Ebony had the feeling she was going to say more but for some reason had changed her mind. Hope sprang within her; maybe Nanny wasn't going to go on with the lecture this time. Then Nanny cleared her throat and continued to say, "I will not stand for your disobedience …"

Ebony inwardly sighed and as she concentrated on the floral wallpaper before her, she took in every line, detail and shade of colour of the dark floral pattern before her eyes, until even when she closed her eyelids, it was imprinted onto the back of them. She hoped that by doing so she did not have to listen to Nanny's voice because it would just fade away.

Three hours later, Nanny threw open the door and swooped upon Scruffy who had been faithfully lying at its entrance. She picked him up by the scruff of the neck, causing him to whimper, turned back towards Ebony and said, "Stay here while I deal with *this.*" She brought Scruffy's face up to hers. "I will teach you not to bite me."

"NO!" screamed Ebony, as she hurried to the door that slammed shut in front of her face.

Ebony grabbed at the solid oak door and leaned her head up against it. *Not again.* She waited for a minute, then with her heart pounding in her throat, carefully and quietly opened the door.

She looked down the hallway. Nanny was heading away from her, towards the flight of stairs. Scruffy, still dangling in mid-air, was whimpering.

Ebony tiptoed along the hall carpet, her ears straining for any other sound. She heard the click of a door as it opened or closed somewhere deep in the heart of the mansion. The ticking of the grandfather clock sounded louder, as it always did at this time of day. It seemed to vibrate through the body of the walls, through the floor, through the very air itself. Other than that there wasn't any other sound. So she crept up to the end of the hall and looked over the banisters down into the foyer, three storeys below. Nanny was heading for the kitchen.

"Blast!" whispered Ebony through gritted teeth, then scrambled back to Nanny's office. She rushed up to the only window in the room, small, long and narrow, and peered out. The vegetable garden at the back of the mansion was shrouded in darkness. The reflective glow of the light, escaping from the many narrow windows running the length of the building, created a patchwork effect on the ground. The rain was splashing large drops onto the paths. Ebony pressed her face up against the cold windowpane. She looked through the runnels of rain trickling down the glass to where the laundry door was located. Instantly a large band of yellow light shot across a pathway, and a dark figure, with Scruffy dangling from its hand, walked into the light. Leaves fluttered across the paving as the silhouetted form walked up to a small wooden garden shed sitting on the very edge of the dark shadows. Ebony watched as Nanny, seemingly oblivious to the rain, opened the door, brought Scruffy up to her face, shook him then threw him inside, slamming the door shut.

Ebony dragged herself away from the window and reluctantly returned to the corner of the room where she waited for the return of her tormentor.

41

The Gribbles looked behind them to find the single guard had been joined by two others. They then looked towards the only way out, to see sunlight glinting off thick black shiny armour, as more creatures than they could count hovered over the ground, billowing dust into the air. Their large iridescent wings deafened the air with a whirring sound and the dust rose higher and higher forming dense clouds that made it hard to see. Trillium faltered. They were trapped.

All of a sudden, somewhere high above them, a loud booming voice roared with the words, "WHERE DID *THAT* COME FROM?"

A loud whooshing sound thundered through the air. The black insects dispersed. A massive black blade crashed into the soil. It hit the ground with such force that half of it disappeared into the earth. The ground shuddered and the Gribbles were knocked off their feet. Whimbrel's body crashed to the ground. Congar squealed, turning bright red. A few seconds later the blade heaved to one side and the ground shuddered, making the plant sway. The blade released itself from the earth, and soil and rubble tumbled from its edges as it lifted high into the air.

Someone screamed, "MOVE!" while others yelled, "Run!"

The Gribbles quickly picked Whimbrel up and ran out into the daylight, dodging the dead leaves covered in lethal spines. The whooshing sound came again, now from behind them. The blade slashed through the air, crashing deep into the soil again. As the blade released itself from the soil once more, the earth shook and the plant tilted. Everyone was thrown to the ground again. Sharp spines tumbled out of the air.

Trillium looked up to see a huge giant had filled the sky, and he froze.

"Trillium," yelled Grigwell. Trillium did not move. "Trillium!" yelled Grigwell, again. Trillium looked back to the group as a part of his mind told him to do something, while another part said, *But I never knew ... It's huge. No. Huge isn't the word ... maybe ... maybe ...*

"TRILLIUM!" screamed Grigwell.

Trillium looked at Grigwell and realised everyone else had picked themselves up and were grabbing at his brother's body. He quickly realised that he should be doing the same, so he seized one of his brother's arms and helped to half-drag, half-pull him into the surrounding vegetation. Soil and rubble were continuing to plummet back to the earth, stems creaked and groaned behind them. Then the huge silvery plant crashed onto the very vegetation under which they had now taken refuge; it was pushing down, down, down on top of them all.

"RUN!" screamed Quintell.

Everyone, dragging the dead weight of Whimbrel's body between them, stumbled forward as spines stabbed through the air, through the leaves, slicing down, missing each Gribble by a fraction of a hair, until Fluellen screamed. Whimbrel's body tilted to one side as she let go of him. Trillium spun around to see her holding her arm. A trickle of blood seeped out from between her four stubby fingers. Sticking out of the ground quivering, was a spine immediately beside her. Mercifully the spines had stopped falling. Silence, blessed silence, then a booming voice from the sky above thundered, "THAT'S THE END OF THAT!"

Creaking and groaning resonated all around them as the huge plant was dragged across the roof of their world. Needle-sharp spines filled the air once more, falling around them. Someone screamed, "RUN!"

The Gribbles staggered forward, pushing and pulling Whimbrel's limp body until finally they tumbled out into the bright mossy clearing, nearly collapsing with relief. The Cloud Dancers dashed forward. The Gribbles instantly dragged and pushed Whimbrel's body across the back of the nearest Cloud Dancer, and as the Gribbles clambered into their saddle chairs, everyone screamed. "FLY! FLY! FLY AWAY!"

42

Hooves clattered within the ancient hollow log as the Cloud Dancers finally heaved themselves to a standstill. Quintell leapt out of his saddle chair and yelled, "Tillia, quickly, take Whimbrel to the back of the log."

Trotting forward, Tillia, with Whimbrel's body slumped across her back, went as far as she could without hitting her head on the roof. Then Quintell yelled, "Stop! Get him off! Quick! Hurry! We must keep him warm."

"Is he all right?" called out Trillium, as he grasped his brother's hand. It still felt cold.

"What was that voice?" inquired Fluellen. "Back there, where did it come from?"

"It was a gi—" Trillium began to explain but Quintell yelled out, "Quiet! Everyone be quiet. Get him off. Fluellen, go and get some bedding ready and set up the Fire Stones. We must keep Whimbrel warm."

As Fluellen turned to leave, Quintell continued to say, "Put the bedding as far back as you can, out of the draughts. I'll be back soon." Quintell trotted over to the side of the log, disappearing into the darkness, as Grigwell said, "Tillia, please lie down."

Tillia blinked her big dewy eyes, and sinking onto her knees, did as she'd been asked.

"Trillium, take his arms," commanded Grigwell. "I'll take his legs … One … two … lift."

They strained under Whimbrel's weight, and slowly both pulled until his body slid off Tillia's back. Trillium gritted his teeth as he and Grigwell staggered to the back of the log with their burden.

A soft glow from some Fire Stones shone ahead of them, and Trillium stumbled on the dark uneven floor.

"Hold him! Hold him!" yelled Grigwell.

Trillium suddenly found Fluellen by his side taking hold of one of Whimbrel's arms. "Over here," said Fluellen, nodding towards the light and the blankets she'd laid on the floor as instructed.

The three of them carefully laid Whimbrel down on top of the bedding as Quintell returned carrying a dark bundle of cloth.

"Good, good, good," he said as he put it down. "More blankets, more blankets. Cover him up. Keep him warm until I'm ready."

"What do you want me to do?" asked Trillium, as he made a pillow from a folded blanket and gently slid it under his brother's head.

"Comfort him. It's most important he is calm and warm," replied Quintell, as he started to untie the cloth bundle. "Grigwell, get some more Fire Stones working. Fluellen, more blankets. Congar, please do what you can for him."

Trillium watched as Congar snuggled up next to the top of Whimbrel's flat head. He started singing a song that filled the hollow log. It was barely above a whisper, it was of indescribable beauty, and yet full of heart-wrenching sorrow. It was bouncing out of the shadows, being absorbed into the wood, into the very being of every creature that listened to it.

Trillium cradled Whimbrel's right hand in his as Fluellen wrapped more blankets over Whimbrel's body. "Fluellen, you're bleeding again," said Trillium.

Quintell looked up. "Why didn't you say something?"

Fluellen looked at him but said nothing as he quickly took her arm. He then parted the fabric of her sleeve and looked at the small wound. "Hum. You'll be all right. I'm sorry but I have to take care of Whimbrel first."

Quintell finished untying the cord from the bundle and as the fabric fell onto the floor, the light from the Fire Stones reflected against two small boxes covered in silver leaves. One was bound with green and yellow silk threads, the other in red and purple.

"Wow, what are they?" asked Fluellen.

Without looking up, Quintell said, 'These are my herbal chests."

He opened the curved lids of each one and started rummaging about, picking out one bottle, looking at the label, replacing it and then picking out another. "They hold my powders, tinctures and all the other things I use to heal creatures. My hope is to find something that will heal Whimbrel."

In the meantime, Grigwell placed the last of the small glowing Fire Stones into a pile, one of many he had created in a circle around the group of Gribbles. Trillium, sitting down next to his brother, looked behind the ring of hazy white light to see the Cloud Dancers had created a barrier with their bodies. They lay, head to tail, blocking any breeze, then turned their heads towards the Gribbles crowded around Whimbrel, watching.

"Trillium! Grigwell!" called out Quintell. "Remove his waistcoat and shirt, so I can get to his wounds."

"We're going to have to cut his clothes off," said Grigwell.

"Do as you must," replied Quintell.

"Is there something I can do?" inquired Fluellen.

"Yes, thank you," said Quintell. "I need some water and a piece of clean wadding. I need to clean the wound … There you are," he said as he took up a small red bottle.

Fluellen nodded and trotted towards the pile of supplies. Trillium in the meantime dropped the last of the ragged strips of his brother's shirt onto the floor while Congar never faltered in singing his strange song.

Quintell looked at the large hole in Whimbrel's right shoulder. He pointed to it. "This is the danger." He gently turned Whimbrel on his side. "It passes straight through his shoulder. These other two," he pointed to two smaller wounds further down his back, "aren't as serious."

Fluellen returned with a small wooden bowl of water and some wadding.

"What is Congar doing?" asked Trillium, as he tried to make some sense of the unintelligible words Congar was singing. Trillium rubbed the area of his chest where the small pouch hanging around his neck lay. He only half-registered that the area was getting warm. He had almost forgotten all about the pouch around his neck.

"Poogles," stated Quintell, as he undid the stopper of the red bottle, "can, for a while, bind the mind and the secret parts of a Gribble's heart, within a protective dream state." Quintell tipped a drop of yellow liquid into the water, which started to sizzle. He went on, "The song keeps the inner part of Whimbrel, the part that makes him who he is, safe, while his body is in danger of dying."

"Oh, I see," said Trillium, then quickly turned to look at Quintell. "What? Is Whimbrel going to die?" Trillium clutched at the pouch around his neck which now felt very warm. Quintell looked at Trillium with eyes that had turned into pools of water, but he did not answer. He just turned away and said, as if to himself, "Now, let's see."

He picked up a small cloth pouch from one of his silver chests, opened it and then removed some of the purple powder from it.

"What is that?" asked Trillium.

"I thought of all the Gribbles, you would know, Trillium. Your papa is the Guardian of the Wandoo plants after all. It's their pollen." Quintell carefully placed some of the pollen onto the wad of fabric and spread it around with the tip of his stubby finger, causing the fabric to turn purple.

"Well. Yes. Yes, of course, I do." Trillium averted his eyes and looked at Whimbrel, embarrassed that he had not recognised it.

"Grigwell, lay this over that side of the wound, will you?"

Quintell pointed to the back of Whimbrel's shoulder. "Make sure the pollen is against the wound."

Whimbrel moaned as Grigwell did as he was told. Trillium bit his lip. He watched as Quintell then picked two hollow reeds out of a chest and joined them together.

"Is it in place, Grigwell?" asked Quintell.

"Yes."

"Hold it tight then. Trillium, hold your brother down."

Trillium grasped hold of Whimbrel's left arm and watched Quintell place the tip of the tube into the water and suck up some of the liquid.

Keeping his tongue over the top of the reed, he moved over towards Whimbrel's shoulder. He held the tip of the reed over the open wound, then quickly blew the contents it held deep within it.

Whimbrel screamed and jerked upwards.

"Hold him!" yelled Quintell. "Keep that wadding in place."

Trillium forced Whimbrel back down by grabbing his left shoulder. Fluellen grabbed hold of his other arm. Congar's song grew louder, and Grigwell struggled to hold the wadding against Whimbrel's shoulder in place. Eventually, Whimbrel lay still, though his breathing had become quite rapid.

Thin swirls of white smoke started to twirl out of the wound as Quintell sucked up more liquid and forced it into the hole.

Whimbrel screamed again and jerked as froth slowly started to spill out over the jagged raw edges of flesh.

Trillium could not help but cry out, "What are you doing?"

"Cleaning the wound," explained Quintell. "I'm making sure there will be no infection deep inside." He sat back and watched the swirls of smoke continuing to drift up into the air as the amount of froth grew. "Ah, good, good," he said as the smoke started to turn lavender in colour, and eventually when it turned dark purple, Quintell cried out, "Brilliant! Keep the wadding in place just a little bit longer, Grigwell." Quintell then extracted three small blue feathers from one of his silver chests.

"Are they what I think they are?" asked Grigwell.

"Yep," said Quintell, with glee in his voice.

"What?" spluttered Trillium. He didn't understand what was going on and he did not like it.

"How did you find them?" said Fluellen.

"Explain yourself," demanded Grigwell.

"Oh, I found them in the clearing, when we were searching for signs of Veeleeta. Lucky I picked them up actually." Quintell looked up. There was silence in the air except for Congar's song. "I found seven small ones and the two larger ones with black spots on them."

"A male," said Grigwell, as he continued to hold the fabric in place.

"Pardon?" Quintell's eyebrows furrowed.

"Those feathers belong to a male Swanling. Swanlings have not been seen in the forest for over twenty seasons."

"I know. They are really rare," replied Quintell. "I didn't know what they were at first, not until they dried out. The small ones just looked like bits of blue string when wet."

"A Swanling must have been flying over the forest when the storm hit," said Fluellen. "Perhaps it was good that we knew nothing about it. From what I understand from the old fables, there is no joy to be had when you meet up with a Swanling."

"Well, whatever the reason," said Quintell, as he placed the three small blue feathers in the open lid of one of his chests, not finishing what he was saying. He then took a small stone basin out of the other and continued, "It's a stroke of good fortune for Whimbrel that I found them." He picked up a small black bottle and unplugged the stopper.

"What do you mean?" asked Trillium, again grasping hold of the little pouch around his neck. He instantly felt its warmth from within flowing through the outer covering into his fingers.

He watched as Quintell poured white powder into the stone basin then dropped a single feather on top of it. As the feather touched the surface, a sizzling could be heard, then the feather turned into a small puff of blue smoke. It erupted into the air and fell back down into the basin as a blue powder. "When I combine some of my other compounds with these ..." Quintell added the other two feathers, one at a time, each one turning into powder. Then without finishing what he was saying, he took three small glass bottles from his silver chests and allowed one drop from each of them to fall into the basin. He added a pinch of purple Wandoo powder, took the larger of the black-spotted Swanling feathers, which was bent and battered from being squashed into the small silver chest, and with the quill, stirred the contents of the basin, making a thick creamy blue mixture.

"It means," Quintell continued as he held the basin up, "that by adding these *particular* feathers to my mixture, Whimbrel may be completely healed from his injuries." Quintell then carefully dripped the thick blue mixture, drop by drop, into the wound and as the last of the mixture dripped off the end of the quill, Whimbrel sighed and breathed in deeply.

"Very good," said Quintell, with a pleased look. "Now let's bind this wound before I fix up those other two wounds. Lappa cream will be good enough for them."

Trillium watched Quintell place a large silver leaf over each end of the wound in Whimbrel's shoulder, and bind them in place with some very fine strapping resembling spider webs. "Congar, when you are ready you can leave Whimbrel to his dreams," said Quintell. "Thank you. Thank you very much for all you have done."

Trillium looked down at his brother whose eyes were still shut, but the colour had at least returned to his skin and his breathing was now normal. Trillium looked at Quintell, who was smiling as he repacked the contents of his chests.

"Quintell," asked Trillium. "Is Whimbrel ... really all right?"

"Yes. He will be fine in a few days."

"A few days! But we don't have a few days!" stated Trillium. "What about Veeleeta? How are we ever going to find her now? I'll have to go on my own. Yes, that's it. I can't wait, I just can't!"

Then a thought bubbled up from somewhere and Trillium released his hold on the little pouch which had now grown very hot. Not knowing why, he undid the thong at the back of his neck and held the small pouch out to Quintell.

"Will this help Whimbrel?"

"What are you doing with that?" asked Quintell.

"It's Papa's."

"I know it's Snailum's. What are you doing with it? Snailum has forbidden it to leave the hanging village."

"I ... Mama gave it to me."

"But why?" said Quintell.

"What do you mean, why? She said it would help us succeed."

"Do you even know what's in it?"

"In it? There isn't anything in it. I looked. I could not find anything, but it keeps getting hot. It seems to me, it must mean something … otherwise …" Trillium stopped talking. He felt he was starting to not make sense, even to himself.

Quintell tipped the pouch upside down into the palm of his hand and the reddest ruby anyone had ever seen dropped out and sat sparkling in the glow of the Fire Stones.

"Wow!" exclaimed Fluellen, as Grigwell said, "What?"

"I didn't know," said Trillium, staring at the ruby's glow deep within it.

"That's one of the Sisters of the Depths," Grigwell stated.

"Quintell, explain what is going on."

"There is a fable from the ancient past that these rubies were once used to heal Gribbles of great injuries." Quintell stared down at the ruby on his palm. "I don't know if this is even true, but it is worth a try. Mind you, it's only a fable. But if it can heal Whimbrel faster than I can, then …" Quintell stopped talking, bent down and placed the stone between Whimbrel's eyes. The instant he let go of it, a red haze radiated out from it, flooding its light upon Whimbrel's face.

"What are you doing?" called out Trillium, unable to hide the nervousness in his voice.

Quintell looked up at him but said nothing.

The Gribbles watched the red haze that had now spread all over Whimbrel's body. It seemed to be pulsating, touching his fingers, his toes, wrapping around his body like a cloth. Then, where his heart lay, a darker whirlpool of mist swirled, turning into a funnel, twirling itself up, up, up, towards the roof of the log, growing wider and wider, reflecting its red glow across the wooden surface.

The Gribbles backed off, except for Fluellen; she was moving towards it with her hands held out as if to touch it.

"No!" yelled Quintell. He rushed to catch her but missed. She'd rushed towards it, and as her fingers sank into the mist they started to glow red. She stood with her eyes shut, as still as a tree. Then when the glow dimmed, her hands fell to her side. The mist faded, and the Gribbles all looked to Fluellen. When she turned and looked at them, she was smiling.

"I can see you." She then burst into tears and fell to her knees.

"Fluellen!" Quintell rushed to her side and grabbed hold of her shoulders, forcing her to look at him. "What has happened?"

"The Sister. She has given me the ability to see the energies of this world. I'm no longer blind to it, to any of it."

A collective sigh could be heard.

"But what about Whimbrel?" asked Trillium, looking down at his brother.

"She has healed him of all his hurts," stated Fluellen. "The ones of the body and the ones of the mind."

"But I don't … understand," stammered Trillium.

"How did Snailum come to have one of these?" asked Grigwell, with concern on his face.

"One? You mean there are more?" asked Trillium.

"Yes, the fables say there are seven, but how many there really are I don't know. The Elder will need to know of its existence, Quintell," stated Grigwell. "He will decide if it can stay within the confines of the village. I will need to talk to Snailum about this when we return. He should never have brought it into the village, he knows that."

"It will do you no good," said Quintell. "Snailum will not talk about it."

"Well, if he will not talk to *me*, he *will* talk to the Elder. I will make sure of it!"

43

Ebony slammed the bedroom door shut and threw herself onto her bed. With large racking sobs, she cried into her pillow. It was late, very late, and her heart felt heavy with desperation. How was she ever going to survive the torment from Nanny Windabothem? As she hugged her pillow, the pendant around her neck grew warm.

Veeleeta awoke to find it was dark. Her tummy hurt from lack of food, and tilting her head to one side, she listened as a rasping noise reverberated throughout the room. She jumped out of bed, rushed up to a large stained-glass window and looked up at it. Orange light flickered across its surface. She grabbed a chair, heaved herself up onto it and stood on tiptoes looking out through a corner of clear glass. She bit her lip. Ebony was crying.

Slowly Veeleeta climbed back into bed and as her tummy rumbled, she grabbed hold of it, realising she'd not eaten since the morning. She looked up at the windows and then around the room.

I'm trapped!

Sleep finally overtook Ebony. She breathed deeply as a dream morphed into the shadowy shape of a wooden structure. Its wooden door creaked open, and she fell through the air into the pitch-black abyss.

"Umph," she cried in her dream world. She crashed onto the wooden floor of the garden shed she could not see but now knew all too well since Nanny Windabothem had come to live here.

Scruffy howled. Shadowy shapes leered up around them. Everything swam in front of her eyes. Something soft touched her leg and she screamed. Scruffy howled again and Ebony froze. "What is it, Scruffy?" The door of the shed flew open. Summer sunshine exploded before her eyes, and the black silhouette of a thin figure stood in the entrance. The shape lunged at her and Ebony yelled, "No! Don't!"

"It's just a dream," she yelled as she scrambled out of bed, collapsing to her knees on the rug below. "It's just a dream ... only ... a ... dream."

As Ebony sat back on her heels, she brushed her sweat-stained hair away from her face, sucked in long deep breaths, pulled at her damp sweaty clothes and looked around the dark room. It felt cold; the fire had died to almost nothing. She shivered as the sound of thunder rolled in the distance heralding a storm moving on. She looked through the curtains that had not been drawn shut and watched as lightning flashed across the top of the canopy of Tanglemire Forest.

She then stood up and fumbled her way back to her bed, switched on a bedside lamp, turned, and went over to the castle.

Carefully, Ebony opened up the side of it and whispered, "Veeleeta, are you there?"

"Ebony, is that you?"

44

"**W**himbrel is staying behind!" Trillium jumped up and glared at Grigwell.

"We can't split up," shouted Grigwell, standing to face Trillium's rage. "He can't stay here alone. Others would have to stay behind. We can't afford to—"

"I refuse to be left anywhere," interrupted Whimbrel.

"Whimbrel!" Trillium turned to see his brother slowly walking towards the group, dressed in a shirt Grigwell had loaned him.

"You've recovered," said Grigwell. "Come. Sit."

"Are you all right?" asked Trillium, anxious Whimbrel wasn't as well as he looked.

"I'm fine. I'm fine," answered Whimbrel. "Just a bit shaky, that's all." He gingerly sat down within the circle of Gribbles huddled around the Fire Stones. "There isn't anything to worry about," he added as Congar settled down next to him.

"I still think he should stay behind," persisted Trillium, but Whimbrel gave him a look of defiance and Trillium sat down again, knowing that on this rare occasion, he would not win the argument.

Whimbrel warmed his hands against the Fire Stones and listened as his fellow Gribbles discussed their plans for the journey ahead. He gently picked up Congar and holding him close, whispered, "Thank you." Congar's fur turned pink. "Words can't express what you have done for me."

As the other Gribbles re-saddled and repacked the supplies onto the backs of the Cloud Dancers, Whimbrel walked up to Freeschum and patted his sleek black neck. "It's good to see you again, my friend. For a while, I thought I never would."

"I too am glad to see you."

"I will try not to get into any more trouble." Whimbrel smiled a shy smile then slowly, gingerly, climbed up the foldable steps and seated himself on the saddle chair. As his shoulder twinged, he leaned back in the chair and sighed. "I just need to rest, that's all."

"Here, nibble this." Whimbrel looked down to see Quintell holding a long strip of black string up towards him. "Don't eat it all at once."

"What is it?" asked Whimbrel, as Congar settled onto his lap.

"I will not bore you with the name, it's far too long. Remember, nibble it. Don't eat it all at once." Quintell then clicked the steps in place and turned to leave. Whimbrel called out, "Thank you. I don't know what would have happened to me if you had not helped."

"Thank them all," said Quintell, as he turned to face him. "Without everyone's help, you'd have ended up being a snack for those things." Quintell smiled and turned away.

"Whimbrel." Whimbrel looked to see Trillium walking towards him. "Um … Are you really all right?"

Whimbrel smiled.

"Um … I … I just wanted to say … um … that … Mama and Papa. Well, they'll be pleased." Trillium shuffled his feet and stuffed his hands in his trouser pockets.

Whimbrel smiled again and wondered why Trillium was acting so strangely.

"Um … I … I'm sorry," said Trillium as he looked up at Whimbrel. His cheeks were flushed, "that I've been *soo* hard on you. But I'm glad you're still here." He then turned and rushed off.

Whimbrel watched him go. He wasn't expecting that!

The Cloud Dancers flew out of the hollow log, up above the water's surface, above the swaying mass of golden vegetation, and soared high into the powder-blue sky peppered with fluffy white clouds.

Whimbrel closed his eyes and the warmth of the sun flooded across his face, seeping into every pore of his skin. He breathed in deeply. Then his eyes snapped open as a voice whispered in his ears, *"You're safe. You're released. Live again … again … again."*

The wind whipped around his long nose and kissed him on the cheek. It then joyfully ran its fingers through the plump golden seed heads below him. He sat back and watched in awe as it danced into the distance, leaving behind a soft cool breeze.

He nibbled on the piece of black string and looked at everything around him. The colours were brighter, clearer and sharper. The smells were stronger, more aromatic, and yet somehow more delicate. The breeze felt fresher, cleaner, and now he noticed a chorus of minute voices of bugs, birds and tiny creatures drifting into his ears. He could hear a soft chittering sound and he frowned, wondering where he had heard it before. *Nowhere,* he concluded.

He looked down into the tall, thin, multi-coloured stalks flying under him at great speed and gripped the arms of his saddle chair. Hunkered down, clinging onto individual stalks, was a horde of dark green crusty faces. Large glassy eyes watched as he passed by. Long fine antennae waved back and forth and Whimbrel straightened himself and frowned as he wondered what they were. Then a multitude of whispers grew into voices, singing, *"A message we bring."*

Whimbrel frowned as the voices strengthened. *"For the world is a-changing."* He looked straight ahead but could see nothing. He looked to his left. *"Don't fear. Don't worry,"* the voices continued to say as he looked to his right. *"A message we bring."*

"Where's that coming from?" he said aloud.

The words grew in strength. *"You seek. You seek."* Whimbrel looked to his left again. *"For the world is a-changing."* He looked straight ahead and gasped in awe, as within a blink of an eye, he was surrounded by a whirr of coloured butterfly wings, darting all around him and Freeschum.

Thousands of voices exploded into a chorus, seemingly everywhere. It was a chorus singing a song he didn't understand. Whimbrel pulled Congar closer, leaned forward and nervously patted Freeschum's neck. Leaning back, he eagerly searched through the swirl of colour for his companions, but all sight of them, of the sky and of the earth below, was lost. The multitude of wings whirled, swirled and spiralled around him and his mind lost all sense of direction.

The whirlwind moved through his body, swam through his veins. His breath caught in his throat. His senses threatened to drown him. Then a single butterfly, half the size of him, appeared, hovering in front of him, and as it lowered itself towards the bar supporting the stirrups straddled across Freeschum's shoulders, Whimbrel removed his feet from the stirrups and the butterfly landed deftly upon it. Whimbrel watched as it fluttered its black and white wings, and waved its two long black antennae back and forth. It uncurled what looked like a long tongue, and as it came closer towards him Whimbrel pressed up against the back of the saddle chair, but unable to go any further, the tongue finally reached him and started probing his chest. Whimbrel sat silent until it retracted its probe into a tight coil under its chin, then erupted into song:

"You seek for one who sits and weeps,
Your kin has a heart so sweet,
Danger lingers, and yet draws near,
The Sisters shudder with despair,
They sent us to bring you near,
Before all is lost for one so dear."

Whimbrel blinked. The butterfly lifted from its perch and with a flutter of its wings, was lost within the whirr of the thousands of its own kind. Within a breath, they were scattered to the winds, as if they had been dismissed from their task by a huge hand. He watched as they fluttered away. The bubble of silence burst. The day had turned to night. Stars hung bright in the velvet sky. Beneath him lay a desolate black expanse, so vast he could not see the beginning or the end. It had replaced the mass of golden vegetation. Not a single butterfly was left in sight. All the voices were gone, and something deep down inside him was missing.

45

Scruffy, clean and dry, smelling of spring onions and rosemary, jumped up onto Ebony's four-poster bed.

"Oh, Scruffy," Ebony cried, grabbing hold of him and giving him a hug. "I'm so glad—"

Nanny Windabothem stormed into her room. Ebony looked up and cringed as she towered over her. Scruffy wriggled further back into Ebony's arms and started shivering.

"Why are you still in bed?" snarled Nanny.

"I … I … I feel sick … and … and … and my legs hurt," whispered Ebony, squeezing Scruffy even harder as her body sank deep into her pillows.

There was a knock on the door, and Nanny tossed a look to her side. As the door opened, she returned her cold eyes towards Ebony and said, "I see. Then you had better spend the day in this room and rest. I mean, I *wouldn't* want *you* to be sick. That would *never* do. *Would it?*" Nanny turned on her heels and bumped into Isobel who was walking into the room carrying a breakfast tray. She peered down at it. "A tray indeed," she spat. "It would *never* have happened in *my* day. It would never have been allowed." She stormed out of the room.

"Well," said Isobel, turning around to see if anyone was behind her. "I don't know what has upset Nanny today, but she is fuming – that is, if you haven't quite noticed. Fortunately, it is her day off and she will not be back until late." Isobel smiled as she moved towards Ebony.

"Doesn't she scare you?" asked Ebony, as Isobel set the legs of the tray on top of the bed covers.

Isobel smiled again, then said, "Nanny is only doing what she thinks is best. For instance, she told me the other afternoon that you were *not* allowed to go outside, but what did I do? I let you go out anyway, and what did *you* do? You went and got yourself *lost*." Isobel shuffled the tray in front of Ebony. "Here you go. Shoo, you, you've had yours," she said to Scruffy.

"Had his?" asked Ebony.

"Yes, he was up way too early. He came in from outside, smelling as if he'd rolled in something rotten, I'll be bound. Smelt like stinky old onions. Well, we could not have that. Nanny would have burst a blood vessel. So George gave him another bath. A right terror he was, trying to jump out of the tub. Honestly, if George hadn't caught Scruffy by his back leg I don't know what would have happened. Anyway, once clean and blow-dried, he doesn't smell so bad," Isobel laughed.

"Oh, you should have seen him, Miss Ebony, sitting there all prim and proper, loving the blow dryer, as he was being brushed. A right little lord he was. Anyway, Agnes gave him two helpings of porridge and here he is."

Ebony smiled as she watched Scruffy move to the other end of the bed where he twirled himself around, padded the woollen blanket under him, lay down, sighed as if content and closed his eyes.

Ebony knelt on the floor next to the camphorwood chest sitting at the base of her bed. Veeleeta was standing on top of it wrapped in the corner of a hanky with her tiny arm out to one side. Ebony, using a large tape measure, was wondering if this was the best way to make Veeleeta a dress.

"Oh, hi, Scruff," said Ebony, as she looked up. "It's about time you woke up, lazybones." Scruffy was standing on the end of the bed looking down at them. He seemed to have a frown on his face.

Ebony held up a piece of red and white polka-dotted fabric she'd purloined from an old doll, which was now lying naked on the floor. She held the fabric against Veeleeta's body. "I just need to figure out how to cut this, then I'll have the dress made in a jiffy. It's a bit tiny but I'm sure I can do it."

Minutes ticked by, and with scissors, needle and thread, Veeleeta was finally wearing a brand-new dress. Ebony held up a small mirror in front of her. "What do you think?"

"It's very good," answered Veeleeta. "Thank you very much." Veeleeta spun around and Ebony smiled. Ebony knew the dress wasn't really as good as Isobel could have made, but it was really nice of Veeleeta to like it so much. The stitches were a bit too big, and she could not hem it very well. Tiny bits of fabric seemed to be hanging off it at strange angles but still, it was better than nothing.

"What do you think, Scruff?" Ebony looked up, but Scruffy wasn't there.

"Do you always talk to Scruffy?" asked Veeleeta.

Ebony looked down at Veeleeta and putting her head to one side, said, "Yes. He doesn't talk back to me of course, but I pretend."

"We have a Poogle," said Veeleeta, eventually. "Well, um …

had a Poogle." Veeleeta looked down to the camphorwood chest she was standing on and her long nose drooped. "His name is, was, Congar."

"What's a Poogle?" asked Ebony. "Nanny Jones never mentioned them and why do you talk as if he is not around anymore?"

"Um ... I think he is dead."

"What!" Ebony said, shocked. 'How?"

"Well, when I fell out of the canopy of the forest he fell as well." Tears tumbled down Veeleeta's cheeks. "He was standing on a suspension bridge and it blew away."

"I am *soo* sorry," said Ebony. "What was he like?"

"Well, he came up to about here," said Veeleeta, brightening up a bit as she indicated the middle of her round tummy. "He was fluffy and round. Had no tail. No ears that you can see, but he did have tiny feet that you can't see, because they are hidden under his fur, although he could somehow spread out his fur around his tummy and glide—"

"Glide?" asked Ebony.

"Yes, like this." Veeleeta spread her arms out wide and moved them from side to side.

"Ah, I understand. Like flying squirrels."

"Um, what are they?"

Ebony looked at Veeleeta as if she was thinking. "I think it might be better if I show you a picture. Yes, I will find one in the library. I will do it later. Maybe Congar didn't die. Maybe he was able to glide to safety."

"Do you think so?" Veeleeta looked up with hope in her eyes.

"I don't know, but you never know, he could have, especially if he is as good as a flying squirrel."

"Um," Veeleeta said with a brighter tone to the word. "Well, you should see it when all the Poogles are gliding through the village. It's a sight to behold, especially when they're different colours. Anyway, Congar has a long pointy nose, and he's a reddish-brown colour most of the time."

"Changes colour?" Ebony pondered on that.

"Yes, you know red, pink, yellow, purple, that sort of thing. It depends on how he feels, of course. Oh, also he smells nice."

"Smells?"

"Well, gives off a scent, when you're sad or hurt. It's a scent that fills you up and makes you feel better. He doesn't smell all the time, only when you need his help, and we go, went, everywhere together. He would tell me all about the forest. He's very clever ... and he complained ... a lot ... but I loved him anyway."

"You mean ... you could talk to him?" Ebony looked up to where Scruffy had been standing on the mattress a short time ago. "Wouldn't it be wonderful to talk to Scruffy," she whispered. Looking back to Veeleeta she asked. "Can you talk to Scruffy?"

"Oh, err ... um, I don't know very much at the moment. I've only just started to learn how to speak to other creatures. It's supposed to be very difficult. If Trillium was here, he could talk to any animal in the forest. I'm sure he would be able to talk to him."

"Trillium?"

"He's my oldest brother. Whimbrel's still learning ... He's my other older brother. You know, older than me, but younger than Trillium."

"You have brothers? Do you have any sisters?"

"One, Arleenar, but she's only little, still crawling."

Ebony smiled as she looked at Veeleeta again. "I don't have any brothers or sisters ... but now I have you."

"Um. ... Thank you, Ebony," said Veeleeta, "for going to all this trouble. For the dress, for the food last night and this morning. This fruit, as you call it, is very nice, but I'm sorry you were upset."

"Um," said Ebony, as she looked at the floor. How could she explain to Veeleeta why she had not been able to take her to the tower last night as she had promised her? Taking a deep breath, deciding to say nothing, she looked up at Veeleeta, and said, "Would you like to do something else?"

Then came a knock on the door. Ebony quickly hid Veeleeta back in the castle as Isobel walked into the room. "It's time for lunch, Miss Ebony."

"Thank you. Um … Isobel? Can I ask you where Nanny Windabothem is?"

"I told you, it's her day off. I don't know where she actually is, but I do know she will be back late. Why?"

"Oh, nothing, I was just wondering."

"Anyhow, it's time for lunch."

As Ebony descended the long flight of stairs, her inner voice whispered, *What about Scruffy? … What? Oh? Oh!*

"Scruffy, are you coming?"

Ebony, back in her room, hummed a tune as she gathered some tubes of paint out of a basket, then stopped. She bent over and picked up a pad of watercolour paper near her left foot then moved to the Persian rug and sat down. Ebony tore pieces of paper out of the pad and arranged them across the floor. A ball suddenly landed on top of them. Ebony looked up. Scruffy was standing there looking at her. No sparkle was in his eyes.

"Stop that!" Ebony picked up the ball and threw it to the other end of the room where it landed in a pile of soft toys. She got up and walked over to her castle and opened the side of it. "Do you want to do some painting?"

Veeleeta smiled. "Painting? What is that?"

"Here, I will show you."

Ebony carried Veeleeta over to where she had placed the paper and gently put her down on top of it. Ebony smiled as she sat down. "Now I have some paints to use in different colours." She pointed to the five tubes of paint she had. "And some paper to draw on," she said, pointing to it. "Drat! Hang on a minute. I just have to grab some water. I forgot."

Ebony sprang back up and moved to her basket again. She picked out a miniature copper saucepan and went to her bedside table. She lifted the roses out of the vase, placing them on the polished floor where puddles of water formed, then carefully filled the pot with some water from the vase, replaced the roses, which now had a bit of a bent, lopsided look to them and turned back, saying, "Here we are. Hey, Scruffy, stop that!"

Scruffy's tail had just whisked Veeleeta into the air as he had walked past her.

"Veeleeta, are you all right?" Ebony dashed over to where she was scrambling to stand up.

"Yes," said Veeleeta, a bit shaken up.

Ebony spun around. "Scruffy! What do you think you're doing? Watch where you're walking."

Scruffy turned and looked at Ebony as if he didn't know *what* she was so upset about, but there was a curl to his lips, and a feeling in the back of Ebony's mind seemed to suggest he had done that on purpose.

Ebony, unsure, sat down again, placing the saucepan next to her. "We can use this, Veeleeta."

Ebony squirmed. Scruffy was now walking onto her lap, and it seemed to her that he was deliberately stomping her with heavy feet. "Will you just settle down, or you can get off," she said to him as he lay down and huffed. Then turning to Veeleeta, Ebony said, "I haven't got a brush small enough for you to paint with."

"Don't worry," said Veeleeta. "Just put some of your colours onto the edge of the paper."

Scruffy squirmed in Ebony's lap.

"Behave yourself, Scruffy. Stay put. Now, colours? Oh, you mean paints … right." Ebony squirted several puddles of coloured paint onto the corner of the paper as instructed.

Veeleeta hitched up her new dress, wiggling the four toes on each of her bare oblong feet, and paddled them in a dollop of blue paint. Ebony laughed and clapped her hands as Veeleeta started singing a song in words Ebony did not understand. Veeleeta danced across the paper, leaving a trail of little blue Gribble footprints. When her footprints grew faint, she stepped into a different colour and off she went again, singing, dancing, adding the colour to the pattern.

She then repeated the process, adding more colours, continuing to sing and dance, her nose swaying, as did her dress, until eventually she stopped dancing, stopped singing, stopped moving. She looked down at the pattern she'd created. She placed her hands on her hips and nodded, as if she was satisfied with her work. She then stood on a new sheet of paper, smiled up at Ebony and said, "What do you think?"

"Oh, that's amazing. Isn't that great, Scruffy?" Ebony brushed her hand gently across his head as he lay in her lap, looking at Veeleeta. He huffed and squirmed where he lay.

"You can sign it now," said Ebony, ignoring Scruffy's agitation.

"Sign it. What do you mean?" asked Veeleeta.

"You write your name on the painting, down the bottom."

"Why?"

"People sign them to let other people know they painted it."

"How strange." Veeleeta shrugged her shoulders, dipped a short stubby finger into the paint, and signed the painting.

Ebony looked down at the little squiggle of a signature and the swirling pattern of tiny feet on the paper.

"That's just great," said Ebony, clapping her hands again.

"Look at my feet," Veeleeta laughed as she lifted one up and wiggled her four little toes, showing that they, and her whole oblong foot, were now covered in a multitude of different coloured paints.

Ebony laughed again and said, "Right. Let's hang the picture on the wall first and then I'll clean you up."

Ebony started to push herself off the ground but found that Scruffy was refusing to move off her lap. "Will you just get off?" Ebony growled as she lifted herself up even higher, forcing Scruffy to slide towards the floor. "Oh, for goodness sakes. Get off!" Ebony finally pushed him off her lap, and then stood up. "Honestly, Scruffy, I don't know what has got into you today. If you're going to behave like this, you can go and sit on the bed."

Scruffy stared at Ebony with what looked like shock, then went and slunk back to the bed, jumped up on it, lay down and looked at her as if he was upset. Ebony watched him go and shook her head. *What is wrong with him?* A pinprick of guilt twisted inside her.

She took the painting and pinned it on the wall in a space amongst her other paintings. She then carefully picked Veeleeta up and said, "Come and have a look."

"I'll have to do something like this for my own bedroom," said Veeleeta. "I wonder if asking a beetle to walk through some colours would work."

"A beetle," laughed Ebony. "What a good idea."

Ebony found time passed fast as she and Veeleeta laughed and chatted together while Scruffy lay on the bed watching them. They put more furniture inside the castle, rearranging it into the many hidden rooms. Veeleeta told of the life she lived in her hanging village, which Ebony found absolutely fascinating, wondering what it would be like to live in. Ebony showed Veeleeta the pendant she'd been given by Nanny Jones, and the paintings and the toys she'd made with her. And still Scruffy lay perfectly still … watching.

47

Veeleeta sat in her little room. Ebony had left to go and have lunch and had locked her up in this room again. The silence within felt solid, as if it were everywhere, that was except for the never-ending vibration of sound through the walls of the ticking of a clock coming from Ebony's bedroom.

Veeleeta found it strange to play with someone, especially a giant, and actually enjoy herself. She'd never played with anyone other than Congar. It had never dawned on her that she would want to, or need the companionship of anyone except her family, and Congar of course. She just liked travelling through the ancient forest finding out about things, seeing strange plants, and creatures.

The forest. How she missed it. How she missed her parents, her home, Congar.

She looked around the little room with its bath, now empty of water, and the chair and table she was sitting at. Ebony had found her a much smaller set, one she could actually use. She looked at the flower pot. It was a thoughtful idea, considering the circumstances, and quite a clever one really, enabling her to relieve herself in that way, but really it was a bit crude. When she got back home, she decided, she would just brush over that part of her story.

That's if I make it back home, she thought. The room wasn't anything like her comfy home at all. It was definitely nothing like her lovely bedroom filled with all the little treasures she'd gathered from the forest. She frowned. As much as she liked Ebony, she could not stay. Veeleeta nodded her head. She'd made up her mind. There wasn't anything else for it, she had to escape. She had to get home.

She turned and looked towards the end of the room. There had been a noise. Also, she noticed that there was a sliver of light coming into the room from around the edges of the wall. The wall was opening. She stood up. There was something wrong, she could feel it. Scruffy's face now filled the opening. He was looking at her but there was no kindness in his eyes.

Veeleeta took a deep breath and quickly looked around. Could she make it to the next room?

Scruffy growled and pushed his muzzle further in, his eyes intent on Veeleeta.

"Scruffy," called out Veeleeta. "What are you doing?"

Scruffy's head came towards her, as he had now squeezed his front legs in as well.

Veeleeta risked it. She dashed to a side door and as she disappeared through the doorway, Scruffy growled again. The sound vibrated through the walls. The noise was terrible, as if the walls were going to tumble down, crushing her. She put her hands over her ears and cringed.

"SCRUFFY!" screamed Ebony.

Veeleeta rushed back to the doorway. Scruffy had yelped. She could see that he was being dragged backwards. Veeleeta entered the room, grabbing a chair for support, shocked at what was happening.

Scruffy yelped again, his ears scraping along the side of the walls. His front claws frantically dug into the large rug beneath them, and as he popped out of the room, like a cork from a bottle, the furniture, sitting upon it, tumbled to the floor.

"What are you doing!" yelled Ebony. She released his back legs and turned him around, grabbing him around the chest with both hands, glaring at him. "What the *heck* do you think you are *doing*? *Get away*," she growled at him. "*Get* on that bed." She put him on the ground and pushed him away with so much force he stumbled across the floor.

Ebony then turned and dropped to her knees.

"Veeleeta! Are you all right? Veeleeta!"

48

"You can't come, Scruffy," Ebony said, shaking a finger at Scruffy's sad face. "You have to stay here. What if someone catches us going to the roof? I don't want you getting into any more trouble."

Ebony very quietly opened the bedroom door, with Veeleeta safely cradled in her other hand. Behind her, she heard the scrabble of claws on the wooden floor, then felt the soft hair of Scruffy's body brush past her legs. She knew he was making a dash for the door. She quickly stuck her foot out in front of his face. He stopped abruptly. She turned to face him and growled, "No! I told you. You can't come." Scruffy backed up. "Stay here."

Ebony stuck her head out of the room and looked up and down the hallway. No one was in sight; the mansion was so silent it gave her the shivers. Even the sound of the grandfather clock ticking away the minutes, somewhere deep within its depths, seemed quieter. As she slunk out of her room, Scruffy dashed between her legs and out into the hallway. Ebony stopped. He turned and looked up at her. His tail was wagging, his ears were up, his eyes were bright and his mouth opened in a smile, but Ebony only stared at him, then through gritted teeth said, "Get … inside!"

Scruffy's tail dropped, his ears sagged and the sparkle left his eyes.

"Get inside!" Ebony pointed to the bedroom door. "I can't trust you anymore." Scruffy shuffled back into the room. Ebony slammed the door behind him, cringing at the noise. "How *dare* he defy me like that! What is wrong with him?"

Taking a deep breath to settle herself, she crept along the hall, while her heart pounded in her chest, hardly daring to breathe in case it made a sound.

"You shouldn't have treated him like that," Veeleeta scolded Ebony.

Ebony glanced down towards her. "I know but I'll … I'll make it up to him later. I don't know what has come over him."

"He is sad."

"Sad? What has he got to be sad about? Shh." Before Ebony reached the end of the hall, she stopped. "What's that?" Someone was humming. "It must be Kate."

Soft footfalls could be heard heading away from her. A door opened and then clicked shut somewhere deep within the mansion.

"Phew." Ebony's hands shook. She looked down at Veeleeta again. "Are you all right?"

"Yes," answered Veeleeta, with a slight quaver to her voice.

Ebony then continued to climb up and down stairways. She crept along many tiled hallways, long and short, always ensuring to walk on the thick rugs running their length, knowing they would muffle her footsteps.

"Ebony," whispered Veeleeta eventually.

"Yes."

"Do you ever get lost?"

Ebony didn't answer.

"You do know where you're going?"

"Um … yes … sort of," answered Ebony.

It's a good question, said Ebony to herself as she desperately tried to remember the one and only time Nanny Jones had taken her to the section of the mansion where there was a painting of blue birds above a doorway, the very doorway she was now looking for. She had taken her to the top of the tower to gaze at the stars through a telescope and learn their names.

Ebony looked atop every door she came upon and started to wonder if maybe she was looking in the wrong wing of the mansion.

Then she came to a T-junction; it was the end of a hall. She remembered this bit. A long hallway led off to her left, another went off to her right. Straight in front of her was a flagstone wall. A large bay of windows, edged by ornate orange-and-brown brocade, floor-to-ceiling curtains, was just off to the right. To the right of

258

them was a dark wooden door. Above it was the very painting she'd been searching for. It had a large flock of blue birds flying over a forest. Ebony crouched near the corner of the walls and looked around. Not even a creak or a groan could be heard; not even a spider could be seen scurrying back to its web. She made a dash for the door, grasped the round black wrought-iron handle and pushed.

"Open up. Please open," she hissed, and twisting the handle she could sense a latch had lifted. The heavy door swung inward on its well-oiled hinges. *Thank goodness.* She dashed inside. A niggling feeling bothered the back of her mind, but she took no notice as she closed the door just enough to allow a small sliver of light to still shine through the gap. She turned back to face the darkness. In the shadows she could see that she was in a round room. The hint of well-worn stone steps curved off to the left, disappearing into the darkness. She looked up into the pitch-black void above her. It felt like a huge heavy emptiness and her body shuddered at the thought of what was hidden within the cold empty tower.

"It's very dark in here," said Veeleeta.

"It's all right. We will be fine," lied Ebony. She swallowed hard as she tried to lose the terror that had just risen in her throat when she realised the rest of the staircase disappeared into the darkness ahead and she was actually going to have to go into it.

Ebony's hand trembled as she searched for the solid wall. Upon touching the cool brickwork, she sighed then slid her fingers along its rough surface, her feet shuffling towards the first step.

Ebony's heart beat faster, and dark visions of spiders, rats and ghosts crowded her mind as she clambered up the ancient stairway. The light in the stairwell was fading when Ebony crinkled her nose and said, "What's that smell? It smells like a dirty toilet."

"Toilet. What's that?" squeaked Veeleeta's tiny voice. "Is everything all right?"

"Yes. Yes. I'm fine. I'll explain later." Ebony took one more step, turned the corner of the stairway and was plunged into the darkest, thickest, inkiest blackness she'd ever known. It was as if the air around her had suddenly become solid. Veeleeta gasped.

"It's … it's all right, Veeleeta," whispered Ebony, but she could hear sounds of things hiding in the darkest corners. Something was scurrying away from her. "Don't … don't worry." A cold hand gripped at Ebony's heart and she flattened her back up against the cold stone, pulling Veeleeta even closer to her. Ebony's breathing grew deeper, heavier and raspier as if she now had a knot in her throat. Visions of unknown fears filled her mind. It felt as if she was swimming in a whirlpool and she told herself, *Calm down. Calm down. Breathe … slowly. Bre-ath-e! You'll be all right.*

Then as her thoughts settled, and her breathing calmed, she pushed herself away from the safety of the wall. Her fingers fumbled across the rough surface of the stonework again. Her footfalls softly echoed around her as she continued to climb the stone steps she could not see.

"Ebony, I'm scared." Veeleeta's small voice trembled.

"It's all right," Ebony assured her, even though her own voice shook. "Don't worry. We're nearly there." She cupped her hand around Veeleeta's tiny warm body just a little bit tighter, then told herself, *Don't squash her … I will not!*

Step after step Ebony carried on, forever upwards, and then a coolness caressed her cheek. She peered into the darkness ahead.

"Look!"

Pinpricks of light had appeared at the top of the stairs. "Oh, thank goodness," she sighed. Then as she progressed up the few remaining steps, the tiny dots grew into small shafts of sunlight stabbing into the darkness.

"The hatchway." Ebony quickened her pace.

Upon reaching the top of the stairs, she felt she was in a small room. The slashes of light indicated a doorway that was only a quarter of the height of a normal door, and Ebony gingerly lowered herself onto her knees, continuing to hold Veeleeta to her chest.

There was another small shaft of light peeking through a tiny hole halfway down on the right-hand side.

"The keyhole," she called out and fumbling just above this dot of light, found the door handle, grabbed hold of it and pulled. "Open up. Open … up."

It wouldn't budge.

"Ebony, maybe we should go back. I don't want to be trapped in here."

"It's all right, Veeleeta. Don't worry. There must be a key somewhere." Ebony's fingers started searching in the darkness.

"Don't you know?"

"Yes of course I do … Well actually, no, I don't, but it must be here somewhere. It's only logical." Ebony's fingers continued to run along the edge of the dusty frame. "Let's see … Ugh!"

"What?"

"Spider webs." Ebony shivered.

"Ebony!" cried Veeleeta, as she grabbed hold of one of Ebony's fingers. "Spiders. What are they?"

"Don't worry, I'll show you a picture … Aha. Here we are. I've found it."

Ebony's fingers felt around a small metal key that was cool and clean to the touch. Another niggle worried her, but again she took no note.

The key was sitting on a small nail located up on the right-hand side of the wooden frame of the hatchway, just like the key to the back door of the kitchen.

She inserted the key into the keyhole and it turned very stiffly. With a bit more force, a loud click echoed in her ears and she pulled on the handle again. Still, it wouldn't budge. Frustrated, Ebony pushed the little door and it flung open. The afternoon sun chased the darkness away. Ebony poked her head out, blinked and took in a deep breath of the cool fresh air.

"Aha … thank goodness. There you are, Veeleeta, we made it."

Ebony shuffled forward and then stood up. The breeze caressed her face and playfully tousled her long hair as if greeting her for the first time, and she looked around. She was standing in an area not more than a few feet wide, and yet its length disappeared on either side of her around the large curve of the building. The outer edge was surrounded by a wide stone parapet and as she looked over the top of it, she sucked in her breath and instantly backed away. "Crumbs!"

She'd never been very good with heights. Taking another deep breath and willing herself to be brave and not look down, she slowly moved over to the edge. She hesitantly rested her hand on the lichen-covered stonework. She looked out to the forest surrounding her on all sides as far as she could see. It was clothed in its finest greenery with the occasional tree splashed with pink, yellow and light grey. *Light grey? That's a strange colour for a tree to be,* she absentmindedly thought.

"Ebony, what are you doing?" Veeleeta's muffled voice said.

"Oh, sorry." Ebony gently placed Veeleeta on top of the parapet, making sure that her hand kept her from getting too close to the edge. "Veeleeta, you live in there, somewhere." She pointed in the direction of the huge forest spreading across the entire horizon.

Veeleeta stood on her tiptoes and grabbed hold of the side of Ebony's hand, then gasped. Her nose drooped and her skin turned pale as she stared out into the distance.

"Veeleeta, is everything ok?"

Veeleeta didn't say anything. Silent tears were running down her pale cheeks.

"I'm sure we can work out where you live," lied Ebony.

Still, Veeleeta said nothing. As the silence grew, Ebony growled to herself, *This is all my fault … I should have left her in the forest.* Ebony's eyes looked at the stone floor and watched as a bug scuttled into a small mound of moss between the crevices of the ancient stonework.

When she looked up again, Veeleeta was sitting down, her little body shaking and her shoulders trembling.

"Veeleeta, please, it will be all right. Somehow it will be all right."

"No, it will not," sobbed Veeleeta. "I'm never going to see my family ever again."

Ebony looked down at Veeleeta's tiny body, and as her heart started to ache for the Gribble's pain, tears trickled down her own cheeks. She didn't have a clue where Veeleeta lived in the forest, let alone how to get her back there.

"Veeleeta," Ebony called softly. "Please stop crying. I'm sure we can figure something out … Veeleeta … Please."

Veeleeta slowly lifted her head and stood up. She looked out across the forest and mumbled, "I never knew the forest was so big. No, not big. That's not the word for it. Huge. Yes, that's the word … No … huge isn't correct, maybe …"

"Veeleeta," Ebony called softly as she got down onto her knees. She was now on the same eye level as Veeleeta, who slowly turned and looked into Ebony's eyes. "I'm so sorry, Veeleeta," said Ebony. "I didn't mean to hurt you. Really I didn't. I just didn't know what you were, when I first found you. I was so excited, and I didn't know what to do. I didn't think … about you, only about what I wanted." Ebony's voice trailed away, knowing that finally she had told the truth.

"I understand. I do. Really I do," said Veeleeta, in a voice that quivered as she spoke. "But all I want to do is go home. You do understand, don't you?"

Ebony said nothing. Her heart ached and her eyes became blurred with tears.

"You're right," continued Veeleeta. "I'm sure you will think of something."

A tiny sparkle of light, off to Ebony's left, reflected off the spire of the church steeple far in the distance. "Do you see the little red roofs and the church steeple?" Ebony pointed to it. "My Nanny Jones lives in that village now. She's going to get married and have a child of her own one day." A pain shot through Ebony's heart and she rubbed her chest where the pendant lay; the area had grown warm.

Ebony continued to look at the village as a little voice whispered inside her brain, *The sun is going down.*

So? she answered.

The … sun … is … going down! the voice yelled and then as if some kind of fog within her mind had lifted, Ebony said aloud, "Crumbs! Nanny!"

Ebony scooped Veeleeta up in her hand.

"We have to get out of here," she said, as she clambered through the hatch, closed and locked the door, replaced the key on its nail and then stopped.

"What's the matter?" called out Veeleeta. Ebony didn't answer. Her eyes had flared as they desperately tried to readjust to the darkness all around her. *You have no time for this,* she scolded herself. Quickly placing her right shoulder against the wall, she rushed down the steps as fast as she dared, even though she could not see where she was going. *SLOW DOWN!* she screamed at herself, as her fingers flew across the rough surface of the stone. *Slow down!* Her footfalls echoed all around her and as she finally clambered around the last curve of the spiral staircase, she looked down the flight of steps to the circular floor below. *Oh, thank goodness. It's getting lighter,* she thought, but, as she went down two more steps, she frowned. *There is too much light.* She could now see that the large wooden door was wide open. *I didn't leave it like that.*

Scruffy barked and rushed through the doorway. Ebony stopped.

"What are you doing here? I left you in the bedroom."

"Well, well, well, if it isn't little Miss Ebony."

49

"What is that?" Whimbrel cried, looking upon an immense dark structure that travelled right up into the sky, blocking out wide bands of stars, taking up the whole world. He trembled as he looked upon rows of windows sparkling with yellow light, looking like eyes watching him, but there were also large sections of utter darkness interspersed between them.

"Quick. Hide!" yelled Grigwell.

"Where?" Whimbrel shouted back.

"Follow us."

Stellman, the Cloud Dancer that Grigwell rode, dashed forward and headed for a splash of dark greenery to his left. He dived under the leaves of an unusual plant and the rest of the group followed. The Gribbles quickly dismounted. They pushed past stems and leaves of strange plants, eventually huddling under a protective cloak of interwoven vegetation that blocked out much of the radiated light.

"What is it?" whispered Whimbrel, as he peeped through a gap in the leaves. A shiver ran down his back. The structure wavered then started toppling towards him. He cringed, closing his eyes, waiting for it to fall but it never came. He looked back up. It was still there, solid. It had not moved.

Someone touched him on the arm. He flinched then looked to his left. Grigwell had crawled up next to him. "Come."

He, and everyone else, slowly moved towards the base of a large boulder and huddled together.

"We have reached the giant's home," whispered Quintell.

"Is that what it is?" said Whimbrel.

Quintell glanced at him and went on. "We have arrived under the cover of darkness, which is a blessing. I thought it would take us another day to get here after our detour."

"It must have been the butterflies," said Grigwell.

"What do you mean?" asked Quintell.

"They must have somehow—"

"The song," interrupted Whimbrel. "It sang me a song."

"What song? Who sang you a song?" inquired Trillium.

"The butterfly. There was a big black and white butterfly in the middle of them all. It sang a song to me."

"I don't understand," said Trillium.

"Sing it," commanded Grigwell, before Whimbrel could reply.

Whimbrel looked at him and blushed. He twiddled his stubby fingers, shuffled his feet and then, taking a deep breath, sang.

"What does it mean?" asked Fluellen, after Whimbrel had finished.

"It means," said Grigwell, "that we're in the right place."

Suddenly a bright red light flared from the middle of Trillium's chest. Out of the middle of it, a tingly high-pitched crystalline voice screeched out Veeleeta's name.

Whimbrel looked at Trillium and shaded his anxious eyes.

"HELP HIM!" someone screamed. Whimbrel thought it might have been him.

"HOW?" someone else screamed back. No one moved as Trillium stood with his arms spread out wide, his eyes shut, and a look of fright frozen upon his face.

The light from Trillium's chest started fading, then as it disappeared, he collapsed to the ground.

"Trillium!" Whimbrel rushed to his side, as did the other Gribbles.

Trillium's eyes opened and he blinked them rapidly. He tried to say something but nothing came out of his mouth. He slowly sat up, took in a deep breath and grabbed at his chest. He undid the buttons on his tunic, removed the small pouch from around his neck and tipped the ruby onto his palm.

Everyone leaned in to have a look. A tiny sparkle of light lingered deep within its centre, and as they looked further in,

Bedlow Manor

it seemed as if a small face looked back at them. They all stepped back with shock, then leaned in again for a closer look.

"That's amazing," said Quintell. "I wonder ..." but Quintell's words faded away.

Whimbrel looked up and said, "You wonder what?"

Quintell didn't answer; he just looked up at the giant's home.

"Grigwell, didn't you say this ruby was one of the Sisters from the Depths?" asked Fluellen.

"Yes."

"I don't want to sound ignorant, but is that a title given to all the rubies or is it the name of this *particular* ruby?"

"There are seven Sisters of the Depths," said Whimbrel, and everyone turned to look at him. "They are the servants of the Swanlings. They do their bidding. This is their doing."

"How do you know this?" asked Grigwell.

"It's common knowledge," answered Whimbrel.

"No, actually ... it is ... not," answered Grigwell. Everyone, even the Cloud Dancers, stared at Whimbrel now. "What else is common knowledge?" asked Grigwell.

Whimbrel shrugged and then winced as he clutched at his arm. "I don't know. All I do know is that this ruby is announcing that it is here."

"Announcing it to whom? How do you know this?" enquired Quintell.

Again, Whimbrel shook his head to indicate that he did not know.

Quintell looked at Grigwell, then at the ruby, then up at Trillium. "We ... I mean your papa and I ... didn't think ... didn't know the stone could do anything, other than heal Gribbles, that is. We had been able to find out that much about it, but we knew no more."

"What do you mean?" enquired Trillium, standing up.

"Your papa and his companion, at the time," continued Quintell, "were each given a ruby as a gift by the Swanlings."

"Why didn't you tell us this before?" questioned Trillium.

"How?" asked Fluellen. "Why did they do that?"

"Why did the Swanlings give this to Papa?" asked Trillium.

"Why didn't he tell us about it?" complained Whimbrel.

Quintell didn't answer.

"Quintell," called Grigwell softly. Receiving no reply, he called again, "Quintell."

Quintell looked up.

"If this Sister is here," said Grigwell, "and it is announcing that it *is*, then are you saying that it's calling out to another Sister ... in there?" He pointed to the giant's home.

Quintell nodded yes.

"This means that ... Papa's companion ... is in there as well," stated Trillium.

Quintell nodded again.

"Do you mean Veeleeta has it?" asked Fluellen.

"No."

"Do you mean there is another Gribble in there?" asked Whimbrel.

"No." Quintell dropped his gaze towards the ruby again. "I mean Veeleeta might be, but no ..."

"Then who ... or what?" asked Grigwell, with a touch of irritation in his voice. "What are you talking about?"

Quintell looked up. "It's a giant."

"What!"

"How?"

"What do you mean?"

"It was a child of the giants twenty summers ago. It got lost in the forest. Your papa saved it ... This isn't the time to discuss it," said Quintell, as he quickly snatched the ruby from Trillium's palm and replaced it in the pouch.

"How can you say that?" questioned Trillium, snatching the pouch back. "We need to know."

"No! Quintell is right," stated Grigwell. "We must save Veeleeta first. There is a real puzzle here, a real conundrum," Grigwell turned towards Quintell, "and one day I will be only too glad to sit down with you and Snailum and work it all out."

"It will do you no good," said Quintell. "I told you before, Snailum will not talk about it."

"We will see," said Grigwell. "But in the meantime, we must rescue Veeleeta."

Whimbrel turned and looked up at the huge mansion. It was as if it was staring back down at them all, like some huge dark menace. "And how are we going to do that? Look at the size of that thing. There is no way we can search for Veeleeta tonight."

50

Veeleeta found herself flying through the air and landing with an *umph* in a corner of a cold stone step. Looking up, she saw Ebony bending down towards Scruffy. She was pointing her finger at him and hissing the word, "Stay!" Ebony then stood up and walked down the few remaining steps, leaving Veeleeta where she was.

Veeleeta, covered in dust and cobwebs, scrambled to her feet in time to see Ebony reach the base of the spiral staircase. A huge giant hand emerged out of the shadows and grabbed hold of Ebony's arm. Veeleeta's eyes opened in wonder and fear. Then a harsh voice echoed within the tower. "*What* were you doing up there?"

"N-nothing, Nanny," stammered Ebony. Her shoulders slumped as the hand, which had now grown an arm, dragged her towards the doorway.

"Don't lie to me," the voice spat. The thin silhouette of a tall, thin giant pulled Ebony out into the lit hallway beyond. "I know you were up to something. I've seen the rooms in your ..." The words faded away.

Veeleeta looked at Scruffy. He had started walking down the stairs, away from her.

"Scruffy," she called out as she rushed up to the edge of the step. He stopped and turned his head back towards her. His eyes looked at her as if she were a wonder.

The light in the hallway abruptly switched off and Veeleeta gasped as she was plunged into darkness. "Ebony said, um ... you were to stay here ... with me," stammered Veeleeta.

Scruffy's huge body, silhouetted against the evening light pouring through the doorway, stood rigid. Veeleeta was unsure what to do. If only Trillium was here, he would be able to understand Scruffy's language and explain to him she needed his help. As her night vision now allowed her to see him much better than before, even though the shadows still flickered across his face every time he moved, she decided that the only thing she could do was attempt to communicate with him. She had to get him to understand.

"Scruffy," Veeleeta said, taking it slowly. "I … need … your … help."

A growl from within Scruffy's chest resonated through the room. Veeleeta shivered. A little voice in the back of her mind was niggling at her. *There is something wrong, something very wrong. He is not listening to me.*

"Scruffy," Veeleeta called out as he moved towards her. *Be careful,* her inner voice warned. His large black eyes were staring at her. Then he stopped and tilted his head to one side as if he was thinking, looking at something that wasn't there.

Veeleeta cringed and slowly backed up into the corner between the step and the rock wall.

Scruffy's head bent down and he looked at her, making his eyes darker, and it was difficult to know what he was thinking about, but she could feel him staring at her again nonetheless.

"Scruffy!" squeaked Veeleeta's little voice. "What are you doing?"

He moved in very close now. He bared his teeth.

Veeleeta gasped and flattened herself against the cold hard stone. She could discern Scruffy's huge mouth, full of sharp teeth. It was coming nearer until Veeleeta could smell his breath. His nose was now so close she could have touched it. She gulped.

Willing herself to be brave, she suddenly stood up straight with her hands outstretched before her, then using the edge of her tiny hand, she hit the base of Scruffy's nose with it. Scruffy whimpered and backed off, shaking his head. Veeleeta stood rigid with her feet slightly apart, hands up in front of herself. "I'll attack you again, Scruffy, if you try to hurt me."

Scruffy shook his head again and turned away, heading down the stairs.

"Where are you going?" cried Veeleeta. She dashed to the edge of the step. "Scruffy. You can't leave me here … E-Ebony said you had to stay here … with me."

But Scruffy continued to shake his head and trotted out into the hallway, disappearing from view.

Well, you did a good job there, Veeleeta, she said to herself.

She looked at the walls surrounding her, but all she could see were shadows bleeding into the blackness. She shivered and scurried back into the corner of the step, pressing her body against the cold stone. The air was tainted with a sour smell she could taste but she did not know where it was coming from.

The minutes ticked by and she wondered what had happened to Ebony. Was she ever going to come back? *What is going to happen to me now?* Her heart sank at the thought.

Veeleeta crept up to the edge of the step again, looking down at the pale moonlight splashed across the flagstone floor beyond the door. *It's getting darker by the minute. I've got to get out of here.* She looked at the step below, so very far away. She looked behind her. The next step was so high above her, she knew she could not reach it. Its smooth surface would make it impossible to climb up it. She did the only thing she could: she settled herself back down in the cold dusty corner and waited. Her tummy rumbled from lack of food, and she shivered from the cold that had started to seep into her tiny body.

Veeleeta awoke, surprised she'd even slept. All her senses were tingling. She leaned forward and looked around, feeling something was wrong. Patches of faded moonlight still reflected onto the dark floor below. A scraping sound came from above. She stiffened and looked in its direction. Something squeaked and scuttled below her. She scrambled forward and saw the silhouette of a large sleek creature scurry across the flagstones, only to be lost in the edge of the darkness below. It had whiskers on the end of its pointy nose and a very long tail. A shiver ran down Veeleeta's spine, and she rushed back to the corner of her prison.

She listened to the scuttling, scratching, screeching sound moving over the steps below her, and eventually, she moved hesitantly to the edge of her step and peered over it again. Two small bright-red eyes blinked into existence. Veeleeta snapped herself back against the corner of the hard stone. Everywhere she looked, red eyes were now blinking in the darkness, getting closer and closer with every second. High-pitched squeaking and screeching reverberated out of the pitch-black shadows, and she held her breath as a foul smell, so sharp it made her eyes water, filled the air. Gasping for breath she gulped in large amounts of the tainted air, and coughed and coughed. She felt sick.

What is that stench?

It reminded her of when her papa cleaned out the pipes of the waste areas of their hanging house.

Veeleeta froze, all thoughts gone. Two dark sleek shadows had appeared from the step below, and as they solidified into black silhouettes, large unknown creatures leaned up against the edge of the step she was sitting on. Two pairs of red eyes stared at her. The smell of rotten food drifted into her nostrils. She didn't dare look, but something told her she had to. She looked above her. Another set of eyes had blinked into existence. Veeleeta's mind started to spin. She could not think. A tiny voice squeaked inside her, *what am I going to do?* but there was no answer, just a sick swirling sensation that had built up in the pit of her stomach. She turned to face her doom.

Suddenly the eyes blinked out. The sound of scuttling exploded all around her. The creatures rushed off, screeching in all directions back into the darkness from where they had come. Veeleeta faced the nothingness that lay before her, to find that huge shadows were now flickering over the surface of the walls surrounding her. She crawled forward. A ball of pale light bobbed in the darkness, floating above the flagstone. Veeleeta pressed back into the corner of the step. Silence hung in the air as the light moved closer. She tried to make herself as small as she could. She tried to close her eyes but they refused to shut. The flickering light was now level with her step. Her mind yelled, *It's coming to get me! It's going to drag me away to Chareen. Move! Run! … Where to?* She gasped. A floating hand stretched out to grab hold of her, and everything went black.

"It's not fair! It's not fair!" Whimbrel yelled as he kicked out at a pebble on the ground, and cringed as his foot found it. "Why have I got to stay behind?" He sucked in his long nose, making it look like a short snout, then crossed his arms and glared at Freeschum. *It's not his fault,* he told himself. He sighed, letting his shoulders and nose slump as he uncrossed his arms and let them fall to his side.

Freeschum looked up with a disinterested expression, then returned to inspecting his toenails as he lay in the shade of a large-leafed plant.

"Do the washing up, Whimbrel," Whimbrel continued moaning as he paced up and down. "Do the packing, Whimbrel. Feed the Cloud Dancers, Whimbrel."

Whimbrel caught Freeschum looking up at him again and he threw himself down on a blanket and winced at the slight pain in his shoulder. He crossed his arms again. "Why could I not go with them? The butterfly gave *me* the message about Veeleeta, not them. It's not fair. They wouldn't even listen to me. Oh no, and now here I'm stuck looking after the *supplies.* Even Congar got to go with them. It's *not* fair. Just because Fluellen has her sight back and thinks she can work out where Veeleeta is. It's not fair." Whimbrel put his chin down on his chest, and his nose slumped accordingly.

"What was that?"

A thud came from somewhere behind him. He got up and crept past the boulders and through the tangle of stems and leaves. He pulled back a large furry silver-grey leaf. A field of rough grey stones flowing across the landscape in front of him was revealed, and he froze. A huge, brown, short-haired creature, with four large feet, a long tail and a shiny black nose was walking towards him.

"Whimbrel."

Whimbrel flinched and turned to see Freeschum, who had walked up quietly behind him.

"Don't do that," whispered Whimbrel through clenched teeth. "Look." He pointed towards the creature. "What do you think?"

"About?" questioned Freeschum.

"About that." Whimbrel shook his arm in the creature's direction. "Don't you think it could have been the creature that left the prints in the clearing? Trillium said it had four large feet, and look at the size of them. They would fit the tracks he told me about." Whimbrel turned and looked at Freeschum, whose eyes stared back at him with no readable expression. "Well?" he asked.

Freeschum said nothing.

"Well, I think it is." Whimbrel turned back to watch the creature as it sauntered closer. "Wait here. I'll be back in a moment."

Whimbrel crawled back to the supplies and quickly pulled a Peeloo torch from a backpack. Carrying it over his good shoulder, he silently returned to Freeschum's side.

"You're doing what?" asked Freeschum.

"I'm going to find out if it took Veeleeta."

"Unwise."

Whimbrel snorted, then slapped his hand over his mouth. *Quiet!* he scolded himself.

The creature was very close now. Whimbrel could hear it breathing. He and Freeschum crept through the undergrowth to their left and watched as a black and white butterfly fluttered past the creature's nose.

I wonder if that's the same one that sang to me? thought Whimbrel. He whispered to Freeschum, "Fly up to the creature's head."

"Unwise."

"Just do it," he growled, and he climbed into the saddle chair, resting his torch across his lap.

Freeschum flew out from amongst the plants, keeping close to the ground. He headed straight towards the creature that had stopped to watch the butterfly fluttering in front of its face. While the creature was distracted, Whimbrel lifted the torch and settled it under his right arm. He scrambled up onto the saddle chair and crouched, holding on tight to the arm of the saddle chair as Freeschum flew up in front of the creature's nose.

This is crazy, yelled Whimbrel at himself, but before he could think another thought he had thrown himself out of his saddle chair, landing on the bridge of the creature's muzzle which was covered in short thick hair. He immediately stood up amongst the rough spiky hair, waved his glowing torch in front of its eyes, and yelled, "Stop!"

The creature frowned and stared at him.

"Where is Veeleeta?" Whimbrel brandished his glowing torch in front of its eyes.

The creature now glared at Whimbrel, then, as if realisation had dawned, it lifted its bushy eyebrows and opened its eyes wide.

"Where is Veeleeta?"

The creature continued to look at him as if it hadn't understood the question or worse, was refusing to answer it.

I'll get you to tell me where my sister is, Whimbrel said to himself. He turned around and lifted his Peeloo torch high into the air, then bringing the glowing end down, he jabbed it onto the creature's shiny black nose. Flesh sizzled, and a sickening waft of smoke trailed up into the air. The creature yelped, threw its head up and dashed off. Whimbrel fell forward with an *umph* and the wind was knocked out of him. The torch, dropping out of his hand, toppled to the ground. He hung on tight to the strands of hair as Freeschum yelled out, "Whimbrel, hold on! Hold on! Hold! On!"

Whimbrel slid from side to side as the creature yelped and bucked, thrashing its head to and fro. It then stopped, raised one of its enormous paws up to its nose and raked large black claws along the side of it. Whimbrel groaned as one of them caught his shoulder and lifted him high into the air, whereupon he landed with a thud on the hard rocky ground. Gingerly he stood up and rubbed his shoulder, then he felt hot breath, smelling of spicy herbs, rush over his body. He froze. He looked at bared teeth, huge, white and sharp, that were now within touching distance. A low rumble vibrated up from somewhere deep within the creature's chest. He looked up at the huge black shiny nose quivering and sniffing him, and then the creature bent its head low, and piercing brown eyes, flashing with fire, glared back at him. Whimbrel took a step back.

The creature shook its head.

Whimbrel planted his feet on the ground, braced himself and then yelled up to it, "Where's my sister? Where's Veeleeta?"

Freeschum landed next to him, and sighing with relief, Whimbrel quickly clambered back into the saddle chair.

Freeschum asked, "You are well?"

"Yes. Get me closer. We can't back out now. It seems it understands me, even if I don't understand what it's saying. That's a start."

Freeschum flew up to the creature's eye level and hovered in front of its face.

"Where's my sister?"

Then as if the creature did actually understand what was being said, the fire instantly died from within its eyes. It turned and looked at the home of the giants, turned back and looked at Whimbrel with piercing eyes.

Veeleeta bolted upright and breathed deeply. Gone was the smothering darkness of the tower, the creatures with red glowing eyes; now there was only soft daylight. Gone was the biting cold that had seeped into every particle of her body; now the air was warm and felt like one of her mama's hugs. It made her eyes prickle with tears just at the thought. Gone was the foul stench that had made her stomach churn. Now the air was filled with the scent of roses. *Roses* ... Veeleeta's mind pondered as it struggled to remember. She looked up at the paintings on the wall, then at the two huge stained-glass windows opposite her. "I'm back. I'm back in the castle. But how?"

The bedroom wall slid open and pale morning light framed Ebony's smiling face. "Oh, Veeleeta, I'm so glad you're all right."

"Ebony! That was you?" Veeleeta jumped out of bed and rushed towards Ebony.

"Yes, and I'm *so* sorry about last night but I ... I just could not think of what else to do. When Nanny turned up like that, I just could not think. It would be terrible if she knew about you. She must never find out ... I don't know what she'd do to you."

"Ebony ..." whispered Veeleeta, as she slowed her steps. "I was very frightened. There ... there were huge creatures there, with big red eyes, and *terrifying* noises." Veeleeta stopped and held her hands out in front of her in a subconscious plea for Ebony to understand how frightened she'd been. "If you had not come and saved me, I don't know what would have happened." Veeleeta's arms fell to her sides and her shoulders slumped, her long nose drooped.

"I'm so sorry, Veeleeta. I just didn't know what else to do. You are all right, aren't you?"

"Yes … but I'm … I mean I want—" Veeleeta looked up, and pleaded with her eyes for Ebony to understand.

"I'm so glad," Ebony interrupted. "Are you hungry?" Ebony lifted the edge of her nightie out of the way and pushed herself off the floor. "I'll get you something to eat."

"Ebony."

"Yes." Ebony slowly dropped back to her knees. "Yes, of course, silly of me. I forgot. We have to think about what we're going to do to … um, get you back home. In the meantime, you could tell me some more stories about your village. It sounds so exciting."

"Ebony … I have to talk—"

"It must be so interesting" Ebony interrupted again, "with Poogles, and Cloud Dancers, and all those other amazing creatures …"

"Ebony—" said Veeleeta, again.

"What did you call them? Babacoots at the Glade of Sharon. No, that's not right. Shanno … no … um … Sharoon."

"Ebony—" called Veeleeta.

"No. It's all right, I'll get the name in a minute. Let me see—"

"EBONY!" screamed Veeleeta.

Ebony stopped babbling and looked down at Veeleeta. She bit her lip.

"I've been so pleased to know you," said Veeleeta, in a soft voice. "Really I have, but I've—"

"We could do some more painting," whispered Ebony. Her eyes filled with tears and her cheeks flushed. She scratched her skin where the pendant lay.

"Ebony. I miss my family."

Ebony looked back at Veeleeta as a tear trickled down her freckled cheek.

"I have to go home," said Veeleeta. "I *need* to go home … I'm *soo* sorry. I really am, but … I cannot stay. I just can't."

"But … don't you like it here? Don't you like … me?"

"Yes … Yes, of course, I do … I like it very much. You've shown me things I would *never* have seen. The forest. I never knew it was so huge. Giants. You were only stories told around the Fire

Stones. I never believed that you, giants I mean, actually existed but here you are."

Veeleeta smiled as she splayed her hands out in front of her and said, "But I'm sorry, I really am. I just can't stay here any longer. I have to go home."

"I understand," whispered Ebony, sounding as if she didn't really want to understand.

Veeleeta looked up into Ebony's face. Her cheeks were flushed pink. Her freckles had turned dark as tears continued to trickle over the top of them. Then Ebony slumped in front of the castle, turning her back on Veeleeta, and said, "Why is it everyone I love leaves?" She sat hugging her knees and added, "My parents are always going away. They are never here, well, not for very long anyway."

Veeleeta climbed up the folds of Ebony's nightdress, making her way to Ebony's shoulder.

"Now you want to go away."

Veeleeta walked across the top of Ebony's left arm.

"My grandmother died. Nanny Jones left and even Isobel will leave me one day." Ebony dropped her head and started to sob.

Veeleeta ran along Ebony's hand and jumped onto the top of her left knee.

"I ... I ... treated Nanny Jones ... so ... so ... very badly," Ebony whispered between her sobs. "She had always been so lovely to me, and I love her so much, but she left me anyway. She'd been my only nanny ever since I was a baby, and that was a long time ago, but a year and a half ago, when my parents told me she was leaving ... I ... I just could not believe it. They sat me down. I always know something is wrong when they sit me down. It's always bad news. But I never dreamed she would leave me."

"I'm sorry, Ebony, but really I ..."

"I screamed at her," Ebony said, looking into Veeleeta's eyes. "I tried to stop myself, but my mouth wouldn't shut up. I told her that she could not go."

Veeleeta sat down on top of Ebony's knee and looked at her.

"I just could not stop screaming. I begged her not to go. But she didn't say anything. She just stood up and walked out of the room. I lost my head. I started throwing things." Ebony burst into tears.

Veeleeta patted Ebony on the knee and said, "What happened?"

The minutes ticked by and Veeleeta wondered, *How am I ever going to be able to leave now?*

Ebony stopped crying, her body relaxed and she looked up at Veeleeta who asked again, "What happened?"

"My father picked me up and took me to my room, but I think I kicked him on the shin or something like that. I can't remember really."

Veeleeta put her hands over her mouth and stared at Ebony.

"I didn't mean it. Really I didn't. I was just so upset."

"I'm sure he understands," Veeleeta said as she patted Ebony's knee again. "Papas do, you know." Veeleeta felt her heart sink inside her.

"Do they? Then why did they send me away to boarding school? Why did they listen to that doctor, and Nanny Windabothem? She planned it all," said Ebony, with anger in her voice. "She talked everyone into getting rid of me. I never see anyone anymore." There was real sadness and bitterness catching in her throat. "Mum and Dad are always away on business, ever since I was very young. They are never here. I now have to stay at boarding school all the time. I *hate* it."

"Oh ... um ... but your dad must love you. Look at the beautiful gift he gave you," Veeleeta said, while a tiny voice inside her head cried, *This is terrible. Just terrible. I'll never be able to go home now.*

Ebony flicked her head back towards the castle, then turned back and looked at Veeleeta. "Maybe. I suppose. They are always bringing me gifts from all over the world, but I don't want gifts, I just want them to stay home. I would give them all back if only they would stay home with *me*. And I don't think I will ever see my Nanny Jones again."

Veeleeta stared at her. "Why?"

"Oh, because I ... I told her I hated her." Ebony bit her lip, then burst into tears again. "I don't! Really I don't. She's like a second mother to me. I miss her *soo* much."

"I'm sure she knows that." Veeleeta leaned forward and continued to pat Ebony's knee, not knowing what else to do as a tear trickled down her own cheek. All hope of leaving was now lost. "She wouldn't have sent you that lovely necklace if she believed you really hated her."

Ebony looked up and smiled a half-hearted smile, and then grasped the pendant lying around her neck.

"She didn't come to my party." Ebony's eyes were red-rimmed, and her cheeks were blotchy. Silence filled the space between them. "I'm so glad you're here, Veeleeta. I've not told anyone about what I did. I've been feeling so terrible. Thank you. I ... I feel a lot better."

"Oh, but you have ... What is her name? Nanny Winda ... Windabothem."

"She hates me," Ebony said, letting go of the pendant.

"Oh, surely not."

"She's not really a nanny, not like Nanny Jones was. She just insists that I call her that. She's only been here for a year and a half, but she has hated me from the very first day she turned up. Do you know what she did? I put on my best dress, the one covered in lavender flowers. Nanny Jones had always said that I looked a real picture in it. Scruffy and I made her a daisy chain as a gift ..." Ebony then fell into silence, as if she was remembering something.

"What's a daisy chain? I've never heard of them."

"Oh, well," said Ebony, with a strangled laugh in her voice. "They are made out of tiny pink and white daisies, the ones that grow in the fields by the thousands. I linked them all together and made one for Scruffy, but he lost his. I think he did that on purpose. I made one for Nanny as a welcoming gift ... but I found it later."

Ebony looked down at her nightie, and then looked back up at Veeleeta again and said, "It was sitting on a hall table all scrunched up into a tight ball. Why did she do that? She destroyed it!" Tears trickled down Ebony's cheeks. "I was only trying to be nice."

Veeleeta bit her lip and said, "Did Nanny Windabothem like your beautiful dress?"

"No. No, she did not." Ebony frowned. "Before I was sent away to boarding school, she took everything away. All my dresses, my paintings, my toys, and hid them away in a cupboard. I've now found out that she lied to everyone, saying I had got rid of them myself because I was so upset about my grandmother dying and Nanny Jones leaving. But it was her. She did it all. I've got most of it back now because my mother and father came home for my birthday, but not the clothes though. I'm sure Nanny didn't want my parents to know. The more I think about it the more I'm convinced that's why the lights were not working in my bedroom. I'm now sure that's why Nanny sneaked out of the room at my birthday party, so she could put it all back before my parents found out. Nanny never allowed me to go anywhere, to see anyone," said Ebony, in a whisper, "and if I did something wrong, well …" She shivered and looked back at Veeleeta. "She wasn't very nice to me."

"Oh," whispered Veeleeta, as her own body shivered. *How can giants treat each other like this? Gribbles would never be so cruel to … to … anything.* "What's a birthday party?"

Ebony looked surprised. "It's a party, with gifts, and music to celebrate when you were born."

"Oh. We don't have birthday parties."

"What! Oh, I'm sorry."

Silence fell between them.

Eventually, Veeleeta asked, "What are you going to do?"

"Do? Do! I will do what I've always done. I will cope. Something has to change soon. My father's always saying that the best thing about life is that it never stays the same way for long."

Veeleeta tilted her head to one side. "What does that mean?"

Ebony shrugged her shoulders. "I don't know. I assume it means that something will happen, that my life will get better or worse." She laughed in a half-hearted way. "Maybe Nanny Jones will come back, and my parents will stop travelling the world, and maybe the sky will turn pink, and elephants will fall from the sky as daisies grow beneath them," she continued as she waved her arms around.

Veeleeta looked up and smiled. "Um. That would be a good thing, I suppose but … err … what … what are elephants?"

"Ah … Oh, um … ah … They are great big animals, huge actually." Veeleeta's eyes grew wide as Ebony spread her arms to indicate their size. "They are grey, have great big ears that flap about." Ebony pantomimed the antics. "They have a long trunk something like ... err ...but ... um, bigger." Ebony almost whispered the last few words as she looked straight at Veeleeta's long nose. "It will never happen though," said Ebony, dejectedly. "Nanny Jones is getting married. She wants to have a child of her own." Her voice sounded very sad, and Veeleeta felt there was resentment hidden within her words.

Silence fell between them again as the clock on the mantelpiece continued to tick away the minutes.

"Come on, we can't sit around here all day," said Ebony suddenly, and she held her hand out flat for Veeleeta to climb onto. "We have to work out a way to get you home."

"Get me home," said Veeleeta, then smiled as her heart seemed to skip a beat for sheer joy. She'd thought she was doomed to spend her whole life trapped here with Ebony, but now ... now there was a chance.

Ebony picked Veeleeta up and with a bit of a wobble, stood up, turned around and looking at the gifts her parents had given her, and all the toys and the paintings that filled the room, she lifted Veeleeta up to her face, smiled, then said with a bit of a croaky voice, "I will miss you terribly. It's been so long since I've had a friend to talk to and to share things with. Even though I've only known you for such a short time, it feels like you're ... the sister I never had." Ebony blushed as she looked into Veeleeta's eyes.

"I'm sorry, Ebony. I wish I—" Veeleeta froze as her eyes fixed on something that lay behind Ebony.

Ebony spun around. Staring back at them from the doorway was Nanny Windabothem.

Ebony's heart skipped a beat, momentarily frozen at the sight of Nanny standing in the doorway, then a switch flicked on in her brain. She instantly recognised the danger, and encased Veeleeta within a protective cage of fingers in her left hand and flung both hands behind her back.

"Oh, no you don't, young lady," cried Nanny Windabothem,

and within four strides she was towering over her. "So … I knew you were up to something."

A shiver ran down Ebony's spine.

"When I found Scruffy in your room last night, alone, I knew my suspicions had been right. I saw those rooms set up in that castle of yours. The little bed that had been slept in. The bath that had been used. The soap. The pot plant. I wondered. I must admit you had me intrigued. I knew you were hiding something. I just didn't know what!"

Nanny's hands darted out and grabbed hold of Ebony's arms.

"Let me go! Let me go!" yelled Ebony.

"Show me what you're hiding," demanded Nanny.

Ebony struggled to stop both arms from being forced forwards but Nanny dug her fingernails in the soft part of the muscle, and Ebony cried out in pain, her arms went limp. In desperation, Ebony twisted away from her, enabling one arm to break free. Her other, still held fast in Nanny's vice-like grip, only just managed to keep hold of Veeleeta.

Nanny, now using both hands, dragged Ebony's left arm forward, until she was close enough so she could see her cage of fingers.

Veeleeta screamed.

"What is that?" Nanny Windabothem stared at Ebony's hand as one of her hands released its grip, and then holding her palm up said, "Give it to me."

Ebony didn't answer but looked at the open palm. Indecision bubbled forth, and she told herself, *You can't give her Veeleeta … But if I don't, you know what she will do to me.*

"Give it to me!" demanded Nanny Windabothem.

Ebony's body went limp, her fingers slackened as she slowly started to uncurl her fingers. *Don't! Stop!* Ebony yelled at herself. *You can't do this! Stop! She's your friend.*

Suddenly Ebony stiffened, snapped her fingers around Veeleeta again and yelled, "Let go of me!"

"Oh, no you don't," growled Nanny as she closed her hand even more tightly around Ebony's arm.

287

"Get away from me. You can't have her."

"Her?" Nanny forced Ebony's fist even closer to her face. She opened her eyes wide as Veeleeta squeaked, "Ebony! Help me!"

Ebony kicked out at Nanny, catching her on the shin.

"Ow! Cut that out, missy. How dare you. Settle down. I only want to look at what you've found ... Ouch!" yelled Nanny, as Ebony kicked her again, throwing her free arm up towards Nanny's face, fingers poised to scratch. Nanny's eye flinched at the movement. She made a grab for Ebony's arm but missed, and as her hand fell to her side her fingers curled around Ebony's pendant, and with the downward momentum, the silver chain freed itself from Ebony's neck.

"NOO!" screamed Ebony, as she wriggled and squirmed and made a grab for it, but Nanny turned sideways out of Ebony's reach.

"Give it back," Ebony yelled. "It's mine! Give it back! You can't have it. Let me go!"

Nanny opened her palm and looked down at the silver pendant. She turned to face Ebony, and suddenly it was as if all the air had been sucked out of the room. She released her hold on Ebony, who instantly stopped fighting and took a step back, panting.

"What's this?" demanded Nanny, her fingers twitching as the pendant sat in her palm.

Ebony glared into Nanny's eyes. "It's my gift from Nanny Jones."

"And that?" Nanny looked at Veeleeta who was still clutched in Ebony's hand.

"It's a Gribble," she answered.

"A Gribble? But how can that be? They are only make-believe."

"No, they aren't ... See?" Ebony released her fingers, just a fraction, revealing Veeleeta, who was crouched, petrified, in the middle of her palm. A tingle ran down Ebony's spine as if something had just happened, and she'd missed it.

"How can that be?" said Nanny again, as she looked down at the small creature then at Ebony.

"I've promised to take it back home." *Don't say any more,* Ebony told herself.

"Home? ... My sis ..." Nanny started to say as she looked down at the creature again. "This can't be true." She looked up at Ebony. "How did you? Where did you ...?"

"In the forest, the other night. She fell out of the trees." *What are you doing?* Ebony complained to the part of her that just wouldn't shut up!

"Why didn't you tell me?" asked Nanny, in a soft voice.

Ebony laughed. It was a laugh full of sarcasm, a laugh she could not stop herself from releasing.

What are you doing? a tiny voice inside her mind cried out as it cringed at the thought of what could happen now.

Nanny stared at Ebony, who couldn't stop herself from saying, "After the way you've treated me ever since you came here?"

The tiny voice inside her head stamped up and down with rage, *Shut up! Shut up! Shut up! Do you want to get us all into trouble?*

Nanny stared down at Veeleeta and a shiver ran across Ebony's shoulders, as if an icy draught had just entered the room. She looked at Nanny and frowned.

What is she doing?

I don't know, she answered herself as she brought her hands closer to her chest, then froze.

Soft words were being spoken. Nanny was mumbling to herself, "The other Gribbles will come ... I know ... They'll take her away just like they did ... I know, I know."

"What is happening, Ebony?" asked Veeleeta.

Ebony opened her fingers and looked at her. "I don't know."

Ebony frowned and listened as Nanny continued to mumble in a voice barely above a whisper. "She's just so trusting ... I know ... It's a failing of hers ... I know ... you must ... I know."

Nanny's hand darted out, swooping Veeleeta off Ebony's palm.

The instant she did so, a bright red light exploded all around, and Ebony screamed, "NOO!"

53

Whimbrel and Freeschum flew behind the large brown creature as it trotted towards the back of the mansion. It led them up to a set of steps flaring at the base in a wide arc. As they ascended the six steps, they passed clay pots festooned with flowering herbs and plants, up to a narrow landing where a huge dark-brown door with a square hole at the base of it sat. The creature pushed its head against something that was covering the hole and started to move through it. Whimbrel gasped as it seemed to him as if the creature was now disappearing bit by bit. Whimbrel hesitantly encouraged Freeschum onwards and looking from beneath the creature, he could now see that it was actually inside the building. Relief surged through him as he realised that this hole was just another door within a door especially made for the creature so it could enter the building.

When the creature was halfway through the hole, it stopped moving. Whimbrel waited for it to do something but it just waited. So with grim determination he urged Freeschum onwards, squeezing themselves between the creature's stomach and the doorframe. The tips of Freeschum's wings flickered against the creature's tummy, making it shiver, causing Freeschum to shoot forward, free of the creature's body.

Once through, the flap fell back into position, and Whimbrel found himself in a very large room. It was filled with two huge white square solid objects with knobs in rows high along the top of it. There were so many things in the room and he didn't know what any of them were. Except for the one and only thing he did recognise. It was a basket sitting on the floor with what looked like fabric in it. It was so immense in size it made his mind spin.

The creature then led them through that room and out into another room that was gigantic. Whimbrel cringed. He had never seen anything like it. It reminded him of the kitchen in his own home, but this was enormous. The legs of the wooden table, sitting in the middle of the room, looked as thick as tree trunks. The tiles on the floor spread out into the distance. High above him pots and pans, of a size that boggled his mind, hung from hooks suspended on chains from a large pole. Freeschum froze, and Whimbrel did the same. A song filled the room. Whimbrel looked in the direction of the sound and stopped breathing.

A giant was standing with its back to them. Its head was nodding in time with the tune. Whimbrel was sure it was a female, because it wore clothing similar to his mama, and she was singing, "… to loving you-u-u … dah, dah, dah … dah, dah, dah. In the Springtime-e-e … hmm … hmm … hmm."

Freeschum instantly flew behind a wooden table leg as the giant turned and started padding its way across the enormous floor in soft shoes. It was old, in that it had wrinkles and grey hair, and its shoulders were stooped.

"… hmm … tra-la-la, tra-la-la … You are my love-e-e-e … hmm … hmm, hmm." The giant had now crossed the floor and picked up a large metal pot.

Freeschum quickly flew into the shadows of an almighty cupboard and hid as the brown creature walked out of the kitchen door, which was located on the opposite side of the room.

"… hmm … hmm … don't leave me … hmm … hmm," the giant continued to sing. "Oh. Drat."

A loud clanging came from Whimbrel's right, and Whimbrel clapped his hands over his ears. The giant stooped and picked up a metal pot that had fallen to the floor, then moved towards the sink under the window.

Freeschum dashed for the doorway. Whimbrel breathed, not realising he had even held his breath. They had made it to the shadow of a room that was long and thin, and yet very high. He looked ahead; the creature seemed to have waited for them.

The creature turned and walked down the long room. Freeschum flew up next to him.

"That was a near thing," whispered Whimbrel. The creature continued to walk on, its claws echoing on the tiles. "Can't you walk any quieter?" whispered Whimbrel. "We will be caught for sure." The creature cocked an ear in his direction but kept on walking.

At the end of the hallway, the creature stopped and stuck its nose around the corner and sniffed the air. It then walked out into a large foyer, and Whimbrel gasped in awe.

The creature stopped and turned to look at Freeschum, who was still hovering in the shadows.

"It's so big," said Whimbrel, looking from side to side.

The creature looked around at the vast expanse of the foyer with its statues and paintings and the huge crystal chandelier hanging from the ceiling three storeys high. It then turned and led them up a flight of carpeted stairs, along a hall full of doors, then stopped when Whimbrel said, "Everything is so big." Whimbrel looked down through the railings, down, down, down to the black and white patchwork tiles they had just travelled over, mumbling, "No. Big isn't the word ... Huge ... No ... that's not the word. Enormous. Yes, that's it."

The creature's chest rumbled and Whimbrel looked at it. It had continued up a flight of stairs. Freeschum followed as it padded along another hallway filled with more doors. "How would anyone find their way out of this place? It's like a Treen Warren," commented Whimbrel.

The creature growled, and Whimbrel felt he was being told to be quiet, but he could not help but look at the immense space they were travelling through. They came to another flight of stairs, and just as the creature put a paw on the first step, a dark-haired female giant walked down towards them. The creature froze, and Freeschum ducked under its chest.

"Hello, Scruffy, my dear," the giant said, stopping in front of him. "Are you going to see your mistress? Watch out, darling, Nanny's on the prowl." It patted Scruffy on the head, and he felt his chin hit something solid under it. A tiny squeal could be heard.

The giant stopped patting him, stood up straight and said, "What was that? Mice again, I suppose."

Scruffy watched the giant walk down the hall and out of sight.

As he started walking up to the top of the stairs, Freeschum and Whimbrel flew out from under him and Whimbrel breathed a deep sigh and tried to stop himself from trembling.

Scruffy led them along another hallway, and eventually stopped in front of a huge white door. It was shut.

Scruffy looked up at the door then looked at Whimbrel. Whimbrel looked up at it, wondering what Scruffy was doing.

When he kept on looking at the door and back at him, Whimbrel realised that he was going to have to figure out how to open it. He spied the long silver handle. "I see." Seconds ticked by. "Right, Freeschum, let's have a look at this. Fly me up there, please. I think if we pull on it somehow, we might be able to open this door."

Freeschum did as he was asked, and when close enough to the silver handle, Whimbrel jumped on top of it. He balanced on its edge and travelled along its length, forcing the long narrow handle down towards the floor with his weight.

A loud *click* sounded, and the door slowly opened.

54

Ebony threw her hands up in front of her eyes to protect them against the red glow. The air was filled with a tinkling crystal voice screaming, "VEE-L-E-E-TA!"

Something solid hit the wooden floorboards with a thud and Veeleeta screamed with fright.

The brightness dimmed and Ebony looked around her. "What the heck was that?" she said.

On the polished wooden floorboards, Nanny's thin body now lay prostrate, her legs splayed apart. Her eyes were shut as if she were asleep. Her arms lay straight by her sides, and in one clenched fist sat Veeleeta, crying. From the other hand, the one holding the pendant, a red light was glowing between her fingers.

Ebony instantly dropped to her knees and prised Nanny's fingers away from Veeleeta. She snatched her out of her grasp, jumped up and held Veeleeta close to her chest. She backed away from the silent, rigid form of Nanny Windabothem.

"What's wrong with her?" asked Ebony.

"I … I don't know," answered Veeleeta.

The bedroom door flew open and Isobel burst in.

"Miss Ebony. Are you all right? I heard—" She stopped. "What is wrong with Miss Windabothem?" Isobel flew to Nanny's side and dropped to her knees. "Has she had a heart attack? I knew all that bitterness would get to her one day."

Isobel felt the pulse in her neck. "Well, that's fine." She quickly put her cheek up against the lady's thin lips. "She is still breathing." Isobel looked into Nanny's face. "She still has colour in her cheeks. Well, if you can call it colour. Normal for her though." Isobel sat back on her heels. "What's that in her hand?"

Nanny's hand had now turned into a glowing ball of red light.

"It's my pendant," said Ebony. "The one Nanny Jones gave me. She snatched it away."

"We've got to get her to let go of it." Isobel pulled on her fingers and quickly let go.

"What's wrong?"

"Her fingers feel like ice."

Isobel leaned over Nanny's prostrate form and felt her other hand. "That feels fine. Warm, I mean." She checked her cheek. "Warm." Checked her arms. "Warm." Her legs. "Warm. It's only this hand." Isobel pulled and tugged, and winced. "Her hand is freezing. Come on, let go," Isobel said as she pulled on the fingers that would not give up the treasure they held. Eventually, Isobel sat back upon her heels again. "What are we going to do? We can't just leave her like this."

"You're asking me!" said Ebony. "You're the adult. I don't know. Phone the doctor, I suppose."

"Yes. Yes, you are right. He needs to know about this," said Isobel, pushing herself off her knees. "What happened? He'll want to know."

"She grabbed hold of my necklace, then grabbed hold of Veeleeta," said Ebony. "There was a flash of light and a voice."

"A voice?"

"Yes ... Yes, it called out Veeleeta's name. Nanny then fell on the floor."

"And what is a Veeleeta?" asked Isobel.

"This is Veeleeta," said Ebony, uncupping her hand so Isobel could see her. Veeleeta cringed.

Isobel's mouth dropped open and she slowly sank back upon her knees, and stared at the Gribble. Her eyes moved up to Ebony's. "That's ... amazing. What is it? Where did it come from? How did you end up with it? How did it get here?"

"It's a Gribble, and it came from the forest. I brought it home on the night I got lost."

Isobel looked back down at it, and then as if she'd suddenly remembered something, she straightened herself and said, "Right. In the meantime—"

Isobel stopped talking. A single beam of white light shot out from Nanny's hand and lingered over the top of her forehead. The light grew into a large, flat, circular disk. As Ebony, Veeleeta and Isobel watched, an image appeared on its shimmering surface like a movie screen.

Two young girls, ten and eleven years of age, were running through a field of wildflowers on a sunny day. A voice, sweet and yet dark, filled Ebony's bedroom. Ebony looked around her room, then back to the vision.

"Rose. Rose. Where have you been? Why did you leave?" a voice said as the two girls on the screen kept running.

"Sister. Sister, my heart cries for you," another voice called out, as the sound of someone sobbing in the distance could be heard.

The two little girls, one with long blonde hair, the other with short dark hair, flopped onto the soft springy turf and took in deep breaths as they smelled the freshness of spring.

"Rose, where did you go?" asked the girl with the short dark hair. "Our uncle and aunty were terribly upset." She shivered. "They searched for you for weeks. I cried and cried."

"Oh, Heather, I'm *soo* sorry. Did they hurt you?" Rose laid a gentle hand on Heather's arm. Heather nodded and mumbled, "I ... I ... um ... I wish I could have come with you."

"I didn't mean to get lost. I'm *soo* sorry, but oh, it was wonderful," Rose said as if she'd not heard the hurt in her sister's voice. She tossed her long blonde locks behind her, and the silver pendant, hanging from a chain around her neck, danced in the sunlight. "It was so delightful. Even though I was lost in that great big forest, I met a creature there that helped me get back to you."

"A creature?" inquired Heather, sitting up and turning to look at her sister.

"Yes. It was only tiny. He only came up to my ankle."

"He?"

"His name is Snailum. He was *soo* wonderful. He lives in the trees with the other Gribbles."

Veeleeta whispered, "Papa."

Ebony looked down at her, then turned back to look at the image, as Heather asked, "Gribbles? What are they? And where did you get that lovely necklace?"

"It was a gift from some beautiful creatures. They are called Swanlings. They have blue feathers all over them with *huge* wings. Blue faces and long black feathers flowing down their backs like hair. They gave it to me." Rose held the pendant up to Heather's astonished eyes. "It has a ruby inside it."

"You must tell me everything. You must. You simply must," pleaded Heather. "I will come with you next time. You must take me away with you. You *must* take me to see the Gribbles. Anything has to be better than living with *them*." Heather shivered again.

"I promise, Heather. I promise. You are right; anything has to be better than living with *them*. We will have such an amazing time. I promise, Heather, I promise."

Visions of the two little girls laughing and talking faded as the darkness ate away at the edges of the light, and Heather's voice called out, "Rose. Where are you? Rose. Why did you leave me behind? You promised. You promised."

The sound of a slap echoed through the air of Ebony's bedroom. A child cried out, "You promised. Rose. You promised. Why did you leave me behind?" Sobbing radiated around the room.

The shadowy shape of a large burly man stood towering over Heather's small body as she cowered in the corner of a dark, dank room. He lifted his belt high into the air and slapped down hard. A voice boomed, "You liar!"

"I didn't lie! I didn't lie!" yelled Heather. "They took her away. The Gribbles took her away. She promised. She promised."

Again the belt was raised high in the air, and slapped down hard again, again and again. "She promised," she sobbed. "She promised."

A door, heavy, made of metal, clanged shut, utter darkness instantly enveloping everything.

"Heather … Heather," a soft tinkling crystalline voice called out, from the heart of the pendant being held in Nanny Windabothem's hand. *"Why do you weep?"*

"She promised," a tiny frightened voice answered. A pale light started to grow in the middle of the screen, revealing Heather sobbing as she lay shivering in the dark, dank, desperate corner. "She left me behind with *them.*"

"She had no choice," the voice replied.

"Yes, she did," spat Heather. "She left me behind, and I hate her for it."

"Love still sits in a corner of your heart and weeps for the sister who was lost."

"No. No. It doesn't ... I don't. The Gribbles came. They took her away. She left me behind. She promised, and she left me behind. She never came back. She promised."

"The Gribbles would never do such a thing."

"Yes, they did ... They did ... They did."

"Heather ... Sweet child ... She didn't leave you," the crystalline voice tinkled.

"Yes, she did. She did ... She did!"

"Heather ... Child ... Strangers tore your heart in two."

"No."

"There was no choice for Rose to stay or leave. There was no choice at all. She was taken away in the dark of the night."

Heather said nothing.

"She was saved by strangers. They searched for you, but lies were told. Your aunty and uncle lied. They lied. They lied. You could not be found as you sat, hidden in the cellar, in the deep dark corner, all those days and nights. They lied. They lied. They lied. You could not be found. You could not be saved."

Heather stayed silent.

"Rose searched for you, time and time again, but you remained lost to her ... She is here."

Heather still said nothing.

"She is here," the crystalline voice repeated.

"It ... it makes no difference," whispered Heather. "Where ... is ... she?"

"Not far, not far at all ... at all ... at all ... at all," the crystal voice

echoed as it faded away. The image vanished. The light surrounding Nanny's hand blinked out and as her fingers uncurled, the silver pendant fell to the wooden floor.

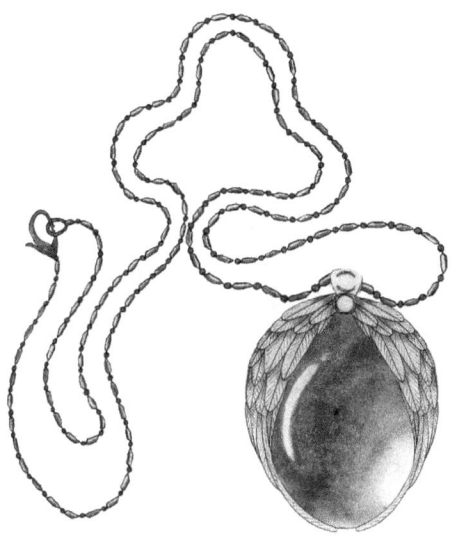

Isobel picked up the silver necklace from the floor and turned back to look at Ebony. Then as her gaze moved behind her, she said, "What was that?"

"What was what?" asked Ebony, turning around.

"I thought ..." whispered Isobel, as she walked towards the open windows.

"What?"

"No, it must be the shock." Isobel stood perfectly still, continuing to look out past the lace curtains.

"What did you see?" asked Ebony. All she could see was the summer sunshine and the blue sky beyond.

"I'm being silly," answered Isobel.

"Isobel! Answer me. We can't stand around. We have to do something to help Nanny."

Isobel turned and looked at Ebony. "It's just ... I thought I saw a tiny flying thing. Blue. About this big." Isobel held her hand up, and with her thumb and forefinger bent, she created a gap indicating the size of a large plum. "It had wings, and a long neck, and four large feet, and I am pretty sure there was something sitting on its back."

Ebony stared out of the window again. There was now a white puffy cloud slowly sauntering across the sky. A thought bubbled up from somewhere deep inside her mind. As it slowly reached the surface and popped into existence, her eyes opened wide, and she mouthed the words, "Cloud Dancers."

Ebony looked at the pictures on the wall. Her eyes found the one she was looking for. There were long-necked creatures with large round feet, coloured bodies and delicate coloured wings flying through painted trees. She looked down at Veeleeta who was still sitting on her left palm, and whispered, "They are here."

"Who are here?" asked Veeleeta and Isobel, in unison.

"What?" said Ebony, looking up not realising she'd been heard.

"Who are here?" asked Isobel again.

"Err..."

"We don't have time for this," said Isobel. "I'm going to phone the doctor. We have to help Nanny. We can't just leave her there like this." She moved towards the bedroom door.

"Right, you go and do that," said Ebony.

They are here, she told herself. *They've come to take Veeleeta home ... I know.*

There was a loud click and the bedroom door opened, just a fraction. Ebony held her breath. Isobel stopped a foot away from the door as if she'd suddenly been frozen to the spot. They watched it swing open, and as Scruffy trotted in, Ebony breathed a sigh of relief.

Isobel slammed the door shut behind him. "Thank goodness, it's only you," she said as she took a step back. "I thought it was someone ... else ... What have you got on your back?" She peered down and gasped. "Ebony, look!" Isobel pointed to Scruffy as if she could not believe what she was seeing. "What are they?"

"What is what?" asked Ebony, hurrying forward then stopping in her tracks. It was as if one of her paintings had come to life. Balancing on Scruffy's back was another Gribble and a black Cloud Dancer.

"Whimbrel!" yelled Veeleeta, and instantly threw herself out of Ebony's hand and plummeted to the floor below.

"NO!" screamed Ebony and Isobel. Ebony dropped onto her knees and caught Veeleeta just before she hit the floorboards. Pain shuddered through her body as an unknown voice yelled, "Vee ... lee ... ta!"

As Ebony's hands automatically enclosed Veeleeta in a cage of fingers, the voice screamed, "LET HER GO!"

Ebony, who had fallen forward, looked up. A black Cloud Dancer was now flying in front of her face. Sitting on top of it was another Gribble. *Wow!* a part of her brain yelled, as another part looked out from behind a corner and cried, *No!*

Ebony scrambled onto her sore knees, pulling Veeleeta, still cupped within her grasp, up to her chest. She looked, with wide eyes and open mouth, as the Cloud Dancer, about the size of a grapefruit, flew even closer. She could see the Gribble sitting on its back was larger than Veeleeta. She had a feeling it was a boy. She stammered, "You ... you ... you ..." but she found the words just faded away. Slowly, unwillingly, she brought her hands forward and just as slowly uncupped her fingers. Veeleeta sat in the middle of her palm.

"Whimbrel! Oh, Whimbrel," Veeleeta called out as she crawled up to the very edge of Ebony's fingers, and hung onto them. "I thought I would never see you again." She burst into tears.

"Quickly! Veeleeta! Jump!" called Whimbrel, as the Cloud Dancer flew even closer. "We must escape. Quickly!" Whimbrel stretched his hand out towards her, but she didn't move, she just sobbed, "It's all right, Whimbrel. We're quite safe. Ebony would never hurt us."

A scrambling sound erupted from behind them and everyone turned to look. Ebony gasped, quickly enclosed Veeleeta in a cage of protective fingers again and hid her hands behind her back.

Nanny Windabothem was sitting up and looking around.

"Quick! Hide," Ebony hissed as she turned to look at Whimbrel. When he didn't immediately move, she stepped in front of them, to hide them from Nanny's view.

"Oh, Isobel. There you are," said Nanny Windabothem. "Could you please come and help me? I seem to have fallen down."

Isobel rushed over and, grabbing Nanny's arms with both hands, helped her to her feet. Nanny Windabothem stood up with a bit of a wobble.

"Thank you," said Nanny, straightening her brown dress. She slid her hand across her hair, which had now not only become frizzled at the edges but was gleaming with long thin bands of white hair entwined within her dark hair.

Ebony stared straight at her, and as if time had slowed down, she watched as Nanny Windabothem turned in her direction.

"I must apologise, Miss Ebony." The words Nanny spoke bounced around in Ebony's brain as an echo bounces in a cave, and her mind went momentarily blank. "I will just go and," said Nanny, "lie down for a little while. I'm feeling a bit … odd."

Nanny Windabothem nodded and moved towards the bedroom door.

"Excuse me, *Heather!*" called out Isobel.

Ebony looked at Isobel and then watched, horrified, as Nanny, who had stopped with her fingers still reaching for the door handle, turned and looked back at Isobel.

"Yes?" she said, but then Nanny's brow furrowed and her eyes seemed to be looking at something Ebony could not see. The seconds ticked by. Silence, except for the never-ending ticking of the clock on the mantelpiece, filled the room and Nanny blinked. A calm expression came across her face, and she finally said, "Excuse me, Miss Ebony, but if you don't mind, I will have a breakfast tray sent up for you today. I really must lie down. I'm sorry to say this, but I really do feel a bit strange."

Nanny nodded again then as she opened the door she stopped, slowly turned and said, "Miss Ebony, your parents phoned. They wanted me to let you know that they have decided to retire from business. They'll be arriving home in about a week. Also, you will not be going back to boarding school." Her brow furrowed, and then she looked into Ebony's eyes, smiled awkwardly, turned and left the room.

Ebony looked up at Isobel with a tear in her eye. Isobel looked down at Ebony and smiled. "I'm *soo* pleased for you, Miss Ebony."

"Isn't it fantastic?" said Ebony, then smiled again and took a big breath. Her head felt very light. She could not believe that all her dreams were coming true ... well, almost. She slowly turned to Isobel and said, "What did you do that for? With Nanny."

"Just checking. If she is Heather, then who is Rose? And where is she if she is so close by?"

"I wouldn't have a clue."

"Didn't Nanny Jones give you that necklace? It looked like the same as the one we saw in the vision," stated Isobel.

"Yes. Maybe. But ... but she can't possibly be related to *her*," said Ebony, pointing to the bedroom door Nanny Windabothem had just walked through.

"I'm just saying."

"That's ridiculous. They don't even have the same last name. They don't even look the same. They don't even ... even ... No. You're wrong. You're wrong. You have to be."

Isobel shrugged, lifted an eyebrow and smiled. Ebony had the feeling that she'd just said something stupid. "Well, at least you don't have to phone for the doctor now," added Ebony.

"I think I will. He'll want to know about this. He's been a bit worried about you."

Ebony flinched as the Cloud Dancer now flew out from behind her and hovered in front of her face.

"Where is my sister?" demanded Whimbrel.

"We will not hurt you," said Ebony.

This is amazing, an excited part of her mind called out. *Are you mad!* she scolded herself. *He's come to take her away.*

Ebony stared at Whimbrel.

I know, she told herself as sadness settled in her heart. *But she'll leave no matter what happens. Everyone does. I can't keep her, she is not a pet!*

I know that! she spat back herself. *She is my friend.* And Ebony's heart ached, because she now knew for certain that she had just lost Veeleeta forever.

"LET HER GO!" screamed Whimbrel.

Ebony blinked and looked at his fierce face. His cheeks had turned red, and his long nose had scrunched up into a short snout.

Tears welled in Ebony's eyes and she moved towards her bed and gently placed Veeleeta on top of the bedding.

Freeschum landed next to her.

"Veeleeta! Quickly!" called out Whimbrel, but Veeleeta did not move. "Come to me," he called again, and then Freeschum took a step back as Isobel moved towards the bed. Towering over him, she looked down. "It has been a pleasure to meet you," she said, "and your flying thing ... err ... creature."

"He's a Cloud Dancer," called out Veeleeta. "Freeschum is his name. This is my brother Whimbrel."

"Ah," said Isobel, turning her head from Veeleeta back to Whimbrel and leaning closer. The Cloud Dancer took another step back. "I hope I will get to see you again one day ... Whimbrel, is it?" Isobel stood up straight and turned to leave. "Oh, and this is yours, I think." She handed Ebony the silver necklace.

"Um ... thank you," said Ebony, marvelling at how the clasp was not broken, enabling her to secure it around her neck as Isobel left the room.

"I'm glad your mama and papa will be home soon," said Veeleeta.

Ebony looked down at her.

"It makes it a bit easier to say ... goodbye," Veeleeta added.

Ebony dropped to her knees and leaned up against the bedding, folding her arms across the top of it. She looked at Veeleeta through blurred vision. "I will tell Nanny Jones all about you," said Ebony, in a croaky voice. "I will make sure of it." She gave Veeleeta a half-hearted smile.

Veeleeta smiled back at her.

Whimbrel, who had dismounted, grabbed Veeleeta by the arm and started to drag her over to Freeschum.

"Whimbrel, it's all right. Stop it. Everything is all right." Veeleeta wrenched her arm free of his grasp, and Whimbrel scrambled up into the saddle chair. He reached his arm down and called out, "Come on! Come on! What are you doing?"

Veeleeta walked up to the edge of the bed and looked down at Scruffy sitting on the floor. "Scruffy. Thank you for bringing my brother here. I will never forget it." She turned to Ebony and said, "I'm so pleased to have met you, Ebony." Veeleeta touched the tip of her long nose onto Ebony's hand. She smiled and walked back to Whimbrel.

Ebony looked down at where Veeleeta's nose had touched her skin. She thought she could just see a faint glow, but then no, it was gone.

Ebony looked up and saw Veeleeta take her brother's arm. He winced and sighed as he helped Veeleeta sit in front of him, and the instant Veeleeta was settled, Freeschum took to the air and flew straight for the open window.

Ebony watched as they flew out into the wide-open space beyond, then panic gripped her, and she yelled, "No! Don't go!"

She dashed up to the window seat and leaned out of the window. She only half-registered that Scruffy had jumped up next to her and was looking out of the window as well. She grabbed hold of the edge of the windowsill with both hands, leaned out further, then gasped, "Crumbs!"

Ebony felt as if she'd walked into a fog. No sound could she hear, no birds, wind, not even her own breathing. Hovering in mid-air in front of her were six more Cloud Dancers, each one looking like a rainbow of colour. Four had Gribbles riding on them, two did not.

She watched as the black Cloud Dancer flew towards the group, and as they grew closer the group rushed forward, crowding around them.

Ebony's eyes travelled to the mass of trees surrounding her home. *Ancient. That's the word for that place,* she said to herself. *Ancient and mysterious. I wonder how many other Gribbles really live in there.*

"Ebony," a tiny voice inside her head called. It sounded like Veeleeta's but how could that be?

I wonder what else lives in that forest, Ebony's mind continued to ponder. She didn't know that there were so many strange creatures living within it. Selenites. Tooreens. Poogles. All sorts of things.

"Ebony."

Ebony blinked and saw Veeleeta in front of her. She was sitting bareback on a pink and white Cloud Dancer, holding onto a thin rope around its neck. It had powder-blue spots on its hindquarters and white wings.

"Veeleeta? What are you … I thought you were leaving!" Ebony said, scratching where the pendant lay against her skin, the area having grown warm again.

"This is Tillia," said Veeleeta with pride in her voice, as she patted the Cloud Dancer's neck.

"Oh? Oh!" Ebony said as memories popped into her mind of Veeleeta telling her stories of how she'd dreamt of riding Tillia one day but *only* if Tillia would allow it. She looked at Veeleeta who had a great big smile on her tiny face. "And you were right. Congar did not die. He is over there with Trillium." Veeleeta turned and pointed back to the group of Cloud Dancers hovering nearby.

Ebony smiled but it was a smile full of sadness, and tears prickled her eyes. She knew Veeleeta would never come back to her now.

"This is Grigwell." Veeleeta indicated a larger Gribble who had just flown into view on the back of a blue Cloud Dancer with a white splash across its chest. "And this is the Cloud Dancer Stellman." Ebony looked into the Cloud Dancer's eyes and felt that somehow it knew all about her, and she wasn't sure if that was a good thing or not. She quickly looked at the Gribble on its back and smiled. Ebony then turned back to Veeleeta, leaned further out of the window and whispered, "I thought you were my friend."

"I am your friend, Ebony."

"Then why … I know I said …" stammered Ebony, and then looked down at the gardens so far away. *How can I tell her I don't want her to leave?* The spicy perfume of her white rose, growing up to her very windows, three storeys high, drifted up to her. She took in a deep breath of its heady scent, allowing it to flow through her senses, giving her the strength to say the words she so desperately wanted to say. She looked back at Veeleeta, and said, "If you leave, I will not have a friend. I will not have anyone to talk to. I will not have anyone to share things with. I'm going to be all alone ... again." Then in a whisper, she added, "I will only have ... myself ... to talk to."

Ebony looked into Veeleeta's dark eyes and saw a sparkle within them, and hoped beyond all hope that somehow Veeleeta would stay.

"I am your friend, Ebony," repeated Veeleeta, in a gentle comforting tone. Veeleeta then looked at the Gribble next to her and said, "Grigwell."

"This isn't a good idea, Veeleeta," answered Grigwell.

"You said you wanted to meet them."

"Yes but ..." Grigwell looked nervous.

"You promised."

"Yes but ..."

"Grigwell."

"Oh, all right, but no good will come of this."

Stellman moved forward, and Ebony was surprised to see that he wasn't heading towards her, but to Scruffy.

"Grigwell," called out Veeleeta, from behind him. "Don't worry about Scruffy. He will not hurt you. Will you, Scruffy?"

Ebony noticed that Scruffy looked at Veeleeta as if he had actually understood what she'd just said. She then watched in wonder as the Cloud Dancer moved closer. Scruffy watched as it hovered in front of his nose. Grigwell tentatively stretched out a hand and a corner of Scruffy's lip lifted revealing his sharp white teeth. A rumble emanated from deep within Scruffy's chest. Grigwell withdrew his hand and Stellman backed off.

"Scruffy," called out Veeleeta, in a tone that clearly held a warning.

Scruffy looked at her again and Ebony placed a firm hand on his back. She didn't know what was going on, but whatever it was, she had the feeling it was very important. The last thing she wanted was Scruffy taking a snap at another Gribble. Scruffy licked his lips and Grigwell gasped as Scruffy's pink tongue darted out and ran along his row of sharp teeth. Scruffy gulped, shut his mouth and stood rigid. Grigwell urged Stellman forward, flying straight up to Scruffy's glossy black nose. Grigwell then held out his hand.

Ebony pressed her hand firmer on Scruffy's back then watched, fascinated, as the Cloud Dancer turned sideways, allowing Grigwell to press his little hand onto the surface of Scruffy's nose. Scruffy's eyes opened wide and then closed. The seconds flew by and Scruffy didn't move. When Grigwell finally removed his hand, an imprint of it glowed bright yellow against the jet black of Scruffy's nose, then slowly the print faded away.

Scruffy opened his eyes and Stellman withdrew and flew back to hover next to Tillia and Veeleeta. Ebony looked at Grigwell, and then to Scruffy, who was now watching the Gribbles. She looked back at Veeleeta who was smiling.

"What just happened?" asked Ebony, but all Veeleeta did was smile, raise her little hand and wave goodbye. "I will see you again someday, Ebony," she called out. "I promise."

No! a tiny voice inside Ebony's mind yelled, then she sighed and reluctantly waved back as she watched the group of Cloud Dancers leave.

A lonely little tear trickled over Ebony's freckled cheek and she placed her arm around Scruffy. As she watched the group of Gribbles disappear into the distance, she said, "I'm going to miss her."

"Well, I'm not. I'm glad she's gone."

"That's not very … n-i-c-e." Ebony turned to look at him.

Scruffy had a twinkle in his eyes she'd never seen before. She quickly swept him into her arms, crushed him to her chest and said, "Scruffy. You can talk!"

Thanks to the Humans

How does one thank all the humans who have helped me to get to this point? How do I thank the energies of this world, that have woven the threads of my life in such a way, this book is now a reality?

I started writing this story on the 6th June 2006, and I finished it almost 14 years later. Many times I considered giving up, but through all the tears and tantrums, there was a determination to see it through. Why, because I want to build a miniature fantasy world, using my models made from gourds and re-cycled objects, and I needed a story to go with it. The book you now hold in your hands is the beginning of that story.

And why did I self-publish? Because my first book is just so important to me because I like to control things, because I want to have my story written the way I want it written (for right or wrong, good or bad), because I want to hold a book in my hands and to know that I stuck with my dream, and here is the proof.

If I was to write all the reasons why this book is being held by you now, and all the people I have met along the way, it would read like a map. If I had not met one person, I would not have met another, and another and another and so it goes on, each of them helping me either in **BIG** ways or in tiny ways.

When I needed an answer, the energies of this earth supplied it. Like the time I was sitting in a park watching fireworks and a dog I did not know dashed up to me and sat on my lap and 'shook right down to his paws.' I had so many, many little things like that, that came into my life to add spice to my story.

When ideas popped into my head, I believe it is because my subconscious has already written the book, and when the time was right, bubbles of inspiration popped into existence. The more I delve into this fantasy world of mine, the more I find out about it, and so now both of us are learning what is around the corner of the next branch, or plant in this fantasy world of mine.

Enough about me though, first, I would like to thank my mother, Sheila, my daughters, Tammy and Samantha, and my life partner, Garry. Without their love and support, I would never have continued on with this journey of writing this story, for this length of time.

I would also like to thank my grandmother, Agnes. I travelled to England and had the delight to read the first chapter of my story to her when she was aged 99. She passed away, just before turning 102. Thank you with all my heart and I miss you terribly.

I would definitely like to thank Jeff Gilberthorpe, who without his encouragment and support I may never have written again. Thank you, Catherine Scalley, who suggested I apply to the Gold Coast Council Writers Course run by Louise Cusack. I would also like to thank Louise for teaching us for two years. I learned so much. I would also like to thank the Gold Coast Council. I was so chuffed to be accepted into the writing course. It was there I met the most amazing group of people. Some of the group eventually became the Parana Writers Club, who went on to win awards in their own right. I now have friends that have helped me in more ways than they know. So a special thank you goes to the following people who have gone above and beyond for me and also helped me in so many ways that my life has been sent off in an amazing direction. Rebecca Fraser (Author of *Curtis Creed and the Lore of the Ocean*). Angela Sunde (Author of *Pond Magic*). Janis Hanely. David Stringer (Author of I*slands of The Heart*) Helen Stubbs (the author of many books),Tom Betts and not, but in the way least, Kerry. Thank you very much all of you, for letting me know I'm not alone.

I would like to thank Barbara Dyer, Sarah Davies, Isobel Sheppard (the author of many books), Simeon Beatty, Rowena Zande, Edwina Shaw the author of many books, Louise Zedda-Simpson, for helping with the editing, advice and support, and Gail Tagarro for helping to polish my story one last time.

To Sarah and Ashley Kuzmanov, for their enlightenment into how a child felt about my story, which I'm happy to say was very positive. It has been a long time since I have been a child, and my memories are fading.

There are also all those people I talked to at the many shows I displayed my models at over the past 30 years, all the people on the internet, all the people who have sent me messages of support, all the people who have patiently listened to my thoughts, wondering if this book will ever get finished.

I would like to thank Andrew McIntosh who illustrated the front cover. He has done an outstanding job and I love his work, he has such a talent and I have had many compliments. Thank you.

I would also like to thank Andy McDermott, of Publicious, who has helped bring this book from the computer to the physical, so you can now hold it in your hands. I am sure that there were times he wondered if I would ever finish it. Thank you very much for helping me bring a little bit of magic into my life and, I am hoping, it will bring some magic into other people's lives as well.

I would just like to add that it is a strange thing we call life. If a friend of my mother's (Joane Hopley) had not asked her to ask me if I would display my models at the 125th Anniversary of the Canungra State School I would probably never have met Doug Reiser. Why do I mention this man? It turns out his daughter went to the school and he saw my work at the event. So, as my display was a great success, I went looking for other places to display it. I eventually ended up contacting the Gold Coast Show and it was Doug I talked to. It was a shock that he knew of my work but he invited me to the show and I have been displaying my work there for 20 years. I was, unknown to me, on a new path of my life, the one I want to stay on. It is there I met Jeff Gilberthorpe. So it is with great sadness that in January 2021 Doug Reiser died but my thanks to him never will.

Author & Illustrations within the book
N. J. Tierney

Nicola J. Tierney lives on the Gold Coast, Australia, far away from where she was born in England, 1960.

Her interest in the tiny, minute, detailed way this world works was sparked when she was very young and is the main reason she builds miniature fantasy houses out of gourds and recycled objects now. Her aim is to build a world big enough for her to walk around in.

Her love of fantasy worlds (sparked by devouring the Narnia Chronicles by C. S. Lewis when she was young) have been with her longer than she can remember. Her determination to make her dreams a reality has been a driving force in her life – this is just one of the many things she wants to achieve to bring some magic into people's lives.

www.facebook.com/TheGribblesGiftAuthor
www.facebook.com/TanglemireForestNoOrdinaryWorld
www.facebook.com/TanglemireForestRetailShop

Cover Illustration
Andrew McIntosh

Andrew McIntosh is a freelance digital illustrator from Melbourne, Australia.

Ever since Andrew can remember, he has had a pencil and paper on hand.

He started his artistic career in the video games industry focusing on Pixel art, 3D modelling and UI design.

In his spare time, Andrew paints whimsical characters and scenes which are greatly inspired by nature.

Since 2015, Andrew has pursued his aspiration to illustrate children's books and hopes to write one of his own in the future.

www.andrewmcintoshart.com

Tanglemire Forest No Ordinary World is a miniature fantasy world made by Nicola Tierney (the author of The Gribble's Gift). She has been making thing's since she was three, now she is much older, she is making a fantasy world out of gourds and re-cycled objects, which fits with her ethos of this world.

She displays her models at shows, schools and has private showings. She live:

Veeleeta's house
   (real model)

The models are the inspiration for the book, and the book has helped inspire the models. They are entwined just as Nicola is entwined within them. If you want to know more about Nicola all you have to do is look to her models, it's all there for those who choose to see.

It's Nicola's long-held desire to make her models into a display so large that she, and anyone else who would like to join her, can literally walk around in a giant fantasy world like no other.

Dreams are made to be fulfilled and Nicola will continue doggedly trying to make hers come true.

To learn more about her work it would be best to go to her Facebook Page Tanglemire Forest No Ordinary World as there isn't enough space here to tell you, the how and why Nicola is making this village.

Veeleeta's bedroom (real model)

One of the drawings
based on a hanging
house, built and
illustrated
by
N. J. Tierney

The

Swanling

Child

The world can change in enexpected ways

The next book
in the fantasy trilogy
by
N.J. Tierney
from the fantasy forest
Tanglemire Forest

Hanging village of Pooreena
South East of
Tanglemire Forest
early evening

www.ingramcontent.com/pod-product-compliance
Lightning Source LLC
Chambersburg PA
CBHW061514020726
47502CB00006B/2071

* 9 780648 811107 *